'Big, isn't it?' Maximin said, with half-suppressed pride.

'It is big,' I agreed, trying to sound nonchalant. I wanted to put something into my voice that would say I too had seen big cities – Genoa, for example, and Pisa – and that Rome was just a larger version of these. But my voice trailed off as I looked again at the whole. In and around the central district, I saw clusters of buildings so huge I could barely conceive how they had been designed and constructed: the Imperial Palace, the baths built by Diocletian and the great Colosseum – a stone amphitheatre so large that eighty thousand people at a time could watch the games that used to be held there.

But even as we rode in, and I strained to look up at the buildings on either side of the road, I could see that Rome, like everywhere else in my world, had seen better days.

A colossal statue of some god or emperor had collapsed on itself, and the body parts had been left where they fell, to be gradually buried under the accumulating rubbish of half a century. Every-where was the smell of damp brisk dust and rotting filth. Here, as back home, pigs snuffed around for sustenance.

We passed through whole districts of silent, built-in desolation. Every now and again, my gaze was drawn by a movement in one of the upper windows of the buildings. I looked up to see a child's face showing pale and thin against the blackness behind. It gave me a long and mournful inspection, and then vanished.

ABOUT THE AUTHOR

Richard Blake is a lecturer, historian, broadcaster and writer who lives in Kent

CONSPIRACIES OF ROME

Richard Blake

HODDER

First published in Great Britain in 2008 by Hodder & Stoughton
An Hachette Livre UK company

First published in paperback in 2008

6

A CIP catalogue record for this title is
available from the British Library

ISBN 978 0 340 95113 2

Typeset in Plantin by Hewer Text UK Ltd, Edinburgh
Printed and bound by Clays Ltd, St Ives plc

Hodder & Stoughton policy is to use papers that
are natural, renewable and recyclable products
and made from wood grown in sustainable forests.
The logging and manufacturing processes are
expected to conform to the environmental
regulations of the country of origin.

Hodder & Stoughton Ltd
338 Euston Road
London NW1 3BH

www.hodder.co.uk

For my wife Andrea

ACKNOWLEDGEMENTS

The verses on p.127 are based on *A Letter from Italy, to the Right Honourable Charles Lord Halifax, in the Year 1701,* by Joseph Addison

The verses on p.222 are the opening lines from Book III of *De Rerum Natura* by Titus Lucretius Carus, *c*70 BC

The verses on p.289 are from Poem III by Gaius Valerius Catullus, *c*60 BC

PROLOGUE

I, Aelric of Richborough, also known as Alaric of Britain and by sundry other names throughout the Greek Empire and in the realms of the Saracens, in this six hundred and eighty-fourth year of our Lord Jesus Christ, and in the second year of the second Pope Leo, and in the twenty-fifth year of the fourth Emperor Constantine, and in my own ninety-fifth year, sit here in the monastery at Jarrow to write the history of my life.

And that's as far as I got yesterday afternoon. I got called in, you see, to take over the mathematics class for that lunatic monk from Spain Abbot Benedict engaged against my advice. He'd been faint again from scourging himself – not a wise act at any time, let alone in this ghastly climate. By the time I'd remembered enough to cane into the boys, I was pretty knocked out. So I came back here to my cell to recover myself with hot beer and took to my bed.

When I woke this morning, I looked again at my opening, and thought to burn it. I didn't feel up to continuing.

Am I at last going senile? Am I no longer good for extended composition? At my age, there'd be no shame in that. Far off in Canterbury, Archbishop Theodore is only eighty-eight, and is getting decidedly past it.

I'll not deny my pretty boy looks are long gone. I saw my reflection a few days back, and I reminded myself of nothing so much as one of the unwrapped mummies they sell in Alexandria – brown teeth sticking through shrivelled lips, a few wisps of hair hanging at random from my scalp. The beauteous Alaric – or Aelric: call me what you will – whose face shone more brightly than the moon, is long gone.

But the great Flavius Alaric, Light of the North, Scholar of Scholars, author of histories, intelligence reports, libels, begging letters, flattery, smutty poems, and so much more – he remains very much still here, magnificent even in his external decay.

No – what had me holding up the sheet of papyrus over my little charcoal brazier was one of my very rare stabs of conscience.

'Why don't you write your life?' Benedict asked me again the other day, after he'd watched me on my best behaviour in the advanced Latin class – that is, not ogling every boy without spots. 'God has blessed you with so many years, and these have been crowded with so many worthy deeds. A full record would be so very *edifying*.'

Is Benedict wholly ignorant of all I've got up to in the past eighty-odd years? Since he lacks any noticeable taste for irony, I suppose he is. Perhaps it's for the best if he remains ignorant.

Then again, a refugee does have some obligation to those who take him in. So, here I sit, a moth-eaten blanket over my knees, the rain falling in sheets outside my window, pen in hand. Benedict wants a full record of my life, and a full record he shall have. But since he said nothing about a comprehensible record, I will, my Latin opening aside, write in the privacy of Greek. If I am obliged at last to tell the whole truth about myself, I feel a coordinate obligation not to shock the sensibilities of my good if enthusiastic hosts.

I don't know who you are, my Dear Reader, and I don't know where or when you are. But I do suspect you will be less pained by the truth than good Benedict. And I do promise that the truth I shall write will indeed be the truth and nothing but the truth.

I

I begin my narrative of truth with that day early in the October of 608. I was eighteen and was seven months into my job as interpreter and general secretary to Maximin. He was a fat little priest from Ravenna who'd come over to join the work of the still rather new mission to claim England for the Faith.

'I was sent here to fish for the souls of men,' he said as he sat carefully down under a tree. 'Clement brought over a whole village last month, and he does it by singing to the natives. I'll not be outdone.'

He washed down an opium pill with his beer and looked at the sky. It hadn't clouded over yet, and the day was looking set to be fine and warm till evening.

'I think we should pray for the rain to hold off,' he said. 'I want a nice rich smell for when the people come by.'

'Don't you think, Reverend Father,' I said, looking up from the job in hand – that is, rubbing our churl assistant all over with a dead cat – 'they might recognise us? Word does get round, you know, about resurrections from the dead.'

'Oh, think nothing of that,' said Maximin with a stretch of his legs. He took another swig on his beer and leant confidentially forward. 'We're a good mile outside Canterbury. These are people who probably have no contact with the fishermen of Deal we ourselves fished for the Faith last Sunday. They've certainly never so much as heard of the miracle-working Maximin.'

He refrained from giving himself one of his little hugs and switched into broken English for the sake of the churl.

'The Old Gods of your race, and of every other,' he said, 'are demons who have, through God's High Sufferance, for the trial of

3

man, transformed themselves into objects of worship. They must be driven out from your sacred groves back to the Hell to which they were confined after their Fall from Grace.'

Very likely! I thought. The Old Gods were just as much a fraud as the new one. 'Keep still!' I hissed at the churl while Maximin was looking at the sky again. 'If this thing bursts and I get mess over me again, I'll give you a right good kicking when we're alone.'

'Your Honour surely needs some time for sleeping,' he mumbled slyly.

Maximin went back into Latin. 'Do you think they might have some food with them when they come back from the fields? I'm beginning to feel rather hungry . . .'

Thus, like thieves lying in wait, we readied ourselves for our miracle of the day. I was my usual convincing self as the young freeman who'd just happened to find a dead churl under some bushes. Speaking for myself, I'd not have got off the horse for that unshod foot sticking out. Maximin performed nobly as the missionary who'd just happened to be riding by on his donkey. The churl stayed absolutely still until Maximin had finished getting the villagers to gather round and join him in the call on God.

I've seen more convincing pantomimes booed mercilessly in Constantinople. In Kent, this one was enough to have a dozen men begging for the 'magic water' of the priests. And they gave the pair of us some of their bread and cheese.

Now we were back in Canterbury. Maximin was off writing up his brief report on the proceedings. Without that, the others wouldn't go out and baptise the wonder-stricken villagers. I was alone in the mission library. The autumnal heat was leaching more new smells from the plaster on the walls. This mingled with the smell of book dust and of the latrines outside. A few late flies buzzed overhead.

I should have been working on the dictionary of English and Latin that Bishop Lawrence had commanded me to prepare once he'd discovered I was an educated native. Now the mission was into unlimited expansion, barely any of the priests who were pouring into Kent and fanning into the neighbouring kingdoms

4

knew a word of English. If still alive, the older missionaries who'd come over with Augustine were now stretched very thin. And the other English converts had poor Latin.

That landed me with a job I just didn't have the skills in those days to do at all, let alone do well. You try taking an unwritten language, in which the words for basic things are different every few miles, and squeezing it into the categories of Latin grammar.

I shoved the wooden writing tablets aside, buried my face in my hands and thought [again] of Edwina. She was the one bright point in my life.

Maximin had sensed some of my pain. In his good and practical way, he was talking now about accelerated ordination for me into the priesthood. It made sense. I had no place among my own people. At the same time, I wasn't really one with the missionaries.

But Edwina stood between me and that idea. Our illicit relationship had begun shortly after my arrival from Richborough. Almost every night since then, we'd been meeting long after dark behind her father's stable to entertain ourselves till dawn with her grey fingers fringed the Kentish sky.

Like one of those ancient novelists, I could fill up pages with accounts of what we did, and how often. But I won't. Either you've had a lot of sex when young and in love or you haven't. If you haven't, no mere words will convey the ecstatic union of bodies and souls. If you have, there is no need of words.

But now the weather was turning against us, and there was another, more specific, problem to consider. When she'd explained about monthly flows and their absence, I was young enough and stupid enough to be as much pleased as alarmed. Edwina was simply alarmed. I'd suggested we should run away to France. She'd asked the usual womanly questions about what to do there and how to eat. I'd given the answers usual of youth. They'd failed to convince.

I jumped at the touch of a hand on my shoulder. I grabbed at a writing tablet and prepared to explain that I'd been trying to think of an English phrase to stand as equivalent for the Latin '*Saluatio*'.

But it wasn't Maximin who stood behind me, or anyone else who had a right to know how I was passing the afternoon.

'Oh, it's you', I said coldly to the churl assistant. I put my hands down into my robe to hide their trembling. 'You should know your sort aren't allowed near the books. What do you want?'

The low creature squinted back at me, a knowing grin only half wiped from his face.

'Be pleased, Your Honour,' he said, 'I won't say if you've been catching up on your sleep.'

He dodged back as I stood and wheeled round at him. He wouldn't get away with this again now we were alone.

'You listen here,' I said, trying not to sound alarmed. 'One word from you to anyone about me, and you'll be shitting your own teeth tomorrow. Do you understand?'

He looked back at me for just a moment longer than gave him the right to get away with unscathed. At last, though, he lowered his eyes and made a submissive bow. I let the matter drop.

'So what do you want?' I repeated.

'The master will have you know he is out of pills,' the churl replied.

Not more opium for Maximin? This would be my second trip to the market in as many days. I'd been getting his lead box refilled ever since he took me on. He'd soon given up explaining that the pills were for his rheumatism, and I've never been one to judge the weaknesses of others. But a second round of fifty pills so soon after the first? Much more of this, and I'd find myself teaching English to someone far less easy to get along with.

I relaxed the muscles in my face. No point in letting an inferior see I was annoyed. Stupid as he was, he'd see a means of using that.

'I suppose the reverend father gave you some coin,' I said. 'The stallholder doesn't give credit.'

The churl bowed again, showing empty hands. Well, I still had some of the change I'd kept from another shopping mission, for Bishop Lawrence. Maximin would be too bombed out on his last dose to wonder what I was doing with money of my own.

The churl shuffling along behind me, I stepped out into the crowded main street of Canterbury.

It was always a joyous sight. Richborough – the nearest I've had to a home town – had once been the main port into a very rich province. But there was no recovery from the comprehensive smashing up my people had given it after the invasion. In short, it was a dump. Even the few people who still lived there knew that. Canterbury, though, was a living place. The streets between the churches were narrow, and crowded with the usual wood-and-thatch houses. But the city had a rush and general feeling of life, and to me, in those days, it was the ultimate in civility. There were churches and administrative buildings going up all over. Much of the material was cannibalised from ruins – there was a regular train of carts trundling up and down from London, then still abandoned. But it was all cleaned and made to look fresh. It must have been the first proper stone- and brick-work since my people took over from the Romans.

Hundreds of missionaries and their retainers filled the streets, all dressed in what to me seemed fine clothes and talking Latin together with other languages I didn't know.

And there were stalls and little shops everywhere, selling things I'd never before seen. No man of taste and culture would have sniffed at the manky things on offer in those early days. But when you've never done more than read about olives and olive oil and pepper and opium and the like, it was almost magical to stand looking at them.

'Begging Your Honour's pardon,' the churl whimpered from behind me, 'but the pill man is moved to the other side of the market.'

He pointed into the side street that would take us there without having to jostle through the square. Then again, my feet would get muddy.

The decision was almost made for me.

'Hello, Aelric. Looking lost again away from your fields?'

It was the bishop's secretary with a few of his hangers-on. They tittered on cue at his joke.

'When will you come and teach English to me?' he added with a knowing smirk. His fat, beardless face was sweaty from lunch in some tavern. 'I can show you a better time in Canterbury than that sad loser Maximin.'

'I have important business,' I said haughtily to hide my distaste. 'I have no time for conversations in the street.'

I certainly had none for creatures like him. For all his airs and graces, he was just a French barbarian – hardly one up on me. And he spoke Latin like a dog.

I hurried into the side street. Now I was out of the sun, I could feel a chill in the autumnal air. I thought again about Edwina. We'd agreed to meet in the usual place as soon as she could get her servant woman off to bed. The thought of being with her was enough to start a thrill that radiated gently through my body.

I thought so hard about the dark, brown hair, about those fine, regular features, about all the ripe perfection of her fourteen years, that I paid no attention to the scuffling just behind me. The crashing blow to the back of my head was a complete surprise.

I came to in one of the masonry carts, trussed up like a bundle of wood. We jolted east over a broken road until I was black and blue from the communicated rapid motion. I had the answer to my continually shouted question late that evening. Soaked by the rain that had been falling almost since I'd woken, and so frozen I couldn't have stood when cut loose without the support of the two strong men who held me tight, I found myself outside the hunting lodge Ethelbert had near Rochester.

2

The gleemen were singing an old battle song as I was pushed into the high single room of the lodge. It was built in the traditional style – a layer of reeds on the trampled earth of the floor, a central hole in the thatch covering that let rain in from the drizzle above while not doing much with the smoke from the great fire below. The damp wood smoke competed with the smell of farting. I quickly gathered that the company had been feasting for hours. Sitting pulling meat off a whole roast sheep were Ethelbert and about thirty of his cronies and retainers. Snarling and yapping, their dogs ran among them.

'Well, just look what the fucking cat's brought in!' roared Ethelbert, pulling himself unsteadily to his feet.

The music stopped. He staggered towards me, his feet kicking up the reeds and the stinking filth below them. He nearly tripped over something that lay out of sight, and one of his retainers had to run forward and steady him.

Ethelbert stopped for an extended fart. He took a gulp from his drinking horn. He looked round to make sure every pair of eyes was turned in his direction.

If you read the history that I – or, more likely now, little Bede – will write, King Ethelbert is one of the heroes in the conversion of England. Because his Frankish wife was born into the Faith, he was the first ruler to welcome the missionaries. That's why the Church made him a saint.

The Ethelbert I knew was a pop-eyed monster with skin complaints and a partiality to other men's wives. He'd put on even more weight than when I'd last seen him, a few months before my mother died. In the flickering light cast by the wall torches and the cooking fire, his face shone with sweat and mutton grease. There was that exultant tone to his voice that I remembered well from when he was minded to let everyone around him know who was the absolute boss.

'You've been a bad boy', he said, his voice dropping to what a stranger might have taken for good humour. 'You've been making that two-backed beast with someone you shouldn't never have looked at. You've dishonoured my best man's daughter. You've dishonoured him. You've dishonoured me.'

He stopped a few feet from where I was held fast, and gloated as I tried without the slightest effect to wriggle free.

'Come on, my lad', he said with a smile that showed a good dozen of his riddled teeth, 'speak up.'

'I can explain,' I croaked. How I could explain I had no idea. I didn't know how much he knew. I guessed Edwina had been to one of the household women to ask about herbs. But effective lying needs some awareness of what the other party knows.

Besides, I was hardly able to keep the tears back. I knew what he could do, and was beginning to shake with terror as well as the cold.

'I – I . . .'

And that was all the speaking Ethelbert wanted. He dropped the façade of good humour and reverted to his more usual tyrannical mode.

'You fucking piece of shit!' he screamed at me, his large face purple with rage, veins in his forehead swollen. 'I gave you your life. I gave you food from my table. I gave you everything. And this is how you repay me.'

He jerked his head over to the company. Alfred sat there among the others. He was somewhat less demure in his bearing than I'd seen him among the missionaries. And if he didn't seem inclined to embrace me as a son-in-law, he didn't seem that put out either by his daughter's dishonour. He raised his horn and grinned at me.

Ethelbert continued: 'You snake. You fucker. You fucking piece of shit. Do you know what we're going to do to you?'

He put his face close to mine. I could smell the sour breath – all rotting teeth and vomity beer and food. His jowls shook.

'See that ladder over there?' he snarled. 'I'm having you splayed on that like a rabbit ripe for gutting. I'll have you begging for death before I'm done with you, you fucking piece of fucking shit.'

He stopped. He opened his mouth wide. A belch came out, followed by a stream of mutton juice. It ran down his chin onto his front.

I spoke quickly. 'Sir, I am of noble birth. I am of your own house. I claim my right as a freeman to face my accuser, sword in hand. I claim my right under ancient custom.'

I looked across at Alfred. He was really grinning now, his sword pulled halfway out. I couldn't last long against him even in a fair contest. He must have been twice my weight and size. But anything was preferable to what Ethelbert had in mind for me.

It might have been better if I'd gone on to add an appeal to the whole company: If Ethelbert could do this to a noble's son, after all, what might he one day do to their sons?

No time. Ethelbert recovered himself.

'Don't give me none of that poof talk,' he screamed, all control gone. He landed a great punch in my stomach.

He took me by surprise. If I hadn't been held fast on both sides, I'd have gone down like a fallen roof tile. I slumped into the grasp of his men, gagging and coughing. He aimed a kick at my balls, but missed, his nailed boot opening a gash in my thigh.

I tried to scream, but only a croak issued. I was numb with terror. This couldn't be happening. It was surely a nightmare. In a minute, I'd wake in the mission library and go back to thinking how to lay my hands on enough cash to get myself and Edwina across the Channel.

But I was awake and this was really happening. I was in the absolute power of a filthy barbarian tyrant. I'd seen any number of times what he could do when the mood took him. Now he had me. I could have shat myself, but had nothing in my guts but wind.

'Don't you dare lecture me like some fucking priest about your fucking so-called rights,' he continued. 'You lost your free status when your father tried to fuck me over. That made you nothing. You're only alive now because I didn't kill you then.

'By the time I'm done with you, my boy, you'll wish the sweating sickness had taken you as well as your brothers.'

There was a blur of motion just out of sight on my left. Then: 'He'll be lower than me – lower than me!'

It was the churl who'd lured me into that side street. He reeled into sight, clutching uncontrollably at himself. A copper bracelet shone new from his withered wrist.

'Let me cut his hair off, Lord King. Give me his golden hair.'

I can't say if my hair back then was my best point. There's no doubt, though, it completed me as a vision of loveliness. It was this that had first brought me to Edwin's attention at those interminable banquets where I'd acted as interpreter between Bishop Lawrence and her father. I'd even turned the heads of quite a few of the priests. '*Non Anglus*,' they used to coo at me as they'd reach up to pat my curls, '*sed angelus*' – 'not English but an angel.'

But it had never struck me before that a churl could even notice these things, let alone envy them. His shrill, demented pleading almost took my mind off the greater horrors as I looked at him properly for the first time.

It was a brief interlude. Ethelbert kicked him out of the way. This was his show, and he wasn't sharing it with anyone – least of all a churl.

He stepped right up to me. He embraced me and suddenly kissed me. He forced his slimy tongue deep into my mouth and flickered it against my throat. I could feel his swollen cock throbbing against me through his breeches. I tried to pull away, but was held fast in a grip tighter than iron.

Ethelbert stepped back, now under control. He gave me another of his exultant grins.

'Hey, Alfred,' he called over in a light voice. 'Do you want this little shitbag afterwards to comb your daughter's hair? He'll be safe enough then with her. Or do you want him in your fields with the other churls? Do you want him with or without eyes?'

'No, please,' I whispered.

But I was lifted bodily and carried towards the ladder over by the far wall. I squirmed and jerked about like a landed fish. But it was to the same lack of effect. I was caught. There were a few laughs and appreciative murmurs as my legs were forced apart and I was tied in place with leather bands.

'Come on, look lively,' Ethelbert shouted, wheeling round to take in the whole display of his power. 'Get that poncy tunic of his up. Let's have a butcher's at what he's still got under there. Two sheep, Alfred, it's no bigger than a baby's finger.

'Not that it makes any difference now,' he went on to Alfred, 'but do you really believe it was this snivelling little piece of shit who got your girl up the duff?' He turned back to me and grasped at my clothing, leering maniacally up at me.

'Give me a knife,' he snapped at one of his retainers. As I heard the rasp of iron on leather, he had second thoughts. 'No – first get me one of them torches. And get me some mutton fat.'

As he slowly raised my tunic, I swallowed and began to pray under my breath to the god of the missionaries.

'Halt!'

In a deep-accented English, the word cut through the air like a knife. The room fell silent. Even the dogs ceased their yapping.

'Halt in the name of God and the Church!'

Maximin stood by the door, his sodden robe sticking to his little round body. How did he get here? I thought. He must have flogged his donkey half to death to get over so fast from Canterbury.

He advanced into the room. 'The boy belongs to Holy Mother Church. None may touch him.'

A couple of Ethelbert's men sprang at him, swords drawn. He gave them a brief, contemptuous look, then turned back to Ethelbert.

'Let one hair of this boy's head be harmed', he said in the strong, dramatic voice he used for preaching, 'and you will answer to Holy

Mother Church in this life and to God Our Father in the life that is to come. 'I tell you this as the representative in this room of the universal bishop in Rome who sits in the place of Our Lord's Apostle Peter.'

There was a laugh at the back of the room. We weren't ten years into the first mission to England, and these savages didn't care either way for the Faith. A word from Ethelbert, and they'd cut him down before he could draw breath again.

But Ethelbert had dropped on his knees, his face grey with fear. It may have been thoughts of hellfire. More likely, it was thoughts of Queen Berthe. She was hard at work, building more new churches than her husband had fathered bastards. The last thing he wanted was the whole kingdom excommunicated.

No one – certainly never in public before his senior men – had spoken like this to him before. Yes, he'd been defied, but no one had ever denied his authority to do as he liked when he liked. And yet he was grovelling among the filthy rushes on his own floor before a little, soft-handed foreigner.

You can forget all those fake miracles the Church lays on for the simple. So far in Maximin's service, those were all I'd seen. He'd explained them to me as necessary frauds for getting a barbarous race to accept a truth not otherwise communicable.

Now, for the first time, I was seeing the real thing. I've seen more like it since then. These priests have a courage born of belief that none of the heroes in our old epics come close to matching. You can kill them. You can burn their shrines and wipe your arse with their books. You will never touch the fundamentals of their imperium over the soul. Rome's conquest of Britain was by the sword, and by the sword it was lost. Its conquest of England has been by men like Maximin, and this will never be lost.

'Reverend Father,' Ethelbert cried. 'This boy is a criminal. He has sinned against God, and he has broken our law too. He must be punished according to our law.' He looked desperately round for confirmation. There was a mutter of agreement from somewhere. Otherwise, the room was now as tense and silent as in a village just

14

before a promised miracle. Though not sheathed, the swords were all now pointing down. The churl who'd betrayed me was repeating his dead act, his face pushed deep into the reeds as if to avoid notice.

'He has sinned against God, that much is sure,' Maximin continued, with a grim look in my direction. 'But he stands within the Church, and he shall be judged within the Church. Give him up to me now, King Ethelbert. I speak with full authority.'

'What judgement shall the Church make against him?' Ethelbert whispered.

'None less than His Holiness in Rome shall decide the penance,' Maximin replied.

I thought he had gone too far now, but Ethelbert remained kneeling.

'We leave for Rome before Advent,' Maximin added. 'Depending on the penance, the boy may never return.' He pointed at my guards. 'Untie him and give him to me.' Ethelbert nodded to them. I felt a knife brush cold against my wrists, and the blood came back into my hands. I stumbled forward. Someone held me from falling.

Maximin beckoned me to follow him and walked towards the door. As I walked past him, Ethelbert, still kneeling, said in a voice so low I wasn't certain I heard him: 'If I catch you in my realms after this man has left for Rome, I'll have your balls on a church plate, and fuck the priests.'

The man was a stinking bastard. Some years later, I rejoiced when I heard about his death. It was from some disgusting pox he'd caught off one of his whores. The priests put out their usual rot about the deaths of those who have advanced the Faith – angelic choirs above, flowery smells, and all that – but my source told me he died screaming while maggots dropped out of his burst scrotum.

When we were about fifty yards down the cart track towards the road, the music started up again. I turned to Maximin in the darkness. I was shaking.

'What will we do next?' I asked.

15

'As I said,' he replied blandly, 'we are going to Rome. You have penance to seek there. And I have been sent to gather more books for the mission library. After that, I have no idea. But I have no doubt you will find our trip of interest.'

I heard the rattle of his pillbox.

3

I was dreaming again last night. I'd normally be glad of that. My bodily pleasures may be less than they were. But the dreams remain as vivid as always.

Sadly, this wasn't one of the good dreams. I was back in the early March of the year I moved to Canterbury. It was the late afternoon, and I'd just arrived back in Richborough from some business I'd been transacting inland – that is to say, I'd been stealing. Instead of my mother mending clothes, I found the renegade monk Auxilius in the ruined storehouse where we'd been dumped by Ethelbert. He was giving her the last rites while his woman cleaned vomit off the floor.

She'd eaten something bad Ethelbert had sent over. It had been fast, Auxilius told me. Between her falling down outside the privy and dying had been barely enough time to get her baptised.

'Baptised?' I asked.

'Yes,' Auxilius replied firmly, but looking away from me. 'She died in the Faith.'

Was she poisoned? I'd put nothing past Ethelbert. But it was more likely he'd simply killed her with the more than usually shitty food he had taken to sending us. He'd been going off her in the past year, and his charity was going the way of desire. My half-sister sat in a corner clutching a broken doll and weeping quietly. My mother lay still quieter on the rush bed.

Given any control, I'd have stopped the dream there. But it had carried on regardless of my own will, every sight and sound and smell as clearly recalled as if I'd been standing there again.

Spring was coming on early. The birds were singing outside. The trees were beginning to bud. But a shaft of sunlight came through the open door and played on my mother's dead features. I could remember when she had been so beautiful and strong. It had only been a few years before. A young fisherman had used to come and sing to her from outside the house while she tried to look scandalised. But then she had grown so suddenly old and pinched. Now she was dead. It hadn't been much of a life, and now it was all over at the age of thirty-two.

Little wonder I woke crying again. I pulled the window open and ignored the rain as I waited for dawn and then the call to morning prayers.

It wasn't all bad in Richborough, you know. I was too young to remember the time before Ethelbert had killed my father and taken our lands. While they were alive, my brothers would tell me what scraps they could themselves remember. My mother never spoke of the past.

So Richborough was all I really had. I was happy enough there as a child. I'd run about with the other boys, playing at hide-and-seek in the empty shells of the administrative buildings. Often, I'd climb onto the broken walls to watch the grey, surging waves of the Channel.

I even got an education there. When I was seven, I went to the school run by Auxilius. He'd killed a man in France. Even under King Chilperic, that was considered not quite proper for a man of the cloth. So he'd gone on the run. Safe in Richborough, he'd taken a wife and some students.

He used to teach in a little church that still had most of its roof. 'I am a man of God,' he would say. 'Therefore, God's house is mine.'

To be fair, no one else wanted the place. The few Christians left in town were even more lapsed than he was. He taught me and a few of the other boys in town. In return, we dug his garden and took him drink and whatever food we could lift from the local villages. What I remember most about him is his pockmarked face and his habit of blowing his nose on the ragged hem of his monastic robe – I don't think he had any other clothes. But he was a good teacher.

He started me on scratching the letters and syllable combinations on bits of broken roof tile. Then he taught me the use of a stylus he'd dug out of the ruined basilica. Bronze, a point at one end, a flat blade at the other, this had been used in the old days for writing on wax tablets. In small things as in great, Auxilius believed in the old ways, and he had me and the others smearing mutton fat on small pieces of board. He would dictate. When I'd got it right, I had to wipe the fat smooth and start on the next task.

On hot days, he'd take us round what was left of the town, getting us to read the inscriptions. Or we'd go out to one of the graveyards. In those days, the stones were still in place, not yet taken off to build into walls. To my knowledge, he never instructed anyone in the Faith. But he could really bring the stick out for linguistic faults. He wasn't interested in teaching the debased, conversational Latin of our age. What he gave us was the pure language. '*Petere fontes*,' he used to say as he let us read from the few books he'd stolen before going on the run from his monastery – 'Go to the sources.'

If I now preside over the greatest centre of learning this side of the Balkans, it is due to the start Auxilius gave me in that crumbling church, with a pigsty at one end and a tree pushing up the mosaic pavement in the middle.

I saw him again only once after my mother's funeral. As soon as he heard the news, Ethelbert relieved me of any family duties I might have inherited. He took my half-sister away – she was his child, after all, and he was thinking to marry her to one of his grade-two retainers. Then he had me thrown into the street. His men turned up on the third day after the funeral. They took a silver brooch that had been my mother's only remnant of our old standing, and chased me out of the house.

What Ethelbert wanted with the place I never did learn, but it was one of the few buildings in town with a sound roof. As I picked up my only change of clothes, which they'd tossed into the mud, his men advised me to go sell my arse in Canterbury if I didn't want to starve.

But that sealed reference to Maximin from Auxilius saved me from both. How they knew each other is unimportant. Why they were in touch is simple. The work of claiming England for the Faith was more important than remembering old and distant crimes.

When I wasn't out faking miracles with Maximin, I'd sit in the mission library to continue my education. I can't say the majority of the books there were to my taste. They were mostly lives of saints or diatribes against the Arian and Monophysite heresies. Bishop Lawrence was always very hot against these, and he had the missionaries asking incomprehensible questions of the converts about the relative status of the Father and the Son. I had enough trouble myself with the orthodoxy of three gods in one, and soon gave up on interpreting the questions Maximin put through me.

What I loved was the small collection of ancient writings that had been sent over from Rome. Opening a volume of Cicero was like stepping from deep shadow into the sunlight. This meant far more to me than the matter of baptism. It was through Cicero that I made my first acquaintance with the sceptics and with the great master of all wisdom – Epicurus. Oh, what a revelation he was through Cicero. It was as if a lamp had been set alight in my head. Or perhaps it was that I'd been given words to express what I already knew by instinct – that happiness, rightly understood, is the purpose of life; that knowledge of the world as it is must be the key to happiness; that the world works according to laws that we can investigate through our own rational faculties; that no authority, whether religious or secular, should be allowed to stand in the way of our individual search for the 'good life'.

I was young. The Church was part of an obviously higher civilisation than my own. I was eating its bread. I was in a part of the world where its priests were necessarily all devout believers. I might have been got properly for the Church. But, good and often greatly good man as he was, Maximin was the last person to be set over anyone of intelligence whose mind was already inclined to scepticism. With his endless pious frauds, he gave me no reason to believe in the claims of the Church. With the little that I read and the much more that I inferred in the mission library, I had every reason *not* to believe a word of those claims.

But for the knock on the head, I suppose I might have given in to Maximin's urging and gone into the Church. He was increasingly sure he could get the rules set aside in my favour. After my last appointment with Ethelbert, though, there could be no more talk of accelerated ordination, or any other place for me in the English Church.

It was to be Rome now or nothing.

In the event, it was nearly both.

4

There is no pleasure, I have always thought, at once so selfish and yet so intense as a good shit. And I'd just had a very good one. Its cause was last night's meal, our first real one in a couple of days – Italian bread, olives, fish from the sea, which we'd roasted on the beach, and a big jar of wine we'd got in return for some of our bread.

We were on the Aurelian Way, somewhere between Populonium and Telamon. Rome was still a few days along the road. I'd dodged off the road for my shit, leaving Maximin to fix breakfast, and was now washing myself in a little stream that ran down to the sea. Birds sang in the trees around me. Above, a spring sun shone from a cloudless sky, warming me after the night frost.

That, though – considerable as it was – marked the limits of my pleasure. I'd grown up in a world of ruins, and nothing much should have affected me. But my people had moved into England centuries before, and had completed their work of destruction long before I was born. We'd driven out the Romans, pushing them west and southwest, or across the Channel, and had looted and burned until precious little remained. By my time, we held the land, and the few bits of town that were left had become wretched, crumbling places, the ruins mostly decorously hidden under little mounds. Until the missionaries turned up and began the rebuilding, it was a world of balance, in which the old was passing out of memory and the new becoming immemorial.

Italy was different. The signs were all around us of recent, savage destruction. Coming out of France, we'd entered an active war zone. This wasn't the half-hearted fighting within the royal family that had been slowly ruining France for generations. It was nasty stuff. Farms and villages and whole towns were abandoned. Whole regions that still, here and there, showed signs of formerly dense habitation, had reverted to wilderness. The roads remained – they were constructed of solid basalt on deep foundations. But they passed mostly through a desert, going for whole days from nowhere to nowhere else.

It was all such a pity. Until just a few generations before I was born, Italy had been much the same as in ancient times. There was no emperor in Rome or Ravenna, and the Eastern capital, Constantinople, had no authority here. But the territory had passed under quite a decent barbarian, who'd tried to keep up the civilised decencies.

Then that fool Justinian had reached out from Constantinople, eager to reunite all the provinces under his rule. It wasn't enough for him to be emperor in the East and to enjoy a vague primacy over the new barbarian kingdoms of the West. He wanted it all.

After twenty years of hard fighting, and the plague, there wasn't that much left of Italy worth ruling. Since then, it had drifted further towards ruin. With the more settled barbarians shattered, and the imperial forces barely strong enough to collect the taxes, it hadn't taken much for the Lombards to break in and really tear things apart.

A nasty lot, the Lombards. They were rather like my own people. They'd recently improved somewhat by taking to the Faith – even if this was the usual Arian heresy. They'd also sort of agreed to stabilise the frontiers between their bits of Italy and the fragments left to the Empire. But it was all very grim. There might be hopes of peace, but its reality was a fading memory.

After passing though a thin strip of imperial territory on the coast, Maximin and I had gone into Lombard territory. Except for the fact we had to hand over all our silver and persuade some barbarous priest got up in stolen finery that we weren't wholly convinced by the Nicene Creed, we'd been let through unmolested. Now we were back in the part of imperial territory that surrounded Rome. At least, that was the theory. But there had

23

been another hard winter, and a bit of plague the year before had got the Lombards back into a mood for localised plunder.

We'd come across evidence of this the day before. Maximin had urged me up the road all afternoon, telling me about a nice monastery outside Populonium that would put us up for the night. Just before sunset, we arrived by a pile of smoking ruins. A plundering band had got there a few days earlier and somehow broken through the fortification. There was a bit of food left in an undamaged outhouse – hence our nice dinner. But the monastery itself was no more. We'd smelt what we found there from a good quarter-mile away. But two-score rotting bodies, many hideously mutilated before death, was a dispiriting sight. Maximin had studied with the abbot, and was naturally upset to find parts of the man carefully draped around what remained of the chapel.

I found a couple of books that hadn't been consumed by the flames, but they were too heavy to carry away, and weren't worth the effort. At every monastery we'd stopped at along the way to beg a meal and a warm place for the night, I'd charmed my way into what library was available. In the evenings, I'd read. By day on the road, when not talking with Maximin, I thought about what I'd read. It was a good continuing of my education. But this was a dead monastery. There was nothing here for me.

'We could spend the night here,' I'd suggested, looking round the outhouse. It's surprising what bad smells you can get used to after a couple of hours, and it would be warmer than bedding down again by the side of the road, and perhaps safer.

Maximin wasn't so sure. 'This repose of the godly has been made into a house of Satan,' he'd insisted.

So we'd gathered up what food we could carry and started along the road again, turning after a while to the seashore, where some fishermen were looking for somewhere safe to put in for the night.

We'd slept eventually in a little copse by the shore, waking in terror every time we heard the undergrowth rustle. Now it was morning, and I was sitting by the stream deliberately washing my bum.

All the signs were for a lovely day ahead. During our passage of France, Maximin had kept me cheerful in the bitter cold and rain by teaching me Greek – he'd recite from *The Acts of the Apostles*, and let me struggle to compare this with what I could remember of the Latin version I'd read in Canterbury – and by assuring me that the world would soon come to an end. It was because of this, he said, that he'd volunteered for the English mission. Augustine and company and Pope Gregory were of a different opinion. They saw the mission as one of permanent occupation. Maximin's interest, though, was in getting as many souls converted before the Second Coming of Christ. This would atone for his many sins. What these were, he never let on – I imagine he'd had a few impure thoughts twenty years before: his lack of scruple in advancing the Faith was evidently not something that had ever preyed on his mind. So he declaimed on and on about the approaching end, warming to his theme whenever we passed another derelict villa, or, once into Italy, some present evidence of the decline and fall.

For myself, the decline and fall seemed purely a human matter. The trees still blossomed. The birds still sang in the trees. The warm Italian sun still shone as it surely always had. And it was a lovely sun – quite unlike anything I'd seen in Kent. It bathed the land in a beautiful golden light, and was reflected back in the living greens and pinks of the vegetation, and in the deep blue of the sea. It could even make the human devastation all around less bleak than it might otherwise have been.

If the world really was coming to an end, that was not a fact taken into account by the armies of ants scurrying around me to collect building materials for their nest, or by the rabbits hopping about on the other side of the stream. Beyond all doubt, there had been a big change in human affairs – whether good or bad on balance, I leave to you. But the greater universe went undisturbed about its normal business.

I heard a cry from the embanked road about twenty yards back. It was Maximin crying loud in Latin: 'My sons, I am but a lone priest on my way to Rome. Take these wretched morsels of food, but spare my life. Spare me in the name of our Common Father in Heaven.' He began a prayer, then switched into Greek without any change of tone: 'Save yourself, my boy, for I am surely lost. I have two brutes upon me.'

5

I pulled myself together and raced silently up the slope to the road. I crawled into the ditch beside it and darted my head up and then down again. Two mounted men had caught Maximin. They were big, ugly creatures, in furs and leather armour – possibly from the raiding gang that had taken the monastery. Whatever they might have done, it was plain they had no intention of letting Maximin pass unmolested. They were dismounted, both swaying gently as they passed a wineskin back and forth. They were turned away from me, swords still sheathed, and were laughing at Maximin while he begged at their feet.

'You fucking old blackbird,' one of them rasped in Vulgar Latin. 'Do you think we give a shit about you and your Triple God?' He sucked in a mouthful of wine and recited: 'The Father is greater than the Son, and separate from him.'

He continued with a garbled account of the Arian heresy, while Maximin nodded eagerly, doubtless considering whether they'd spare him if he pretended to convert.

They were enjoying themselves too much to make an early end of Maximin. The drink had made them merry in their brutal way. Perhaps they would let him go. But I doubted this. I knew their sort. They'd soon grow bored, or their drunken mood would change in some other way, and then Maximin would be another bloody heap to frighten later passers-by as we'd in turn been frightened by the half-eaten corpses that had dotted the road every few miles from Pisa.

I thought quickly. I'd acquired a good sword from a drowned brigand outside Paris. I had this in my hand. But there were two of them, and each was a match for me in open fight. What to do?

Taking Maximin's advice wasn't an option. Once you've walked several hundred miles with someone, in generally disgusting weather, through dangerous country, you're pretty well best friends. Besides, I owed him. I owed him my life. I owed him my further education. I owed him whatever prospects might present themselves in this world outside England. I owed him – and, unless you're one of those degenerate Latins or Greeks whose sophisticated treachery is losing or has lost them control of the world, I don't need to say more than that.

I bobbed up again. They were still looking at Maximin. I waved to him. His eyes remained fixed on the bandits.

'I have a silver crucifix in my baggage,' he said in a wheedling tone. He jerked his eyes over to the far side of the road. Fortunately, one of the horses was sniffing at the baggage, concealing the fact that there was too much for one man to carry. The bigger of the two grunted and went over to look. By the horse, he steadied himself and stopped for a piss.

That was my chance. I was up and across the road before either had a chance to look round. I swung my sword high and got the one by Maximin a blow to the unprotected head. He went straight down.

With a shout of rage, the other had his breeches up and his sword out almost before I'd got my own sword clear and steadied myself from its recoil. He came at me, a dark stain growing down his left trouser leg. I jumped back, slashing at him.

He grinned at me, an ugly scar running down his face into the straggly yellow beard. He stretched up and threw his arms wide, taunting me. 'Come on, you miserable little fucker. See what you can do with a man who's looking at you.' He stamped on the ground and spat. 'Come on. I want my breakfast!'

I circled him, carefully staying out of sword reach. He seemed unbelievably big and heavy. He must have been pillaging and murdering since before I was born. He had armour. I had none. How I'd beat him I had no idea. I tried reasoning with him.

'Get on your horse and be off,' I said. 'We saw Imperials just down the road.'

No luck. He took advantage of the effort I put into the words and lunged at me. An inch to the right and he'd have had me.

I danced back again and waved my sword. It felt suddenly heavy and twisted in my sweating hand. He stepped forward at me. His arm and sword were both longer than mine. I swung at him. Apart from a bit of playing back in Kent, and a quick running skirmish on the road in France, this was my first swordplay. Hardly moving, he parried me with a flick of his wrist. I staggered and nearly lost my sword as steel clashed on steel.

Without warning, he lunged forward again, sword arm outstretched. Again, he nearly had me. It was only because I was still swaying about that he missed. As it was, he sliced a long cut into my tunic. He wheeled around, forcing me to look at him with the sun behind.

I was breathing hard. He'd hardly raised a sweat. I could see he was enjoying himself.

'Oh, fuck,' I thought. This was a shitty hole I'd dug for myself. He'd skewer me with that blade of his and then turn back to Maximin, whose show of Arianism would have no chance now. I couldn't even run away. He'd get on that horse of his and ride me down in no time. From the corner of my eye, I could see the wineskin deflating as it spilled its deep red content over the road. Not, you will agree, the most inspiring image in the circumstances!

Thwack!

Maximin had struck him a great blow across the back with his walking staff. The armour protected Yellow Beard from direct harm, but he was now fighting on two fronts. He swung round to wave his sword at Maximin, who fell back, jabbing at him with his staff.

'Fuck you!' I shouted, stabbing uselessly at the leather skirt that protected his buttock.

He wheeled back to me, ignoring Maximin while he dealt with the greater threat. He lunged at me again. This time, I stepped out of his way and threw a random slash in his direction. Glory be – I felt a crunch of steel on flesh and bone. I'd got the wrist of his sword arm. He fell back with a scream of pain and fear. I'd gone deep and his sword fell to the road. He had it up at once in his left hand. But I now had the advantage. Sober, he'd only have been enraged by the slashed skin and muscle, and hacked all the harder with his good arm. But the wine and the intensifying sun were doing their silent work.

He was backing away towards his horse, Maximin and I now facing him. I slashed again at him, roaring to raise my strength. But he knocked me away this time. I slashed again, and this time got him on the right forearm. Blood spurted. I lunged now, aiming at his throat. I fell short, but let him see my bloody sword. His face grey, he dropped his sword and ran for the horse. I followed.

As he got to the horse, he turned back, knife in hand. But knife against sword is nothing, especially in the left hand. I could see terror and defeat in his eyes. I stabbed with an exultant yell. The blow glanced off his leather breastplate, but got him into a deeper panic. He bellowed like an ox taken to slaughter. All he wanted now was to get clear of me, but I was too close to let him on the horse.

I stabbed again, and got him in the left shoulder. I stabbed again, and pushed straight through the fleshy part of his arm. He fell to his knees, babbling and raising his bloodied arms for mercy. I got the point of my sword between his neck and the edge of his breastplate, and pushed down with all my strength. As I pulled it out, he died with a gurgling, blood-frothing sigh. I watched as the life went out of his eyes.

Suddenly tired and aching, I stood looking down at him. I felt the need of another night's sleep.

'Aelric, the other one's alive!'

I turned. He was twisting on the ground, covering his face and head as Maximin beat at him with his walking staff. I crossed over to them, and flopped onto the ground by the fallen man's head, my sword at his throat.

He was the theologian. I was sure I'd killed him with that heavy first blow. Instead, I'd only knocked him out, hardly drawing blood.

'Quarter!' he croaked in English, looking up at me.

My strength recovering, I took his hair in my left hand, pushing my sword harder against his throat. 'So, what brings you to this sunny clime?' I asked in the same language.

The answer was obvious. Quite a few of my people had joined with Alboin in the first invasions. There never were that many true Lombards, and they'd increased their numbers by offering a share of the booty to any band of savages who would go in with them. Though the majority had gone away after he'd made it clear this would be his kingdom, some had stayed, and the occasional bravo still drifted over when England seemed too dull. I'd probably just killed one of them. Here was another.

'You're English, mate!' He made an attempt at conviviality. 'Well, it's a time since I could share thoughts of home. What's your name?'

'I am Aelric, son of Ethelwulf of Rainham,' I answered flatly.

'Ethelwulf. He was a mate in the old days. Perhaps you was the boy I saw on his knees. You was a pretty child. You won't remember me, but I remember you. Let us up – we can't talk like this.'

I said nothing, my sword still pressed against his throat.

'Look in our saddlebags,' he whined. 'It's all yours. Go on, look.'

I nodded to Maximin. He came back with two leather bags. From the heavy chink as he put them down, I knew their contents. They were filled with golden solidi. But these weren't the debased, shapeless copies I'd seen once or twice in England and more often in France. They were the smooth, regular coins of the Empire, imperial head on one side, 'CONOB' clearly imprinted on the other. There must have been two full sets of seventy-two to the pound. They were new and identical. Each of them had the same defect on the 'B', which was raised a little above the four other letters, indicating that they came from the same die.

I saw all this later. For the moment, I glanced at the coins, but my sword hand didn't waver.

'Look, mate,' the theologian whined again, 'I can show you more of them – bags and bags of them. Just let us up. We can talk over all the news from home. Then we can go and get the others. Fair shares for all, there can be!'

'Tell me where they are,' I asked in my flat voice. I pressed harder so a line of blood showed along the blade. 'Tell me now.'

'Yeah, yeah – don't let's be unfriendly,' the theologian cried, trying to push his neck still closer to the ground. 'Just take the sword away, and I'll tell you everything.'

'Where are they?' I asked.

'South along the road – about five miles,' he babbled, breaking now and then into Latin. 'We brung them down from Tarquini. There's a ten-man guard on them – not good Englishmen, like us: just runaway slaves and other trash. We can take them together, no prob.'

He paused and looked ingratiating. 'I see'd you cut up Bertwald right good. We won't have no trouble with the others . . . Now, give us a drink, mate.'

I said nothing.

He continued: 'We was ordered to wait there by the Saint Antony Shrine for instructions. Some Roman or summink was to come and tell us, or such. We didn't know right, but we was to wait there – that's all we was told on delivery.'

He spoke on in quick gasps in his strange mingling of languages. They were on some business, of which they knew nothing, for the Lombard authorities. They were to take delivery of a consignment of gold and a very holy relic – the nose of Saint Vexilla. They had no idea what would happen. They'd been told simply to wait for further instructions that would be obvious when they came.

'All very hush hush,' the theologian continued, trying to lick some moisture onto his dry lips. 'Bertwald and me, we just grabbed what was rightly ours and was on our way back to Pavia. Come on, mate, I'm gasping for a drink. Don't keep me down like this. The fucking sun's in me eyes.'

Nothing more to learn here, I thought.

'My father was not Ethelwulf. I have heard of no Ethelwulf of Rainham,' I said. I drew the sword across his throat, cutting from under one ear right up to the other.

'Oh, shit and fuck!' I'd never cut a throat before, and wasn't prepared for the fountain of blood. It went all over my face and hair and soaked my sleeve. I was mucky enough already from all that crawling in the ditch and the other death fight. But that was just washing muck. This would take hours of scrubbing, and still there'd be a stain on the grey wool of my tunic. Add to this the sword-thrust, and I'd be shabby as a churl. Of course, I had no other clothes with me.

'Fuck!' I pushed the jerking, gurgling body away. More blood splashed onto my trousers.

'Was that quite in order, my son?' asked Maximin. He sat on a slightly raised paving stone, looking with evident disapproval at the pool of blood now creeping towards him. I couldn't tell if he was objecting to the dispatch or to the mess, or even to the attendant language – though English is a tongue rich in obscenities, and he must have picked up most of them in Canterbury.

'He had it coming,' I snapped. 'If he and his friend weren't involved in doing over that monastery, I've no doubt they'd have done similar elsewhere . . . And a dead bandit is always better than a live one.'

Maximin didn't argue. He was probably thinking as I was – that if we'd stayed in that outhouse, none of this might have been necessary. In any case, we seldom argued now about matters of defence and violence. As I said, we'd been together on the road for months.

Back in England, he'd played me by the book. He'd led me round Canterbury and had me begging forgiveness in every church for my many sins with Edwina – and had me confessing them chapter and verse to the other missionaries, who had rolled their eyes and hugged themselves.

He'd still tried to lecture me on Christian humility back in Amiens, when I'd had cause to beat a cutpurse to pulp. Since then, we'd been pushing steadily through a dense mass of two-legged vermin. Even someone less intelligent than Maximin would soon have learnt the difference between a being created in God's image and a particle of scum fit only to be kicked or beaten or stabbed or otherwise repelled in the shortest order.

We rolled the bodies into the ditch. I took a vicious little knife from the theologian's belt. And we loaded our baggage onto the horses. Maximin plainly didn't like the thought of climbing onto what seemed the more placid of the beasts. I can't say I was a skilled rider. But we were better off on horseback than on foot. Just because we'd got through this attempt on our lives didn't mean the roads would now be clear all the way to Rome.

As I dressed myself after washing down at the stream again – Maximin and the horses this time in clear view – and then ate breakfast, I was increasingly aware of the two-pound weight of gold swinging from my belt. It was a nice, comfortable weight, and I couldn't help thinking how, without putting myself in too much danger, I might before the next morning increase it.

6

'You'll look lush, sir – really, truly lush.' The younger of the tailors spoke with unforced enthusiasm as he looked up at me, his mouth full of pins.

'Indeed, sir, you will,' the other added, holding up the dented bronze mirror. 'For a lady, is it, sir? Is she pretty? Will you be marrying her in Rome? Or simply *visiting* her?'

I ignored the questions and looked at what I could see of myself in the mirror. They were right. I looked remarkably fine. I'd looked good in Canterbury. But that was before all the walking and other exercise. I now looked ravishing. As I stared into that mirror, I had to work hard to repress a little stiffy I felt coming on.

Populonium, on the other hand, had seen better days. It had once been a rich little port town and a seaside retreat for the less wealthy of the Roman higher classes. Now, it was mostly ruined within its walls. The port remained, but the trade was largely gone. Still, it had its own bishop, and there was enough local demand to keep a few dusty shops going in the unruined centre.

We'd been lucky in finding the tailors. I had thought it unlikely we could get anything sufficiently good to be convincing in such short order. But the sight of one solidus had led, after a hushed and rapid conversation I hadn't been able to catch, to the appearance of a most beautiful suit of clothes. They were, Maximin assured me, in the fashion of the wealthy young – tight linen trousers, loose woollen tunic, dyed blue and drawn in at the waist, and a little scarlet cloak. Ignore the slight pissy stain around the crotch and the neatly mended rent in the tunic under the heart – was that a darkness on the blue of the wool or a trick of the light? – and I could have passed easily among the grander passengers on the road, who'd been hurrying by on horseback, surrounded by armed bodyguards. Even the soft leather boots fitted, once they were reduced with a thick insole. At least the brimmed cap might have been made for me.

'Tell me,' I asked Maximin in Greek – I raised my arm as directed as a loose fold in the tunic was pinned back for adjustment – 'who was Saint Vexilla?'

Maximin drifted out of his tipsy reverie. He'd taken in a good two pints of wine since our encounter of earlier that day. He looked into his empty cup, looked at the jug beside him, sighed, and put his cup down. 'Saint Vexilla,' he explained, sitting up a little, 'was a beauteous and noble virgin in the time of Diocletian. She was pledged by her family for the idolatrous cult of Vesta. Then began the seventh and the last great persecution of the Faith. The martyrs of our Church were as the stars in the sky, or as the sands of the Libyan desert—'

'Yes,' said I. The wine was leading him into declamatory mode, and I wanted information, not a sermon.

He drew himself together and continued. 'The tyrant, unlike earlier persecutors, was not satisfied with the blood of our martyrs. He also wanted to extirpate our books and other holy objects. His decree went out, that all copies of the Scriptures should be delivered up for consignment to the flames.

'One day, as she was carried through Rome in her chair, Vexilla was approached by an ancient retainer, who was secretly of the Faith. "Take these precious books in safekeeping," he begged her, giving her the Gospels according to Saint Matthew and Saint Mark. "There cannot be another day before I am caught. My old body is as nothing, O gracious lady, but save these precious books."

'Vexilla took and read and, by the working of the Holy Spirit, was converted to the Faith. And so it became her mission to go about Rome, gathering up whichever of our books could be saved from the flames.

'One day, she was betrayed by her own brother to the authorities. She was bound and taken before Caesar himself. He looked

36

grimly at her, his evil face as hard and smooth as the stone of his idols. "Deny this sordid cult, and you shall be freed with full honour," he said. "Deny this cult and deliver up to us the writings we know you to have harboured."

'But Vexilla was obdurate. And so the tyrant had her given over to torture. A club studded with iron hooks was heated till red, and drawn across her white, virginal flesh . . .'

I won't enumerate the tortures some lying monk had written with one hand. It was the usual stuff – drops of blood turning to rose petals where they fell, slaves brought in to rape her struck impotent or made to ejaculate stinking pus before they could touch her, and so on and so forth. Eventually, she was slowly broiled in a bath of molten lead while she prayed in a voice of unearthly sweetness.

All lies, of course. I've never seen a miracle but I've also seen how it was done. Why therefore believe a word about miracles I haven't seen?

But, after one of his opium pills, Maximin continued. About fifty years after her alleged death, alleged parts of Vexilla turned up on the now booming market for relics, and were alleged to have miraculous properties. Her nose was a particular treasure – a single kiss to the cloth covering it was a sure cure for all respiratory disorders. It had eventually come into the possession of the Church of the Apostles in Rome, and there it should still have been – only now a band of heretical barbarians had it in their clutches.

'We must get it back,' Maximin said, his face red with anger at the impiety.

'We certainly must,' I agreed, thinking of the gold.

'In his mysterious goodness, God has surely put in our path an opportunity to expiate all our many sins. To take back such a mighty relic and restore it to its proper keeping . . .'

Maximin fell silent, pouring another cup and doubtless thinking of his soul. I stood admiring myself as the tailors fussed and chattered around me, and thought of the gold.

* * *

Young as I was, I already knew the most important fact of all about money – that, in this world, you can't fart without the stuff. If you aren't lucky enough to inherit from your ancestors, you must somehow get it for yourself. From my early childhood, I could just recall a rude level of comfort. All other memories were of supplementing Ethelbert's castoffs by living on my wits. Whether I'd ever see England again, or make my way in life on the shores of the Mediterranean, I was determined not to pass another day as a mendicant pilgrim. I'd live or die with money in my purse. So here we were in Populonium, getting prepared for a deception that – if successful – would, ten thousand times over and more, beat all the highway robberies in which I used to assist on the Wessex border.

I'd seen to the horses on our first arrival in town. Though big and powerful, those taken from the bandits had to be replaced. They were too recognisable and didn't fit with our chosen image. There was a market in front of the main church, and I'd made a good exchange with a Frankish dealer. The two beasts we had, plus a little gold, got us a white and very striking horse for me and a smaller but still fast gelding for Maximin.

I knew a low profile was essential. But after transacting the horse business, I couldn't resist a look around the town. As said, it was mostly in ruins, but it was still more in one piece than Richborough; and it had a few curiosities I hadn't seen elsewhere on our journey.

Built into the nave of the church, for example, was the remnant of a very ancient building. About twenty feet across, it had been a circle of columns with a tiled roof. A temple of some kind, I had no doubt. But I'd now seen any number of converted uses along the way. What made this one interesting was the evident age of the temple and the inscriptions on lead plates that still covered some of the columns where the roof overhung. Most of these were in standard Latin and recorded thanks in stereotyped form for births, marriages and cures. Some of the older ones, though, were in often very strange Latin – letters added in words, letters written back to front, unexpected variations of grammar. Some weren't even in Latin at all, but in a language unknown to Maximin, if for the most part in Latin script. More faded than the rough Latin inscriptions, these were very finely made.

And as I stood outside that church, with the market bustling away behind me, and the sun of an Italian spring burning down almost directly above, I'd seen in a burst of inner enlightenment a complete cycle of history. The Romans had taken this land from an earlier race – taken the land, the cities and the religion. They had grown in strength and wisdom, their language growing with them. Then had come the decline. Impoverished, ravaged by barbarians, in no place sufficient in numbers to fill the spaces within their ancient walls, the modern Latins jabbered and bargained in a language as broken as the stones of their cities.

Maximin might think this evident decline heralded the end of the world. Probably men of that earlier race thought the same when they were dispossessed. I had stumbled all by myself on the main difference of secular focus between the Church and the ancients – the difference between viewing history as a straight line, going from Adam and Eve, through Christ, to the Second Coming and Final Judgement, and viewing it as an endlessly repeated cycle of progress and decay.

I don't know how long I stood looking at those lead plates, but Maximin had eventually coughed and nodded my attention to someone who was watching us from within the market. A tall, swarthy ruffian, with grizzled hair and a patch over his left eye, he was plainly on the lookout for something. He'd been talking to the horse dealer, and was now looking at us.

I didn't like the look of him, and Maximin had agreed. So off we'd sloped to the tailors in search of something grand enough to hide the fact that I was just another barbarian on the make.

'How long before I can have them?' I'd asked in an affected Roman drawl imitated from Bishop Lawrence back in Canterbury. I don't suppose it would for a moment have convinced a real member of the nobility. But I was finding a considerable talent for mimicry – it goes with the talent for languages – and it worked on the tailors.

'For you, sir, before the close of business,' they said together.

'Indeed, yes, sir – you'll look lush in the rays of the setting sun. Your lady in Rome will hardly recognise you.'

'Is she pretty, sir?' the younger tailor asked. 'Do you sigh for her? Does she sigh for you? Ho!'

He ended with an expulsion of breath I took for a sigh. Were these people taking the piss, I wondered? Probably not. They lived in a world that had been turned upside down half a dozen times. I decided they were simply touched in the head, and ignored their chatter. For all my elegant Latin, they must have known they were dealing with an obvious barbarian whose sword had fresh notches cut in the blade.

'Is she pretty, sir? Are you thrilled by her embrace? She will be thrilled by you. Can we follow your horse down to the city gate? You really are our finest customer this year.'

7

We were clear of the place just as the sun was setting. We trotted back along the road towards Rome. The shrine of Saint Antony, Maximin told me, was about a mile outside Populonium, a hundred yards off the road. On a slight rise in the land, it was a useful gathering point for bandits, as it gave them a good view – without they themselves being seen – of all traffic along the road.

For this reason, we made sure to start our deception some while before coming to the shrine. I held myself upright on the horse, proud and stiff. Maximin followed behind, bowed in silent prayer. We turned left off the road, following a little path that led upwards through bushes. We heard the subdued whining of horses long before we reached the shrine.

'Who goes there?' The harsh Latin cut through the darkness.

'Your instructions,' I said with slow precision, continuing forward.

Actually, I was feeling the need for another shit – not this time from dinner, but from pure nerves. Back on that sunny road, while the birds sang in the trees, and in Populonium, the plan had seemed daring but safe. Now, in the darkness, no moon yet risen, the temperature dropping, surrounded by roughs who weren't likely to be as unprepared and stupid as the two I'd killed earlier, it all became less daring than foolhardy. How could I know these people hadn't seen us ride past earlier in the day? We'd looked different, granted – but we were still two. Would they accept me as a young Roman noble? I had the clothes, and could mimic the accent and surface mannerisms. But I was still a big blond barbarian. How could I know they hadn't already had those mysterious 'instructions' of which the theologian had spoken? How could I know he had uttered a word of truth?

To be sure, he'd lied about the nature of the guards. They weren't the 'runaway slaves' of his description, but were big Englishmen, speaking the dialect of Wessex. And, dark as it was, I could see something in the way they bore themselves that told me they weren't simple bandits. There was an order in the little camp and a general discipline that chilled me.

We rode straight among them. They had a little fire going in a hollow, and were getting some game ready to cook. I stayed on horseback, looking down at them with a lordly confidence I didn't feel. Maximin dismounted and began a silent and exaggeratedly devout prayer in front of the shrine, which appeared so far as I could see to be an old tomb with a cross stuck on top.

'They've sent a fucking boy out to deal with us!' The words were in English, spat out with evident contempt. 'Can't these Latins keep their bumboys out of anything?'

'Kill them both.' Another voice came out of the darkness. 'I told you this whole fucking business was dodgy. Take delivery of that stuff, sit here for two days, and then do the bidding of some boy and a priest. Something stinks, and it ain't my cock. Kill them both, I say, and take the gold. We've been here long enough.' He was another big man with a moustache that, in the shadows made by the fire, seemed to stretch down to his waist. 'Next he'll be saying One-Eye sent them.'

'Your mission is completed,' I drawled, a note of slight impatience in my voice. 'Get the stuff loaded for me and be off back to Pavia.' Probably feeling my tension, the horse shifted under me and whinnied. I brought it back under control.

'I don't have all night to sit here with you,' I added, now evidently impatient.

'I thought—' the first voice replied.

'You aren't paid to think,' I snapped. 'You were told to wait here for instructions. I've brought your instructions. You load up for me and get yourselves off.'

I tried to work One-Eye into the instructions, but wasn't sure which way to go with him. So I added: 'Do I need to get down and count that gold myself?'

Suddenly shifty, the first voice told me there was no need for that. Did I think they were just 'fucking bandits'?

'What I think is my business,' I said slowly. 'Now, I didn't come here to trade words. I want everything piled up in front of me and a light to see it by.'

I'd done the trick. A lump of burning wood was pulled from the fire and a couple of men scurried back and forth in the pool of light with more of the type of leather bag I'd seen that morning. I could hear the subdued music of coin every time one thumped onto the ground.

'I count twenty-eight,' I said, raising my voice. 'Where are the rest?'

'You came late with your instructions.' The voice was nervous, almost whining.

'I said we didn't need no extra help,' a new voice muttered in English. 'Those fuckers will get us our hands chopped off. "Trust you to believe a couple of Kentish cunts",' the voice went on, quoting a line from a song I'd heard an age before in a Winchester tavern.

'You'll hear about the missing gold when I've made my report . . .' I added: 'Now for the other stuff.'

Big Moustache came forward with a larger bag. From it he pulled a small casket. Even in the poor light, I could see its elaborate making – all gold set with jewels.

'We ain't touched nothing,' he said. 'We know the Faith.' He passed it to Maximin.

'Thank you, my son.' Maximin's voice was hoarse. He set the casket on the ground and opened it. His hands shook as he drew back a little cloth inside. He looked reverently on the contents for some while, then closed everything up. 'Our Common Father will take note of your piety on the Final Day.'

'You'll want these as well,' said Big Moustache. He reached into the back again and drew out three sealed letters. He passed them up to me. Without looking at them, I handed them down to Maximin. He gave them a cursory glance and put them beside the casket.

'Right,' I said, now businesslike, 'get twenty of those bags into my saddlebag. The rest goes with Father Constantine.' I nodded to Maximin.

To steady my now horribly frayed nerves, I counted silently to fifty as the saddlebags were packed. At last it was all done.

As we were ready to depart, the first voice asked: 'What password shall we take back with us?'

'Canterbury,' I answered, saying the first word that came into my head. I gave it in the English form, 'Cantwaraburg'. I bit my tongue and cursed my nerves. I could feel the suspicious glances.

I laughed, adding: 'Say you spoke with Flavius Aurelianus. They will understand.'

At last we picked our way on horseback down to the road. The smooth slabs underneath, I forced back the impulse to spur my horse to a wild gallop. Whatever had possessed me to open my mouth like that? I suppose it was that we'd been deep into a long day. I'd woken that morning, a shabby barbarian travelling with a priest who was barely less shabby, heading into a future that involved poncing my bread off others. I'd then killed two men in short order, taking over a tidy sum in gold. Now I'd just swindled another twenty-eight bags of gold from a band of mercenaries, any one of whom could have cut me down in the blink of an eye. Whatever I now got up to in Rome would be done in style. I was nervous. I was tired. Even so, I'd been stupid as a churl, and no one could blame me for wanting to get away while it was still in my power to do so.

A few hundred yards along the road, we broke into a steady trot. The gold was evenly distributed on each side of me, and the horse seemed hardly to feel the additional weight. A small but bright moon was now coming up in the sky with a star or two beside. We could make out the dreary waste that extended on our left, far into the distance. Way over on our right, the sea gently lapped the shore.

As we passed our fifth milestone, I began to breathe more easily. 'How far to Telamon?' I asked Maximin. I'd asked that the previous day, but had forgotten the answer with all that came between.

'With horses on this road,' Maximin said shortly, 'I'd say we'll be there tomorrow afternoon.'

'There used to be an inn about halfway there from Populonium. We can rest there.'

He looked nervously around. 'I don't feel too happy about sleeping in the open again.'

I agreed. We were now decidedly worth robbing. Besides, we had the means to make the last stages to Rome like persons of quality. I saw no reason why we shouldn't do so, heart and soul. I opened my mouth to speak. Before I could even form the words, I clutched the reins in a spasm of fear.

Ahead, a horseman was galloping towards us. He was moving at a furious pace. It was no time at all before he'd passed from a tiny speck, only recognisable by the clatter of hooves in the silence of the night, to a solid presence just in front of us. About twenty yards away, he stopped and waited for us to come up to him. In the pale moonshine, I saw the glint of his half-drawn sword. And I could see the darkness about his left eye.

'Singular courage,' said One-Eye in accented Latin, 'to be out alone on this road now.' He let his sword slide back into its scabbard.

Did he recognise us from earlier? I'd then been in very different clothes. But Maximin was the same as ever, and there couldn't have been many of my age in that region with my hair. Also, we'd seen him in Populonium. Why and when had he left? Why was he now racing back there? I was suddenly conscious of my sword, loose in its scabbard.

'Greetings, my son,' said Maximin, his voice bright and steady, 'and a benediction upon your head. If you and like you are all we shall see this night, God will have smiled on us.'

One-Eye looked keenly at me. His good eye glittered cold in the moonlight. 'You must be in a hurry for Rome – if that's where you want to be,' he said, speaking evenly. 'Have you seen anything back along the road that so drives you forward?'

'Nothing,' said I in my best drawl. 'We have business in Rome that will wait no longer.' I added: 'What do you think we might have seen?'

'Perhaps nothing,' came the reply. The face was now in shadow, but I could still feel the cold and searching look upon me. Was he looking at me or at my clothes? 'Perhaps nothing at all,' he repeated. 'Or perhaps two men. Or perhaps more . . . This road is not always as lonely as it seems, nor as safe.'

We hadn't yet passed again the spot where I'd killed the men. It had been a hot day, and those bodies must now be decidedly on the turn. Unless One-Eye had been in a gallop from before we'd seen him – and even then, he'd have needed a leather nose – he must have noticed some smell.

He continued to face in my direction, ignoring Maximin even when speaking with him. Was he thinking of some other question? Or was he merely setting me firmly into his memory?

He confirmed there was still an inn further along the road, though seemed deliberately vague about its distance. He spoke of other matters with Maximin. A casual listener might have found these matters unconnected with our journey. I could tell he was fishing for information.

Maximin answered him readily enough. An accomplished liar, he had no trouble keeping up a flow of chatter that gave out nothing of substance.

At last, though, One-Eye raised his hand in a gesture of parting and was on his way past us. He was no longer galloping. Whatever emergency had brought him tearing along the road seemed over for the moment.

While just within easy conversation distance, he turned and looked back. 'You have good Latin for a barbarian,' he observed. For the first time, I could hear a smile in his voice. 'I may hear it again.'

With that, he was off. So were we. Every so often, I turned to look back. One-Eye kept up a steady trot that, as we both moved further apart, took him down to an indeterminate patch of darkness on the bright road, and then to a moving dot, and then to nothingness. We were alone again.

8

Mindful of the extra weight, we still didn't want to push the horses. But the bright, silent stillness of that road was having its effect on us. The moon was now fully risen, and while the colour was bleached out, all around was clearly visible. There was no wind to disturb the dust on the road. The only noise was the striking of eight hooves on the paving stones and our own occasional and listless conversation.

By tacit consent, we chose not to discuss what we'd done that evening. The brief exultation of the getaway had worn off. I'd got the money. Now I had to make sure to keep it. We'd ride through the night, I told myself. We'd surely reach the inn by early morning. We'd eat. We'd sleep. We'd wash. I'd change into the less beautiful and well-fitting suit of clothes the tailors had found in a box. Then we'd join with the largest and best-armed group of travellers who were heading on to Rome. There, we'd make whatever introductions were in the detailed orders that Maximin had received in Canterbury but had never bothered sharing with me. After that – well, I had a few ideas of my own forming, and most of these didn't bear discussing with Maximin; but I'd need to see that gigantic city for myself before deciding anything for certain.

In the meantime, we rode alone along that straight and inter-minable streak of whiteness.

'Maximin,' I asked, trying to make conversation, 'who maintains this road? Is it still the emperor?'

'If maintained at all,' he answered, 'it won't be by the emperor. The roads in Italy aren't like the ones in France. They were built more solidly in ancient times. They were kept up until recent times. I suppose, even now, the exarch takes a certain interest. This is a main military road that keeps Rome in touch with Pisa and with the Frankish allies when we need help against the Lombards.'

I shuddered in the dead silence that followed his words. 'So the emperor doesn't rule in Italy?' I asked with another attempt at making conversation.

'The emperor rules all from Constantinople,' Maximin answered, 'but no longer directly. Be aware that in ancient times, the One Empire of the World was divided in two. There was the East, which gradually turned Greek, and which had fairly defensible borders – the Persians on one side, the Danubian provinces on the other. And there was the West, which had too long a border on the Rhine. The barbarians couldn't be kept out.'

I knew all this, but it kept that ghastly silence at bay. I tried to pretend it was all just like the day before yesterday, when Maximin lectured and I listened and learned.

'You know what happened in England. Your ancestors turned up and smashed everything in their barbarian rage against all that was good and civilised. Here in Italy, it was very different. We had no emperor of our own, but the Goths weren't so bad. Emperor Justinian decided on his great reconquest about eighty years ago. It was harder than he'd thought. There were twenty years of unexpectedly hard fighting – towns burnt, farming wrecked, Rome taken and retaken, plague and famine all over. By the time his eunuch general Narses had cleared out the last of the Goths, much of Italy was devastated.

'It might not have been so bad, if Narses had been left in charge. Having conquered, he knew how to leave things alone. But the next emperor wasn't happy with the tax receipts or the spending on defence, and tried to recall him in humiliating circumstances. In revenge, Narses called in the Lombards. You can see the rest for yourself. What remains of Italy is ruled by the emperor's exarch, who sits in Ravenna—'

He broke off and put his hand suddenly up. We stopped. All around us was absolutely silent. Then, as my ears adjusted, I heard the gentle lapping of the waves far over on our right. Ahead, a fox darted onto the road. It stopped and looked at us. Then it was gone. Maximin breathed again.

'If only we hadn't stopped at the monastery,' he said wistfully, 'we'd be well towards Telamon by now. There would be more traffic on the roads.'

Well, I'd argued long with him over that. But it hadn't turned out too badly, I thought now to myself. Certainly, I'd not have changed things for the world. I reached back and patted my full saddlebags. I couldn't hear the gold move, but I felt its heavy and satisfying bulge under my hand.

We rode on. Maximin made a feeble effort to draw my attention to the white ruins on our left of single buildings and more substantial settlements. But his ancestral recollections of a settled, teeming Italy had charm tonight for neither of us. We rode in silence, slow along that ever straight, and ever interminable road. It had survived the race that built it and, for all I knew, would survive those that came after.

Now I heard a noise. It came from behind us – just a brief snatch of something so faint I told myself it was my ragged nerves. I focused and listened again, and heard nothing but ourselves. We rode slowly on in silence.

It seemed to come again. 'Some nocturnal animal or the lapping of the sea,' Maximin muttered.

I stopped again. 'Maximin,' I whispered.

We listened again in silence. There was nothing. There was surely nothing.

My horse neighed suddenly. I almost fell off with shock at the unexpected loudness. I muttered an obscenity in Latin that I'd heard earlier back in Populonium. I came out with a little laugh and prepared a witticism. But Maximin reached over and put a hand on my shoulder. We looked back along the road. Far in the distance, there seemed to be a slight blur in the moonlight. It was as if a little cloud had fallen from the sky. We stared again, straining our eyes in the moonlight. It seemed dazzlingly bright – unless you really wanted to see something. Then it might have been a single candle in a church at midnight.

'They're after us!' Maximin's voice was soft but urgent. Now I heard the noise clearly – a distant clatter of many hooves on the paving stones. As yet, the riders were visible only from the dust they threw up behind them.

I made the obvious calculations. I failed to see how One-Eye, even at speed, could have got back to the mercenaries and then brought them over so fast. But they were after us, and coming on at full speed.

Now we did spur the horses. The long silence of the road was over. All was suddenly a clashing of hooves on the hard surface of the road, and a panting of horses and the internal sounds that go with hard jolting, and the sound of wind in my hair.

For all his uncertainty of touch with the gelding, Maximin was ahead of me by a full horse-length. Either fear was discovering a riding ability until now unknown, or the gold was dragging me back. I thought of lightening my saddlebags. But greed and the knowledge that the delay would be compensated by no amount of lightening had me just digging in the spurs and using my whip. I darted forward, catching up with Maximin.

For a while, we kept the noise at a steady level behind us. We flew along the straight, raised length of the road. The stones flashed past beneath us. I remember the brief but heavy stench of death as we passed where we'd stopped the night before.

Even Maximin was lighter than our pursuers in their armour, and our horses were better bred for speed than theirs. I almost began to feel better as we raced along. I got my body into a rhythm that made lighter work of me for the horse. We'd surely outrun those clumsy great Englishmen.

But what they lacked in speed, they more than recovered in stamina. There is a limit to what unskilled riders can do with whip and spur, and, little by little, the sounds behind increased in volume. I tried to tell myself they were strung out along the road, and that only one or two of them were beginning to catch up. Perhaps these would fall back.

I didn't dare break the rhythm of my body by looking round. But I knew they weren't strung out. These were experienced riders.

They knew the road. They knew perfectly well how much time they had. If they hadn't caught up with us already, it was so they could keep together.

Now, to the rising clatter of hooves were added the cries of pursuit, and then the faint jingle of harness. Even had we been able to get off that road without being seen, there was no cover on either side. Straight as an arrow, it stretched on before us in the moonlight.

Some years later, I slowed a pursuit by throwing little three-pointed spikes onto the road behind me. On another occasion, I outran a band of Avar raiders by throwing coins over my shoulder. Now, I didn't even think to empty the loose gold from my purse – and, if I had, I might have doubted its effect on men frantic to recover a much larger sum.

I still couldn't – still didn't dare – turn my head to look behind. But they can't have been a half-mile behind as I felt my horse begin to flag. I dug in my spurs and shouted at the beast to get a move on. For a moment, I felt a quickening of speed. But it was a momentary quickening. The horse was already approaching the limit of its endurance.

Maximin looked round for me and slowed his own horse. 'Ride on,' I called to him. 'We can outrun them. Ride on!'

I knew I was lying. But I wanted him at least to get away. This was all my fault. If anyone had to suffer for it, that duty was mine. 'Ride on!' I called again.

'Stop right there, you fuckers!' came the words in English so close behind I could hear they came from Big Moustache. For all that sounds travel oddly by night, I knew they were just a few hundred yards behind. And they were closing on us.

I could hear the panting of their own horses. I could hear the grunted obscenities in at least two languages.

'Don't let the fat one get away,' I heard one call, nearly frantic with the strain of pursuit. 'Get either side of him.'

They were so close, we were almost a single group. I pushed my head into the mane, and dug in my spurs for a final, desperate effort of speed. But I was falling behind. Only his continual looking back and waving me on kept Maximin from flying ahead. I could almost feel the approach. I imagined a hand reaching for the reins, and at last the swing of the heavy sword . . .

As we came to a slight incline in the road, and my horse eased to a diminishing canter, the clatter behind ceased abruptly with a babble of obscenities. At first, I paid no attention.

'Faster, faster, fuck you!' I snarled at the horse. I dug my spurs viciously into its flanks. I plied the whip to every point I could reach without falling off. But, as the poor thing continued slowing, I realised we were indeed without pursuers.

I didn't look round. But I did lift my head and look forward. At the top of the incline, as if come from nowhere, sat a band of mounted soldiers. It took a few moments for me to realise what was happening. How long had my head been down? Until then, the road ahead had been empty. Was I imagining the soldiers? Was this some mirage, brought by my own imagination to lessen the horror of the killing blow from behind? But the soldiers were real enough. Like fish scales, their armour glittered in the moonlight. They sat in perfect formation, parting on either side as my horse staggered through.

I saw Maximin already dismounted, talking to one of the men and pointing wearily back at our pursuers. As my horse came to a spontaneous halt, I fell to the ground. Every muscle suddenly ached. My clothes were wringing with sweat. Until I felt the smooth, stable warmth of the slab under my cheek, I hadn't realised how cold I'd become in the night air. I shivered. I was too exhausted otherwise even to pant.

There was a shout of orders in a language I didn't know, and the men were off in pursuit of the now fleeing pursuers. The renewed clatter of hooves faded into the distance. Maximin knelt by me, pouring water between my parched lips and uttering soothing words.

'Whatever were you doing so late on the road?' a new voice came in Greek.

I opened my eyes. An officer with a great dark beard stood looking down at me, his steel helmet a cone of light.

'They were chasing us,' I whispered feebly in Latin. Not much of an answer – but it was the truth.

'We are on business for the universal bishop,' Maximin added in Greek. He seemed almost his usual self. 'We have a relic of the highest value to give back into his holy keeping.'

The officer grunted an order to a couple of men who hadn't joined in the pursuit. They poured water for my poor shattered horse and began sponging the gore from its flanks. One of them gave a disapproving look at my bloody whip and at the smear of blood that led from it to near my right hand. 'Your arse will hurt like buggery tomorrow,' he said in jocular but accented Latin.

I nodded feebly. I was hurting badly enough already. The pain would soon be ready to blot out the relief of not having been caught by those English bastards.

'Welcome to the Empire of the Greeks,' said Maximin, fully himself again and without any hint now of exhaustion. He nodded to the soldier, who went back to his work of sponging. He continued in English: 'I don't think we shall go beyond mentioning the relic.'

9

I was lucky in my first view of Rome. It was on a Monday and, according to the modern style, was the twenty-first day of April in the year 609. The spell of drizzle that had been with us for the last few days of our journey on the road was now lifted. Before riding on ahead into the city, one of the soldiers who'd accompanied us told me that spring was now here with no chance of a relapse.

We entered through the Pancratian Gate and, the great wall of Aurelian behind, we rested our horses atop the Janiculum Hill. We dismounted and ate a little breakfast of bread and cheese. From here, in the morning sun, we could see the Seven Hills and appreciate the city as a whole.

I had never seen anything so gigantic or magnificent. Within the immense circuit of its walls, Rome spread out for miles across in all directions. There was still a mist in the lower parts, and this prevented a full view. But I could clearly trace the circuit of those walls, and I knew that everything inside was Rome. It was so vast, you could have dropped in the whole area of Canterbury and Richborough together, and had room to do it dozens of times over.

As long as I could remember, I'd been hearing about Rome. I'd heard about it from Auxilius, who'd never been here. I'd read about it in the mission library. I'd heard about it from the missionaries. I'd heard much from Maximin, who'd been here so often he nearly counted as a native. But nothing had prepared me for anything so terrifyingly wonderful.

One of the ancient emperors – one from long before the seat of Empire was transferred to Constantinople – could find no better way to apprehend the size of his capital than to have all the cobwebs gathered from every building and heaped before him. It is often only in the accumulation of the individually small that you can make sense of the inconceivably vast.

No one did any such for me. Instead, I just stood there, gawping at the unimagined size of it all, and trying not to let Maximin see how overwhelmed I was.

'Big, isn't it?' he said with a half-suppressed pride, shaking out his napkin for the little birds that twittered round and reaching for his bridle.

'It is big,' I agreed, trying to sound nonchalant. I wanted to put something into my voice that would say I too had seen big cities – Genoa, for example, and Pisa – and that Rome was just a larger version of these. But my voice trailed off as I looked again over the whole. In and around the central district, I saw clusters of buildings so huge I could barely conceive how they had been designed and constructed. Standing out most clearly in the general vastness were the Imperial Palace on the Palatine Hill and the baths built by Diocletian far over to the left. These dominated the city, dwarfing everything around them in height and sheer mass. Largely obscured by the palace was another mountainous building that I later found out was the great Colosseum – a stone amphitheatre so large that eighty thousand people at a time could watch the games that used to be held there.

But even as we rode in, and I strained to look up at the buildings on either side of the road, I could see that Rome, like everywhere else in my world, had seen better days.

This had, indeed, been apparent even before we reached the gate. There was a time when Rome was served by eleven aqueducts – long arched structures carrying in three hundred million gallons of water every day. These fed the baths, the fountains, and many private houses. They poured into fishponds and even great artificial lakes. But in the sieges of Rome that had attended the War of Reconquest, the aqueducts had all been cut. Some had been patched up afterwards. But most remained cut. The baths and the fountains were now all dry. The ponds that remained had become stinking, pestilential sewers.

I had seen how the aqueducts were cut on the last stretch of the Aurelian Way. For several miles, this is joined by the route of an aqueduct built by Trajan. About a mile from the city, the top level of arches had been smashed away, and the continual gush of water that still came down from the hills had made the surrounding land into a marsh. Projecting from the rippled mud were the usual ruins – only there were so many of these, it was apparent that the city had once extended far beyond the walls.

Inside the walls, the city was falling into or was already in ruins. The great public buildings mostly remained. These were built of stone or massive brick arches. They had been stripped of their ornaments. The very marble facing had been pulled off the lower walls, leaving exposed courses of brickwork, with regular notches where the marble had once been attached. Here and there, too high easily to reach, massive bronze decorations showed something of what the old effect must have been. Below that, all was mean and bare. Every dozen yards or so, I saw plinths half-buried in the rubbish. The bronze statues advertised by the lush flattery of the inscriptions were all gone.

But, so long as the roofs were sound, the main structures survived. They were still surviving when I was last there, hobbling out of the emperor's reach with a price on my head. Probably they will always be there. The less solid structures were already collapsing, though. We rode down streets of apparently magnificent buildings that towered seven or eight storeys above the ground. But I could see daylight through the bare upper windows, where roofs and floors had fallen in. Sometimes, only the façade stood up, the rest having collapsed upon itself. Sometimes, the façades themselves had collapsed forward into the street.

Most of the side streets were choked with rubble. In the main streets down which we passed, rubble had usually been piled back against the walls, where it lay covered in grass and rubbish. Mostly, the middle parts of the streets were clear, and we directed our horses over radically worn but still serviceable paving stones. Occasionally, though, what had originally been a wide avenue was now so constricted that we had to dismount and lead the

57

horses over little hills of broken masonry. We did this by what had once been a junction of five wide streets. A colossal statue of some god or emperor had collapsed on itself, and the body parts had been left where they fell, to be gradually buried under the accumulating rubbish of half a century.

Everywhere was the smell of damp brickdust and rotting filth. I could have shut my eyes and sworn I was back in Richborough. Here, as back home, pigs snuffed around for sustenance. Little clouds of steam swirled on the ground as the sun gained in power. Those streets reminded me of nothing so much as rows of blackened, broken teeth, the occasional soundness only emphasised the neighbouring decay.

We passed through whole districts of silent, built-up desolation. In ancient times, I am told, there had been over a million inhabitants. Now, the decline of power and trade and the ravages of war and plague had reduced the population to around thirty thousand.

Of course, this was a larger population than I had ever seen. I doubt if Canterbury – when I first arrived there – had more than five hundred people. But it's all a matter of proportion. Canterbury was small enough to bustle even with five hundred people – the main street was often so crowded, you had to take your turn to get down it. Thirty thousand people in a city built to house a million produced an effect of almost total desertion.

Every now and again, my gaze was drawn upwards by a movement in one of the upper windows of the buildings. I'd catch a brief view of someone pulling back to avoid being seen. Once, I looked up to see a child's face, showing pale and thin against the blackness behind. It gave me a long and mournful inspection, and then vanished.

It was around the churches and other religious buildings that the remaining population of common people was now clustered. These people squatted in the former palaces of the great, or had built squalid hovels from reused blocks.

As we crossed the Tiber and approached the central districts, we began to see people in the street. They shuffled about, mostly in rags, shopping at little stalls that sold spoiled fruit and old clothes and dried fish so stinking it would have turned a dog's stomach.

Here and there, I did see people dressed in respectable clothes. I even saw a covered chair carried by four slaves. But persons of quality, I later found, usually stayed indoors until the sun was well and truly up, and the more dangerous human trash had vanished until the return of darkness.

We even went by a few of the great houses that hadn't been given over to the poor. Heavily fortified, all remaining ancient elegances bricked up, they glowered blankly over the streets they faced.

We passed into what had once been a grand square hundreds of feet across, in which the central decorative column was toppled over and lay in broken sections, and the buildings on two sides were burnt out. Here, we were accosted by about a dozen raddled old whores and some scabby rent boys. They dragged themselves behind us, offering their services. Though dwarfed by the surrounding vastness, the noise of their cries was the first we'd heard since passing through the gate.

> Come, lie with me, O pretty lad!
> And give me money and be glad

Some ancient creature of probably female sex struck up, though I thought long after it might have been a eunuch. The song was taken up by a few others, building to a choral detailing of inventive though unlikely pleasures.

Maximin ignored the various prostitutes. I gave them a momentary glance. I hadn't had a fuck in months, nor a wank in days. But I could easily resist these charms. I kicked one of the boys over as he came too close, and half drew my sword as one of the whores held up supplicating hands that seemed almost to drip contagion.

Such was the posterity of the great *Populus Romanus* that once had set the world to order. Such was the fallen magnificence of a city that had once been adorned with the plunder of the world.

IO

At length, we reached the Lateran, which lay on the far side of the city from where we'd entered. Part of it, indeed, was joined to the southern wall. It stood out from its surroundings in bright, jarring glory. Many centuries ago, it was built as a palace for some noble family. Then it was confiscated by one of the emperors and used as government offices. Then it was given – I think by the Great Constantine – to the pope in his capacity as bishop of Rome. Since then, it had been altered and extended to become the main residence of the pope and the administrative heart of the Roman Church and all those churches that looked to Rome for guidance.

It loomed before us in a jumbled mass of porticoes and arches. The square in front of it was crowded with beggars and other scum. I could smell their diseased bodies at twenty feet. Fortunately, they saw the glower on my face and kept a reasonable distance.

First, we presented the letters of introduction that Bishop Lawrence had given Maximin. These were accepted by a priest sitting at a desk in the great reception hall behind the gate. A fat creature of uncertain age and sex, he looked at the battered but still sealed letter with plain contempt. 'His Holiness is away from Rome. Nothing can be transacted in his absence. Come back next month,' he drawled, reaching for another dried fig.

A few silver coins bought better manners. He told us he would do what he could, and we should return the following afternoon.

Next stop was the Church Bank, housed in one of the cellars. Armed guards stood outside a monumental brick arch that led down into what I cannot imagine once had been. Now, it was brightly lit and filled with dark, sharp Syrians, who darted here and there among parchment ledgers and sheaves of papyrus. Every movement threw up clouds of dust into the dank, unventilated air of the bank.

This was my introduction to banking. I hadn't at all liked Maximin's idea when we'd unloaded the horses and dragged those bags into the Lateran. I was appalled when he said we should hand it all over to these shifty Orientals. I said it would be safer with the whores outside. It still took some explaining to me what a good idea banks were.

Of course, it all depends on where you bank your cash. I lost a small fortune when the Saracens took Antioch. Every bank in the city closed its doors as the cash boxes were plundered. I did in the end get some of it back from Omar – but only after shedding my foreskin in a pretence conversion, and then he paid in silver that took forever to carry away.

Not that I did too badly from the deal. When that pig of an Emperor Constantine – the present one, that is – caught me out and confiscated my house and fortune and tried to have me blinded, I still had something beyond his reach in Antioch. It paid for my escape and the bribes along the way. It still pays for little delicacies that I have sent to me in Jarrow, along with the occasional new book and quire of papyrus. I have a great-grandson who looks after this. I have never seen him, but I understand he is a perfect little Saracen.

But the Church Bank was an excellent choice. Handling and backed by the vast revenues of the Church, it has never closed its doors. Not even when, about thirty years after opening my account there, Exarch Isaac marched over from Ravenna to plunder the Lateran, did the bank suspend its activities. It is the greatest if least observed power of the West. In those days, it was still flexing its muscles as the imperial hold on Italy slackened. Even so, it transacted an immense business. Money came in from the papal estates all over the West and in the Empire. Money went out.

Recently, the pope had taken over the costs of Roman defence. After the last big siege, about ten years previously, Pope Gregory had made a separate peace with the Lombards under which he paid them five hundred pounds of gold every year. There was the cost of a food dole for the dirty parasites in Rome. There were bribes to state and Church officials in Constantinople. There was the occasional sub to the emperor himself when his finances became desperate – that is, every few months.

Entering Rome with twenty-eight pounds of gold in the saddlebags and two around my waist, I'd thought we were unimaginably rich. The Syrian clerks didn't turn a hair as I dumped bag after bag onto the table. They opened a few bags at random, tested the coin, and just weighed the rest. Most of it went unopened into another vault even deeper underground. They gave us a little parchment book with our names and addresses and the weight of the amount deposited. Being still a distrustful barbarian, I kept hold of the two pounds I'd killed for. All the while, big boxes of coin came back and forth, each one accompanied by a sheet of papyrus covered in writing by many hands.

Now to our lodgings. Back in Canterbury, Maximin had been given an introduction to some monastery nearby the old Praetorian Camp. This would give us a floor to sleep on and our bare fill. But we had gone somewhat up in the world in the past few days, and Maximin saw no sinful indulgence in revising our arrangements.

'Let us give our places to some other poor souls who cannot afford what God has placed within our reach,' he'd explained in Tarquini, as he sent ahead. 'So long as we do not enjoy it to the exclusion of our spiritual needs,' he'd added with a monitory wave of his finger, 'it is our duty to take what luxury God has made possible.'

'Indeed,' I said, with an attempt at meekness. I was wondering where the brothels might be, and what excuses I'd be able to make to get away from Maximin.

Luxury for him was the house of Marcella on the Caelian Hill, with a fair view from its roof down to the southeastern wall and the country beyond. Looking away from this, one could see the still noble shell of the Imperial Palace on the Palatine.

Usefully close to the Lateran, the house was a sizeable place, in a district still populated and reasonably wealthy and therefore un-ruined. Two storeys high, it was built around a central garden. The external walls were as blank and windowless as a fortress's. There was a double gate in, which showed that Rome had never been a very peaceful city. Other similar houses lined the street on both sides. The paving stones were unbroken, and were kept clear of weeds and rubbish.

All within was delightful. The rooms were light and airy. There was fresh plaster on many of the walls. The furniture was ill-matched, having been picked up in various auctions. But, un-formed as my taste then was in such matters, I could see that many pieces were of remarkable workmanship. I was most struck by a table in the entrance hall – ebony legs in the shape of caryatids, the top a single sheet of blue glass two inches thick. Rather big even for that big hall, it supported a crystal vase filled every day with freshly cut flowers.

In Richborough, we'd all lived in one big room. In Canterbury, I'd slept in a dormitory with the other monks, and it had needed great care not to wake the others as I went out for my nightly exercise with Edwina. Otherwise, I'd slept in common rooms in taverns, in monasteries, or by the side of the road with Maximin. Now, I had my own suite of rooms on the upper floor. I entered through a door with a lock that led off a corridor. Within, I had a fine living chamber, where I could eat and work if I felt disinclined to share my company. Through a connecting doorway was a bedroom – with a bed, with a mattress, with linen coverings, with a lead chamber pot underneath.

'Piss only in there, if you please,' Marcella had said when I drew it out. 'We use it for bleaching the clothes.'

Through another door was my own bathroom. At the time, the Claudian Aqueduct was back in a semblance of working order, and the house drew water from it. There was no longer any furnace to heat the water in the main bathhouse downstairs, but I could have a bath whenever I pleased to have the slaves bring up cold water. In his own suite, across the corridor, Maximin sniffed at the idea of a cold bath. But a childhood spent swimming in the sea off Richborough had prepared me for the very gentle chill of the Roman water supply.

But I haven't described the toilets! These were in a low building in a corner of the garden. There was a bank of five stone seats, each one in the shape of an omega. You sat yourself down. You shat. You reached through the opening between your legs and cleaned yourself with a vinegary sponge on a stick. I could see there used to be a time when the shit and piss fell into a little channel and was washed away into sewers that led down to the Tiber. Nowadays, though, the water hadn't the pressure to reach here, and so buckets were placed under the seats and emptied before they could overflow.

It was delightful! I'd never imagined such delicacy of living. The poets and sermonisers I'd read had declaimed against warm baths and silken sheets. But none had thought to mention this. It must have been to them an accepted fact of civilisation. Never was cleanliness made easier or more elegant.

'Right, my lad,' said I as I sat sponging myself for the first time, 'it'll need more than for Ethelbert to change his mind before you set foot in boring, dumpy old England again.'

I have no idea how old Marcella was. With her scrawny arms and black wig and hard, painted face, she could have been anywhere between fifty and eighty. She tyrannised her slaves and as many of her guests as she could terrify into line.

'This is a respectable house for respectable guests,' she'd said as she'd showed us round. 'I'll have no excessive drinking in the rooms, nor any gambling, nor male or female callers after dark.

'And you can keep your hands off my slaves!'

This last was thrown in my direction. I took my eyes off one of the maids who was scrubbing the steps down to the garden, her tits bobbling most provocatively, and tried to look demure. But my amorous propensities were well and truly excited, and I marked that girl down for a delivery of bread and cheese or whatever to my room as soon as the Pleiades had set around the midnight hour. I'd not lie alone that night, I was sure.

Before dying in one of the plagues, Marcella's husband had been a middling imperial official. She'd then had the house adapted for paying guests, and had managed very well ever since. Her guests were a mixed lot – merchants from the East, the poorer sorts of diplomat, officials on business from Constantinople who didn't fancy being put up in what was left of the Imperial Palace. With her rates, and assuming a three-quarter occupancy, she must have taken about three pounds of gold a year, of which two-thirds could have been profit. In a city like Constantinople or Alexandria, this would have bought solid comfort. In Rome, where coin was short outside the Church, it let her put on all manner of airs and graces, and think herself the equal of the ancient senators.

'Of course, we fair dote on learning in my house,' she'd said, throwing open the door to her library.

Also on the upper floor, the library was across the garden, just opposite my rooms. About fifty volumes, with scorched covers and water-stained pages, her collection was an incongruous mass. I don't doubt she'd got that too at auction – a job lot of stuff collected from ruined houses after one of the sieges or internal riots. Much of it, not surprisingly, was religious. Some of it, though, was of interest for me. I took down some volumes translated from Greek on mathematical theory, together with a brief work on the construction of drains. Marcella saw me and pulled out a papyrus notebook.

'Your name and the title, if you please,' she said briskly. 'I find this avoids much unpleasantness.'

She looked at my name and pulled a face sour even by her standards. 'Where are you from?' she asked. 'You're not a barbarian, surely?'

'He is a good Christian boy from the old province of Britain,' Maximin hastily explained. 'He is my secretary, and will assist in the collection of more books for the missionary libraries there.'

She sniffed and launched into a long boast about some remote ancestor of one of her late husband's cousins – a senator, she claimed, who'd run a chain of wine shops in London. I forget the details of all this. Its burden, though, was that she distrusted barbarians and refused to have them as guests.

Though it still exists in the Empire, this distinction between barbarian and citizen has broken down in Italy. When I was first there, though, it was still sharply drawn. You can imagine I was somewhat put out by having it drawn against me. I only felt happier with Marcella when, shortly after, she took in a whole party of Franks, accepting their silver with what passed with her for a happy smile.

While I recovered my composure, she prosed on about a London she seemed to have confused with somewhere in Africa. She was cut short by one of the household slaves. There was a man at the door, asking for Maximin. A slave, he was shown into one of the common rooms on the ground floor. The urban prefect awaited us at our earliest convenience.

'I wonder what took him so long?' Maximin grunted.

II

In olden times, the city had been governed from the Basilica built by Constantine. In those days, the urban prefect had enjoyed dominion in the emperor's name over Rome and its external suburbs. The prefect sat there still – though his correct title even then, I think, had changed to duke of Rome – and we hurried to be in his presence.

We repassed the Colosseum after coming down from the Caelian. It made anyone beside it look like an ant. It dwarfed even the huge buildings that surrounded it. I wanted to stop and look at it, but Maximin said we were in a hurry.

'We can have a little tour once our business is finished,' he said soothingly, as I looked about within this massive landscape of stone and brick. I wanted to run about, looking at everything. I wanted to see what shops there might be, and what was in them for sale. To look properly about this great city would take months, and then there would still be much to see. I wanted to make a start. Seeing some imperial official, to say who we were and get his formal consent to our remaining in the place, struck me as a dry and almost useless proceeding.

But Maximin had fussed about in his room with documents, and insisted I shouldn't put on my fine suit. Then we'd come straight out. Now we were hurrying past things of endless interest.

The Basilica was a block further down on our left, just before the main Forum. It was interesting in itself. Being the main government building, it had suffered in the general sacks by the Goths and Vandals, but had escaped the more continuous predations of the Roman people. Therefore, it retained all its marble facing and most of the bronze tiles on its roof. The Basilica was adorned in the manner usual for ancient buildings – marble portico, colonnades, niches for statues, and so forth. But the dominant feature was its immense size. It sat on a sheet of concrete three hundred feet long and two hundred wide. Raised on each side of the width were a line of barrel vaults extending down the length. Connecting these was a great central vaulted nave, two hundred and fifty feet long, eighty wide, and a hundred and twenty high. Still smaller than the Colosseum, the building towered over us as we approached. Two giants walking abreast could have entered through the main bronze door.

The great hall inside was a shimmering mass of many-coloured marbles, lit from windows high up in the vaults. At the far end sat a colossal statue of Constantine. There were still traces of gold leaf on the upper parts. But even bare and white, it was an impressive sight. The head alone was bigger than most houses. To the right and left of the hall, staircases led to warrens of offices and smaller public rooms. On each side, about fifty feet up, were long galleries giving an overall view of the hall.

As we entered, the prefect sat before the statue of Constantine. A small man with a dark beard and a white robe fringed with purple, he was hearing a law case. Beside him on stands were icons of the emperor and empress. Slightly away from these, though at the same height, was an icon of the pope. In front of him, their clients in cowed silence, two lawyers were arguing at interminable length about some defective building works.

As we sat unobtrusively by one of the smaller statues, I gathered that the plaintiff had engaged the defendants to repair a drain. But as nobody in Rome nowadays knew anything about the correct gradient for water, there had been a flood and the plaintiff's house had been undermined. Now the lawyers were making the most of the work put their way. Listening to their slow, turgid delivery, I was unable to work out if they were being paid by the word uttered or by the time needed to utter their words.

Otherwise, the hall was empty. It had plainly been built with crowds in mind. The prefect would once have sat among a vast

68

concourse of litigants and petitioners, all jostling and shouting for his attention. Now he sat almost alone. There hadn't even been beggars outside. The sunbeams moved slowly across the dusty, tiled floor, and the lawyers droned on.

I coughed. The sound echoed round the empty hall. The prefect looked up from his doze, saw us and stood.

'This is a case of gross negligence,' he said in the very correct Latin of someone who has learnt it as a foreign language. The exarch had recently taken to appointing Greek officials to the post, there being so few Romans willing or competent to discharge the remaining duties.

'I give judgement for the plaintiff. I will settle the damages in my written judgement, which you will receive on the Ides of next month. You can pay the appropriate clerking fee as you leave. You are all dismissed.'

With that, he was walking quickly over to us, his legal business forgotten. One of the litigants cried out in a thick German accent that he hadn't received justice. He had used the best engineers available, and could show the receipts. He would be taking his case to the Lateran, where justice went on the merits of the case, not the size of the bribe. The prefect ignored this.

'Welcome to Rome,' he said warmly, reaching out a hand to Maximin. 'I've heard so much about your adventures on the road, and am eager to hear all about it at first hand.'

He took us into his private office at the far left end of the hall. A lavishly marbled room with high windows, this was piled high with books and documents mainly covered in dust. He sat at his desk, we before him. A slave appeared with a pitcher of wine. Three generous servings were made. He drained his in a single gulp and reached out his cup for another. Maximin did the same, then gave a brief and expurgated account of all we had done since that morning outside Populonium. 'But for you and your forethought in sending out guards,' he concluded, 'we should certainly now be dead men. We give all thanks to you,' he paused, 'and, of course, to the divine prudence of the emperor, whose benevolence shines upon us all.'

He raised his cup suggestively. The slave leaned forward again.

The prefect smiled. He probably didn't receive much flattery, and anything was welcome.

'I was given information of something odd happening outside Populonium,' he said, 'and sent a force to investigate. I did give orders that any armed barbarians were to be arrested and brought back to Rome. Here, they could be tried according to the divine justice of the emperor. I was thinking of something lingering for them – something perhaps with boiling oil. Or we still have the two lions. Rex and Regina would have liked some good barbarian flesh – so much tastier than the local trash I must generally feed them.'

He shrugged. 'But something seems to have gone wrong with the transmission of orders. There was a fight, but no prisoners were taken. Getting any orders obeyed is a constant trouble now His Holiness has taken over most payments. A pity. The people would have appreciated a good show . . .

'Now,' he said, changing the subject, 'I understand you relieved those barbarians of a large sum in gold.'

I looked up sharply. How could the prefect have known that? I thought of those shifty Syrians at the bank. So much for Maximin's lecture on the confidentiality of bankers. I only hoped he was right about their honesty.

He continued with a smile: 'You have nothing to fear on that account. I've had no complaints about stolen money. There are no claimants about to demand an enquiry of restitution. You may, of course, make some voluntary gift to my men. If you send it to me, I will ensure it reaches the proper hands. However,' he paused, 'I believe there were other objects taken from the barbarians – objects recovered, that is, that may have identifiable owners.'

Maximin broke in: 'God made us His humble instruments in the recovery of a most holy relic. This, of course, is a matter for His Holiness. I shall see him tomorrow and give the relic directly into his own hands.'

'Not tomorrow, you won't,' the prefect said. 'Boniface erupted all over a while back in a rash of bleeding sores. Since the relics didn't work in his case, the doctors have sent him off to Naples for the volcanic mud baths. I doubt he will be back before next month. As the highest civil power in Rome, I will take delivery of the relic. It is intended for the consecration of the new Church of St Mary – that is, for the consecration of the old temple of the demons Jupiter, Venus and Mars.'

He crossed himself, and continued: 'I have full authority to take possession of all stolen goods that may be recovered.'

'With respect,' said Maximin, 'this is a matter for Holy Mother Church. I have an appointment at the Lateran tomorrow, and will hand the holy relic back into the hands of those whose lawful property it is.'

It was obvious that, whatever fancy title he might have, the prefect had no authority in practice to compel anything. He dipped his finger in wine and traced a circle in the dust that covered his desk. 'Very well,' he said at length, in a flat and only slightly disappointed voice. 'If that is how you want to play, so be it.'

He paused again, then asked: 'What brings you and your young friend to Rome?'

Maximin explained our mission to gather books for Canterbury, passing me off as a convert of the utmost piety. The prefect shot me a brief but penetrating glance, as if looking for any trace of piety. I looked humbly down, hoping he had seen other than an educated brigand.

'I think a month from today should be sufficient for your purposes,' he said. 'I doubt you will have any trouble gathering all the books you could ever want in this place. I don't even think the owners will insist on your making copies to take away. And it would be a shame to deprive the furthermost Britons of two such holy and effective missionaries of the Faith.

'I will have your residence permits sent over to your lodgings tomorrow or the day after. Please note they will not entitle you to receive anything from the papal dole.'

With that, the prefect rose, our audience at an end. As he rose, he knocked over his cup, spilling red wine over a heap of papers. He scowled and brushed them all onto the floor, shattering the cup, and sat heavily down again with his back to us.

12

Our business over, Maximin and I continued deeper into the Forum. This had once been the civil and religious centre of Rome. But times now were altered, and its buildings were no longer in use. Some had fallen down. Most had been locked shut. We passed by the Julian Basilica – big, though far smaller than the place we had just visited. Its great doors were secured with bars and a rusted padlock. As ever, its marble facing had been mostly stripped. The bronze statues that had once been crowded outside were evidenced only by their plinths. I think it was the Vandals who had stripped all the bronze they could carry in their leisurely sack of about a hundred and fifty years before.

It was the same for the Temple of Concord and even the Senate House – this hadn't been used for generations. The Temple of Vesta we'd already seen. This was an elegant little building – the old temples, by the way, were generally built smaller than churches, which follow the basilica pattern. The reason is that temples were never meant to hold large numbers of worshippers, but housed the cult statues, the main worship taking place in the open. The Temple of Vesta had been broken open, and was in use as a cow shed. Other buildings had fallen down, and I couldn't identify their function even by the broken inscriptions.

Once or twice, I turned to ask Maximin. He'd known Rome from any number of visits. Sometimes, he'd answer with a firm confidence that I was willing to trust. Quite often, even he was vague about the former uses of these falling or fallen buildings.

'It was a temple to some demon,' he said, pointing up at the great Temple of Jupiter that still loomed above us on the Capitoline Hill. 'As with all the others, it was closed over two hundred years ago on

73

the orders of Caesar. God willing, it may soon fall down – or be turned to some holy purpose. So many were the demons who resided in this city before men were brought to the True Faith of Our Lord and Saviour, Jesus Christ. Even now, they wander the Earth, tempting the unwary to blasphemy or heresy.'

Knowing Maximin as I did, I mastered the urge to sniff. I resolved instead to get him again when he was feeling less devout. Plainly, Rome was in no need of temples. With the decay of power and population, it also had little need of administrative buildings. But it would be nice to know what all these places had been.

It didn't help that the Tiber had risen in the past hundred years, and the Forum was now regularly flooded. We mostly walked over compacted mud several feet higher than the old pavements.

Just in front of the Julian Basilica, though, the ground had been cleared, and there was a gleaming new column set up with a golden statue on top. About fifty feet up, the statue was a crude lump of bronze. It looked barely human. It made a shocking change from the smooth perfection of the marble statues we'd just seen in the Basilica or still dotted here and there about the city. The thin leaf covering was coming off. But the column was an elegant, fluted thing. Untouched by the elements, it had obviously been salvaged from some ruined interior – like all other new work in Rome.

This was my first sight of the Column of Phocas. The inscription on its base – placed over another that had been chiselled out – said everything. Part of it read:

We have erected a dazzling golden statue of His Majesty, our Lord Phocas, the Eternal Emperor, the *Triumphator* crowned of God, in return for countless good deeds, for the establishing of peace in Italy, and for the preservation of freedom.

It had been set up a year or so before by the pope in the presence of Exarch Smaragdus, over from Ravenna, in honour of the emperor. In recent years, pope and emperor had not always been at one. The emperor saw Italy as an outpost. It was a place where taxes should be collected rather than spent. His main concerns were the Persians across the Euphrates and the barbarians beyond the

Danube. It took up all the work of diplomacy and strategy to bribe or otherwise to conciliate, or repel these groups by arms from the taxpaying provinces.

The pope, of course, saw things differently. He'd taken effective control over Rome and some other parts of Italy, and was dealing with the Lombards as if he were a sovereign prince. The treaty Pope Gregory had made some years earlier was technically an act of treason. But the days when an emperor could arrest and replace a pope – as Justinian had – were long past.

Then there was the matter of religious primacy. As the successor of Saint Peter, and bishop of Rome, the pope claimed a supreme status above all the other churchmen and an equality with the emperor himself. Pope Gregory had taken up and refurbished the old claim to be regarded as the universal bishop.

So long as they could, the emperors in Constantinople had deprecated or ignored this claim. But then Phocas had taken power by murdering the legitimate emperor, and had run into endless domestic and foreign challenges. Gregory, though old and dying, was still the most effective pope in hundreds of years. It was he who'd sent out the mission to England.

He'd seized his chance with Phocas. In return for some gross but vague flattery – of which this column, set up after his death, was one instance – and a more effective, though less public, series of bribes, the emperor had conceded the title of universal bishop and tacitly accepted the temporal supremacy of the pope in Rome. The gift of one of the larger temples for conversion to a church was a minor thing besides.

We bumped into one of the lawyers we'd seen earlier, pissing against a fallen column outside the Senate House. He gave us a little papyrus slip advertising his name and services, and launched into an overblown declamation on the splendid ceremony that had attended the dedication of the column. There was the exarch himself. There was Pope Boniface, just consecrated after a nine-month interval that had followed the sudden death of the previous Boniface – in those days, popes couldn't be consecrated without the imperial warrant, and Phocas had held out for a bigger bribe.

'There was,' the lawyer said, spreading his arms dramatically, 'a multitude of the highest dignitaries that came from all four corners of the universe, and all the glory and magnitude of the great Roman People assembled here in the very navel of the universe.'

It took an entire handful of copper to get the spouting wretch off our backs – I thought he'd follow us back to Marcella's. Instead, he stuffed the coins into his purse and slouched off towards a wine shop set up under the Arch of Septimius Severus.

On the way back, I thought several times we were followed. As ever, the streets were mostly empty, and our shoes rasped loud on the paving stones. But could I hear a soft patter of feet behind us? I knew already Rome was a dangerous place, and cursed myself for leaving my sword behind when we'd set out to see the prefect. My knife would be of limited use against more than one attacker. But every time I stopped and looked round, the street behind was empty and silent. Was it an echo? It might have been. I only heard the noise when we were moving.

'It'll be dark soon,' said Maximin. 'Rome can be frightening when the light has gone. Let's hurry back.'

We quickened our pace. So did the footsteps behind. But if they were there, they kept a regular distance, and we didn't look round again.

At the top of the hill, there were some slaves lounging by a little shrine and other people going about their late afternoon errands. There was a sound of hammering from one of the houses as some roofing tiles were replaced. Soon, we were back at Marcella's. With the inner gate shut behind us, we felt safer.

We'd felt safe too early. Our rooms had been searched. It was a clever job. I'd not have noticed, except the book on drains I'd borrowed earlier was turned over, its spine facing right instead of left. And the little green stone Edwina had once given me was fallen out of the fold in my cloak where I'd stored it.

Had it been my rooms only, I'd have concluded it was the slaves going about their business or looking for things to steal. But Maximin's papers had been gone through. He was always very neat about these, and had spent an age when he unpacked in arranging these into the right order. He swore they had all been disarranged. Yet when Maximin checked the money he'd left on full display, none was missing. Nor was his silver crucifix. Whoever had been in wasn't after cash. We called for Marcella. She was distraught.

'But he was such a well-spoken gentleman,' she wailed, looking at the papers on Maximin's table. 'He swore he was sent by you from the prefect's office to get some things you'd forgotten. This is a respectable house for respectable people. We've never had this sort of thing before.'

'What did he look like?' I asked.

He was a tall, dark man, she explained among a mass of irrelevant detail, with a scar and an eye patch. 'He was ever so polite. He knew your names and where you'd gone, and everything. I had no reason on earth to believe he could be a common thief.'

She fell into a chair, fanning herself with a battered ostrich feather. 'Gretel! Gretel!' she screamed. 'Where are you? Where have you gone, you lazy good-for-nothing bitch?'

The little maid I'd earlier seen scrubbing the step came silently into the room. She was a stunner – and by the sideways look she threw me, I could see she thought the same of me. The moment I heard Maximin snoring across the corridor, I told myself, I'd have her. For a moment, I clean forgot the matter in hand.

'Gretel, you little Lombard bitch, you hear me well. You don't never let strangers into the house again. You hear me? You don't let no one in. I say who comes and goes in this house, and don't you forget – else I'll sell you into the brothel God made you to furnish.' She heaved herself up. 'O fie, sirs! Just look at the refuse we have to buy nowadays. Even persons of quality – such as I myself – is hard put to find slaves what aren't uppity. Shall I have her whipped for you?'

'I don't think that will be necessary,' said Maximin. He could have added it wasn't Gretel in any event who'd let One-Eye into our rooms.

'Where is the relic?' I asked quietly.

With a look of concern, Maximin took me down to the stable beside the toilets. Except for the gold, he'd left his share of the loot in his saddlebag. There it still was. The groom told us One-Eye had been in, but had only time to check my bags before an Ethiopian diplomat had come in and started demanding who he was. He'd gone off pretty directly.

'There was something furtive about him,' the diplomat said to me. 'I hadn't seen him in the house before, and I didn't think he was a new guest. If I'd thought he was trying to steal one of my horses, of course I'd have killed him on the spot. As it was, I challenged him, and he sloped off without saying anything.'

I'd met the diplomat earlier in the day. We'd bumped into each other as I was going in to try out the toilets. He'd smiled at me and bowed most politely as I'd passed him. Of medium height, very thin and black all over, he was the first person of his sort I'd ever seen. Assuming you, my Dear Reader, are English, I imagine you've never seen people like him. But I assure you, there are people who are black all over. They come from parts of the world where perpetual exposure to the sun causes the skin to blacken with permanent effect. And for some reason I can't explain, their skin burns not only in the exposed areas.

For all his physical oddities, though, he spoke excellent Latin. I later found he also knew Greek and several Eastern languages beside his own. Now we lounged together just inside the stables, quietly comparing notes on the delights of Rome. He'd been here about a month longer, and had found his way round pretty well. We agreed I should let him take me soon on one of his 'missions of pleasure'. From the way he grinned and rolled his eyes, these missions were rather less than spiritual.

Just as we were turning back to a discussion of what One-Eye might have been after, Maximin was calling me over.

'God be praised,' he said. 'This Ethiopian has saved the Church from a second violation. But for him, the relic would surely have been stolen again.'

He showed us the leather bag into which the English mercenaries had stuffed things. It was undisturbed. Maximin explained to the diplomat about the relic and its significance. There followed an interminable flourish of crossings and mutual flattery.

'So he followed us all the way back to Rome,' I broke in, 'to steal Saint Vexilla's nose?'

I wanted to speculate on the value of the jewelled casket containing the relic. None of the cash in our rooms had been touched; and that together was worth much more than the casket. But Maximin gave me a dark look that said, 'Shut up: this man is a stranger.' The diplomat wandered off to look at his own horses.

Maximin took the leather bag containing the casket straight up to his room. 'Who else has a key to our rooms?' he asked Marcella.

'Only me, Reverend Father,' she answered.

'Good. Pray see to it that only you and I go into these rooms in future.'

With that it was over. Not very hungry, I skipped dinner. Normally, I'd have had a Greek lesson from Maximin. We were past the scraps of literature he could remember and were well into conversational practice. I said I felt tired after the long day. From the loud snores I soon heard, so was he. I put down the mathematical text I'd been reading and went to the door.

I feasted that night on bread and cheese. Oh, glory was it to be young. If only I could be again . . .

13

'The English mission,' the dispensator said with an attempt at the declamatory style, 'is more than the work of bringing over a race of barbarians on the edge of the world. It is a new and vital project of the Church.'

He'd been addressing us for what seemed half the day, standing within the arc of a semicircle of seats; other, lesser dignitaries seated beside him, all in their best white and purple robes. Maximin and I sat before him, ourselves in the best clothes we'd been able to find on the last lap of our journey to Rome.

No one dared look bored. No one dared plead other business. The dispensator was in fact, though not in theory, the main Church official in Rome, and therefore the most important man in Rome. He handled the accounts, authorised payments, and supervised the whole administration of the Church and its ancillary functions.

Maximin had been exceeding glad to crawl out of bed and have the summons pressed into his hand. Splashing water over his face, he explained this was another sign of our step up in the world. Back in Canterbury, Bishop Lawrence had told him to report to someone of far less importance. Now we were barely short of honoured guests.

The great hall of the Lateran is a wonderful place for a meeting – cool, though not too cool, good light, good acoustics, a fine coffered vault high above, glittering mosaics of Christ and Saint Peter covering the walls.

Probably enjoying their faint echo, the dispensator repeated his phrase about a 'new and vital project of the Church'. He sucked in his withered cheeks, and looked round to bask in the consent of all around him. Then, with a lurch from bombast into a diplomatic jargon I could only understand much later, he continued.

For all the intriguing that had bought it, the title of universal bishop meant nothing in the East, where the Churches hated or feared or despised all things Roman. It meant little in much of the West, where the Churches claimed an autonomy of discipline based on their own long foundation, and mostly dealt with Rome though their local kings. But the English Church was a new Church, subject directly to Rome. Bishops were appointed by Rome. Local rulers were to be honoured, but obeyed only so far as was consistent with a primary loyalty to Rome. So far as England was concerned, the Lateran was '*omnium orbis ecclesiarum Mater et Caput*' – the Mother and Head of all the Churches of the world.

There was, the dispensator granted, a Celtic Church in the country that had survived my people's invasion. This Church denied the primacy of Rome, and held heretical views about the date of Easter – as if this latter would have counted but for the former dereliction. Our duty was to bring the Celts over. If they refused our hand of loving friendship, we should use all secular means available to smash them.

On the model established for England, a new order was to be established in the West, and then elsewhere – of a unified, centralised Church, subject in all matters to Rome. The dispensator quoted the relevant text of Scripture: 'Thou art Peter, and upon this rock I will build my church; and the gates of hell shall not prevail against it.'

He gave it in Latin – '*Tu es Petrus et super hanc petram . . .*'

The pun, you see, is the same in Greek and Latin – though I hope you will also notice that it isn't a very good pun. 'Peter' and '*petra*' are not substantives of the same gender. Now, would God really sanction a universal Church based on such slipshod grammar? I don't think so. Indeed, I assume Christ addressed Peter in Aramaic, which I know pretty well, and the pun doesn't work. Nor does it in Coptic or Syriac or Hebrew or Slavic or Germanic or English.

I looked at that semicircle of the great sitting still in their formal robes. Some of the faces were ravaged by fanatic penances, others softened by lives of sybaritic luxury. Some were educated men. Others could truly boast that they had never opened a single book of pagan learning. But they had an absolutely common purpose. This was the aggrandisement of their Church. They had taken this from those who went before them. They would hand it on to those who followed. You can achieve much in your own lifetime. But this is nothing compared to what can be done in the lifetime of a corporate entity. This never tires and never sleeps and never grows old and feeble. It recovers from mistakes and reverses. Like the waves on Richborough beach, individual follows individual, sometimes pressing forward, sometimes falling back. But the tide comes in with unbroken force. It can, by sheer perseverance, change the manners of whole nations, and can by unending repetition make statements that, considered rationally, are nonsense, gain acceptance even by the wise as self-evident truths.

Such I gathered from my first real encounter with the Imperial Church of Rome.

That was what made our book-gathering mission so important. I had thought the books were brought over to entertain the likes of me. Not so – or not entirely so. Through the English Church, Rome would conquer not only by example. Our nation was to be reshaped as a race of Christians and Christian missionaries. Our priests would then be sent forth – to France, to Germany, to Spain, even back to Italy – with purified Latin and no tinge of heresy and no loyalty but to Rome, to reshape all other nations in the image established for us. The books were not incidental. They were central to the plan.

'So, Maximin of Ravenna,' the dispensator concluded at length, 'you have our fullest confidence. You have unlimited funding. State what you have achieved for us in England, and state what more you want of us.'

Maximin stood and began a monstrously long speech of his own. He'd been working on this ever since we took ship from Richborough. We were told of the conversion of Ethelbert and his many works of piety. I barely recognised the drunken, demented savage I'd last seen with mutton fat dripping off his chin and a gelding knife in his hand.

From this, we proceeded to the multitudes of converts – true enough, if you allow for the fact that their sacred trees had all been cut down and their witch doctors killed or chased out of Kent. I was produced as evidence of the miracles of learning that my people could achieve. One of the clerics gave me a long and appreciative inspection, abstractedly wetting his lips. The others marvelled at my command of the language as I uttered a few sentences in Latin.

Then there were the official miracles. Oh, I had trouble keeping a straight face during that recitation of lies. Did Maximin believe it? I rather think he did. I'm sure he believed all his own lies. I am myself an accomplished liar. But I've always felt constrained by a clear distinction in my mind between the truth of a matter and what I was saying at any one moment. Maximin was a natural liar. He really should have tried a career in diplomacy or intelligence or finance. He'd have prospered.

Needless to say, everyone else believed him. His description of how, on Bishop Lawrence's approach, the sacred grove outside Dover had spontaneously uprooted itself and run into the sea drew murmurs of pious approbation. When I was with Theodore last Christmas, I made a point of struggling to Dover. The rotted stumps were still in place – untouched since I had myself supervised the churls with their axes. The timbers still roofed the little church we'd started in the same place.

And we got the promise of books. This being said, the assumption of the meeting was rather different from my original understanding. I thought Maximin was here for books, and I was tagging along. Now, it seemed, I was to be the primary collector of books. Maximin was to be given other duties in Rome.

I wasn't told this in so many words. But it was so. I can't say I was put out. Find the right man for the job has ever been the practice of the Church. Or, when the right man appears, adapt the job.

Afterwards, in his drab little office, the dispensator made the necessary arrangements with us.

'We have a considerable library here in the Lateran,' he said. 'It dates back to before the Triumph of the Faith, and has been much enlarged over the years. We had a good harvest after the great wars. So many noble palaces lay in ruins. Our people went digging out their libraries, rescuing what could be repaired . . .

'Martin, I'll be glad of your presence,' he called suddenly in a raised voice.

A clerk entered from an adjoining room. Taller, thinner, somewhat older than me, he had the freckles and red hair I hadn't seen since I was deep into Wessex. I suddenly realised what a contrast I must have made beside all those sallow little Mediterraneans. Though he was dressed in good linen, and though he dressed his hair with obvious attention to effect, something about his cringing manner suggested he was a slave.

'Martin handles all my correspondence with the East,' the dispensator explained. 'Though growing up in Constantinople, he is originally from an island to the west of Britain. I can assure you, however, he is neither a Celtic heretic nor a Greek semischismatic. He is a true son of the Church. He has my trust in all things. He has drawn an entry permit for the young man to our own library.'

Martin handed over a sheet of parchment covered in the smooth, clear hand of the Roman Chancery.

The dispensator continued: 'He has also drawn an introduction to Anicius, an elderly nobleman of eccentric views who still has a library in his house. You'll not find much there of spiritual sustenance. But one must read the pagan classics for their style.'

Martin handed over another sheet drawn in similar form.

The dispensator paused, looking at Maximin. Martin remained where he was and coughed gently.

'Oh, yes. The young man' – he squinted at my name on the report – 'Alaric, is it not? Is that a Gothic name?'

I didn't correct the error. So began my life as Alaric rather than as Aelric.

'Alaric,' the dispensator continued with another look at the spelling of my name, 'will need a team of copyists for our library. In many cases, our books exist in only a single copy, and we cannot possibly spare these. They will need to be copied. Anicius is poor, and may doubtless be brought to an arrangement for the surrender of originals. Martin has very kindly volunteered to guide young Alaric in the obtaining of books and in supervising the copyists.

'Now,' the dispensator stopped for a moment and looked up at a filing rack beside the little window of his office, 'I understand that the pair of you, in the course of your journey here, have acquired a considerable sum of money.' He pressed his fingers together, a hard look now coming into his eyes.

Fucking bankers! I swore to myself. They'd so far shown themselves about as discreet as a drunken old woman.

'Holy Mother Church, therefore,' the dispensator continued, 'will look to you to bear the whole cost of acquiring and arranging for the transport of books. This is, you will agree, very much to your advantage. We had in mind a fairly small gift in the first instance for the Canterbury library. Now, of course, you may gather as you please. Martin will help in the matter of the books. He is also fluent in Greek. This is nowadays an unusual accomplishment in our Church – indeed, Saint Gregory spent many years in Constantinople before becoming pope, and returned with not a word of Greek. We find Latin sufficient for our modern purposes.

'Yet it is our intention that the English should, when the time is right, study Greek as well as Latin. It may not presently be useful, but it would make sense to take advantage of your opportunity and to form the basis of a Greek library in Canterbury. Martin will assist in the selection of the appropriate texts.'

At last, we came to the relic. Maximin reached into his satchel and handed this over. The dispensator assured himself all was in order and looked up, now smiling. 'Holy Mother Church is in debt to both of you,' he said. 'This precious relic of Saint Vexilla was stolen not ten days ago. It was an audacious robbery – in the very church where I sometimes pray.'

Another clerk entered, this one in the rough, dark robe of a monk. He bowed silently and placed a sealed letter on the desk. The dispensator gave it a brief glance. 'I will read this later,' he said to the monk, 'when I have time and am alone. No reply for the moment.'

The clerk opened his mouth for what looked a protest, but checked himself. He bowed again and left. I saw Maximin stare at this letter, a curious look on his face. As if he'd noticed this look, the dispensator neatly covered the letter with a sheet of papyrus.

'You did well,' he continued, looking back to the relic, 'not to hand it over to the prefect. You know how these Greeks like to set their paws on the holiest things of the Faith.' He turned to me. 'You know, young man, these Greeks have no sense of the holy. I can't call them heretics, but there is something not altogether right about them.

'Many years ago, when Saint Gregory was newly our pope, some Greek monks turned up in Rome. They were caught digging for the bodies of ancient martyrs by the Church of St Paul. When we examined them, they said they wanted relics to take back to Constantinople. They were proposing to touch relics that must be handled – if at all – only wearing gloves. They even said it was their national custom to wash the bones of saints. Did you ever hear such grossness? You'll be relieved to hear they were struck dead as they left the city! Some while later, the empress wrote from Constantinople, asking for the head of Saint Paul. She probably wanted it on her dressing table. It took all our diplomacy to say no without giving offence.'

Back to Maximin: 'You need fear nothing of the prefect. He will do as we tell him.'

Martin came back with us to Marcella's. It was convenient that we should put him up while he showed me round the libraries, and so we took a small room for him on the ground floor. He'd be close by the toilets – but this was more than one step up from the slaves of the other guests: they were bedded down all together in the second stable building.

86

Gretel passed me as I loitered by the glass table. I thought of giving her a quick grope, but Marcella was about, screaming over an egg someone had smashed on one of her limestone floors. Worse, I found on the table an invite for Maximin and me to have dinner at some noble house near the Baths of Diocletian. Unless we rode, that would mean a walk through half the city, and I'd be back too shattered to enjoy myself. Already, I was feeling the effect of not sleeping much the night before, and was beginning to wilt in every sense.

'Is there some way of getting out of this?' I asked Maximin, showing him the pompous invite that covered half a regular sheet of papyrus.

'Dear me, no,' said Maximin. 'You really do need to mingle with these people. Some of them still have their family libraries, and you never know what you might find there. Go and enjoy yourself, and make some useful friends.'

All very well for him. He had an excuse for crying off the dinner. There was to be a meeting of Italian bishops the day after next. He'd been asked to address them on the English mission. Now, he was hard at work on another of his speeches.

14

I set out with Martin just as night was coming on. It had clouded over in the late afternoon and was looking set for rain. I put on a nice travelling cloak I'd bought earlier in the day. Maximin lent his own tatty cloak to Martin, who was assigned to guide me and supply some force of numbers should there be trouble in the street.

As yesterday and earlier in that day, I heard the soft patter of feet as we walked down the empty, darkening streets. It seemed that whoever wanted the relic hadn't noticed we had given it back. But there was much else now. Rome comes to life at night. There are more people – shifty, dirty wretches obviously out for mischief of various kinds. But mostly there are the rats.

There could be millions of these in Rome. Certainly, there are more rats than people. So far as I can tell, they live during the day in the old sewers and in the deeper stretches of the ruins. At night, they all come out to gorge themselves on whatever rubbish has been deposited in the streets. They scuttled out of our path, but swarmed all around with a muted cacophony of squeaks and scratching. In the remains of the light, I could see the tide of brown bodies streaming around our feet. I pulled my sword out and skewered one that was moving slower than the others. I tossed it over against the wall. At once, in a little frenzy, the others were upon its twitching body, three deep, tearing at it and each other.

'They have their uses,' Martin said. 'They eat dead animals, which keeps the streets a little cleaner. In Constantinople I was told that, when their coats turn black, you can expect the plague.'

Interesting. I've heard that one many times since, and it is true, so far as I can tell. I think there is some power in the contagion that changes them. I do know that they often die first.

I thought to start a conversation with Martin, but couldn't think of an opening that wasn't horribly contrived. In truth, I've never been very comfortable with slaves. They're fine for sleeping with, but I find conversation embarrassing. I think the reason is that I grew up without them.

Yes, we have our churls in England. But they are so low as to be almost different beings. Excepting a few barked orders, there is no communication with them. It is the same elsewhere. I've come across whole races in my time, fit for nothing else but enslavement.

Unlike some of the old philosophers I've read, and some of the less worldly Christians, I've no objection to slavery in principle. There are some jobs so shitty – digging the fields, working the mines, rowing in galleys, and so forth – that they can only be got done under compulsion. And so there is an economy in nature that supplies certain answers to certain problems. But I've never got used to the idea of owning rational beings and setting them to work in areas where paid labour would be more humane and less costly. Secretaries come right into that category. I rather think even the higher household servants do.

I know most of the ancients disagreed. They used slaves even as tutors to their children. The modern Greeks still do. That diplomat I came across at Marcella's went one step further. He had a slave to wipe his arse. He'd take his place and sit talking about commodity prices with me beside him, and a slave would reach under and wipe him, while he continued as if nothing odd were happening.

Then, with Martin, there was the matter of his nationality. My people took the country from his people, and they hate us for it. Until I was small, they rationalised their hatred by calling us heathens. Then the missionaries turned up, and we started to become better Christians than they. So they thought up some trifling difference over dates and made it a big issue of orthodoxy – not caring if it made them into heretics in the eyes of Rome. When I was first in Canterbury, one of their bishops came through on his way to some business in Brittany. He wouldn't set foot in our church. He wouldn't even open the very nice letter Bishop Lawrence sent inviting him to have dinner.

A while back, I did some historical research on the synod our bishops had arranged at Whitby some years back. Because they had more learning, and had come straight from the Roman mould, they were able to trick the poor Celts back into communion. But that hasn't stopped them from hating us still.

So Martin and I walked largely in silence down those black, deserted streets, while the rats scurried away from us and something human followed discreetly behind. A fine rain began to soak us through our outer clothes. What desultory conversation we managed was wholly about the matter of assembling the materials and personnel for the copying that was to start tomorrow.

We smelt the surrounds of the house from a distance. At first, it was a pungent, aromatic smell, as of heavily spiced food. As we drew closer, the smell grew stronger, until it almost overpowered us. It was the olfactory equivalent of a deafening noise. Someone had been digging up the drains across the road from the house – possibly to repair them – and the whole neighbourhood was using the hole to dispose of shit and general waste. A combination of frequent rains and the hot spring sun had started some kind of fermentation.

The rats seemed to love it – jumping in and out, and even swimming in the filth – so far as I could see from the little lantern we carried. I pressed a wet fold of my cloak to my face as we hurried past.

The house where dinner was arranged was scarcely better. The windows were shuttered against the smell, but it followed us in nevertheless. 'You are the main attraction for tonight, sir,' Martin had told me. 'You should arrive last.' That's why we set out so late.

When we arrived, the dinner party was already in full swing.

Perhaps swing is not the correct word. You may have read descriptions of noble dinner parties in the old days – the many courses, the entertainments, the witty conversation. For all the efforts made, this one didn't come up to the old standards. The host and his guests lay self-consciously on their rickety eating couches, not much cleaner than the beggars outside the Lateran. With the disruption of the water supply and the closure of the public baths, cleanliness had gone out of fashion among the upper classes in Rome. Most didn't seem to have bathed in years. From their dirty hands and fingernails, many didn't seem even to wash that often.

Now, bodies aren't much of a problem where cleanliness is concerned. Washing helps the work of nature, but she herself manages to slough most of the dirt off an ordinary body. The real problem is clothes. Whether or not you wash, if you don't change your clothes, you invariably stink. And these creatures stank. They added another bright strand to the tapestry of smells that drifted in from the street. They wore the togas I'd seen on the ancient statues of senators – only these didn't hang in neat and elaborate folds, but drooped in grey and brown wrinkles, following the shapeless contours of those who wore them.

They looked mainly to be in late middle age – most balding, and with lean, saggy faces. As I entered – Martin was taken off to the slave quarters – they were stuffing themselves from dishes of what smelt like bad cabbage served by a few scrawny slaves. The few lamps were of good bronze workmanship, but were burning meat dripping rather than oil. They threw out as much foul smoke as light, and I walked in to stinging, streaming eyes.

'We bid welcome to Alaric of Britain,' a particularly dirty old man cried, pulling himself up from his couch. A battered wreath on his head, he was the host, I gathered. His name had been on the invite, though I forgot this almost at once, and it is unlikely to come back into my memory now. All eyes turned in my direction, and there was a little round of applause.

'Here is the one who slew twelve barbarians with his own hand, yet is versed in all the wisdom of our ancient fathers,' he went on. 'Accept, O golden hero from the farthermost land of unending night, the welcome and gratitude of the mighty Roman Senate!' The host raised his wine cup in greeting, or to have it refilled.

I was led to a couch at the front of the room where I could be seen, and was invited to arrange myself on it. This had once been a fine piece, and still had some of its ivory trimming. But it was warped and cracked with age, and there was a long, black stain running down its length where generations of greasy togas had rubbed against it. I carefully lay down, glad to have ordered other clothes from the tailor Marcella had recommended.

The food looked as bad as it smelt. I swear some of the smaller and less obviously bad meats were baked rat. I avoided the meats of whatever kind, and the uncooked dried fish. I accepted a dish of olives that didn't look too mouldy, and crunched on some stale bread that still had the papal dole mark on its underside. The wine was surprisingly good, and I sipped on this without mixing in any of the brackish water I was offered.

Never mind the attendant circumstances, it's the quality of conversation that really makes a gathering. As you might expect, though, this was dire. The everyday language of these people was the radically degraded Latin of the City. It's easier for us barbarians: we learn Latin as a foreign language, and can, if not always do, learn its purest form. And the dialect can even be forcefully expressive when spoken with feeling, as I could hear when Marcella really lost her temper. But in their mouths, it sounded grotesque. Their drawls were so exaggerated and slow, I almost wanted to finish their sentences for them. Anything they did say in the pure language had obviously been got from the classics, adapted for its purpose, and carefully memorised. There was no conversation as this is normally understood. Instead, the guests made little set speeches, looking in my direction whenever about to say something they thought specially apt. They generally spoke of their present wealth and the glorious deeds of their ancestors. One gave a long description of his alleged estates in Africa that, when he could remember the correct order of words, scanned as elegiac couplets. Some of this was clever enough to bear listening to, though I never did learn the name of the poet.

At length they thought me sufficiently impressed by this display of leisured learning, and fell silent, indicating it was my turn to speak.

I gave the usual brief and censored account of my journey to Rome. It shouldn't have taken that long to get through, only everyone kept interrupting me with expressions of wonder at how well I spoke. 'Such milky copiousness of words!' one exclaimed. 'Such grace and purity of diction!' cried another.

Someone else asked if the sun ever shone in England, and if there were headless giants in London. When I ignored the second question and explained that the weather was wetter and cooler than in Italy, they gave me a round of applause, then raised their cups. 'The first Alaric took Rome by starvation,' someone with stained false teeth and a slipping wig simpered, 'this Alaric has taken it by storm!'

When the applause for that – admittedly spontaneous – witticism had died away, another added: 'He has the name of the uncouth barbarian, Alaric, but surely the face and body of the Grecian Apollo.' More applause. More raising of cups.

Dear God, I thought to myself, how much longer? Maximin was snoring happily in his bed. Gretel would soon give up on me for the night and go to her own. And here I was, pinned down by a pack of bores whose grandfathers had probably used their last worthwhile books to cook dinner.

'But surely you embarrass our young friend with such flattery? Let us respect his simple modesty.' This was a new voice, young and firm and unaffected. It came from the back of the room. I strained through the smoky gloom and saw someone who'd come in late or whom I'd missed when I first came in. About thirty, well dressed, with a neat little black beard and hair very close cropped, but for a neat fringe that hung over his forehead, he sat on his couch with a napkin between it and himself. He swung his trousered legs back and forth. Like me, he was ignoring the food but making free with the wine.

'Lucius!' Our host reared up again. 'I'm so glad you could make our company. How delightful to see you again.'

'How was Constantinople?' the wigged man asked Lucius. 'Caesar is well?'

Lucius stretched his legs and took another sip of the wine. 'Both were about as well when I left them as one might expect,' he said. 'The Persians are rampaging through Syria. There are Slavs pouring across the Danube. The exarch of Africa has revolted.

His Eternal Gloryship Phocas, Ruler of the Universe, is quaking in his palace. He's run out of everything he can tax or borrow, and is now murdering his way through the Senate so he can confiscate enough to keep his guards in wine and whores and the scum of Constantinople quiet with chariot races. I could hardly tear myself away from the place.'

The wigged man turned serious. 'Is it that bad?' he asked. 'Will the East fall like we did?' He paused suddenly, looking round. 'Naturally, I take it for granted that Caesar will be victorious – ever triumphant.'

'I shouldn't worry about informers,' Lucius said with a slight note of scorn. 'In Constantinople, yes. They are everywhere. You can't fart without worrying someone might twist it into a treason. But not here in Rome. There's bugger all here worth confiscating – unless you're desperate enough to lay hands on Holy Mother Church. In any event, His Holiness stands between us and Caesar.

'As for the military collapse, yes, that is bad. I think the Persians mean what they say. I don't believe this time they are interested only in a bit of plunder and a few indemnities to buy them off. They want permanent rule over Egypt and Syria, which are the only provinces left in the Empire that can pay tribute. And I think they've made a deal with the Slavs. The attacks I heard about were too close in time and purpose to be accidental.

'I promise you – the next time those Eastern senators come visiting their cousins here, they won't be so stuck up about our faded grandeur. They'll be down at the Lateran, cadging their own tickets for the bread dole.'

His words came in quick, nervous bursts, with flashes of profound bitterness. As he finished, the room stayed silent. There was nothing more to be said. Rome had gone. Everywhere else had gone. Only Constantinople remained for these broken-down wretches as the bright beacon of civilised order in a world turning visibly grey. Eventually, some old man at the back asked in a quavering voice if any oil would be included in the next papal dole. A debate gradually started up – more natural and interesting than anything I'd yet heard. They even sat up on their couches into a more normal position.

Lucius stood in front of me, his hand out. 'You can be sure, the only reason I came here tonight was to meet the famous Alaric of Britain. Did you really kill a dozen Lombards with your bare hands, rescue the nose of Saint Vexilla, and carry away half a ton of gold?'

'Not exactly, and not alone,' I answered.

He laughed and introduced himself. Lucius Decius Basilius, the last of a truly great house, had come to this dreary gathering to take me as a friend. He was just back from Ravenna, and before that from Constantinople, where he'd been trying to charm Phocas into revoking the confiscation of his murdered uncle's estates in Cyprus. No luck there, he told me, but it was plain he could still afford a bath and a decent suit of clothes. In any gathering, he'd have stood out by his looks and energy. Now, he was almost dazzling.

He leaned forward, 'Listen, I only came here tonight to say hello. I must get away directly for something else. But . . .' He paused. 'It was my intention to invite you to dinner tomorrow night. But I can see you've had enough of these stinking paupers. I'm astonished they're waiting so long to touch you for a loan. Why not come away with me? I think I can show you something you won't forget in a hurry – or want to forget.'

'Anything better in mind?' I asked, looking queasily at a cluster of mould I'd just found in my crust.

'Plenty. Come with me if you want to stay awake.'

We crept out of the dining hall. The senators were deep in argument about something to do with double entitlements of dole for anyone who left his house to the Church. They had forgotten about me for the moment.

'I'll tell Uncle you were suitably overwhelmed by senatorial grandeur,' said Lucius, speaking low as we quietly prepared to leave. 'Tell these people you're off, and they'll all be expecting a goodbye kiss – on the mouth.'

My flesh crawled at the thought of actually touching these beings.

'You leave things with me,' said Lucius as we began a move for the door.

Martin met us by the main door. He'd been fed in the slave quarters, and there was a smear of something on his face still more disgusting than I'd been offered. 'Sir,' he said with a respectful nod of his head, 'you told the reverend father you would be home not too late. Won't he be worried?'

'Is this your slave?' asked Lucius.

'He was lent by the dispensator,' I said.

'I see,' Lucius said coldly, 'a slave of Holy Mother Church.' To Martin: 'Your master is now with me. I'll have one of my slaves escort you home.'

'But, sir . . .' Martin spoke to me, his face red, his manner nervous.

'Your master is with me,' Lucius repeated, his voice now silky as well as cold. 'I commend your attention to duty. But while you're on loan from the dispensator, you'll do the bidding of who feeds you. Do you understand?'

With a look on his face half sulky, half alarmed, Martin bowed low before us. He knew better than to argue with a man like Lucius.

'Tell Maximin I'll be fine,' I added, trying to sound reassuring, but unable to meet his eye. Without another word, Martin turned and went.

'Come with me,' said Lucius. 'I think I can show you something pretty good tonight.' He stepped out. I followed.

15

The rain had cleared, and a bright and nearly full moon lit our path down towards the Forum. Its light concealed the full ruin of the buildings around us, and I felt some idea of how Rome had appeared in its days of glory. We passed through streets that were now reasonably frequented – a few whores, a priest about some business, a small band of thieves who'd have been mad to take on Lucius, me and the armed slaves of our escort. The rats were confining themselves to the side streets. I couldn't tell if we were followed. We made too much noise of our own.

As we went, Lucius told me something about the gathering we had just left. They were all cousins or uncles or other relatives by blood or marriage. The Roman upper classes had always been a close group. Now, after generations without a new family to join the group, intermarriage and adoption had made them virtually a single family. Following the great wars and the attendant collapse, they were all variously hard up. Some survived on remittances sent from relatives in the East, others on the same papal charity as the ordinary Romans.

Every so often, Lucius would stop and draw my attention to some building. Before it was gutted in a fire, this had been the town house of the Praetextatus family. This had once been the main police building, but was now a monastery. Here had once stood a golden statue of Theodosius. Here had been a temple of Minerva.

It was the best guided tour I've ever had. Every building, every place of note, was illustrated with some anecdote to bring it to life. His family had been big in Rome since before Diocletian. This was his city, and he'd made sure to know it from the foundations up.

We skirted the Forum, turning left. We passed the Basilica on our right. We came to the Colosseum, looming gigantic in the moonlight. I'd noticed the day before with Maximin that all the entrances were locked and rusted. But there was one little door I hadn't seen.

Lucius stopped before it. He turned to face me. 'Look, I don't know you, but I like you, and I think I can trust you. I want you to promise me that what you see tonight you won't share with another living being. Can I have that promise?'

'A hard promise to exact when I don't have a clue what I'm to see,' I said.

'Then I'll make you a promise,' said Lucius. 'Nothing you see here tonight will violate the natural law that all peoples have in common. You will see no harm done to any person or any legitimate interest. Will that do for you? If not, we have to part here. I'll have some slaves take you back to your lodgings.'

I'd probably have settled for less than that assurance. I hadn't known Lucius longer than I'd needed for a few cups of wine to wear off. But something about him had captivated me as surely as if I'd known him since childhood. Some people require time to make you realise how special they are. I'd known Maximin for months before I made that realisation, and still it had taken months longer on the road with him before I understood exactly how remarkable he was and how greatly I revered him. It had taken a year for him to grow on me as friend and father and tutor. Lucius had managed all of that in a short conversational walk through Rome.

Of course, I made him the promise he asked. With one necessary exception you'll hear about in proper time, whatever I saw tonight wouldn't be for another living being. If I were some cavilling lawyer, I might say I'm keeping the promise even now: were you alive on that night?

He rapped gently on the door. 'Basilius,' he said.

The door opened a little for a face to look out, and then noiselessly all the way. Someone in a hood beckoned us in. The door swung shut behind us.

98

I stood a moment in darkness. Then my eyes adjusted. There was some light from a window high overhead. By this, I saw we were in some kind of entrance chamber. Over by the far wall, there was a staircase leading down. With the confidence of someone who knew his way, Lucius walked quickly down. The rest of us followed.

We went through a tunnel perhaps fifty feet long. There was almost no light, but I had the impression of doors every so often on either side of us. There was a cold draught from an open doorway on my right that carried a blast of something long since dead. Then we came up a flight of steps, rounded a corner, and I found myself in the Great Arena of Flavius – a place for so many centuries the spiritual home of the Roman People.

In those times, the Colosseum had been filled day after day with an immense multitude. There were the common people, bathed and in their best clothes. There were the senators, solemn in the white and purple robes of their status. There were the elegant ladies, dressed in coloured silks and chatting excitedly. Overhead on hot days was a great awning to keep off the full rays of the sun. Presiding over all from his high box, watching all and being seen by all, was the emperor, clothed in deepest purple.

I don't know the purpose of the little door we had used, but the iron gates of the main entrances were still there, now rusted shut. I stood in the arena, looking around. Once, the roar of the crowd would have been terrifying, as an endless procession of criminals, prisoners of war, Christians and the gladiators were moved into that place to entertain with their offerings of blood and death. Now, the moon shone brilliant on the pale, silent benches.

The games, I later discovered, had never got over Constantine's adoption of the Faith. When he rebuilt Constantinople as his New Rome, he'd permitted neither pagan temples nor an amphitheatre. Instead, he and his successors had contented themselves with an immense circus for chariot racing, which had soon come to give as much excitement as the old games, though without the same unwilling blood, except when it came to public executions.

In Rome, things had continued much as before, though under noble patronage. At last, about a hundred years after the switch to Christianity, some Eastern monk – Telemachus, his name – had run into the arena during a particularly bloody contest, trying to part the gladiators. The outraged mob stoned him to death and insisted that the games should continue. But the emperor was got at by his priests and banned the games.

For some while after, the Colosseum was used for wild beast hunts and executions. But then the money ran out and the doors were locked shut. Since then, the place had stood empty like the other main public buildings. Those that hadn't yet fallen down or been destroyed were subject to further orders – from the prefect, or the exarch, or the emperor himself. In most cases, orders had never come.

And so the Colosseum stood in empty silence. Every so often, someone bribed a permit out of the prefect to take away materials for building. But the sands of the arena had for generations before my visit been unstained by human blood.

While a little cloud obscured the moon, I heard a shuffling far across the sands. As the cloud passed, I saw a dark procession approaching us in the still night air. Perhaps five men were coming towards us. They were dressed from their hoods down in black. Behind them, slaves carried a small brazier heaped with glowing coals. Behind them came some black animal led with a chain that shone silver in the moonlight.

'O Basilius, my lord, you are come at last to this place of silent magic. You are come to commune with the God and to seek what the future may hold for you. The sacrifice is prepared for your performing. Make ready for the solemn compact with the Ancient One who was before we became. Make ready.'

It was the first of the hooded procession who spoke in a deep, resonant voice. It filled that vast stone valley with its volume. The brazier was set down in the centre of the arena. Beside it was placed a wooden table and chairs. Beyond this, a black stone cube of about three feet was already standing.

As Lucius stepped forward, a slave met him with a bowl of water and black cloths. He bowed his head, looking away, as Lucius washed his hands with slow, deliberate movements. Lucius shook his head as the slave looked quizzically at me.

'This time, he is here only to observe,' he explained. 'Perhaps next time.'

Lucius fell silent, stood still beside the stone. The others started a slow, rhythmical chant:

> O God immortal, to whom
> Is the Empire of Life and Death,
> And the Realm of Silent Shades,
> And all the places covered by night –
> Make unto us, your servants,
> Visible what is dark,
> Showing what is now,
> And what once was,
> And what is yet to become.
> This offering we make to you,
> That you may give to us.
> Accept, accept, O God Immortal,
> And give unto us in return.

As the chanting died away, the hooded priest cried three times for silence. '*Procul, O procul, este profani*' he added. 'Away, away, be all unclean.'

Lucius moved to face the stone altar with the east before him, his arms stretched out. His lips moved in silent prayer. I strained to hear what he might be asking, but his lips moved without a voice.

As he finished and his arms came down beside him, what I now saw was a goat with a perfectly black hide was brought forward. Water was dribbled on its head, as in a baptism.

'See,' the hooded priest intoned, 'the beast is unafraid. All is ready according to ancient custom.'

Lucius covered his head with a fold of his cloak. He took the goat by its chain. Slaves lifted it with practised ease onto the altar before him. The hooded man uncovered a knife that had been carried by one of the others. He held it up in the moonlight. It had no glint. Lucius took the knife in his right hand. Holding the goat with his left hand, he drew the knife with a single motion, and stepped quickly back as the animal sank twitching onto the block. I saw no blood, but heard it gushing onto the altar.

'The Lord has given a clean death,' the hooded priest spoke again. 'The beast has moved without sense of motion into the realms of darkness. It is as ancient custom requires.' He took out another knife and slit open the goat's belly, drawing out its entrails. He examined these by the light of a small lantern.

'O Noble Basilius, great seed of ancient greatness,' he intoned, 'you have asked for what you would have, and the God has granted all that you ask. Behold, the liver is unspotted. The entrails are pure throughout. Your sacrifice is accepted. Let the God give all that you ask in the manner of His choosing. His will shall prevail!'

Lucius placed his hands on the now-still goat and drew them away, black in the moonlight. He prayed silently again for a short while, then nodded.

The animal was skinned, its hide and entrails thrown on the fire, which now burned black. There was a sprinkling of oil and wine on the altar. Wine was spilled onto the ground with another brief invocation. The rest of the goat was cut into strips and roasted on the clear part of the coals. We all sat together round the table, now set with bread and wine, and waited for our share to be cooked. Slaves and free sat mingled together, drinking the same wine.

And that was it. I had attended my first pagan sacrifice.

It was obvious at the time we had done something illegal. If this sort of thing got the priests in Kent in a regular sweat, there seemed no saying what they would think of seeing it done in Rome, barely a mile from the Lateran. I later learnt that it carried the same penalties as treason – that is, the punishment could be really unpleasant. I once saw a high government official in Constantinople ripped apart by hyenas in the Circus – and he had only consulted an old oracle outside the city gates. We had performed a nocturnal sacrifice in full, if undiscriminating, semblance of the ancient custom. No wonder it had all been so furtive.

'Surely, the Ancient Gods have no power in the modern age?' I asked the priest diplomatically. He sat beside me at the table, now unhooded. His narrow face and thin white beard went strangely with his deep voice. I could have questioned their existence, but thought that might not be in the best taste, given the circumstances.

'The Ancient Gods are not dead,' he answered. 'They merely sleep in stones and in the quiet places, ready to be called forth by sacrifice of blood.'

'And the Almighty God of the Churches,' I asked, 'whose priests have conquered the world – what of Him?'

The priest frowned, pouring out more wine for himself. 'The Galileans worship nothing more than the tribal God of the Jews. They have raised him above his proper status, and in his triumph the world has grown old.

'In former ages, the smoke of sacrifice rose above every temple. Every God and every Goddess would have its proper worship. Then, the beasts of sacrifice were brought in full daylight, with sound of flutes and cymbals. Women and little children would join the joyous procession. There would be games and readings of poetry. Beautiful works of art would be raised in celebration of the gifts showered upon us by the Gods. In those days, the arms of Rome were triumphant everywhere, from the furthermost limits of the world to the shores of the Indian Ocean. Then the Galilean worship took hold – first among the slaves and the rabble of every city, then among the women of the higher classes, then at last on the emperor himself. Since Constantine disestablished the ancient worship, all has gone ill. Our cities are empty. Barbarians have taken our lands. The Persian is upon the East.

'The Galileans cannot even agree among themselves. The Ancient Gods were never jealous. Each had his proper place, and never complained if another had finer temples or a more numerous worship. Now, the supposed One God has many cults, and the various devotees hate each other more than they hate the barbarians and the Persians, with whom they make common cause as the mood takes them.' The priest finished and turned back for a second helping of meat.

'And the Gods are with us yet.' One of the priest's deputies now spoke, a fanatical gleam in his eye. 'Did you not feel the God's presence as we called Him forth?'

Of course I hadn't. Before, during and after the sacrifice, all around had been the same so far as I was concerned. It was a fine spring night – but just like any other. Nevertheless, I'd had enough experience of Church miracles not to go stating the obvious. So I slightly changed the subject, asking which of the Gods had been invoked.

'His name is not to be mentioned,' the priest replied. 'There are words and names that are only to be whispered, even among the initiated.'

'But, my dear boy,' Lucius broke in, 'did your priests ever serve such an excellent meal after one of their interminable, corpse-worshipping services? I think not.' He grinned, all solemnity gone, and began a scandalous story about some deacon who had been found dead of a stroke in a brothel, dressed in nothing but a slave collar and a bag over his head. To keep the story even reasonably quiet, the dispensator had been required to buy all the whores out of slavery and then get them forgiveness for all the sins they had committed and might again in future commit. I nearly choked on a piece of bread as he pranced around doing a perfect imitation of the dispensator's pompous manner – the dispensator turned out, by the way, to be yet another of his relatives.

Good food, excellent wine, the moon high overhead, the air still, the slight chill of the night banished by the coals of the brazier, and excellent conversation from Lucius, and much of interest from the other diners – this was everything the other dinner hadn't been.

Afterwards, Lucius took me on a tour of the Colosseum. The gates to the upper reaches were locked and rusted shut, so the imperial box and the better seats were off limits. I was told there was a network of tunnels underneath the arena, where the animals and human victims had waited their turn in the open. This too was barred to us. But we had free run of the lower galleries and arcades, where there had once been shops and brothels and offices and rooms for private entertainment.

By one of the main processional gates to the arena, Lucius stopped and pointed to a slab of stone fixed to the wall. It commemorated the charity of one Decius Marius Venantius Basilius, '*Praefectus Urbanus, Patricius, Consul Ordinarius*'. After some earthquake had damaged the arena and podium, he had paid for repairs out of his own pocket. To this benefactor of the public – if not, perhaps, of the performers – Lucius was great-great-grand-son.

'My family had money in those days,' he said. 'We could pay for repairs to this place as easily as I now pay the bill in a wine shop. We had estates in Italy and Sicily and Africa, as well as in the East.'

'What happened?' I asked.

'All we had in Italy was taken by the Lombards. In Africa, the desert took everything more slowly, but just as surely. My grand-father left what we had in Sicily to the Church – he was a regular Galilean, you see. As for the East, my mother's family lost that just recently to that lowlife bastard Phocas. I am left with a house in Rome I can't afford to run, and a few blocks of tenements that haven't yet fallen down.' He shrugged and smiled in the dim light. 'But the future is bright. I have brains. I have luck. I have the blessing of the Gods, for what that may be worth. And I glory in the friends I seem to make everywhere.

'You, of course, are the latest.'

I looked at the inscription. Lucius seemed greatly proud of it. But it was clearly a wretched thing. The letters were of uneven height. The word form '*sumptu*' – from '*sumptus*', meaning 'ex-pense' – was misspelled as '*sumpu*', though might this not be an indication to actual pronunciation in the past? I wondered vaguely at the time. So the money had still been there for this Basilius: there was, even so, a decline in the things on which it could be spent.

We moved on, and Lucius told me about his rejection of the Faith. It had happened when he was fifteen. He'd spent a summer on the family estates in Sicily. Some villagers there still worshipped as their ancestors had since time immemorial.

'I looked at this sweet communion with the natural world. I looked at the ghastly worship of body parts and the meaningless words of the *Credo*. What more could I do but embrace the Truth?' he asked.

We stood together by a little iron gate that led down to the lower chambers. We looked across the arena. The moon was setting. The coals were dying down. The priest and his assistants were clearing away the remains of the sacrifice. The eastern sky would soon be fringed with pink.

'What are you doing for dinner tomorrow?' Lucius asked as we prepared to leave. 'I did, after all, intend to have you to myself then.'

I said that was for Maximin to decide, but I'd do my best. I liked Lucius. He might be as superstitious in his own way as the priests he despised. His superstition might be a failed one. But he was an engaging companion. And – I'll confess – I was flattered to be treated as an equal by the closest I'd ever seen to the noble Romans of old.

I, you must always bear in mind, was also of noble blood. Ethelbert might have taken the lands. We might have fallen on hard times. But the blood was still there. No one could take that from us.

So Lucius and I were equals. But it was nice to be treated as an equal.

16

'We haven't been in Rome two days,' Maximin shouted, 'and already you're out all night – drinking, whoring and gambling, I've no doubt.'

He was angry. No, he was furious. I hadn't seen him so lose control before. His face was red. His hands shook. He walked restlessly up and down in my public room. Martin sat quietly, looking at the wall. He looked embarrassed – yet also still frightened.

'I haven't made a big point of this – though it's in my full report – but you came here to seek penance for your existing sins, not to commit fresh ones.' He went to a detailed recitation of what I'd been up to in Canterbury. Martin heard it all.

I tried to explain that I'd been in perfectly safe company. But I couldn't think of anything convincing to say that wasn't other than an admission of what he'd accused me of doing, or a confession of truth that might kill him from shock.

He calmed down a little. 'Listen, my son, you may think I want you to live like a monk. I don't. But I must warn you – Rome is a dangerous city. You know we're being followed everywhere. You know our rooms have been searched. Don't you ask yourself why?' He didn't pause for an answer, but continued, 'There are things here that you can't begin to understand – wickedness upon wickedness upon wickedness. It is the home of our Holy Mother Church. Before then, it was the home of all vileness and sin, and this is with it still. Rome is evil. Rome is dangerous. I want us out of here in the time given by the prefect. Between now and then, I don't want you to go out alone.'

I tried to tell him about my walk though the city with Lucius, and how safe we'd been. Maximin wasn't interested.

'The dangers of which I speak are not to be repelled by a few armed slaves. There are evils outside this house that will swallow you whole. I don't want you ever to go out alone at night again. You go with me. You go with Martin. Or you stay in this house.'

The lecture was over. Maximin went back to his big speech. I slunk off to bed, wondering what he could have meant by his 'full report' – hadn't he given that the day before? How many of these meetings were there to be?

Martin had disappeared. Slaves can always make themselves scarce when they need to. Gretel was nowhere to be seen. In any event, I was shattered. I'd felt quite full of myself as I threw stones over the outer gate of the house to get the attention of Marcella's watchman. I'd felt good groping my way upstairs. Then I'd tripped over Maximin's boots, put out for cleaning, and his door had flown open. Now, all I wanted was to get some sleep. I pulled up the bedclothes, barely noticing how some smell of Gretel still clung to them.

When I woke, the sun was pouring into the room. No one had disturbed me, and I'd lost much of the morning. Previous lack of sleep and a bellyful of wine had given me a ferocious headache. I looked out into the corridor and stopped a slave. Soon, a couple of them were carrying water up for a bath.

I eased myself into the cold water. It did seem colder than at Richborough. But cleanliness has a price that must usually be paid. After a while, I got used to the chill, and sat there scrubbing myself. And I began to feel more human. I started to think of Edwina – not the Edwina of untutored passion, but an Edwina who knew all the wicked things Gretel had introduced me to the night before last. That really perked me up.

Better still, as I was drying myself, there was a knock at the door. The tailors had finished some of the clothes I had ordered. Some things still needed a few touches to be perfect. But the suit of blue I'd ordered fitted exactly. It was in the mixed Roman and barbarian style then the fashion in Italy – both trousers and tunic. I'd specified it should follow the shape of my body without being tight.

The tailors had done an excellent job. I looked down at my reflection in the bath water and loved what I saw.

I went downstairs and showed myself to Marcella and the slaves. They agreed. I saw Gretel's mouth fall open with wonder and with lust. That night, I'd not disappoint either of us, I told myself. Marcella was so pleased she had me go out into the street to show off to the neighbours and passers-by what manner of guests she was able to attract. Sure enough, every head turned as I walked up and down in the hot Roman sun. This was our first hot day in Italy. Until then, the days had been like the best days of a Kentish summer. Now the sun burned with a wondrously pleasing heat.

I thought I could order a little cap to go with the suit: it would really set off those golden curls. Or would it? I was considering whether to imitate Lucius and have it all cut short but for a fringe. It was a very neat style. And it was the fashion. On the other hand, those curls were part of my charm. I pondered the question as others in the street nodded and smiled at me.

As we prepared for an early lunch, Maximin seemed a little recovered from the morning. He glanced at the fine clothing and grunted, making no comment otherwise. He was at his writing table, looking up a reference in one of Marcella's books. He closed this, marking his place with a piece of scrap. He looked at me and sighed.

'It is your intention, I take it, to visit *one* of the libraries today?'

'Oh yes,' said I brightly, still thinking about caps. 'I asked Martin yesterday to find some copying secretaries. We'll soon be turning out as many books for Canterbury as we can ship there.'

As we were about to go downstairs, a messenger was shown in. He was the monkish clerk we'd seen yesterday. The dispensator was calling Maximin to an unscheduled meeting in his office.

'At your earliest convenience,' the clerk emphasised.

Maximin looked unusually troubled as we ate lunch. Silent, he ate little, instead drinking much.

'Shall we go together down to the Lateran?' I asked.

Maximin gave me a bleary look. 'I don't think you have time for waiting around any longer,' he said with a glance at my white boots. 'You'd better get moving. I'll follow you down to the Lateran when I've sorted some papers.'

Down at the Lateran, Martin had indeed found and assembled the copying secretaries. There were twenty of them. There was little demand for their services in Rome, and so we had got the hire of them all for much less than the bill that would follow from the tailor.

I think they had been there much of the day when I finally arrived. All solid, respectable slaves in early middle age, they had the inky hands and crabbed posture of their occupation. All rose to greet me as I was shown into the room. Good slaves never show impatience or disappointment. I might have kept them waiting all day and all night before seeing them: still they'd have stood before me with the same polite looks.

I motioned them to sit, and began the little speech I'd prepared. Turning the phrases over in my head, it had seemed an easy matter to give the thing. I'd imagined how the sound of my balanced, melodious Latin would fill the room, and leave my audience crying out for more. But this was my first ever speech, and, even if it was to slaves, I found my mouth was dry. Worse, I began to shake.

The slaves continued to stand, their looks still mechanically polite. I opened my mouth again, now desperate for the constriction in my throat to clear and for some sound to issue.

'You may find this useful,' Martin whispered, passing a cup of wine.

I drained the cup. I pulled myself together. I opened my mouth and spoke. 'We have been brought together during the next month for a work of the highest importance,' I said. 'As you know, Holy Mother Church expects much of its mission to the English. Churches are rising all over the land. Schools are opening. Soon, there will be English priests to send on missions deeper into the island. All of England is to be reclaimed from the darkness of heathen superstition.

'I have come here to gather and to return with books for the libraries of England. The youth of England are hungry for knowledge of every kind. The books already there are insufficient to satisfy this hunger. If I can send back two hundred books on this first visit, I shall be content.

'I will select the books. Under the direction of Martin, you will copy all that I give you. I want the best copies you can produce. I will provide you with the finest parchment and the best inks. I will feed you all that you can eat and drink. I will have what you produce bound in rich and heavy leather that will protect your work for ages to come, and will let it be used for making further copies. In return, I want copies that the finest Church dignitary here in Rome would not be ashamed to have on his shelves.

'Above all, I want accurate copies. Don't think I'm some pretentious barbarian who can't tell when words are dropped from a passage, or the metre of verse or the prose rhythm is garbled. I shall notice these things. If I think you have been negligent, I shall give you to Martin, who will whip you, and I will have you make the copies again in time that would otherwise have been yours for relaxation. If, on the other hand, you do well, I will reward you so that you look forward to my next visit . . . Do I make myself clear?'

From the expectant muttering among the secretaries, I had. Perhaps I could have done it better. At least I hadn't disgraced myself on the first day.

I suddenly noticed I'd given the whole speech with that wine cup in my hand. And, without noticing, I'd somehow managed to crush it. I passed it to Martin with an attempt at nonchalance that was spoiled when he dropped it on the floor. Everyone looked at it.

'I'm so sorry, sir—' he began.

I cut him off with what I wanted to be a friendly jest, but that turned out when I said it to sound rather spiteful.

I gave up on the effort to look good and motioned everyone toward the books.

Martin first, I second, and the secretaries hurrying behind, we passed through a maze of corridors and public rooms. We moved deep into the interior of the palace. At last, we entered a high, bright room, its windows facing into a large courtyard. This was the first room in the Papal Library.

We were greeted by a birdlike little priest who was the head librarian. He closely inspected the permit Martin had drawn for us.

'All is in order,' he said. 'I have arranged for the scriptorium to be cleared out. I think the writing frames are still in good order, but I'm glad you have brought your own instruments otherwise.'

He took us into another, smaller room. This was still easily big enough for the secretaries, and was cleverly sited, so that the best light, but the minimum of direct sun, fell in through the long windows. The secretaries seemed pleased, and began setting up their instruments.

I went with Martin though the library. It went on for room after room. I had never seen so many books. There must have been tens of thousands of them. In most cases, the titles were embossed on the leather spines. Sometimes, the titles were written on gummed sheets of papyrus. The head librarian did mention a catalogue. But I was as yet unfamiliar with the apparatus of a great research library. So far, I'd never been among more books than could be comprehended by a few moments of walking up and down the shelves.

I wandered about, getting my bearings, seeing what was where. Sadly, nearly all the books were religious. When I had finished exploring, I began pointing at volume after volume to some ordinary slaves Martin had also rounded up. All the books were dirty through years of neglect. I had no intention of touching any until they had at least been dusted. And the slaves had to heave and strain to pull down the largest, heaviest volumes. I stepped back to avoid the clouds of dust they raised. I soon had over a hundred volumes of all sizes dusted and piled on the floor beside my reading table.

This done, the rest was very fast. I skimmed every volume, rejecting all that were badly written or particularly absurd. I had to be tolerant in this second matter. I have never failed to be astonished at the nonsense men can write when they believe God is dictating to them. I rejected a lot, but allowed much through that I'd never, given free choice, put into the hands of the impressionable.

The twin filters of grammar and common sense soon left me with about fifty volumes. These I had carried into the scriptorium, where the secretaries now set to work.

I stayed awhile to watch them, learning much I had never considered. Perhaps you never have either. I'm writing at present on single sheets of papyrus. I fill the whole of one side, and then add the sheet to a growing pile in a wooden box. Copying books is a very different matter. Martin had bought in great stacks of parchment, each sheet of which was around two foot by three. The sheet would ultimately be folded in two across the long side, and then folded again across the new long side. This produces a section of eight sheets. These pages must be written in the right order if they are to make sense when bound. On the first side, on the bottom, there is page eight and then one. Then the sheet must be turned upside down, so that pages four and five can be written at the new bottom. Next the sheet is turned over: pages six and three fall on the obverse of pages five and four, and pages two and seven on the obverse of pages one and eight.

Then there is the matter of the grain. Skin is made of tiny fibres. When it is scraped and dried into parchment, pages must be so written that, when folded into a section, the folds go with, rather than against, the grain. And there is the matter of colour. Parchment is darker on the skin side, and the pages must be arranged so that the two facing pages in a book have the same colour. You can see what care must be taken by a copying secretary. Martin had got parchment mostly of the right size, the grain running down the long side. But mistakes are easily made. On two occasions that afternoon, sheets had to be scrapped. Since we were putting the secretaries under great pressure of time, it would have been unreasonable to punish them for these slips.

'We can get most of the ink sponged off these,' Martin said, regarding the wasted sheets. 'They can be reused when dry.'

Even so, my ambitions had grown beyond what I'd discussed

with him the previous evening. These were only the first books I had in mind for copying at the Lateran. We hadn't even looked at what Anicius might have. Two hundred volumes might be sent to Canterbury. Many more would follow.

You may have noticed in my speech that I said 'send' back to England, not 'take'. I had no intention of going back there myself. Partly it was Ethelbert. Partly, though, it was Rome. Yes, the place might be a stinking slum. But it was the best I'd seen. And, all considered, it was turning out quite a jolly place to be. It might turn better still with Maximin out of the way for part of the year. If he wanted to see France again, he could ride through in the good months, on a good horse, at the head of a caravan, and with an armed guard. Or perhaps the sea journey might be faster and safer. I made a note to check in some of the wine shops down by the river port.

Martin had to go out for a while to order more parchment. 'I don't know how much there is in town,' he said. 'At your likely rate of consumption, we may need to use the dispensator's name to pre-empt every sheet. I'm sure you don't want prices to go through the roof.'

Going back to those books, once written on, each sheet is folded the required number of times, stitched with the other sections, and glued onto a spine. When dry, the pages are cropped so that all the folds except those at the spine are removed. Then it all goes off for binding in wood or leather. The quality of the finished product depends on the skill and care of all those involved in its making. I'm sure you've seen tatty little things that fall apart almost as you read them – faded ink on the pages, gross errors in the text, and so on. What I had in mind for England was something that would last forever and delight all future generations. And I wanted it fast.

Watching the secretaries at work, leafing backwards and forwards for the correct order of pages to copy, was decidedly more interesting than reading all that prosy trash – even if it was to be in pretty editions – I was about to inflict on the English mind.

The room was filled with the gentle murmur of reading. I'd noticed that, like me, Martin read quietly. Everyone else in Rome read aloud, like boys at school.

I had expected Maximin to come and join us when finished with the dispensator. But it seemed his meeting was running longer than expected – or he was still out of sorts with me.

17

I'd discussed with Martin the order of our inspections. First, there was to be the Lateran. We'd start the secretaries, and leave them to their copying – we might have the first completed books within ten days if they applied themselves. Then, we'd go off with just two of the general slaves to see Anicius. Martin said he was very old, and might not appreciate a mob of visitors. Because I'd slept in, we were somewhat behind in our inspections. But I decided to continue with the agreed order. It was late afternoon when we set out from the Lateran for the long walk to the house of Anicius on the Quirinal Hill.

Behind its imposing façade, this was largely a ruin. It had once been a very big palace faced with marble and stucco. It must have dominated the surroundings, both in height and with its sprawl down the hill. Now, the marble was stripped, and the stucco falling off. The roof had fallen in on most of the rooms, leaving only the library rooms, which had been built with brick domes, and some small ancillary buildings. All about were the usual piles of rubbish and the smell of dumped sewage. Unlike on the Caelian, there was no running water on the Quirinal.

We were let in through the still standing gate by a young slave. He led us through the unroofed entrance hall into the library rooms. These were mostly in good order. Water had come through in a few places, but the resulting damage was local to the racks directly underneath. All else was largely intact.

The books were nearly all of a kind I hadn't seen before, and that I doubt you have ever seen. They were made of papyrus. Now, unless you're reading all this in manuscript, rather than in a copy, you may never have seen a sheet of papyrus – since the Saracens took Egypt, the stuff has been in short supply for us.

Martin looked at me with a smile. I suppressed the look of confusion he could plainly see on my face, and reached for one of the books. It was heavier than I'd expected – nothing like the weight of a modern book, but still heavy. It fell through my fingers and, with a crash, came apart on the floor.

'Let me help you, sir,' he said. He reached for another and took it over to a table. 'Look, you have to take it from the leather case if there is one, and then you take it in your right hand, and unroll it a column at a time, winding it onto the outer spindle with your left. Then you wind it all the way back.'

With practised ease, he unrolled the book, showing the slender columns of text. These are written so narrow to avoid excessive strain on the sheets, which are delicate even when new. The text is written larger than in a modern book because the surface is so much rougher than parchment.

'What is papyrus?' I asked. I hated showing ignorance in front of Martin. But I wanted to know.

He stood back from the book he'd opened and let his voice take on a lecturing tone. 'Papyrus,' he said, 'is made from the tall, thick reeds of that name that grow everywhere in the Nile valley. The reeds are harvested. The outer casing is removed, showing a dense inner pith. This is sliced into thin strips, and these are cut into manageable lengths. Strips from the rougher, outer pith are laid lengthways, side by side, into a sheet about fourteen inches across by about eleven high. On top of these are placed further strips from the more tender pith, also side by side, going across. The whole is then pressed very hard and dried. Finally, the better side is rubbed smooth with pumice. The result is a tough, semi-flexible writing sheet.'

He turned back to the book and showed me the joints between the sheets. Papyrus is written on the better side, in columns about two inches wide, each separated by a margin of about one inch. When about thirty sheets have been written, they are glued, side by side, into a very long strip. This is tightly rolled about a wooden spindle with knobs at each end. The outermost sheet is joined to another spindle. The finished book is then sprayed with aromatics to keep insects away and stored in a leather case. Collections of books can be stored in a wooden box. The title is attached as a slip of papyrus to this container. In libraries, such books are stored not on shelves, but in racks, which are often designed to accommodate particular titles.

'The great advantage of papyrus,' Martin continued, 'is its cheapness. A standard sheet here in Rome costs no more than the value of what an industrial slave could produce in two or three days. Parchment, of course, is much more expensive. The ancients used papyrus for all their books, and sometimes built up libraries of hundreds of thousands or even millions of books – though they contained only a tenth of the text that our own style of books can hold. Indeed, papyrus was so much the standard that it was the limitation in terms of the number of sheets in one roll that determined the length of ancient books.'

He stopped his lecture and looked at me, a faintly triumphant smile on his face. Or it might have been more servile politeness. I didn't grudge him the first.

I picked the book up and practised unrolling it. The thing was so old, one of the sheets cracked as I handled it. Martin took it back and showed me how to unroll it more gently. I grunted some thanks.

'I don't know how long the parchment book that we know has been around,' he said, slipping back into didactic mode. 'But the ancients tended to look down on it as a vulgar innovation from the oriental races. It was brought into general use by the Church, influenced by its oriental roots. For hundreds of years now, it has been the standard – papyrus used only for supplemental or impermanent writings. Obviously, Anicius has inherited a great store of ancient writings that reached back to before the Triumph of the Church.'

I had another go with the book. This time, it unrolled and rolled again without breaking. I'm surprised it took so long for the papyrus roll to fall out of general use. Apart from cheapness it has only disadvantages as a book. For example, it can be hard to tell what book you are reading, if the title falls off the case, or if the cases are muddled. The full title is only given on the innermost sheet – so you have to unroll all the way to see what this is. There is no page numbering, which makes any passage hard to find. And it's much harder to skim a papyrus roll than a parchment book. Another problem is that only one side of the sheet can be used for writing, and papyrus is also far more delicate than parchment. The Church and the barbarians might have killed books. But this was a random and occasional massacre. The really great killer was time. These things just don't last in a European climate.

Martin had shown me the basics of reading in the ancient manner. Now he was off again on some errand. I sat alone in the library with a pile of books, carefully unrolling them to see what gems I might find.

It was all precious treasure. If you rule out some Latin translations of Plato, there was nothing religious here. It was all from the great ages of the past, when men wrote about the world as they saw it, rather than as a pack of life-hating bigots had instructed them to think about it.

I went through book after book after book. Most of these – the complete Cicero, for example – I set aside for collection and copying. Others, I couldn't resist reading on the spot. I read and read, and delighted in all that I read. And I'd have read more but for the difficulty of coming to terms with the unfamiliar medium of these books. I read until the light through the high windows began to dim, and one of the Lateran slaves began to talk about going off in search of some lamps.

Careful as I was, though, the books were in very delicate shape. They were all old, and for a long time had not been stored in anything like good conditions. Some were already in pieces as I took them out of their cases. Some fell apart as I unrolled them. But, unlike in the Lateran, I found almost nothing I wanted to reject. As the light began to fade in earnest, I had several hundred books piled on the floor beside the reading table.

'Oh fuck!' I muttered in English as another roll cracked apart in my hands. 'Rub this stuff between your hands, and powder your face with it,' I continued more politely in Latin.

I heard a voice behind me. 'Don't trouble yourself over it, my dear young fellow. It's all worthless stuff in these rooms. I wonder you spend so long poring over it.'

I looked up. An old man had come silently into the room, and stood looking at me from the doorway. Tall, thin, with unkempt hair and beard; this, I supposed, was Anicius. He tottered over and fell into a chair opposite me that I'd rejected for myself as too rickety. It took his weight without a creak. If anything, he was even dirtier than the other nobles, and his stained robe stank of piss. But he had the usual proud look of a noble.

'You have a most remarkable library,' said I.

He brushed the compliment aside with a dismissive wave. 'All worthless,' he continued: 'Crumbling books by dead writers from a dead civilisation. There's nothing here for you.'

'But surely,' I replied, 'there is so much beauty and truth in these books. You are fortunate to have them as your friends.'

'There was a time when I might have agreed with you. One of my ancestors certainly would. He used to sit all day at this very table, writing philosophy in Latin and translating from Greek. That was –' he paused, screwing up his face – 'a long time ago, when even I was a small boy. He came to a bad end, you know: killed by the barbarian who ruled Italy at the time. My family had a long fight to get his property back from the emperor. By the time we got it restituted, there was little enough left worth the having.'

I remained silent, hoping he might tell me something worth hearing. At last, he continued: 'When I was a boy – until I was older than you are now – this was a house of wealth and learning. In those days, Rome was still alive with people. We had baths and fountains and elegant entertainments. You can't imagine how glorious the city then was. I thought then I was a scholar, and I'd give whole days to communing with the great minds of the past. Nowadays, I know better. What is it your Galilean priests cry out when they see some pleasure they don't share? Ah yes, "Vanity of vanities, all is vanity".'

'They have a point, you know.' He waved vaguely at the book racks. 'It took a thousand years to amass all these words. Can you imagine the original work of writing? Can you imagine the continuing work thereafter of copying and recopying to keep them alive? And what do they tell us, now the civilisation for which they were written is dead? They tell us nothing.

'We drowned because of this accumulated weight of learning. It weakened our bodies and minds. It didn't save us from the emperor's Wars of Reconquest, nor from the barbarians, nor from the plague.

'You barbarians have neither learning nor the trade that feeds the wants revealed by learning. Your strong bodies resist the plague. We die.'

I didn't want to be rude, so held my tongue. But I could have told the old fool he was talking rot. My mother couldn't read her own name, and had never owned anything produced more than a few miles distant. She'd still vomited her guts out. My dead brothers had dodged class with Auxilius more often than they'd attended, and they could barely give the sounds of the letters. This noble savage and decadent civilisation stuff has been around since the early Greeks. Search me how long it will stay around. Well, unlike most, I've tried both – and I know which one I prefer.

18

In Anicius's library, I let the old man ramble on.

'The plague,' he said emphatically, 'was the end of my world. It came just after the beginning of the great reconquest. Even as the Greek soldiers sent here by Justinian were advancing against the Goths, the plague advanced against us all.

'There was a summer without heat. Then the sun and moon had shone in many colours. Then the poor began dying in Rome.'

He went into a grisly description of the symptoms – fever and a black mottling, followed by swellings in the groin and armpits. 'All who caught this pestilence sent hither from the city of New Rome died without exception.'

More rot he was speaking. A summer without heat and blue moons! The first, just possibly; the second, not at all. Claims made so greatly against common sense are always to be at least suspected. As for the rest, I was once in Alexandria during an outbreak of plague, and another time in Ctesiphon. He got the symptoms right. But I know now that not everyone dies.

Anicius sat spouting about the deaths until the light had well and truly gone – the multitude of bodies lying unburied in the streets, the riotous living of those who weren't yet stricken, the general collapse of order and morality, the public orgies, as the still living fornicated like rabbits.

Like all who could afford to, he ran away from the city. The plague followed, and soon the country districts were as ravaged as the towns. Here, the crops withered on the ground, and cows wandered, bellowing with pain when there was no one to milk them. It all sounded very nasty. But it seemed to cheer Anicius.

'And so I am all that is left of the old world,' he concluded with a smack of his withered lips that screamed complacency.

There wasn't much replying to this, so I changed the subject.

'My Lord Anicius,' I asked with a humble wave around the library, 'might you have anything by Epicurus?'

The old man's eyes widened. He looked at me as if for the first time. 'And what,' he asked in a suddenly firm voice, 'would you want to know about Epicurus?'

The answer was that I'd pressed every book I could find in Canterbury for mentions of him, and turned over every book I could find in those French monasteries. Now, I was for the first time in a library stuffed with ancient writings. I wanted to know what original works it might contain.

'You'll find much here in Greek,' Anicius said after a pause, 'though I don't think much at all in Latin, which is not a language well adapted to philosophy. But do tell me – what possible interest could a young and clean-minded barbarian have in that ancient trash?'

'Of all the philosophy I've read,' I answered, 'Epicurus comes closest to the truth that I feel.'

Anicius let out a wheezing laugh. He leaned back on the creaking chair. As he gathered his thoughts, he seemed twenty years younger at least. 'The feelings of an uninstructed mind,' he said with a surprising precision, 'are not an appropriate criterion for deciding the truth of a matter. Epicurus was the author of a bestial philosophy. It allows for no nobility of sentiment, no feelings of honour. It preaches a message of individual happiness and of withdrawal from the world.'

Nothing wrong with that, I told myself. So long as happiness is rightly understood – and I'd learnt enough to know the meaning that Epicurus had intended – there is no finer end in life. As for honour and nobility of sentiment, they are good ultimately only for turning the world into a nightmare.

I wondered if it would be presumptuous of me to quote one of the doctrines I'd found in a fragmentary encyclopaedia outside Pisa: 'Of all things that wisdom provides for living one's entire life in happiness, the greatest by far is the possession of friendship.' But the chance had passed. Anicius was warming to his theme.

'You will even find the man's physical theories defective,' he said. 'According to your Epicurus, the world is made of atoms that move through space. As these atoms collide, they form compounds of increasing size and complexity.

'Now if – as Democritus believed – these atoms move constantly in their first course, either they will not collide or they will. If they do not collide, no compounds can be formed, and there will be no universe as we know it. If they do collide, both the collisions and all that flows from them can be known as surely in advance as an archer can tell the flight of his arrow. In this second case, the mind will be trapped in a sequence of absolute necessity, and there can be no room for any freedom of the will.'

'I don't know about Democritus,' I said, 'though I have heard his name. But I do know that Epicurus believed the atoms to swerve from their course in uncaused ways. That surely means—'

'An uncaused swerve?' Anicius broke in with a sneer. 'If the atoms can swerve once from their course, why should they not swerve all the time? Why should there be any observed regularity to the world? Why should the atoms not swerve unpredictably together and unpredictably apart? Why should a new universe not come into being with every heartbeat, and be at once dissolved?'

I hadn't thought of that. I'd picked up scraps of philosophy here and there. I'd had to join much of this for myself. When you're young and largely on your own resources, it's easy to suppose you've reached the truth of a matter. It's invariably a truth that – even if real – doesn't stand up very well to informed criticism.

Anicius saw the look of confusion on my face. He got up and began pacing firmly about the library. His age, his infirmities, his evident depression of spirits forgotten, he took me through a lecture on the importance of logical paradox as a guide to the truth.

Matter could not exist, he told me. There can be no such thing as an indivisible extended atom: whatever has a front side and a back side must also have a middle along which it can be divided. And so if an atom has any extension in space, it must be divisible into two smaller particles. If these have extension, they also must be divisible. This process of division must continue until we are left with an unextended particle. This cannot be further divided.

But two unextended particles, added together, do not make any degree of extension. Nor do a million unextended particles. Nothing comes of nothing. Therefore, any object containing less than an infinity of atoms must be infinitely small. Anything containing an infinity of atoms must be infinitely large.

Since an infinitely large object would leave no room for us, there is no such thing. Nor can infinitely small objects exist.

'Therefore,' Anicius concluded, 'matter does not exist.'

This and much else that he said confused me horribly at the time. It didn't help that Anicius went into Socratic mode – asking me questions that I didn't understand, and then picking my answers apart. From paradoxes that I could understand but not explain, he led me gradually into a cloud of hot air that I later realised was neoplatonism. Again, I'll not trouble you with an account of the 'Single Mind' and its progressively corrupted emanations. By comparison, you'll find arguments over the Monophysite heresy relevant to our everyday concerns. In any event, much of this – if under different names – has seeped into the more learned formulations of our own Christian Faith.

'But what does any of this matter?' Anicius gasped at the end of his lecture. He fell again into his rickety chair and closed his eyes. When they opened again, he was back to normal.

'None of it matters,' he said mournfully. 'The ancient times are gone forever. They will never come again. And soon I shall be dead myself,' he added. 'I shall be dead, and all this corrupt and useless learning can die with me. Already, there is plague again in the poor districts. It always comes back to feed on the living.'

I must have given his gloomily satisfied tone a sceptical look. He leaned suddenly across the table and quoted an old poet: 'After death there is nothing, and death itself is nothing – *Post mortem nihil ipsaque mors nihil.*' His breath nearly threw me backwards onto the floor.

'That isn't your Epicurus,' he hissed. 'But that's what your Epicurus believed. And who knows? Perhaps he was right.'

There wasn't much answering that. I had been considering a reply that poured scorn on Plato and all the other hot-air merchants who'd darkened the light of the Greeks. But while I could counter his ill-informed rant about the end of the world, I had just been given a lecture of a brilliance I'd never before encountered. He might be a semi-demented bore, denouncing a world that had settled him on the backs of slaves charged on pain of death to keep him from falling down. But he had once been something much more than that. I didn't fancy more slicing from that razor mind. I was already feeling rather small.

But it was now that I conceived my true mission in life. This has not been wealth and sex and pleasure of the bestial kind – though I'll not deny I've managed more than the common share of all these. It is something of which Epicurus himself would have approved. My mission has been to save all that I could of the ancient learning.

By the time I met Anicius, the civilisation that had produced all that truth and beauty was dead. Much of its produce was still alive, but was often hanging to life by a single thread. How many other libraries were there in Rome like that of Anicius – filled with books that crumbled to dust almost as you read them? How many Church libraries were there, filled with the occasional gem that would one day be washed clean with vinegar, so it could be covered with some extended graffito about Saint Nemo or some meaningless difference over Church doctrine?

No, the light of learning was going out in Rome. But the Church had big ideas for England. We were to be made into the force that would evangelise the world for it. Why not hitch a ride on that immensely powerful vehicle? What I had copied here in Rome could be stored in England and recopied and recopied again. And when the missionaries went out to convert other lands, they could educate as well.

I began in my mind to form some hexameters in echo of Vergil:

Others with buildings grand may please the sight,
And in their high and gorgeous domes delight;
A nicer touch to the stretched canvas give,
And teach their animated rocks to live.
Let England's Might stand guard on Learning's fate,
And keep each threatened book in pristine state,
To gather all the rays of setting light,
And wait the passing of our own world's night . . .

And that is what I've spent my life doing. Now that I'm old, I can see the tree bear fruit from the seed that I planted. From the monastery where I'm sitting, the missionaries are already preparing for Germany. And they'll be taking perfect copies of the books that I've saved with them. The world wasn't coming to an end when I was young. It was just going through a rough patch. It had been there before and recovered. Things haven't much improved since then. Indeed, they've grown steadily worse. They may get worse still.

But the 'ancient ways' were not gone forever. They would come again. There will one day be a recovery – though I can't say when. And I shall have been its father or grandfather or great-grandfather.

Now, am I hitching a ride on the Church? Or was this always part of the 'plan'? Was it expected that I, or someone like me, would be there at the right moment? That I can't say. But I have no doubt Abbot Benedict and the authorities in Canterbury have been most indulgent hosts. Of course, they knew what sort of old monster they were taking in. And still they took me in.

I know that Anicius was talking like a burst water pipe in that library. But I wasn't listening as I conceived my own plan. I'd need more money, I decided. Even in a world where it was so short, that gold wouldn't begin to pay for what I wanted. Yes, I could get as many books out of Anicius as I wanted. I might get them for free if I'd sit listening to his lectures. But they'd need copying before anything could go off to Canterbury. Even the limited copying I'd ordered earlier in the day would eat up a quarter of what I took on the road from Populonium. How to get more? I'd have to speak to one of the merchants back at Marcella's.

Better still, there was that Ethiopian diplomat. He seemed to know more than most, and had been quite friendly in the toilet. There was always money to be made from commerce, I knew.

'You know, young man, you really must come again,' said Anicius into the pool of light cast by the lamp that had been set beside us. 'It's so long since I last had a chance to hear what the young have to say. It's so very interesting. You must come again. Take whatever of these useless old things you want. But do come again.'

I looked at the pile of books beside me on the floor. But, as I was divided between the thrill of ownership and the need to compose a speech of appropriate thanks, we were interrupted by one of Marcella's slaves. He burst into the room, panting hard.

'I came as fast as I could, sir, once I'd found where you were.'

'What is it?' I asked.

'Sir, the reverend father went out before nightfall. He was – he was drunk, sir. He hasn't come back. No one knows where he is. Please come, sir. My lady is worried.'

19

'But I don't know exactly when he went out, or where,' Marcella wailed.

She was deep into hysterics, and was setting off everyone about her. They clustered round the entrance hall – other guests, slaves, a few neighbours who'd been attracted in by the sound of chaos. The place must have been that way for a while. Only half the lamps had been lit, and some of those were beginning to smoke badly.

'It was around nightfall,' she continued. 'It was ages ago. He went alone, and he ain't back. No one never goes out alone at night in Rome . . . Oh my!'

She pressed both sets of knuckles to her face, in a gesture of fear and despair that chilled my blood. But I at least had to stay rational. In a moment, Maximin would step through the door, announcing he'd been for a stroll before supper. In the meantime, someone had to take charge of this mob.

'Did Maximin tell anyone where he was going?' I shouted, trying to be heard above the babble. No answer.

'For God's sake,' I bellowed now, 'will you please shut the fuck up!'

Silence.

I continued at normal volume: 'Did he say where he was going?'

Gretel stepped forward. Her face had the same ghastly look as her mistress's. 'Sir, I heard him say he had business with the Sisters of the Blessed Theodora.'

'Where is that?'

'I – I don't rightly know, sir.'

'I do,' the old watchman volunteered. 'It's by the Shrine of Saint Tribonius.'

Leaning forward, Martin answered my blank look. 'It's by the Salarian Gate, sir,' he said. Behind the freckles, his pale face shone white in the lamplight.

That was miles away, on the east of the north wall.

'Right,' I said, 'we're going out. I want a search party.'

I pointed to the two largest of the household slaves, and to the two Lateran slaves who'd come back with me. They were big men.

'A solidus for each of you who come with me,' I said. 'Five solidi,' I added, 'and the price of your freedom to any who brings Maximin back safe by morning.'

I turned to Marcella. 'I want these men armed – swords and knives, if you please.' She nodded, fiddling with the key chain she carried so the armoury could be opened. 'And a good stock of torches.'

'Sir,' the old watchman stepped forward. 'I'm no good with a sword now, but I know this city better than anyone.'

'You come too,' I said. 'The same terms.'

I turned to Martin. 'How are you with weapons?' Though weedy, he was, after all, a barbarian. But he shook his head, more scared than ever.

'No matter. Come with me anyway.' I paused, and added: 'Same terms.'

He stared back at me as if I'd hit him, but then went off for his cloak.

Rome this night was a place of nightmares. The sky had clouded over and a slight drizzle was starting. The streets were utterly black and, except for us, empty and silent. Even the rats were few in number. I'd thought of riding ahead. But a horse in these streets at night would have been slower than going on foot. In any event, we had to keep reasonably close together.

We raced down the streets. I kept running ahead, and had to keep slowing down to wait for the others. Wheezing and gasping behind us, the old watchman called out directions for the quickest route to the convent. Even so, it seemed to take an age to get there.

The convent was a high, dark building; more fortress than house. It wasn't possible in the night to see that much of the place, but it loomed forbiddingly above and around the fortified gate. It stood alone, the neighbouring buildings having fallen down or been demolished.

'Open!' I cried, banging hard on the gate with the pommel of my sword. 'We seek information about one of your visitors.'

No response.

I banged again, harder. Two of the slaves shouted in unison.

There was a shuffling sound within. A little slot opened a few feet above my head.

'There are no strangers within,' an old man quavered. 'Go away. We have arms, and know how to use them.'

'I seek a priest who visited you this evening,' I said, trying to sound urgent yet reasonable. 'I need to know if he is safe within.'

'Go away. There are no strangers within. There have been no visitors. There's no priest here. If you want to see the abbess, come back in daylight.'

The slot closed.

'Open this fucking gate,' I roared, 'or I'll have it broken down. Open up now – or I'll wring your fucking old neck.'

No response.

I banged again and again, my sword pommel bouncing back from the solid, nailed timber. A full military assault would have had trouble breaking that down.

'Sir,' Martin pulled at my cloak, 'sir, the reverend father isn't in there. I can get you a search order tomorrow if you want. But we need to look elsewhere now.'

I sheathed my sword. He was right. But where to look? Rome was gigantic, and Maximin could be anywhere. A full search even of the streets would take days at least. I thought quickly. We'd have to break up into smaller parties.

'You two,' I spoke to the Lateran slaves, 'go west.' To the household slaves: 'Go east round the wall. Keep going in decreasing circles. We'll meet in the Forum.'

To the old watchman and Martin: 'You come with me.'

To the old watchman: 'Where is the most crowded place in Rome at night?'

131

'That'll be the Suburra, sir,' he said. That was the central area of the city. We set off as quickly as the old man could hurry.

The Suburra was a place of narrow streets with densely packed buildings – some still very tall, others fallen down. The main streets were brightly lit with torches, and crowded with stinking, verminous trash of all conditions. I saw nobles in their shabby robes, the usual assortment of whores and rent boys plying for trade, food sellers, common people, beggars with limbs missing or covered with hideous sores. I saw a party of barbarian pilgrims, staggering with their crosses and jugs of beer as they gawped up at the remaining high buildings.

Once, I came across a man dressed in very fine clothes. I gathered that one of the slaves carrying him had slipped in the mud and pitched him out of his chair. He now stood screaming over the fallen wretch, while his other three slaves smashed down savage blows with the cudgels they carried for defence. Passers-by stopped to watch and cry encouragement to the three slaves.

In one of the smaller squares, a crowd had gathered to watch some travelling acrobats who'd stretched a rope between the central column and an upper window. Some boys were dancing on this, high overhead. As I watched, one fell off to a round of applause, landing in a net stretched below.

From the crowded wine shops came music and raucous laughter.

But no Maximin.

I suggested going into one of the wine shops and getting help for the search. Martin warned me off. 'At best, sir, they'll be useless. They don't know what the reverend father looks like. They might even try attacking us to get at your money.'

We moved on through now dense crowds of revellers. We found ourselves somehow back near the dancing acrobats. I grabbed at one of the more sober spectators. Had he seen a priest? I sketched Maximin's height and round shape with my hands. He shook his head. I stopped a passer-by, and then another.

No information.

With rising desperation, I ran from the square, not caring if the others were keeping up with me. I stopped people at random. I waved a bag of coins. I begged for any information.

Nothing. No one had seen Maximin.

'You want a priest, big lord?' a rent boy simpered tipsily at me. 'You've come to the wrong place for that. But you'll find one down there if you look hard.' He giggled, pointing down a side street.

I picked my way over fallen masonry. In a little hollow about twenty feet along, I saw someone in a priest's robe lying on his back. He was resting on a broken limb from a colossal statue, his face in shadow. Under the robe around his waist was a bulge and little movements.

I could hear the beating of my heart as I approached. 'Maximin?' I called uncertainly. 'Is that you, Maximin?'

I pulled the robe back. It wasn't Maximin. It was a priest being sucked off by a whore. She looked up at me, the lines of her face showing through the glazed chalk paint that stood out in the light from my torch. She opened her mouth in a black, ragged smile. Her client's great, heavy cock collapsed like a stricken tree.

'I can explain everything, my son,' the priest began in a round voice.

I fought back the throbbing in my head and kicked him hard in the belly, and then again. I stepped back to avoid the jet of winey vomit that came from his mouth. He doubled up like a disturbed hedgehog. The whore reached out for the purse tied to his waist. I kicked her in the face. She flew back, her head cracking against more of the smashed statue. I pulled out my sword and raised it—

'Sir,' Martin was beside me. 'Sir, we must move on. Morning will be with us soon.'

We searched and searched. 'Maximin!' I cried like a maniac as we ran through the endless, silent streets beyond the Suburra. 'Maximin, Maximin – where are you?'

I lost all track of where we could be in that gigantic city. One dark street was very like all others. Some were more ruined, some more blocked with filth and other debris. Some contained a few shifty creatures who scurried to get out of my way. Some were entirely bare of human life.

133

A few times, the cloud cover broke, and a momentary gleam of moonlight supplemented our now dying torches.

Eventually, we reached the Forum. The other searchers were there already. They stood in a tight, silent knot beside the Column of Phocas.

The Forum itself was still in darkness. But the first light of the morning sun was lighting the gold of the statue from its head down. Soon it would put all the gloom to flight.

I stopped perhaps five yards from the column. The others stood looking down. Martin hurried forward. As if in one of those dreams where your legs have turned heavy, I forced myself along behind him. At the foot of the column, a little heap lay.

There were strange colours flashing in my head, and I fought to control spasms of shaking as I made myself walk the last few yards.

It was Maximin. The head was covered with a piece of cloth. But it was Maximin. I'd known that already.

The light was strengthening from moment to moment, and I could see all more and more clearly. It was Maximin.

No, it wasn't Maximin – it was his body. His body was carefully laid out, the arms folded across his chest. His head was a bloody mass. Blood oozed through the robe. The rats had been at him and had left droppings all around.

The others stood back.

'Maximin,' I whispered. 'Oh, Maximin.'

I fell to my knees beside him. I raised his cold, little body in a tight embrace. I kissed his grey face. I buried my face in the bloody robe. I wept so that I could hardly breathe for the lump in my throat. Bright flashes of memory ripped through my mind. I saw him in Canterbury when I was first shown into the office he'd shared in a little hut. 'I really want to learn English well,' I heard him say, his face oddly soft and sallow in comparison to the northern faces I'd known before. 'Do you think it can be done before Christmas?'

I was distantly aware of the arms that parted us as we were both lifted for carrying back to the house on the Caelian Hill.

20

The doctor spoke in a prissy, detached voice, as if giving a lecture. 'There is a contusion here, and another here.' He pointed at places on the back of the head. 'However –' he pulled back the sheet, again revealing the pale, washed flesh – 'I believe death was immediately caused by this wound here.'

He pointed to a little puncture just under the ribcage. 'This looks like the stab from a military sword. It was made with a force and precision that indicated some professional skill.' He lifted the right hand. 'Three fingers missing here. They weren't found? No – the rats didn't carry them away. Not, at least, from where he was found.'

He answered questions from others. I stood silent in the store-room beside the kitchens where the body had been laid out.

'But even without the other marks, this would indicate a desperate struggle. The victim was struck from behind. He fell –' pointing to the scuffed knees – 'but he didn't go down. He was up and round. You say he carried a staff? This wasn't found either? I imagine he defended himself. That would explain the lost fingers and the gashes on both arms.

'The stab was upwards, indicating he was on his feet to the last. Bearing in mind the struggle, I'd say there were at least two attackers.'

I gripped the back of a chair to hold myself up. Marcella had pumped me with wine and something else that tasted bitter. My head was aching, but otherwise clear. But the sudden view of Maximin's naked body was bringing back the shakes.

'You say he was found with his purse still about him,' the doctor continued. 'Even had it been taken, I wouldn't say this was a common robbery. That generally involves a knife in the back or a garrotte. The killers here were men with regular arms.'

He stopped and thought. 'I'm guessing here, but I have the feeling that the blows to the head were not intended to cause death. More likely, the intention was to disable the victim so he could be taken elsewhere . . . I can't explain the stab wound. An accident, perhaps, or a sudden change of plan. As it is, I haven't examined where he was found. But I'm told there was little blood on the ground, and he was laid out. These are facts consistent with a killing elsewhere. On why the body was moved to where it was found, and its arrangement, I cannot possibly comment.'

There was a question from the diplomat. He spoke clearly and in good Latin. But I had to shake my head in the unaccountably useless effort to understand what he was saying. It was a strange trick my mind had been playing with me on and off all morning.

'When did he die?' I finally made myself hear the diplomat say.

'From the condition of the body now, and from the intense activity that preceded death,' the doctor answered, 'I'd say around the early part of yesterday evening. The Forum isn't busy at night, but I can't imagine that the body could have lain undiscovered long there. It would have been left there shortly before you found it. But that is a matter for others to decide. I am not an investigator.'

He replaced the sheet, turning to face us. 'I shall need to make a further and more detailed examination. But I will do this in private. You can have my written report later today. In the meantime –' he looked at me – 'I think the young man would benefit from sleep. I can prescribe . . .' He reached into his bag.

I shook my head. I needed to stay awake.

I remember almost nothing of the journey back. I recall waiting at the front gate, supported on both sides, watching the sun turn the tiles of the neighbouring houses a deep red. I recall being helped by Martin and Gretel into a hot bath. I recall being dressed. I recall being held in Marcella's arms during a fit of sobs, as she comforted me like a child with little lullabies. I remember pressing the gold I'd promised into grateful hands. Above all, I remember standing beside Maximin's body before it had been washed and prepared for the doctor. Marcella's potion was just taking effect, putting me into a mood of calm detachment. I was alone. I took up one of the cold, stiffening hands and held it to my breast. The skin was already grown flabby, and it moved oddly over the bones beneath.

'By all that you held holy,' I said in Latin, 'I will avenge you.'

I switched into English, as what I had to say was for no one else. 'I swear by whatever God or gods may reign in Heaven – I swear by my honour and the love that I bear you – that I will avenge you. I will not rest. I will care nothing for my own safety or comfort. I will regard no laws, human or divine. I will find who did this to you – and I will destroy him. Wherever you have gone, my friend, my father, my everything, you will not go unaccompanied.'

Now the doctor had arrived and was setting out his instruments in that little room, and we were being moved out into the hall.

'We must take this to the prefect, sir,' the old watchman told me. He was right. There wasn't much in Rome of order. But there was a law, and its formalities had to be observed.

'He will eat something first,' said Marcella in a voice that cut off all chance of objection. 'He can't go down to the Basilica in this heat with nothing but wine in his poor belly.'

As if from nowhere, slaves appeared with bread and olives. I ate without enthusiasm or much awareness.

Out in the street, among the householders and slaves about their normal business, I felt a little more human. Some gave me sorrowful looks. One of the neighbours I'd seen the night before came over and embraced me, expressing his regrets in a thick accent I couldn't place.

I went down to the Basilica with Martin and the old watchman for support.

'Shocking – perfectly shocking,' said the prefect from behind his desk.

I sat before him, alone in the office. He'd already had the news, and his sympathy extended to pouring me a cup of wine with his own hands.

'A priest, and so brutally slain,' he continued. 'I shall hardly be able to bear reading my copy of the medical report. Have another cup, my dear friend. The wine is from Cyprus. I have it brought in specially. You'll agree it's so much finer on the palate than the local muck. Now –' he leaned across the desk – 'what brings you to see me?'

My mouth fell open. 'I . . . I want to ask what investigation you will begin. Where I come from, we sort these things out ourselves. I will find the killers myself. But I shall need assistance. You are the civil power in Rome. You know this city. You have men who can help with the search. I've come to ask how we can work together in the investigation.'

The prefect smiled indulgently. 'Oh dear me, no. I can't possibly do anything about this. I'm far too busy to sanction any investigation.'

He lifted a pile of reports. 'Can you begin to imagine how many murders there are in Rome? There were forty last month alone. There were two last night, including your friend. Not one has been or can be cleared up.

'No – wait – one was cleared up, I think.' He dug through the pile. 'Ah, yes. A woman was murdered in her bed. That was another shocking crime. Her breasts were sliced off and her privy parts sewn shut. We solved it when the husband confessed to the local baker, then hanged himself. It was to do with disputed paternity of a child. Or something.'

He took the sheet in question and added it to a clear space on his desk. He looked at it with a satisfied smile, and poured more wine.

'It's all to do with resources, you see.' He took in a mouthful of wine and swilled it round before swallowing. 'You can't make bricks without straw.'

'But he was a man of God,' I said, astonished. 'You can't just ignore his being murdered in the street.'

'But was he murdered in the street?' The prefect leaned forward, pressing his fingers together. He switched into Greek: 'What *did* you find outside Populonium?'

A few years on, and I'd have given him back a look of stony incomprehension. As it was, I said nothing, but perceptibly stiffened.

'You have many accomplishments for a barbarian,' he said, pleased with his stratagem – not that I could see its purpose. He switched back into Latin. 'What did you find outside Populonium?' he asked again. 'I had positive orders from –' he waved a hand vaguely in the air – 'from on high to send a mounted unit all the way over to Populonium. You were saved carrying a reasonable amount of gold and what I admit was a most holy relic. But none of this can explain the urgency of my instructions. Tell me – what did you find there?'

'The relic and some other things,' I said in confusion.

'*What* "other things"?'

Yes, what 'other things'? I went cold.

'There were some letters,' I said with dawning horror. 'There were three sealed letters.'

'Letters?' His eyes narrowed. 'Letters from whom? To whom? What was in them?'

'I don't know. Maximin had them.'

'Did he read them?'

'I don't know.'

The prefect shrugged and took up his cup again.

I did know. Maximin had forgotten about the things just as I had. Letters hadn't been on our list of things to grab from those English mercenaries; and since we'd got everything that was on the list, we'd paid no attention to anything else. But it wasn't the gold or the relic that had primarily got that chase under way. What was it they'd said as they caught up? 'Don't let the fat one get away.' They'd have killed me, sure enough. But Maximin had the letters, and they were after him.

Maximin had been reminded of the letters in the dispensator's office. That was why he wanted me out of the way that evening. He'd wanted time to read and think. What had he found? Whatever it was, it must have been big: he'd still been disturbed next morning. That explained his anger with me.

Why hadn't I picked up on this? Why had I spent the morning prancing about in fine clothes? If I hadn't been so full of myself, and I knew I could have got information out of him had I tried, Maximin might still . . .

I checked the thought and focused back on the prefect. He was looking very pleased with himself. I declined another cup.

He sighed. 'I truly would like to help you. But unless you can show me those letters or tell me what was in them, I have nowhere to begin with an investigation.

'Of course,' he added as an afterthought, 'if you wanted to offer a reward for information, I'd be glad to hold the money for you . . .'

As I left his office, I nearly bumped into a slave carrying another jug of wine. The old watchman shrugged when I said how little I'd got. I couldn't say what I had expected. I'd read that the Romans had authorities to investigate and try crimes. Plainly, my sources were old. It would all be down to me – which I supposed was for the best.

21

Back in the house, all was chaos again. Marcella was running about screaming. A cane in her hand, she was lashing out at any slaves within reach. There was a gathering of the other guests out in the garden.

I went into the courtyard. The diplomat was saying something to one of his slaves that I couldn't understand, but, from its tone, sounded humorous.

'What's happening now?' I asked.

'The dispensator's men came just after you left,' he explained in his slow but correct Latin. 'They searched the reverend father's rooms and took all his papers. They were in yours too.'

He smiled, showing the wide gap between his front teeth, and said something more about that cargo of incense from Athens. I'd normally have paid attention – the man was a mine of interesting information about all matters commercial. Now, I rushed upstairs.

They had been in my rooms. Everything written was gone, including the books I'd borrowed from Marcella. Everything else had been thoroughly searched. Maximin's suite was almost bare. Even his spare clothes had been taken.

Gretel filled in the details. Three large men had turned up just as I must have turned the corner away from the house. They'd waved the search order under Marcella's nose and made her open the doors. Aside from an explanation of what the search order allowed, they'd spoken not a word from start to finish.

The diplomat took me aside. 'Is it true that an ethereal light was seen above the reverend father's body when it was found?' he asked. 'This house may have been blessed by the final days of a saint. You should make sure to hold on to some of his property.'

Maximin a saint? He'd been many things, and I'd loved him for all of them. But a saint? I said nothing.

Marcella, though, was relishing the possibility that she had let rooms to a saint. She continued in hysterical mood. 'They haven't got no right to do this to persons of quality such as myself,' she sobbed to no one in particular. 'In my husband's day, the rule with quality was always to ask to come in. Search orders was for everyone lower. Oh, what sad times these is . . . what terrible sad times. This world isn't for much longer, I can tell you.'

So she raved on. But I could see the satisfied glint in her eyes. Having a guest murdered – even away from the house – would not in itself mean good business. But a martyrdom was an entirely different matter. When I got back, I'd seen a couple of well-dressed slaves hanging around in the entrance hall. These had been sent over to enquire about rooms. The city would soon be filling up with assorted dignitaries, you see, for the consecration of the converted temple. For business purposes, Maximin's death had come at just the right moment. Already expecting a full occupancy of her rooms, I had no doubt Marcella was now calculating by how much she could increase her rates. She lashed out with her cane, telling all around her that persons of her quality expected better treatment. But I could see her mind was elsewhere.

I dodged behind her back, making for the exit. This was all too much. Maximin was dead. No one knew who had killed him. No one in any position to know seemed to care. I felt like a man who climbs down a well and then discovers that the friend holding the rope at the top has been called away. From that evening in Ethelbert's palace till now, I'd always been able to turn to Maximin for support or for mere companionship. Now he was gone, and my world was falling apart in confusion and horror.

I wanted to get back to my room and gather my thoughts. But the diplomat saw me. He clutched gently at my sleeve and led me over to the glass table.

'Listen,' he said gently, 'I know this is not the best time – though it is a valid question *when* is the best time for what I have to say. But

I really want your company for breakfast the day after tomorrow, on the Jewish Sabbath Day.

'No, I can't say now. But I will say everything on Saturday. Can I count on your company for breakfast? It will affect both you and your dear friend, the now-blessed Maximin.'

His voice dropped to a whisper. 'Please keep this quiet.' He repeated in an even softer whisper, 'Absolutely quiet.'

He turned back towards Marcella. I escaped into the sunlight. I didn't want to go back to my room. I'd had another thought.

'Where are you going, sir?' Martin had appeared beside me from nowhere.

'To the dispensator, of course. Where else do you think I should be going?' I tried to put a firmness of purpose into my voice that I didn't at all feel. I stepped back into the house. I'd not be needing a cloak in this sunshine.

'Shall I come too, sir?' asked Martin. 'I can get you into the Lateran.'

'I think I can do that for myself,' I said, inspecting myself in a little mirror on the wall. My face looked rather haggard, but I wasn't setting out on a social visit. 'I'll be grateful if you could start preparing the funeral, Martin. If you don't know anyone, speak to the doctor. He must have a recommendation.'

'I don't think, sir, that will be necessary,' he said with a close look. 'The dispensator's men placed a seal on the storeroom door. In view of the rumours circulating, I think the body will soon be removed to the Lateran.'

I ignored the invitation to talk about these 'rumours'. I'd already dismissed them as the gossip of slaves for whom finding a murdered priest wasn't enough. 'We'll speak again when I'm back from the Lateran,' I said.

The dispensator was reading as I walked unannounced into his office. Getting into the Lateran had been easy. Getting into any building is easy, so long as you make it seem to the guards and receptionists or whatever that you are too important to be stopped.

I sat down opposite the dispensator, who continued reading. He must have known I was there. I waited. Eventually, he looked up at me.

'You have an interesting past, young man,' he said, waving his hand over what I could now see was Maximin's report. 'You came here for penance, and penance you shall be given.'

'What is in those letters?' I asked abruptly.

'These letters from Father Maximin?' he asked in return. 'Their contents are for the eyes only of Holy Mother Church.'

'Stop playing with me,' I snapped. 'You know perfectly well what we found outside Populonium. What is in *those* letters?'

'Do you not know that yourself?' The dispensator brushed an invisible speck of dust from his sleeve.

'I didn't read them. I don't know their contents.'

'Too busy with the gold, I imagine,' he said, a hint of a sneer in his voice. 'It might have been well for Father Maximin had you paid more attention when you could.'

'You received a letter during our last meeting, didn't you?' I asked. 'It told you about the letters. As soon as you'd read it, you sent for Maximin. What did you discuss with him? What is in those letters? Who told you about them? What else did you find in his papers?'

The dispensator raised a hand for silence. 'Questions, questions, young man – so many questions. Please be aware that I ask the questions in this city. I do not make it my habit to give answers.'

He closed a file that had lain open on his desk. Its pages had been covered with tiny writing that I hadn't been able to read from where I sat.

'However, so far as I can tell, Father Maximin took the letters out with him last night. They were not found this morning with his body.'

'But surely you had them from him yesterday,' I broke in. 'You called him here in the morning.'

'I sent for him,' the dispensator said. 'He didn't come. I sent for him again. My private secretary did not return. I sent out a search party for him. He was found this morning, dying from a stab wound. I never saw Father Maximin. I saw him last in your company in this office.'

I fell silent. What was going on in this city? 'There are evils,' Maximin had told me, 'that will swallow you whole.' They'd swallowed him instead. What had been in those letters?

I tried again. 'Maximin was my friend and my confessor. I have a duty to find his killers. I need all the information I can get.'

'Duty?' The dispensator's face took on a thin, contemptuous smile. 'You have a duty? Was it not your duty in Canterbury to keep your breeches around your waist? As it is, you caused a potentially serious dispute between the Church and a local ruler who had previously been wholly favourable to our mission.' He tapped Maximin's long report. Then he reached for a sheet of unrolled papyrus. 'If that weren't enough, you hadn't been in Rome two days before you were seen attending a nocturnal sacrifice.'

I slumped back in my chair. I'd come here to find answers. All I was getting was further questions. Yes, I was tired and drunk and drugged, and fighting back a despair that was threatening to reach out and floor me. But the dispensator would have been a match for me even otherwise. I'd burst into his office with some wild idea of getting a full explanation or a promise of justice. Instead, I'd smashed my face into a brick wall. I'd been landed with an accusation that would in all other circumstances have terrified me. Even now, I was baffled.

The dispensator continued: 'You will have noticed that the prefect has much else to do beside the performance of his official duties. But I doubt if even he would take no action were I to send him a formal complaint. The old worship is strictly forbidden. I will not warn you again.'

He looked steadily into my face. I looked uncertainly back, fear at last clawing its way from the back of my mind.

'I am sorry that Father Maximin is dead,' the dispensator added, now in a softer tone. 'He was a good and faithful servant of the Church. But you and he blundered outside Populonium into something beyond your comprehension. He did so from pardonable but unwise zeal, you from simple greed. Little people should keep away from such things.'

He closed the file. He made a mark in black on its papyrus cover and dropped it into an open box. 'His was not the only death in the past day,' he added. 'I have lost a highly valuable assistant, and must now transact a mass of confidential but routine business alone. Brother Ambrose will not be easily replaced. My first priority is to see to the solving of his murder. Perhaps that will lead us to whoever killed Father Maximin. In the meantime –' the dispensator rose, indicating the meeting was at an end – 'you must perform alone the duties that brought the pair of you to Rome. I have excellent reports of the work you did yesterday in two libraries. You have a natural aptitude that you will do well to develop. And that must be your whole duty in this city. You have already intervened in matters that were none of your business. Two men are dead because of that. I will have no further trouble.'

As I was leaving, he called me back. 'There is the matter of the funeral,' he said.

'Yes. I believe you are taking that from me as well.' I was bitter.

'Not at all, young man,' he said smoothly. 'You will have first place among the mourners. So far as I can tell, Father Maximin had no living kin. You are all he had. Nevertheless, he was of the Church, and he must be buried by the Church.' He paused, gathering his words with more than usual care. 'Someone has started a rumour that Father Maximin died in a peculiarly holy state. If this turns out to be the case, it will be fitting to inter him in the new Church of the Virgin and All the Martyrs. The English Church has saints, but has had no martyrs so far. To have the first one buried here in Rome would be useful.'

I opened my mouth to make some protest. I still had some reason and common sense. The dispensator stopped me. 'You will neither confirm nor deny any rumours that you hear. You will remember that you came last upon the body, and are in no position to say what signs attended its first discovery. Pending the conclusion of my enquiry, and my report to His Holiness, the body will be brought here to the Lateran, where it must be embalmed. Do you understand that I require your complete silence?'

I nodded. Did any of this matter?

The meeting was still not ended. The dispensator spoke again. 'How is Martin doing?'

'Very well,' said I. 'Because of him, the mission so far as it regards the books has gone very smoothly. I am grateful to him.'

'I am glad of that. However, I now find myself in need of Martin's services. There is work for him here that would otherwise have been assigned elsewhere. I needed him yesterday even before I lost Brother Ambrose. But tomorrow will not be too late. Please ask him to attend on me here at first light tomorrow. In the meantime, he will remain your guide and general assistant.

'Now, you saw yourself in. I am sure you can see yourself out.'

22

As I walked back into the bright sunshine in the square outside the Lateran, I tried to draw my thoughts together. But it wasn't to much effect. Whatever Marcella had dosed me with was wearing off. I felt I should go back and get some sleep. I hadn't slept at all in a day, and then it had been little more than a nap. I was tired. But I didn't want to go back to my rooms. Everything there reminded me of Maximin. And there would be men taking the body away from me.

And there would – I now realised – be interminable questions about the life and conduct of this latest martyr in the history of Holy Mother Church.

I went to a letter-writer's stall in the square and bought a slip of papyrus and borrowed pen and ink. I wrote a brief note to Martin, passing on the dispensator's message and saying I'd be back later in the day. For a few additional coppers, the stallkeeper undertook to have it delivered.

I crossed the square, avoiding the crowds of priests, beggars and pilgrims who swarmed around the palace. Already, though the consecration was still some while ahead, there were perceptibly more of these than on my first visit.

Choosing at random, I took one of the exit streets, and walked briskly past arcades of bright, cheerful shops. I'd normally have stopped and looked in these. Rome, you see, wasn't just a depopulated slum. If much fallen away from its old magnificence, it was still, here and there, by any other standard, a great and wealthy city. There was a continuing demand for goods and services that had to be satisfied somewhere. And I'd wandered by accident into one of the few districts where life went on much as it always had. But I was in no mood for shopping.

I walked, it seemed forever, through the sometimes crowded, sometimes dead, streets of Rome. I stopped at last by one of the crumbling embankments of the Tiber. I sat down on a stone bench and looked across to the far side.

You could see that there had once been elegant gardens there – trees and shrubs brought in from the limits of the known world, carefully arranged paths, little grottoes, and so on. But nature had long since reclaimed the site, and I looked over at a jumble of local and exotic foliage that seemed to owe nothing to human action. The vividness of the flowers aside – and that glorious Italian light that even I, in my present frame of mind, couldn't wholly ignore – it reminded me a little of the forests back home in Kent.

Down by the river, slave women and the poor did their washing. Some children ran in and out of the water. Their faint cries of joy floated up to me on the still, warm air. These joined the louder chattering of the birds across the river. Closer by, the respectable classes of Rome went about their business – exchanging gossip, doing business, getting up an appetite for lunch. I sat watching in the bright, hot sunshine of a late Roman spring day. Everything was surprisingly normal.

I tried again to gather my thoughts. The dispensator was right. We had blundered outside Populonium into something bigger than we could understand. There was something going on there that had involved using the mercenaries for an exchange of letters and precious things. What was being given in return? I couldn't imagine. The mercenaries had been finished off by the prefect's men. But the matter had followed us to Rome. We had been followed. Our rooms had been searched. Whoever was after us had been willing to take any risk to get those letters back. Finally, Maximin had remembered and read them. But he hadn't told me their contents. Instead, he'd been somehow lured out at night and murdered.

Why had he delayed so long after the summons to the dispensator? I didn't know. I did know he'd been kept from obeying the second summons by the murder of the monkish clerk. It was reasonable to suppose the letters had then been taken from him when he was killed.

What did the prefect know about this? Probably nothing more than he'd revealed that morning. What did the dispensator know? Certainly much more than he was inclined to tell me. Were they working together to get the letters back? Perhaps. Perhaps not.

Where did One-Eye fit into all this? What had he been looking for in Populonium? He must have known about the two men I'd killed – after all, he'd alluded to them. Or did he know I'd killed them, or even that they were dead? Where had he been when he came galloping back along the road towards us? What connection had he with the mercenaries? I didn't see how he could have passed us on the road and then had time to alert them before they came after us. But he'd been the one who had searched our rooms.

The little scraps of information were jumbled together in my head, and I couldn't see my way to fitting them into any satisfactory order. We had blundered into something odd. We had now been ejected from it. I was reminded of a summer storm that bursts into a clear sky, leaves a trail of sudden devastation, and then disappears, leaving the sky clear again. Only this storm had killed Maximin.

Do you think I should have been racing about Rome, looking for his killers? Had I known where to begin, I'd have been racing there even now. But I had nowhere to begin. It's one thing to swear vengeance in a city like Rome. It's another thing to know how and where to exact it.

So I sat on that bench, watching the bright normality of a spring day in Rome and feeling so empty of emotion that I could hardly recognise my own mind. I hadn't until then realised what a large part of my life Maximin had come to fill. Every few moments I had to check myself from thinking I should tell Maximin about the shops, or Maximin about the happy children, or Maximin about the strange colours in the old garden across the river. He was gone, I thought yet again, and I was left in this huge, evil city, alone and poised between savage despair and a vast emptiness of misery that I hadn't felt even after my mother died.

Until the day before, I'd blessed that evening when Maximin had refused my suggestion to sleep over in the ruined monastery. From that decision, everything flowed as logically as the plot of one of those Greek tragedies I'd read in translation. Because of that, we met the two bandits. Because of that, we learnt about the relic and the gold. Because of that, we arrived in Rome not one up from the beggars in the street, but men of means and reputation.

Now, I cursed that decision. If only I'd insisted on staying put, Maximin would still be alive. And I could have insisted. Maximin had come to take my firm advice in such things. Oh, it was his idea to get the relic back. But without the gold as well, I'd soon have talked him out of that. Without the relic, I knew I'd still have talked him into getting the gold. There was no symmetry in the mutual encouragement. And if only I'd paid more attention to his troubled state of mind the previous morning . . .

If only, if only. And now he was stiff and cold and surrounded by onions and cured hams. Worse, he was about to be taken away from me and pickled for use by the Church even after his death. However I looked at the matter, it all seemed to be my fault – my irresolution, my greed, my vanity. And now Maximin was dead, and I was all alone in the world.

My thoughts went in circles. At last, I closed my eyes. I only meant to do so to rest them from the brightness of the sun. But it was as if I'd thrown myself backwards into a dark ravine. I sank into the blackness.

I did dream. But my dreams were mostly of the faint and disconnected sort that you can never remember on waking. My mother was there, and the rats from the streets, and the sacrifice in the Colosseum. One-Eye came and went. I didn't see Maximin. But I felt his presence in all the varied images that flitted through my head. It was a presence half comforting, half sad. He was still with me, but was powerless to help in anything I might now attempt.

One dream I did recall on waking. In this, the figures came to life from a set of triumphal friezes I'd seen attached to a temple in the Forum. They wound in a slow, silent procession through a Forum of buildings that still stood in their ancient freshness. I saw the trumpeters, and the purple chariot of the Triumph, and the purple-clad figure within. Behind came slaves, flinging coins from great baskets to the multitude. Behind this marched the soldiers – thousands of them – and then the prisoners in a long line, their backs bowed from the weight of the heavy chains that fastened them, and from the knowledge of what fate would be theirs once the Triumph had culminated in the Temple of Jupiter.

And every one of those prisoners looked like me.

I woke with a start. The sun had moved from behind me to my front left. It was late afternoon. Someone stood over me, holding up a shade to keep the sun from my face. It was an act of kindness, but I could feel I'd already caught the sun while asleep. Beside me on the bench, Lucius was watching me, on his face a look of polite and patient composure.

'How . . . how long?' I gasped. My mouth was dry as dust.

'A very long time,' Lucius replied, handing me a cup of wine. The slave holding up the shade did look rather strained. 'You really should take more care in the sun. Northern skin can't take the force, you should know.'

'How did you find me?' I croaked.

'You weren't at your lodgings. I spoke to your slave, who said you'd return late. You weren't at the Lateran or in the library of poor old Uncle Anicius. Therefore, you had to be somewhere else in Rome.' He laughed, 'And you'll be sure there are few others in this city who fit your description.' His face turned serious. 'But Alaric, I am most terribly sorry about your loss. I came looking for you as soon as I heard the news. If there is anything I can do – anything – do please ask.'

I gabbled an apology for missing dinner with him the night before. He waved that aside. I told him about the prefect. Lucius turned up his nose. 'The man is useless. The only reason he spends any time in his office is because his rooms in the Imperial Palace have no running water. It's an insult to us all that the exarch doesn't get him recalled. I know the priests have got him by the balls over money. But there's any number of natives here who could do more with the job than this wine-sodden little Greek insert into our lives.'

I decided to tell Lucius the whole story as I knew it. No one else had been willing or able to lift a finger. At least he might be able to offer sympathy.

As I finished, he put up his hand and tugged at his fringe. 'You know, I receive messages from the Gods. Since I became their servant, they have served me in turn. They told me the other evening you were to be my best friend. It was confirmed at our secret sacrifice.'

I said nothing about the alleged secrecy of what had happened in the Colosseum. He'd only have said the Gods would protect him. Beyond doubt, his connections did that – plus, of course, the fact that the Church was rather more worried about heresy than a handful of furtive pagans.

He continued: 'I wish we were deepening our friendship in less terrible circumstances. But you won't deny the power of the Old Gods who brought our paths to cross.' He dropped his earnest tone, continuing: 'I could blame you for not opening those letters when you could. But in your position, I'd not have done that much. I'd have tossed them over my shoulder as I galloped off.'

For the first time that day, I smiled. I could imagine the scene, complete with the look on the face of old Big Moustache as he picked them up and roared for his horse.

'Do you feel up to starting the investigation now?' Lucius added. 'No time like the present, after all.'

'An investigation?' I asked. 'Yes, I will investigate, and I will have revenge – revenge according to the justice of my own people. Back home, we handle these things ourselves. We get hold of whoever's done us over, and take personal revenge, or we make some appeal for customary justice. But here – here, I haven't a clue how to find the killers. They came. They went.'

'Things aren't so very different here nowadays. You do these things for yourself, or they don't get done. . . . Now, my dearest Alaric, I don't pretend I had the best education. You've probably read more books than I've touched. But I do know about knowledge. Some things we know by direct revelation from the Gods. Other things we know by patient collection and judgement of facts. I can't tell you now who killed your friend Maximin. But I can tell you how to find who did. It's a question of slow and patient method. You dig and dig, until something turns up. You just have to know where to begin. And,' he pointed far over to the high buildings that surrounded the Forum, 'that looks to me the obvious place to begin. We still have the light if we hurry.'

Fair point. I pulled myself up and staggered a little from stiffness.

Lucius laid a hand on my arm. 'Listen – are you up to this? We need to act pretty fast if we're to find any evidence over in the Forum. But if you don't feel too good, I can start by myself.'

'No,' said I, 'let's make our start. There may be something important that only I can see.'

So began the investigation.

23

The gold of the statue shone bright in the afternoon sun. The
Column of Phocas cast a long shadow toward the Senate House.
Flowers were already piling up at the spot where Maximin's body
had been found. A mixed crowd of locals and pilgrims had
gathered, and a priest was directing the prayers.

'He was a leader of the mission to far-off Britain, where the light
of the sun is hardly seen. By the power that flowed from the Holy
Ghost through his pure soul and body, he worked miracles without
number, bringing over thousands of converts from the dark
heathenism of their race to the True Faith of Holy Mother Church.
Pray for the soul of the Holy Martyr Maximin. Pray for the
Intercession of Saint Maximin, who will surely soon be seated
at the right hand of our Lord and Saviour Jesus Christ, the only
begotten Son of the Father.'

It was lie after fanciful lie from the grey creature. I'd heard this
sort of stuff so often before. But it shocked me to hear it in
connection with Maximin. Would we be told any truth about
Maximin my friend? About his partiality to red wine? About his
ability to lie with a straight face? About those bursts of good
humour that could make his body shake with laughter? Not a
word. It was all now about the many good works and the utter
orthodoxy of Maximin the candidate saint.

Had I seen this priest earlier, hanging around the dispensator's
office? I probably had. It sickened me.

Lucius and I crossed ourselves with convincing reverence as we
pushed through the crowd to the spot where the body had been
found. Lucius took up some of the flowers that concealed the exact
spot.

'Here, what do you think you're doing?' the priest cried. 'Those flowers are private property. I'll have the dispensator on you.'

'Do you know who I am?' Lucius asked, standing up and looking down at the priest. He spoke in the cold tone he reserved for his inferiors.

The priest did recognise him, and stepped back, a surly look on his face.

'Get that mob out of my way. There is work to be done here.'

Blood had oozed from that wound to the heart, and had soaked through the clothing to leave a clear shape on the ground. Though people had obviously cleaned much away as they took up what relics they could scrub with their cloths, enough remained.

'You say there was little blood here when you found him? That would be consistent with his having been murdered some while before being left. Blood dries. Before then, though, it congeals. Even if last night was fairly cold, there still wouldn't have been a lot of leakage.'

I nodded. The body had been neatly arranged once only, the head closest by the column with a cloth covering. From the mark on the ground, there was no reason to suppose it had been moved or at all repositioned. We looked harder. There was a faint but obvious trail of scrape marks and a few blotches leading back from the column and away from the Senate House.

'Those who carried the body were tired by the time they got it here. It was mostly dragged,' Lucius said. That much was evident. We followed the trail easily enough across the fifteen or so feet of the broken pavement that had been uncovered for the presentation of the column. Then we could trace scuff marks in the dirt and breaks in the weeds that covered the steep slope leading back up to the compacted mud that was the modern ground level in the Forum.

After this, the trail was harder to follow. There was so much rubbish and so many weeds. But there was a trail still to be followed. Carrying the weight of Maximin's body at night through that lot had disturbed things. Occasionally, even before getting to the centre of the Forum, the body must have been dropped and dragged – there were little specks here and there. On a little bush, we found a scrap of cloth that I recognised as a piece of his cloak.

We were followed part of the way by a few idlers who'd grown bored with the prayer meeting back by the column. I wanted to tell them to piss off, but chose to ignore them. Lucius, though, lost patience earlier. He gave an order to his slave, who picked up a stone. Before it had to be thrown, there was a commotion back by the column. I looked back. A man had got up from his knees and was waving his staff.

'I can see! I can see!' he bellowed. 'I have been blind all the days of my life. Now the intercession of Saint Maximin has moved the Lord God our Father to grant me the gift of sight. I can see the face of our reverend father, who directed my prayers, and I see the crucifix he was given by Holy Mother Church. I can look up and see the golden statue of our lord and master the emperor . . .'

I looked at him in contempt. I'd helped arrange this sort of thing any number of times in Kent. He was drowned out in a general howl of devotion. In a moment, everyone was on his belly, rolling or fighting to roll in what was left of the bloodstain. Those who'd followed us were back there in a flash. It reminded me of nothing so much as those dreadful rats when I first saw them. The priest stood back, a satisfied smirk on his face.

'See what beasts this corpse religion makes of men?' Lucius spat out the question. 'Don't you just long for a cleaner and more rational worship?'

'I want my hands round the neck of Maximin's killer,' I said. 'If your Gods can bring me that, I'll worship them as these men worship theirs.'

'Is that a promise?' Lucius asked with a little smile. 'If it is, I'll hold you to it.'

I broke the silence. 'Is that a broken twig?

'No – but here is another mark on the ground. We go this way.'

I thought several times as we worked our way towards the edge of the Forum that we'd lost the trail. But as the thickets became more dense, we saw an increasingly consistent pattern of broken twigs and flattened greenery. It was lucky for this purpose Maximin had been so heavy.

We emerged from the Forum round the back of the Basilica. Here, the pavement was still at ground level, and we could trace the smudges where the body had brushed the ground. As we got closer to the killing spot, we found more evidence of blood.

We followed the trail through the outer arches of the Colosseum. We were moving back towards the Caelian Hill.

Then, as we reached a burnt-out library building at the foot of the hill, we saw the big dark patch we'd been hunting. It was just below the broken portico. Beyond that, for about twenty yards, there were faint scuff marks on the unfrequented pavement leading to the main road up the hill.

'He was set on here.' Lucius pointed to the corner of the side street as it joined the main road. 'He was struck and knocked unconscious. He was dragged – look, see the two lines on the mud patch here as his feet dragged on the ground when he was taken under cover of the portico.'

We returned to the portico. The dark patch of my friend's life blood was a vague circle with a diameter of about four feet. On the edge and leading off – I hadn't taken this in at first – was a confusion of footprints, and the unmistakable signs of a blood-sodden corpse being pulled and then carried off for dumping. A few feet away, hidden in some lengthening grass, were scattered the three broken fragments of Maximin's staff. It had been sliced roughly in half, and one of the halves had had about five inches lopped off.

I breathed hard, fighting back the misery and the nausea. At first, I couldn't make any pattern in the bloody prints. But by measuring with our hands and looking for irregularities in the imprinting leather, we finally made out five distinct sets of prints. Two were of large, heavy men. These were the most frequent going in and out of the circle. One was of a smaller man, who seemed mostly to have stood on the edge, going in perhaps only once.

There were two other sets of prints. These were inconsistent with the others. They went in once to the circle – we could see a clear impression, as if the blood were already congealing when they passed over it. They came out again, leaving increasingly faint prints as they moved back towards the Forum.

'The small man used the sword,' said Lucius. 'The others held your friend on either side. Before then, he fought like a hero – staff against swords. His staff was sliced first in half. Then he defended himself with the part that remained, until this was sliced off by the hand. You say fingers were missing. I fear we should look for them.'

'The question is . . .' My voice was a croak. I started again: 'The question is, why stun him and then bring him over here to be murdered?'

'Something may have gone wrong,' Lucius replied. 'What was meant as a robbery or abduction became a murder. Perhaps your friend recognised someone. There is reason to believe he was left here for some while after death. The two others may have been sent back to remove the body to the Forum, though for reasons I cannot yet imagine.

'But this is guessing. For the moment, we need evidence. I'm afraid we must look for those fingers. They may not tell us much. Then again, they might. At least, they can be added for burial.'

We looked, but no fingers. Perhaps the rats did get them after all. Whatever the case, I was quietly relieved.

The slave produced a small book of waxed wooden tablets. He scraped with his stylus as Lucius gave a dictation – everything plain and matter of fact, with no surmise.

'Always keep a record,' he explained. 'What we are seeing now won't be here tomorrow. Already, much evidence by the Column of Phocas may have gone for good. Always keep a record. Even the least important detail may turn out important – but only if you have it recorded.'

He had manners enough not to show it. But I could see that Lucius was enjoying himself. He was enjoying the challenge of the investigation, and he was enjoying my company as his apprentice.

I was grateful for the help. At the least, I no longer felt alone in that city.

We moved on. Most of the houses in the side street where Maximin seemed to have been grabbed were in ruins. The end house, though, was still sound. It looked inhabited. The upper storey had windows that must have overlooked the Forum.

Lucius nodded to his slave.

'Open for the lord Basilius,' the slave shouted, banging on the flimsy door. 'The noble lord desires information of the house-holder. Open for the lord Basilius.'

Connections really are everything. The slave had no sooner fallen silent than there was a scraping of bolts and the door opened a few inches. An old woman looked suspiciously out – ruined teeth, wrinkles, a few wisps of hair. She must have been a good twenty years younger than I now am. It pleases me to think she looked much worse. Such is the effect of poverty.

'What do you want?'

'Information,' Lucius replied.

'You'll get nothing from me,' she said. 'I'm just a poor old woman. Go away and leave me be.'

She tried to shut the door. But the slave had deftly pushed his right foot into the opening. The old woman made a feeble effort to eject him, then gave up. The door opened wide. We walked in.

I can't be bothered to describe how the place stank. You can imagine that for yourself. Filth and great age so often go naturally together. Even though I make a certain effort, I know that I am hardly a sweet flower to my students. Being half paralysed from a stroke, the old woman had made no effort. I don't know how long she'd been alone. I suppose she was waiting for death to claim her, and in the meantime she was living on the papal charity that supported much of the Roman population.

I don't think the building had originally been a house. It was too small for a house in such a fine location, and had the remains of an elaborate stucco. It must once have been a row of offices. Now what was left was a hovel for the poorest of the poor.

The old woman settled herself into a cot that was the only furniture in the single room of the ground floor, and pulled some rags around her. The light that came through the blocked window just above street level was too poor for me to see the stinking refuse with which she surrounded herself in the cot to keep warm at night. We stood leaning against a wall that seemed cleaner than the others by comparison.

'With proper respect for your many years, mother, we seek information of the highest value,' Lucius opened in a surprisingly charming voice. He allowed a slight emphasis on the words 'highest value'.

'A man of God – a priest, no less, of Holy Mother Church – was set upon last night by vagabonds. They robbed and murdered him just by your house. We are charged by His Holiness himself to bring these enemies of God and man to justice. Did you hear the commotion last night?'

She had. She'd been woken by a sound of shouting outside. She'd crawled upstairs to the disused upper part of the house and looked out of the window. She babbled on for a while about the nothings that flit through the minds of the very senile or uneducated. Then: 'Three men was on him,' she jabbered. 'They pulls him away. They was followed by two others.'

'Two others?' I asked. Lucius hushed me with a movement of his hand.

She drooled awhile from her sagging lips. Her mind seemed to wander. Lucius snapped his fingers impatiently in her face.

She pulled herself together with a look of perhaps habitual alarm – the old, I can tell you, need often to be wary of the young – and continued: 'Two others. They follows close behind. Far down the way, there was sounds of more shouting. I hears fighting. I can't say nothing more.'

She cackled a prayer that the killers might be brought to justice. 'We had a way with bastards like that in the old days.' She jerked her head in the general direction of the Colosseum. 'They was fine display with the animals. Rome was safe in them days – safe as the Emperors' Palace, I tell you.'

I doubted this. Lucius had told me a story the other evening about a young man in the great days of Rome. For a bet, he'd dressed as a woman one night and gone out alone. He was raped before he got forty paces. But it pleases the old to think the past was better. It compensates for the lack of any future.

As Lucius was paying out some small change for her trouble, I spoke up again: 'Can you give any description of the attackers? I know it was a dark night. But did you have any sight of those men?'

She thought. 'They had torches. I seed them once all bright. One, he looks up at me.'

'Can you tell me what he looked like?'

'Big man, he was – big and ugly. Patch he had on one eye.' She cackled at the recollection.

'Your One-Eye, perhaps?' Lucius asked.

Yes, it was One-Eye. He'd been in at the kill.

24

We found no more information in or around that street. No one else owned to seeing or hearing anything. But we'd found enough for today. I was no closer to jumping to a complete account of what had been happening since those two bandits crossed us on the road. Even so, I now had a good idea of how and where Maximin had been killed. And One-Eye was part of the story. As if I needed an atom more of evidence, I knew that this hadn't been a casual robbery and murder.

And Lucius had begun my training in the art of investigation. I tried to persuade Lucius that the letters must have been taken by the killers.

'It's obvious,' I'd said. 'The fact is surely plain.'

'A fact is not a fact until it's been checked,' he'd snapped smartly back. How did I know the letters had even been connected with the death? They probably were, and it was worth making what the lawyers call a rebuttable presumption. But this was open to rejection if further evidence should turn up. And if some connection with the letters was to be presumed, their current whereabouts remained an entirely open question.

Yes, Lucius had set me on the path to finding the killers. We'd reconstructed the main details of the murder. Much remained, of course. I still had no idea why those letters had been worth killing for, or who wanted to recover them so badly. But Lucius had revealed a method of getting answers to my questions. Back home, the truth in these matters was apprehended – if at all – by a sudden assault. Here, it would need to be subdued by a possibly long siege.

I was tired again, and feeling half dead from hunger. Marcella's breakfast aside, I hadn't eaten in over a day. The progress of the afternoon had brought back my appetite. I suggested eating in one of the little cookshops that dotted the centre.

Lucius turned up his nose. 'By all means, eat there if you want. If you'd rather avoid food poisoning, though, come back with me. I don't think I can raise a banquet at short notice, but I can offer something that isn't soaked in herbs to cover the taste of decay.'

We walked back to the Forum, where Lucius had his slave buy me a black cake from a stall set up beside the locked Senate House. This had last been opened, he said, for the acclamation of Phocas, seven years earlier. This had been an embarrassingly chaotic event, he added. It was the first meeting of the Senate in ages, and none of the senators who'd bothered to attend had realised they had to bring their own chairs. They'd had to stand like the congregation of a Greek church.

But I looked dubiously at the cake. It looked more like a block of charcoal than anything edible.

'It won't taste very nice,' Lucius explained, 'but it will perk you up for the time between now and dinner. I may try some for myself later. I can't say what's in it, but priests and lawyers eat the stuff before a long session.'

He was right. The taste was utterly horrid. But I soon felt a comforting warmth that started in my belly and spread rapidly over my whole body. The tiredness fell away from me. Even the misery lost much of its dullness.

As we waited for the drug to take better effect, Lucius showed me several more inscriptions in the Forum that commemorated his ancestors. There was even a marble statue, lying on its back, that he told me was of the Basilius who'd paid to have the Colosseum put in order. Lucius had already paid to have it set up again once, but it had been thrown down again in a bread riot. Since it was too big to take back to his house, he'd decided to have it left until a more permanent solution could be found.

From here, we set off slowly up the Capitoline Hill. I'd recovered some of my drained energy, but still had to stop every so often to steady myself. I'd seen the Temple of Jupiter with Maximin from below. Now, it was coming much closer. If you know anything of history, you'll know that this was the spiritual heart of Rome in the days of the Old Religion. It was here that the formal inspection of entrails took place, and here that the triumphal processions terminated. I think it was here that the Sybelline Books were kept.

After Constans turned up in Rome, some decades later, he stripped the gilt bronze tiles off as many temples as he could easily get at. He didn't touch the Temple of Jupiter, but the pope had the tiles removed to replace those from a now more important building. That was the end of the place. The last time I was in Rome, it was a ruin.

Back then, though, it was still standing more or less as it had for centuries past. Of course, it had lost all its adornments, and the doors had been smashed open so beggars could squat there. In better circumstances, I'd have turned tourist. But we walked right past the temple and continued on our way. We walked along a wide street lined with the ruins of ceremonial buildings, then into a maze of side streets so narrow that even the lowish buildings there kept out the daylight. Some of the bigger tenements in these streets were still inhabited.

'That is the remnant of the Basilius fortune,' Lucius said, pointing. 'I collect the rents in person, and sometimes pay my creditors with the proceeds. I suppose I'll have to shell out something to them next month. But Constantinople and Ravenna aren't cheap places to visit. So, for the moment, they can go fuck themselves.' He laughed and moved on.

We came suddenly into a large square, dominated by a cluster of temple buildings. The main courtyard had once been a colonnaded rectangle. But the columns had mostly been taken off for use elsewhere. The temple, though, remained – itself apparently in all its former glory. I could see brick here and there, but most of the marble facing was still in place. It was easily the biggest temple I'd ever seen – a cylinder about a hundred and fifty feet across, topped by a vast dome that terminated perhaps another hundred and fifty feet above the ground. It was fronted by a portico that, big as it was, seemed nothing by comparison with the main building. I leant against an empty plinth.

'What is that?' I asked, pointing at the building.

'That,' said Lucius, 'is something you have to see, tired as you are.'

He sent the slave off to order food for us at his house. We would follow more slowly behind. 'We'll be safe enough as a pair. It's not even dark yet,' he said.

We'd approached from the side. I moved back from the portico, so I could take it all in from the front. The portico was made of three rows of granite columns topped with Corinthian capitals. Above this was a long entablature. On this was the inscription: 'Marcus Agrippa Son of Lucius Consul for the Third Time Made This'.

'Who was this Agrippa?' I asked.

'He was the son-in-law of the great Augustus,' Lucius replied. 'He built this temple around the time your Galilean carpenter was born.' He looked at me closely. 'Or is he *your* Galilean carpenter?' he asked. 'I'm beginning to wonder what you do actually believe . . . But never mind this.' Lucius turned back into well-informed guide. 'The temple was almost entirely rebuilt by Hadrian a hundred or so years later. You know Hadrian? He was my favourite emperor – a man of great learning and of piety for the Old Gods.

'Do you know about Antinous?' he asked with a change of tone.

I knew something, but shook my head. I'd read something of Hadrian's catamite in the *Encyclopaedia* that Saint Jerome put together. Since I didn't know what of this I should believe, I waited for Lucius to enlighten me. But he shrugged and turned back to his main theme.

'The main structure is all by Hadrian,' he said. 'He left only the portico. He left Agrippa's name because he was always too modest to have his own put on his works.

'Let's go in.'

We walked through the portico and Lucius rapped on the huge bronze door. It wasn't locked, but swung noiselessly open, just enough for a priest to stick his head round.

166

'This building is shut until the consecration,' he said officiously. 'Come back for the ceremony.'

Lucius pushed his usual key in the lock: 'I am Lucius Decius Basilius,' he drawled. 'I go where I please. You will open the door now.'

Another priest looked out, then withdrew his head. There was a whispered conversation inside. Finally the door opened and we entered.

Nothing had prepared me for the astonishing beauty of the interior. It was one great circular room, topped by the coffered, hemispherical dome. The light of a very late afternoon entered obliquely through a hole, or *oculus*, at the centre of the dome. This fell directly on the upper part of the dome, and was then diffused lower onto walls of the most glorious polychrome marble. Around the walls, taking the weight of the dome, was a circle of elegant Corinthians.

The overall impression in that late, golden light was of immense yet restful magnificence. I could hardly reconcile the people of the Rome I knew with the race that could have conceived and built something so completely wonderful. It was like the most beautiful and technically perfect ancient poem, enlarged and made into stone.

We stood awhile in silence, then Lucius said: 'It was built as a temple to all the Gods. Now it is to be stolen and given over to the worship of the Jewish Sky God of the Galileans.'

Then I noticed for the first time the frantic work all around us. I was confused for a moment as to how I could possibly have ignored it. Workmen ran up and down ladders. They were taking down any obvious symbol of the old worship. Already, a giant cross was in place before one of the main recesses. There was a high altar that hadn't yet been set in position.

In another of the recesses I saw a pile of broken statuary. We walked over to this. The disfigured beauty of the Old Gods pierced my heart, lifting me for a moment from my own personal grief.

'The "demons" are to be cast out,' said Lucius flatly. 'When I was last in here, they were still in the places given them long ago.

Now, they have been pulled down, and the smashed fragments are to be burnt for cement. The walls are to be scraped. I am told there are to be twenty-eight cartloads of corpse parts delivered from the catacombs to complete the desecration. They'll need to burn half a ton of incense to cover the stench of death. But these will be old relics. I regret to say your friend looks set to join this lot. He'll be a nice, fresh, convenient martyr to add to the pile and inflame the passions of the mob.'

Would Maximin have wanted this? Probably, he would. 'When is the consecration to be?' I asked.

'Around the Ides of next month, I believe,' said Lucius. 'If Boniface is still sweating pus in Naples – a punishment, be assured, for his impiety here – it may all be delayed. Or this new plague may force delay. Or the dispensator may take his place. That'll please the grisly old creep, I'm in no doubt.

'Do you know, he helped stop my father's legal challenge to the will that left everything to the Church? He was only a deacon back then. Even so, he was in thick with Pope Gregory. If beggaring his own family helped advance him in the corpse cult of the Galileans, he didn't care shit.'

Suddenly: 'Did you miss something? Would you have me speak louder?' Lucius wheeled round and spat the questions at the priest who'd let us in. He'd been following us round the temple.

'My lord Basilius,' the priest answered, looking panicky, 'you speak too freely in this house of God.'

'Well, you can speak freely too – that is, if you want a stick taken to your back one night. Fuck off back to your work, scum, and stop snooping on your betters. Do you hear me?'

The priest walked away with a stiff dignity. The dispensator would have this on this desk well before breakfast, I had no doubt. But Lucius seemed untouchable. Perhaps I was too, if I kept in with him, but my own mouth shut. Just to make sure, though, that something acceptable got back, I turned and ostentatiously crossed myself as we left.

25

Lucius had his house not far away from the temple. I say house, but it was in fact a little palace – and mostly in good condition, once you got past the shabby brick exterior. We passed into a high, wide entrance hall, faced with marble that glowed a gentle pink in the fading light that came from above. In the centre was a fountain that still splashed water over a statue of a naked boy.

A slave bowed low to Lucius and removed a cloth from a little block that I gathered was an altar to the household gods. Lucius took up a gold crucifix that had been placed on the cloth and spat on it, holding it upside down. As the slave took the thing away, Lucius prayed silently and scattered a few petals on the altar. 'I feel cleansed from that,' he said cheerfully. 'Let's eat.'

Dinner was plain but good – bread, olives, a little baked rabbit, and plenty of wine mixed with clean water. We didn't recline in the pompous manner of old, but sat opposite each other at a small table. Slaves stood behind to refill our cups.

I stuffed myself and drank until I saw two lamp flames where only one had been. I began to feel better than I had all day. Drugged cakes are all very well. But nothing beats good food and plenty of wine.

For a while, we discussed the arrangements for the following morning. We reviewed the progress of the day, and planned our course of further questioning.

'Remember,' said Lucius again, 'you keep digging until the truth is exposed. We shall see what we unearth tomorrow.'

I said I'd get Martin to lay in a supply of papyrus for our notes.

We turned to other matters. I wanted to know more about Lucius, and I wanted to know something about Constantinople.

'Tell me,' I asked, struggling with the words – the drink was catching up fast on me – 'about Constantinople. Is it really as grand as people say?'

Lucius put his cup down. 'Compared with Rome,' he said, 'it always used to be decidedly second best. Constantine had the place built in a hurry when he needed a new capital in the East. For the next few hundred years, his buildings kept falling down. Nowadays, though, it has no competition. And it is pretty good, if you can put up with all those dreadful churches. The buildings are huge and still fresh. The place has at least a million people. The nobility is rich. The baths are crowded. The shops have everything you could ever want. It costs the earth to live there, of course. Oh yes, and the emperor's a complete bastard.'

Lucius had my cup refilled, this time with unmixed wine. I asked him about Phocas. 'The Church here in Rome liked him. Was he really that bad?'

'Yes, he is that bad,' Lucius insisted. He elaborated on what he'd said the other evening. Phocas was the most common emperor there had ever been. Lucius was as scandalised by this as by the man's great personal ugliness. He'd been a lowly officer in the army on the Danube. The previous emperor, Maurice, had been unlucky in his wars on the frontier, and had put up taxes. The army had eventually revolted and put up Phocas as emperor. Maurice had found no support at home, and was soon put out of the way. This was the first successful revolution against a legitimate emperor in hundreds of years. The Christian ascendancy had until then stabilised the succession.

Phocas, though, had turned out to be a complete incompetent. The barbarians had overrun the Danube provinces, getting all the way to Athens. Then the Persians had put up an alleged son of Maurice as the legitimate emperor and invaded. For a while, they'd kept up the pretence of keeping an old agreement with Maurice. Now, they'd dropped that and were talking about a permanent conquest of the provinces west of the Euphrates.

As Lucius had said, all this left Phocas in serious trouble. There were no taxes coming in from the East. There was nothing to be got in Italy – not even though he'd restored Smaragdus as exarch, who'd previously been recalled for madness and oppression.

The exarch of Africa had effectively declared independence and was plotting an invasion. The whole Empire was collapsing around Phocas. He was too useless to lift a finger in defence of the Empire, but kept control in the capital with a reign of terror. That was how Lucius had lost his expectancy from his Eastern relative.

'Put to death for plotting, the swine claimed,' he said. 'More like he just wanted the cash.'

I described my similar experiences with Ethelbert back home.

Lucius raised his cup. 'So we have still more in common – both robbed of our birthright by tyrants adored by these slimy clerics in Rome. May they all rot in the underworld.'

He drained his cup. More was added.

'But if the man is so dangerous, what could you have been thinking to go there?' I asked.

'Simple.' Lucius gave one of his charming smiles. 'I hoped I could charm the deformed pile of shit into giving me back some of the confiscated property. I got some inspired piece of flattery written in Greek and went out there to read it to him in person. You won't believe how I sat in the ship practising the words until it sounded as if I really knew the language.

'Then I got to Constantinople and found he could just about follow the prayers in Greek. His only fluency is in a kind of barbarised Latin. Still, I recited my poem, and it was interpreted a couplet at a time for him. I didn't understand it. He didn't understand it. But we both went through the motions. He grinned. He hugged me. He sent me off with a letter of commendation to Boniface and the promise of a consulship – just as soon as he could get round to reviving the office.

'I suppose I should count myself lucky to leave his palace with the head still on my shoulders. There were more executions that day in the Circus. He even had the women and children put down. I was there to see it.'

We sat awhile in silence. For all the horrors Lucius was describing, and for all that were attending me even now, I was feeling oddly comfortable. I was no longer alone, and no longer frightened of being alone. I had a friend – a friend who would surely see me right with Maximin, and perhaps much else besides.

A slave fussed with one of the lamp wicks. Lucius sat up straight. 'But I'm not much of a host. Let me show you the great *domus Basilii*. Parts of it are still worth a look.'

Parts of it were indeed worth a look. None of it had fallen down. The roofs were still sound. The living quarters were simply arranged now, the grander furniture having long since been sold off. But the pieces that remained were nicely matched. The floors were covered with rich mosaics of scenes from the ancient mythology. Though tatty in places and often faded, the plastered walls still had their original paintings – country scenes, hunts, and some very interesting scenes of city life from a Rome not yet fallen into decay.

There wasn't much of a library. What books I saw were mostly full of nonsense – magical spells and the like – from the Old Religion. Possession of these, Lucius carefully explained, was treason in itself. His whole life, he added, was a gigantic and deliberate crime against the modern world. He looked into my face as I scanned one of the pages – it was an incantation against haemorrhoids. How could someone be so rational in some matters, yet so ridiculously superstitious in others?

'Do you believe in anything?' he asked, taking up the question he'd earlier dropped. 'Better an atheist, I suppose, than a Christian. But while I've heard of them, I've never met an atheist. Tell me, Alaric, what are your beliefs?'

'Until yesterday,' I answered, 'I didn't know how a book was made. Do you blame me if I keep an open mind about how many gods, if any, there may be watching over us?'

Lucius had been honest with me. Why should I not be honest with him?

'How old are you, Alaric?' he asked.

'Eighteen.' I suddenly remembered: 'I shall be nineteen come Sunday.'

'Then we must celebrate. But so young and an atheist! I'm sure you get on well with Uncle Anicius. Don't you have any sense of a higher power that directs the world? Even the God of the Galileans exists – though he isn't the Supreme Being the priests say he is. There is a providence in our lives, you know. One day, you will have a sign, just as I did.'

He paused and began a new line of questioning. 'Tell me again, my dearest and golden Alaric, do you believe that laws must always be obeyed?'

A year later, and I'd have stiffened and begun looking round for where spies might be hiding. But I'd grown up in a world where power, if often arbitrary, didn't rely on informers. Besides, I had no reason to distrust Lucius.

'The natural function of law,' I said, trying not to slur my speech too much, 'is to protect life and property. We are therefore obliged to obey the laws of any ruler – whoever he is and by whatever right he rules – that reasonably tend to this object. Any laws that go beyond this don't bind in conscience. Perhaps they should be obeyed in public for the avoidance of scandal. But they should not stop us in private from doing whatever we please.'

Lucius asked if that included laws prompted by the teachings of the Church.

'Yes,' I said. I'd have gone on, but my head was beginning to spin from all the wine, and I could feel myself on the verge of incoherence.

I suppose, my Dear Reader, you will put my blasphemous rejection of what our Most Holy Faith enjoins on both rulers and ruled to my infatuation with Epicurus. Well, Epicurus does say all this and more. But I still hadn't done more than guess that this was his position.

Oddly enough, I'd had all this drawn to my attention by a priest in Canterbury, who'd got me to read an attack on the old British heretic Pelagius. The ignorant churls we were trying to evangelise had never thought about Divine Grace and how to reconcile this with freedom of the will. They'd thought no more of that than they had about the Divine Nature of Christ. But there was a slight fear among the missionaries that the independent views of the

Romanised Britons we'd displaced might somehow have infected my own people.

We moved out of the library, and now stood by a functioning bathhouse. The sudden chill did me good. I let the subject drop.

'I can't always justify the full thing,' Lucius explained as he took me though the complex of steam rooms and hot and cold pools. 'But there's still unlimited water from the local aqueduct, and I can manage a hot tub in the morning. There's a broken tenement down the road. You must come round one morning when I've had the slaves rip some more of the joists out of it to get the boiler up to full pressure. You'll be amazed how glorious the experience can be.

'Then there's the gymnasium. I have a small one inside. But the days are warm enough now to use the larger one outside. You're young enough and active enough to have a natural poise. But you won't believe how much art can add to nature – or how it can extend the effects of nature.'

I accepted the invitation, suggesting I should come back the day after next. This was a Saturday. We eventually agreed the day after that. There would surely be time on Sunday for recreation.

'And here is my bedroom.' He led into a high chamber, its walls faced with marble and painted plaster. I looked with surprise at the frankness of the painted scenes. In the middle of the room was a large bed of ebony heavily trimmed with ivory. It was neatly turned back, revealing the clean silken sheets. A few feet from it stood a small brazier to keep the night chill from the room.

Lucius stood proudly by the bed. 'There is another of these in the next room. We once had more. My ancestors had them specially imported from Alexandria.

'Would you like to have a bed made up for you next door?' he asked. 'It's a way back to the Caelian, and I won't say how exhausted you're beginning to look. Indeed, why not move in as my guest? There's plenty of room here. I know we'll get on very well together.'

A thought was stirring in my fuddled mind. 'Lucius,' I replied, 'I'm really grateful for the invite. But I should be getting back to my lodgings. I need to be up and about there very early.'

I saw his face drop a little.

'As for moving in as your guest,' I added, 'I'll give that strong consideration tomorrow. On the one hand, I feel drawn back there because of Maximin. And there may be evidence to be uncovered that I'll only find by staying there. On the other, I do appreciate I may bring greater detachment to the investigation if I'm away from those direct memories.'

Lucius forced a cloak on me against the night air, and then watched me as I vanished into the blackness. His slaves had me back in no time at Marcella's.

Gretel was up late in the entrance hall, making a good pretence of folding some linen. I was tired. But I was young and fighting sorrow. And the walk back to the Caelian had stirred up that mix of wine and drugs to give me an interestingly endless energy.

26

It was turning out useful for Maximin to be all but a declared saint. Even without the immense pleasure of having Lucius as a guest – even without the gross flattery he sprayed at her in a steady stream – Marcella would have been inclined to give us whatever we wanted.

It was Friday morning, and we had assembled all the guests and household in the entrance hall. They sat facing us. Martin, conveniently returned from the dispensator – he wouldn't say what his mission had been – sat to our left at a writing desk to take a verbatim note of the meeting.

'We need,' said Lucius, opening in his smoothest voice, 'so far as possible to reconstruct the last day on earth of our former Brother in Christ, now Holy Saint Maximin. To this end, we have, our Gracious Lady Hostess kindly permitting,' Marcella almost purred from her raised chair at the front of the household, opposite Martin, 'brought you all together so that you can share any and all knowledge you may have of that sad yet glorious day. Our Gracious Noble Hostess has agreed to overlook any default that the slaves may confess to in giving up such knowledge. Our only concern is to apprehend those enemies of God and man who have committed this act of impiety. Let us therefore begin.'

I rose and addressed the gathering. 'We need to know everything that Saint Maximin did and said on his last day with us. In particular, we know that he received a number of messages throughout the day. We need to know when these came, and who brought them, and – if possible – what they said. We shall be most grateful for any information you can share with us.'

I had thought that getting everyone together like this would be a mistake. Better, I'd said to Lucius, to have people in to a side room one at a time. 'No,' he'd said. Including slaves, there were over thirty people in that house. To question them all would take an age. Besides, what evidence they had might be corrected or supplemented by others if they could also hear it. Even so, I still thought a public enquiry might not reveal very much.

I was wrong. The words were no sooner out of my mouth than the old watchman was on his feet.

'It's my job to see all who come and go in this house,' he said, 'and I remember everything that happened that day.' He looked around to ensure he had full attention, cleared his throat importantly, and continued. 'Shortly after the young sir had gone to his bed, a little boy came to the door. He had a message for the Holy Saint. I said I'd take the message myself. But he said it was private. He'd been told to give the message into the hands of the Saint directly. So I let him through.'

'Who took him up to Maxi . . . to the Saint's rooms?' I asked.

There was a pause, and then Gretel was on her feet. 'I took him up,' she said. Unfortunately, she hadn't gone into Maximin's rooms. She'd only seen that he was writing at his desk. He'd got up and closed the door as the boy entered. The boy had been there a very short while, and then had come out with a papyrus note.

'Would you recognise the boy,' I asked the old watchman, 'if you ever saw him again?'

'Of course, sir. I never forget a face.' To Marcella: 'That's right, isn't it, my lady?' He gave a description that might have fitted every child in Rome above the lowest, unhealthiest class.

Martin's pen scratched away as various slaves began to murmur agreement, commenting on the old watchman's excellent memory for names and faces.

I held up my hand for silence. 'Very well,' I said, 'that was the first visit. Can anyone add to what we have heard? Did anyone else see the child? Does anyone else perhaps know who the child was?'

No real answers here. Others had seen the boy as he was led

through the house, but had nothing to add to what we already knew.

The next visitor Maximin had received was the monk Ambrose – the one, that is, who'd been found dead the previous day. He'd come with an oral message. There was no need to ask what he'd said. I'd been with Maximin and had heard the summons.

I turned to Martin. 'Have you any idea why the dispensator sent his private secretary with that summons?' I'd told Martin when I had met him later down at the Lateran about the summons. But perhaps he had something of his own to offer.

He laid his pen down. 'None, sir. Ambrose never discussed his private work for the dispensator. I only know it was highly confidential. The first I knew of the summons was when you told me about it. The dispensator certainly said nothing to me.'

The old watchman broke in. 'He was found yesterday morning, just down the road. I was on an errand for the mistress just after dawn today. I spoke with the slave who found him dying.'

Lucius sat up. 'We must speak as soon as we possibly can with that slave. Did he tell you anything significant when you met him?' he asked.

'I'm sorry, sir, but I didn't think to ask. I can take you to the slave, though. His master is our local wine dealer. He's a good man.'

Lucius turned to Martin: 'We need a meeting as soon as possible. You can make the arrangements after this meeting.'

I continued. 'After I went down to the Lateran, did the Saint receive any other visitors?'

'Yes, sir, he did.' The old watchman spoke again. 'Some while after you'd gone, another monk arrived at the door. He said he had a private message for the Saint.'

Again, Gretel had shown him up. She hadn't heard what passed between him and Maximin. However, she did suspect he wasn't a monk. 'As I showed him down, he . . . he tried to take liberties with me.' She cast her eyes down in a very good impression of shocked innocence.

'How so?' asked Lucius.

'He tried to touch me on . . . in my secret places. I'll swear he was no monk.'

Well, lechery and monastic vows have often been well acquainted, and at first I was inclined to dismiss Gretel's insistence that the man hadn't been a monk. The way she bounced around, she could have excited a stone idol. Then again, she was no stranger to the world. She'd doubtless been touched up by bishops, let alone monks. Still, she insisted this hadn't been a monk. Either she was holding back on something she didn't want to discuss, or she'd picked something up from his general manner that she wasn't able to describe in words. I suspected the latter.

The old watchman disagreed. 'He was a monk, I'll swear. Man and boy, I've been watching over this house forty years. No wrong 'uns ever got in before. Isn't that so, my lady?'

'It most certainly is,' said Marcella. 'My watchman is the best in Rome, I'll have you all know.'

'Of course he is,' said Lucius smoothly. 'But we know the Evil One can take many forms. Were not even the holy saints of the desert often deceived by devils in human form?'

There was a burst of conversation at this – the thought that Satan himself had been in the house was more exciting than any martyrdom – though, by the look on her face, Marcella didn't think it half so good for business. She opened her mouth, perhaps to defend the old watchman again. Then the diplomat spoke up.

He'd wanted to speak before, but probably was reluctant to follow mere slaves. Now Lucius had spoken, he felt no reserve. He'd seen the monk leaving as he was returning on horseback from a ride outside the city, he said. He'd dismounted and bowed low for a blessing. The monk had walked straight past. 'Now I realise I had been in the presence of the Evil One,' he shuddered in his slow Latin.

I asked for a description. There was none worth having. The man had been hooded. Lucius intervened with more detailed questions about height, possible age and so on – also about the direction from which he'd come and to which he'd gone. Martin wrote down the answers so far as he could, but all was vague and contradictory.

After the pseudo-monk had gone, Maximin spent time in the garden. He'd sat there a long time, drinking and looking at some flowers. The diplomat had some information here. He'd gone into the garden after communing in the stables with his groom.

'I went up to the Saint,' he said. 'I asked for the blessing the monk had refused me.' He looked round proudly. 'I was the last man on earth to receive the Saint's blessing before he was martyred.'

He seemed about to launch into a theological digression. But Lucius checked him. 'Did you discuss anything worldly with the Most Holy Martyr?'

'Yes.' The Ethiopian smiled broadly, showing the gap between his very large and very white front teeth. 'He was drinking deeply, and I joined him for a while in conversation. He was troubled in spirit – but who would not be after grappling with the Evil One? To refresh his spirit, he drank wine, and he spoke of his journey to Rome. He said, and I quote from memory: "Oh, that I might be once more on the road through France. I have never known such happiness as with my young friend. He is like the son I never had. We were so happy when we had none but each other. This city is a place of evil. I wish I were away from it. I wish I had never come. I fear for young Alaric. If only he could know he is among serpents."

'Such were the words of the Saint to me.'

I turned and walked over to the glass table. I steadied my hand on its cool surface. In a moment, I'd fight back the tears that were beginning to sting my eyes. I'd burn them out with pure hatred. For that moment, I knew everyone was looking at me.

'But –' Lucius turned the attention back to himself – 'he gave you no indication of what had passed between him and the hooded visitor?'

No, the conversation had been on other matters. The Ethiopian had nothing to add of any value. I regained control of myself and returned to the front of the gathering. 'Were there any other visitors that day?' I asked.

The old watchman spoke again. 'Yes, sir, there was one more for the Saint. He came just before dark. He stood in the deep shadow under the gate, and I couldn't see his face. He handed me a note. "See that this reaches the hands of Father Maximin," he said to me.'

'Did you see what was in the note?' I asked.

The old watchman was offended. 'No, sir, most certainly not. I never look at the correspondence of my lady's guests. Anyway, sir, I can't read.'

Well, that was a conclusive answer. But a letter. It was probably lost, along with the others. Or it had been taken by the dispensator's men. Even so, I asked: 'Did anyone else see this letter?'

There was a stir at the back of the meeting. Marcella's face took on a look somewhere between anger and embarrassment. An old woman stood up. She was one of the lower slaves in the household. I'd seen her boiling linen in a big pot, and mixing piss with something else to make bleach from it. Looking down at her feet, she was mumbling something.

'Speak up, Griselda,' said Marcella, speaking sharply. It was to no effect. The old woman was simply too nervous to speak in front of so many people. I walked over to her. She pointed to Martin. He reached into his files and took out a slip of parchment. I brightened. Here was the letter. We might have an answer to some of our questions.

'It was in the Saint's clothes,' she explained. Marcella had given her these to wash after the embalmers had called to collect the body. 'I got off most of the blood. I scrubbed and scrubbed, but I couldn't get it all off. I give it to your secretary. Please don't blame me, sir. I tried.'

I took the slip from Martin. She had tried. The parchment was about three inches by two. Except for a dark patch that covered most of the skin side, it was about as clean as when it had first been dried and scraped.

There was no point in blaming the silly old woman. I took the slip over to the old watchman. 'Do you think this might have been what was given to you?' I asked.

'Most certainly, sir. I never forget the size of parchment. That's what I was given.'

It was almost maddening to hold that slip in my hand, yet not be able to read it. Lucius and I went over to the doorway into the garden. We examined the skin side in the sunlight.

'That word there is "letters",' said Lucius. I looked, and perhaps it was. 'Look – "*E-P-I-S-T-O-L-A-S*."' He slowly spelt the letters, pointing at each one. He pointed again. 'Could that be "with you" – "*T-E-C-U-M*"?'

'"Letters with you"?' I broke in. 'Was this a message telling Maximin to go to a certain place and take the letters with him?'

'With respect, sir, those marks could say anything.' Martin had come over to join us. 'I've been looking at the marks for some time, trying to see if anything could be recovered.'

He was probably right. I forced myself to obey the command not to jump to conclusions. I agreed with Lucius about the first word. The second was possible. All else was lost beyond recovery. You can often see the old writing on parchment that is reused. But this had been fresh ink, and the parchment had been scrubbed as clean as it could be.

The last matter was Maximin's departure from the house. I asked who had heard him say where he was going. It was Marcella. She'd stopped him as he was going out. 'You shouldn't be going out alone,' she'd told him. 'Surely let me send one of the slaves with you as a guard.'

But he'd insisted he knew where he was going and would be safe. 'No one will be interested in a shabby old priest,' he'd told her. 'I have business with the Sisters of the Blessed Theodora,' he'd said, adding that he'd be back before late or send a message.

That was it. He'd swallowed two of his opium pills to steady himself from all the wine. He'd gone out. We knew he'd got to the foot of the hill, then been set on. There was much still to be settled, but we now had the outlines of Maximin's last day on earth.

After this, there was no more evidence. There had been other callers that day. But these were all known or had been visiting other guests. I thanked everyone for sparing the time to attend. Lucius made a circuit of the hall, thanking everyone in person – even the slaves. Then he asked one last question: 'Did Holy Saint Maximin burn anything on his last day? Were any ashes cleaned from his room?'

There had been no ashes.

We were to visit the convent in the afternoon. Marcella promised to send over to arrange a meeting there with the abbess. Before that, however, there was the matter of the dying secretary. There might be some scrap of information to be had there. The old watchman made sure his deputy was in place, and set off with Martin to find the wine dealer's slave.

So far, a productive morning, Lucius and I agreed. We hadn't found any answers yet. But we were now mapping the contours of our ignorance. 'Ask enough questions,' said Lucius as we refreshed ourselves on raisins and wine, 'and some of them will answer the others.'

27

The wine dealer had his shop at the foot of the Caelian Hill, just by the road leading to the Lateran. The old watchman and another slave were sitting together in the doorway when we arrived with Martin. From the size and state of the jug at their feet, they'd drunk nearly a gallon of pale wine.

'So, back at last, O little Celt,' the old watchman called. 'Will you have a drink with us now?'

Then he remembered himself and got up to bow to Lucius and me. He pointed at the other slave. 'This is the one you want, sirs,' he said. 'Davus found the dying man.'

Davus was so drunk he could barely stand. I took him by the arm and led him in out of the sun. As my eyes grew accustomed to the dim light within the shop, I saw that we were in a large, cool hall, stacked high and deep with ceramic jars. Each one was labelled with a papyrus slip, showing the vintage and the price per gallon. There were steps leading down to a basement, where perhaps the finer vintages were stored. We sat down at a central table that I guessed was used for letting customers sample the wares.

At first, I thought Davus was too drunk to give us anything. But he drank deep from a jug of red, and seemed to pull himself together. His master was away on business, he explained, and he had been left in charge of the shop. The slave evidently thought himself lucky to be on his own.

Poor master, I thought.

As you might expect, he gave his story in a slow, digressive manner. The previous morning, he'd got up early to open the shop. As he was pulling down the little awning over the entrance, he'd been taken short and had gone over to the entrance to an ancient sewer across the street. Pissing into it, he'd heard a faint groan beneath.

With help from a couple of passing slaves, he'd managed to reach down and get the man out of the sewer. It seemed he'd been stabbed some while before and dumped as if already dead in the sewer. Perhaps his attackers had thought he was dead. He was pale and weak from loss of blood. Davus had sat him up and poured some wine into him. But the manhandling had caused the last of his blood to gush out. With a gasp, he'd died. Shortly after, men from the Lateran had come over and removed the corpse.

'Did he say anything before he died?' I asked. 'Anything at all?'

Davus thought hard. 'He said many things. But he was weak and I had trouble hearing him. One thing he did say clearly. "It was the Column of Phocas," he said. "Destroy the Column of Phocas."'

I looked at Lucius. He looked back at me.

'Whatever could that have meant?' I asked.

'Search me,' said Lucius.

'Perhaps he really said something else, sir,' Martin added.

'No!' cried Davus. 'I know what I heard. He said to destroy the Column of Phocas. I would never make up such disrespect for our lord the emperor. I saw the column going up – and a very fine thing it is, too. Don't you go putting treason in my mouth, you worthless piece of barbarian shit.' He waved a heavy fist at Martin.

The man was clearly an habitual drunk. Yet he was quite sure of what he had heard. We had to accept his description, and try to work out its meaning for ourselves.

Outside, we examined the broken sewer. It was a gash in the road about six feet long. It had been dug up many years earlier for a repair that hadn't been completed. Now, it was choked with so much dirt and rubbish that it would never be used again for carrying away waste. There were holes like this all over Rome. I'd seen a particularly nasty one the other evening. I'd nearly fallen down several before getting used to their random presence.

I thought of sending Martin down to look for any evidence we couldn't see from above. But he was wearing the rather nice clothes he'd put on for the dispensator, and I didn't want to push the rights of borrowed ownership that far. Besides, I doubted if there was anything to be found there.

Lucius wouldn't have thought twice about saving Martin's appearance. But he too didn't seem to think there was anything down there to justify a closer inspection.

Now to the convent. In bright sunshine, even the dumpier parts of Rome can look reasonably cheerful. Certainly, the streets we walked along were better by day than on that dreadful evening. Some of them, as ever, were empty. In others were crowded the dirty rabble of the city. Others were filled with sturdy, brightly clad pilgrims, who were still coming in for the consecration. We moved at a restrained pace. The abbess knew we were to visit. But I didn't think it would be appropriate to arrive too soon after Marcella had arranged for us to be there.

What had seemed a fortress the other night was now visible as a large town house of the old nobility. Though blackened in the usual way by dirt and smoke, the exterior remained imposing – a grand building with the remains of a portico and colonnade about the entrance. This was of marble, and had been mostly broken up and taken off for burning into cement.

The main building was a series of filled-in brick arches, supporting a number of brick domes, most of them still sheathed in lead. It had survived the troubles of the previous seventy years in pretty good shape.

Close by was the shrine of Saint Tribonian. This looked for all the world like a ruined privy. Perhaps it was. I believe Bishop Arius, who caused so much trouble with his heresy, died in a privy in Constantinople. His stomach exploded. It was a miracle, Maximin had explained in Canterbury. A Frankish monk who was inclined to Arianism had later whispered to me it was poison. Of course, that privy was soon demolished and the whole area redeveloped to pre-empt any claims of further miracles. Saint Tribonian, doubtless, had been an orthodox martyr.

Martin knocked on the door. It opened, and an old man – the one from the other night? – bowed and motioned us to enter. He took our weapons and placed them beside his small office. He led us down the carriageway straight into a large courtyard garden. This was neatly maintained, and planted, so far as I could tell, with various medicinal herbs. On the other side, we entered into a hallway, from which doors and passages led off to the interior rooms.

This hall had once been richly decorated with mosaics. These were now crudely painted over with a whitewash that still showed the occasional street scene in its thinner places. The marbles were cracked and broken. It was as if efforts had been made to remove all traces of former wealth from the room.

The rooms through which we passed were empty, but showed signs of recent use. I saw balls of thread and stitching frames in one room; in another a freshly broken loaf of dark bread. From far away inside came a collective whisper of prayers. The ladies of the house did not receive male visitors, and evidently preferred not to be seen by any who did come.

These rooms had also been made plain. In a few cases, a larger room had been divided up using wooden screens that reached to the whitewashed ceiling. A couple of rooms had even been partitioned with rough, unplastered brickwork.

The abbess sat alone on a chair placed in the middle of a library room. Around her I could see shelves of books and racks of papyrus rolls. Her face set sternly, she was dressed from head to toe in black. It was impossible from her face alone to tell what age she was. Early middle age was the best guess I could make.

She motioned to the old slave. He brought another two chairs so that Lucius and I could be seated. Martin stood back against the wall. We'd agreed to make a record of the conversation afterwards from our joint memories.

'You are the men who disturbed our peace two nights ago,' the abbess began in a stiff, clear voice. It was less a question than a statement of fact. I nodded.

'I deeply apologise for any alarm I may have caused in this house,' I began. 'But, Reverend Mother, I was looking for my friend. He said before setting out from his lodgings he was coming here. Before he reached you, however, he was brutally murdered in the street.'

'This world,' she replied, 'is a place of many dangers. I have heard the reports of that murder, and you have my sympathies. My own brother was murdered not long since.'

She sighed and let a fold of her black robe fall down from her body. She wore black underneath. 'They are both now in a finer place. But our nature is to miss those who are parted from us. You have my sympathies.'

'Father Maximin was my friend,' I continued. 'I believe he had no kin, and I was all he had at the end. I disturbed you the other night because it was my duty to find him. I am now here in discharge of my duty to find his killers and bring them to justice.

'I do not think Father Maximin was able to visit you on the night of his death. But are you able to give me the purpose of his visit?'

'Young man, I am not able,' she said. 'You were our only visitor on that night. I was given no notice of any other visit.'

I hadn't expected this emphatic denial of contact. I showed her the parchment. 'This letter was received by Maximin shortly before he went out,' I explained. 'He said as he left that he would be calling at this house.'

She looked at the sheet. 'No such letter could have issued from this house,' she said flatly. 'Parchment is a sinful indulgence for the writing of letters. It is to be used only for copying the Holy Gospels or for recording the lives of the saints. For correspondence, it is our custom to reuse the papyrus from the more profane books in this library.'

She raised her arm and waved it at the surroundings. I looked closely for the first time. There were still many books in place. But I could see a pile of wooden spindles and empty cases over in a corner. Like mice, these women were eating their way through one of the few ancient libraries left in Rome. They were ripping precious manuscripts apart and reusing the sheets for occasional notes.

I was there on other business. But that wasted library was a sight that brought added pain to me. For how much longer would there be any books in Rome worth saving?

She watched me looking at the surrounding waste. 'This house came to me from my grandfather. He was a senator in the old days, and less than attentive to his spiritual duties. I have given the house over to the service of God, so that we poor sisters may offer prayers for the rescue of his soul and the salvation of our own.

'We are not accustomed to receive male visitors. We are not accustomed to receive visitors. The world outside these high walls is a place of sin and sudden death. Within, we have attempted to create a refuge of safety and peaceful contemplation. We maintain that peace by limiting communication to the absolutely necessary.

'Again, I am sorry that your friend is dead. Your own earnestness in seeking justice for him surely testifies to his many good qualities. But your informant is mistaken in saying that he was to visit this house on the night of his death. There was neither visit nor summons to this house. I am sorry that I am not able to help you further.' She spoke with great sadness and equal finality.

And that was all. Back in the street outside, I sent Martin off to the Lateran. Someone had to supervise the work of copying that had continued regardless of all else since I'd set it in motion. With Lucius I retired to a wine shop that he said was above the common run.

28

'Have another cup,' said Lucius, raising the jug. We'd been sitting inside the wine shop much of the afternoon. Around us, various merchants and professional men did business or whiled away the hot afternoon hours. I'd made my record of our conversation with the abbess. We'd then gone over the written notes of the past few days, reviewing the case.

Lucius had been right in his theory of knowledge. By investigating for ourselves and asking questions, we had gathered much in the past day. We knew how and where Maximin had been killed. We knew a small amount about who had killed him – at least, we knew how big their feet were and perhaps how heavy they were.

'I think,' said Lucius, shuffling his notes, 'we are now in a position to jump from facts known to facts reasonably open to guess.

'Maximin was called by the dispensator to hand over those letters. Someone knew he had been called in for this purpose – or thought this was the purpose. He was then told by the next visitor – the pseudo-monk, this was – to wait in the house for further instructions. Finally, he was given a note that told him to take the letters to a certain place. He went out, and was attacked. Your One-Eye was one of the killers, though the pattern of prints indicates he may not have struck the killing blow. That old woman didn't see the murder. But I fail to see why else he could have been there.

'Will you agree this is a reasonable construction of events?'

'Yes,' I said. The whole investigation was becoming an odd source of comfort. In proceeding from the known to the unknown, it wasn't so different from trying to get the meaning of a corrupt text in one of those monastic libraries in France.

I continued: 'We still haven't explained the first visitor. And the further question arises of how the killers knew enough about Maximin's planned movements to stand him down from going to the Lateran. This we haven't answered. Nor do we know why he said he was going to that convent, when he never got there. Nor do we know what Ambrose meant about the Column of Phocas.'

'These are questions that will be answered in due course.'

I took another sip. 'What could Brother Ambrose have meant by his dying words?' I asked again. 'What is this Column of Phocas we must destroy?'

'You've seen the dreadful thing in the Forum. I can't say I know of any other.'

'Yes,' I continued, 'but this is plainly a matter of significance. Ambrose couldn't have known Maximin would be found dumped by the column. Yet he still mentioned it. And dying words are important things.'

Lucius shrugged. '*If* they really were his dying words. We have only the word of a drunken slave. If that is what he said, we still haven't enough information to make even a guess.' He paused. 'I think we should give more thought to the content and whereabouts of those letters.'

I insisted again they had been taken from Maximin. That was now plain. He'd been called out with them.

Lucius rolled his eyes and set his cup heavily on the table. 'Listen to me, my dear boy – if we are to get anywhere with this investigation, we must proceed on the basis of evidence. Just because you cannot find those letters, that is no reason by itself to suppose they were taken. Perhaps they were taken. Perhaps Maximin destroyed them. Perhaps he left them somewhere after he'd read them.

'I'll accept, for the moment, they aren't with the Sisters of the Blessed Theodora – though we do need to explain why Maximin said he was going there. But we need to think where else they might be. Do bear in mind that, if we can recover those letters, we shall almost certainly know why your friend was murdered. We may even know by whom he was murdered. Perhaps they will lead us to One-Eye. Find him, after all, and the matter is probably solved.'

I remained unconvinced. Maximin's papers had been searched. I didn't think the dispensator's men had found anything there. Earlier, with Lucius, I'd searched the stables and other places in Marcella's house where the letters might have been hidden. They couldn't be at the convent – even were the abbess lying, I didn't see how Maximin could have had the time to go there.

I asked about the abbess. Was she yet another of his relatives?

'There is a relationship,' Lucius said, screwing his eyes together. 'My great-grandfather was a cousin of . . .' He broke off. 'I'm related to everyone, though I can't always say exactly how. But today was our first meeting. The woman never leaves the house, so far as I can tell. If you want me to get you back in there for a longer audience, I'll have to think hard for any common acquaintance.'

'I'm not sure we'll need that,' I said.

A slave came over to us. 'My lord Basilius: as agreed, the lawyer Venalianus awaits your instructions.'

Lucius closed his eyes, impatient at his own forgetfulness. 'My dearest Alaric,' he said wearily, 'I have some business at home that went clean out of my head. One of my tenants is making a fuss about a charge for repairs to the common parts. It looks as if the whole thing will end before the prefect unless we can reach a settlement. I hardly need explain that I can't have that! Could you possibly excuse me for this evening? I have no idea how long I'll be with the wretched lawyers. We have tenancy agreements and a trust going back to before I was born. Some of the relevant documentation went in a fire.

'It isn't yet dark. You can get back alone. But I'll send some slaves back here if you feel the need of an escort.'

So long as I had my sword with me, I needed no escort – certainly not in daylight. I agreed to call on Lucius the following day. We'd fix the time by prior message.

'I was hoping that we could dine again,' he said. 'There are so many things to discuss – and not only about this deeply sad matter that has brought us so very close together. Tomorrow, you shall be my guest again. We shall dine in greater style – and for longer. That much I do promise.'

With that, he was off.

I sat a while longer in the wine shop. It was nice to sit there, unregarded, taking in the busy atmosphere. And the wine was rather good. I sat longer there than I'd intended.

I left just as the moon was coming up in the cloudless sky. The streets were silent and empty, except for the usual rats. I traced my way back towards the centre of the city, though I soon realised I had taken a wrong turning – one collapsed façade looks very like another, you know. I thought to turn back and retrace my steps to the last place I definitely recognised.

Then I heard the footsteps behind me.

It was the same soft yet not-too-distant padding on the paving stones that I'd heard those few but long days ago with Maximin as we walked back from the prefect. I turned and pulled out my sword.

'Show yourselves, you filthy bastards,' I shouted. 'Who are you?'

I heard only the scurrying of the rats as they ran away from the sound of my voice.

Staggering a little, I walked quickly back along the street. 'I know you're out there. Come on, you piles of shit – come and show yourselves like men.'

I heard a sound behind me. I turned. At first, I saw nothing special in the patterns of dark and of seemingly intense moonlight. Then my eyes focused.

There were four men facing me in the moonlight. I put aside the question of how they could have got behind me. Those streets could do odd things with echoes. I looked at them. They stood very still. They looked the sort of scrawny street trash I'd seen all over Rome, dipping in and out of the cheaper wine shops, lounging about the more populous squares. Only these men were armed. I could see the dull glint of steel from the knives they had in their hands. Silently, they fanned out and moved closer to me.

A sword betters a knife any day. But there were four of these, and the intention was to take me from more than one direction. I backed away. I'd get a wall behind me. Ideally, I'd get into a doorway – that would cover me on three sides. Even against four knives, a sword would then still be better. If they didn't turn and run, I'd rip a few up and try to keep one for some leisurely questioning.

Such was my plan. But the streets in Rome are a disgrace. I'd have had firmer ground trying to fence on Dover Beach. I stepped back onto a line of fallen brickwork, and the mortar gave way. I fell flat on my back. I heard my sword land with a clank in some shadows.

'Fucking hell!' I muttered as I watched the men come closer. I'd really been too long in that wine shop. I could feel a headache coming on as I looked briefly up at the dark sky.

I was up in a moment, my own knife out. But there was an end of my advantage. Even with my back now against a wall, I was one blade against four. Then again, I was bigger. I slashed out at the nearest. He danced away.

'You've got something we want,' said one of them in a loud yet conversational voice. He was a nasty little brute with his thin arms and pinched face. He didn't look particularly strong. On the other hand, he did look just the sort of man who'd spent his life cutting people up in dark alleys. 'Take us to them letters, boy, and you won't come to no harm. That's a promise.'

'Fuck you, gutter-scum!' I snarled, slashing out again. I sliced the air, a good few feet short of him. 'Shitty-breathed cocksucker!' I added.

He smiled. 'You can make this easy for us or hard for yourself,' he said. 'You'll take us to them letters if you knows what's best for you.'

I pulled myself together. In England or in Rome, knife fighting is all the same. The first rule is not to move around too much. Don't let the enemy see how fast you are. Don't let him gauge how far you can reach. Don't waste energy. Yes, so far I'd broken those rules. But I began now to keep them in a loose, semi-inebriated way. I stood with my knife at waist level, and waited.

'Come on,' the pinched man said impatiently. 'Just give us what we fucking want.'

'You want them. You come and get them,' I snarled. I pulled off my cloak and wrapped it round my left arm.

One of the four moved in just a little too close. I darted at him. I went for the face. That's what you should do. Groin and face for close combat – arms and face from a distance. Don't go for the body. It may be armoured. Otherwise, you may not hit something vital. Arms are good. You may get a tendon. Face is always good. You may get an eye if lucky. Even if not, you'll give your enemy something to think about.

I got him on the forehead, just above an eye. He fell back screaming and clutching at his bloodied eye. A lucky hit, but not at all fatal.

Second rule of knife fighting: don't try to follow up a hit when there's more than one attacking you; not, that is, unless you can get a big advantage thereby. I did follow this one. The three others began at once to close in on my sides. One tried to get behind me. Just in time, I danced back against the wall. Out of action for the time being, the wounded man was dabbing at the stream of blood that ran down his face. He'd be back. But there were only three for the moment.

Cautious now, the three spread wider around me. They were trying to wear me out. As one came close enough, I'd go at him. He'd jump back. The others would move in from another side. The trick is to be fast enough and strong enough to stop them from closing in at once – but not to look too fast and strong: you need another one to chance his luck just too far. If you can't pick them off in this way and level the odds, they will eventually get you.

And these men knew what they were doing. Little by little, they were closing in.

I tried a tactic that had once saved one of my victims on the Wessex border. 'Help! Help!' I roared. 'Bloody murder in the street. A reward for help! You there, go for help!'

I didn't expect any help. But I did just slightly unnerve them. One looked briefly round.

That was the end of this fucker, I can tell you. I darted suddenly to the right, holding the others off with my covered left arm. I lunged, and got him straight in the bladder. I felt the knife jolt as it hit the back of his pelvis, and felt the gush of blood and piss as I pulled it out.

He fell screaming to the ground. A good thrust straight up through the ball bag is best. You get more blood, and the moral effect is greater. But bladders are still good in themselves. Even if it doesn't finish an enemy off in short order, it absolutely disables. And there is the added joy that he'll suppurate in agony for days and days.

Yes, I'd got another one. The only downside was that I'd lost the cover of the wall. I tried to get back there. But the two remaining had got me front and back. I darted sideways again. But they followed me and closed in.

'Maximin!' I cried and lunged forward. There's nothing like a good battle cry. All good soldiers swear by them. They cost a bit in breath. But they can really set you up for a fight, and may unnerve an opponent.

As one of the remaining enemies fell back, I threw my cloak at him, then whipped suddenly round on the other and went for the face. I'd take one more with me. There are worse ways to die than giving out twice what you're getting.

I got the one now in front of me in the throat at close quarters. It was a slicing, parallel blow. I felt the momentary resistance as my knife brushed hard against flesh and gristle. With a little surge of hope, I grabbed him and twisted round with him in front of me for cover.

I looked at the remaining able attacker. It was the pinched man. He stood a few feet away looking back at me. What was he doing? I wondered as I pulled my human shield better into place. I was ready for him to come at me. I was rather hoping he might run away. I was ready to expect anything but stillness.

He opened his mouth in a silent cry. I saw the trickle of dark blood from his mouth. I saw the dark shining point of a sword projecting from his chest. As the sword was pulled back, he fell to his knees. He raised his eyes to heaven, another silent cry on his bloody, frothing lips. It was almost as if he were praying. He fell face forward with a long, rattling sigh. I heard the crack of his skull on a paving stone.

The one I'd just got on the face was nowhere to be seen. Instead, I saw a darker blackness in the shadow of the wall. I heard the sheathing of his sword. I had an impression of great size and bodily power. Before I could collect myself, he turned and was off, still in shadow.

I stood, two fallen men around me, another still alive, but choking out his last in my arms. From the blank, still expression on his face, I saw that the one I'd got in the bladder was dead. I must have got a blood vessel. My legs began to shake. I was in no position to follow the stranger.

'Who are you?' I cried feebly.

No response.

I thought to cry out a few words of thanks. But I could think of nothing appropriate. The stranger was gone. There was silence where he'd been. The shadows now were all of the same darkness.

I pushed the dying man forward. He fell with a crunch onto his face. Still cautious, I knelt down to examine him. I'd got him in the windpipe, sure enough, and he was going fast.

'Who sent you?' I asked, twisting at the now shattered nose. 'Give me his name. Did you kill Maximin?'

The hole in his throat gave a shrill whistle. His lips moved in an obscenity. I reached down and tried to cover the hole, so he could get some air into his lungs. But the damage was too extensive. He was bleeding to death. I'd get nothing from him. No point in further questioning.

But you don't respect the dying moments of someone who's just tried to kill you – and may have killed your best friend in the world. There was no time left for anything elaborate. I thought briefly, then stabbed him short in both eyes. I stood up and watched the bloody tears flow black in the moonlight. I looked on gratified at the bubbling, agonised convulsions in which he finally died.

'*Ite feri, ut se sentiat emori*,' I muttered, quoting one of the madder emperors. 'Strike, but let him know that he's dying.'

A shame I hadn't been able to question him. But I'd got the shitbag too deep into the throat. Annoying for me, if a blessing for him.

My fit of the shakes had passed. Indeed, I felt rather good. I was alive and uninjured. At least three other men who'd intended to change that state of affairs were dead. Perhaps there was a justice in the world, I thought, as I cast round for my lost sword.

I found it. I sheathed it. I stepped into the full moonlight. I looked round to get my bearings, then set off in what I supposed to be the right direction home.

All the while, I was followed down the silent streets. I knew that I was followed behind. Those footsteps were now so familiar, I'd have noticed if they weren't there. But I could have sworn there was someone in front of me. It was just one person, I thought. I never saw anyone, but I knew someone was there. He'd stop some way past each junction, to see which way I'd go. If I turned left or right, this watcher would go silent awhile, and then be heard quietly walking in front of me again.

I kept a hand on my sword. But whoever was following me had no present wish to come any closer. Slowly, and with much turning back on myself, I found my way back to Marcella's house on the Caelian.

29

'Well, you certainly had a busy night.' The Ethiopian diplomat smiled broadly and unstoppered another jar of the fizzy water he'd urged on me in place of the normal wine.

He was right – and I'd only given him the incomplete version. I'd go back to find the house dark and locked up. The old watchman had still been about, however, and he'd let me in. His eyes had opened wide at the bloody mess all over me.

'Sir, you ought to know better by now than to be out alone at night,' he'd said, clutching at the door handle for support and breathing wine fumes at me.

I'd agreed. Certainly, Rome was turning out to be heavier on the wardrobe than I'd expected – another suit that would never look the same, even after cleaning. I'd pressed a silver coin into his hand. 'I don't think we need to upset your lady,' I'd explained. 'These past few days have been hard for her as it is. Just send me up some water, if you can.'

He could and did. And Gretel had brought it. I don't know about you, but killing often makes me lustful, and I was wildly inflamed. I'd ripped off my clothes, washed a bit, and then dragged her into bed. I'd worn the little slut out long before rolling off her, and – according to her later description – snored like a pig till well after dawn.

Now I was having breakfast, as agreed, with the diplomat. I say 'as agreed'. In truth, I'd clean forgotten. He'd invited me after Maximin's death, and I'd have agreed to anything at the time without knowing what I was doing. As if that weren't enough, there were the events of the previous night. But he'd got me out of bed with impeccable manners.

'It's my lady!' Gretel had whispered at the first gentle knock. 'She'll have me flogged for this. She'll sell me to the Lombards – er, back to the Lombards . . .'

'I don't think so,' I'd grunted as I staggered from the bed. 'I'm virtually the son of the Most Holy Saint Maximin. Besides, my rent is up to date – which probably counts for everything with the old witch.'

At last, Gretel had opened the door, and the diplomat had not once commented on the fact that she was stark naked, and smeared with some of the blood I hadn't bothered to wash off myself, and in a hurry to get down to the kitchen before her lateness was observed. His only concern, once I'd taken an age with bathing and dressing, was to have me swear on a nice volume of what I took to be the Gospels in his own language, and a foot-high stack of relics, to absolute silence about whatever I might learn from him.

Of course, I'd sworn. Why not? It was coming back to me that he'd promised to tell me things concerning the death of Maximin. If this was useful to me, I didn't think an oath would stand reasonably in the way of using it. Otherwise, I'd keep quiet in any event.

But he had nothing to say about Maximin beyond repeating his now formulaic regrets.

The reason why we mostly met on the toilet, I found, was that he took his meals alone in his rooms. These were larger and far more lavish than my own. The dining room was hung with blue and yellow silk. Attached to this were dozens of little icons in gold and silver frames. We sat on new ebony chairs, eating a kind of honeyed porridge, while slaves who knew only his language danced attendance on us.

'Tell me, Aelric,' he asked – I almost jumped at the use of my proper name: I hadn't heard it since the murder – 'tell me, what do you know about myrrh?'

'Not much,' said I. 'Isn't it some kind of spice? Together with gold and frankincense, it was brought by the Three Wise Men to the birth of our Lord and Saviour Jesus Christ.'

Bearing in mind the décor around me, I looked down and crossed myself. The diplomat did likewise, and the conversation ground to a momentary halt.

He looked up and continued: 'Myrrh is the basic ingredient of incense, large amounts of which are used by every church. It is a dried, brownish gum that is produced chiefly in Arabia, but also across the Red Sea in my own country. It sells in Constantinople for about its weight in silver. It is cheaper here in Rome, but still expensive.'

'I suppose,' said I, 'the Church will be burning a lot of it next month at the consecration.'

The diplomat smiled. 'The Church will burn an enormous quantity of incense at the consecration. This will be the biggest event since the funeral of Pope Gregory – that is, the Most Holy Saint Gregory.'

More crossing.

'And all this incense will be made up here in Rome. It would normally be imported ready-made from Alexandria. But the East is in such chaos, with these Persian and barbarian and civil wars, that it has been decided to import the ingredients directly.

'The Church has awarded the contract for supplying myrrh to a company with offices in Rome and Syracuse. This is owned by a group of Sicilians and normally handles some of the shipments of grain for the papal bread distribution.

'In negotiating this contract, the dispensator was unusually hard. The company must undertake all the risks of buying and shipping the myrrh. Once in Rome, there is no guarantee that any will be bought by the Church. Only so much as is needed, and when it is needed, will be bought. The company must absorb the cost of any delay and dispose of any surplus entirely by itself. The benefit is that the Church has agreed to pay the same rate here in Rome as in Constantinople and Ravenna for whatever quantity it does decide to buy.

'Three days ago, shares in the company were trading at one solidus each. Then –' he paused, taking a sip of his fizzy water – 'then somebody spread a rumour about an alternative shipment of prepared incense through a trading company based in Athens. The rumour adds that these Athenians have bribed someone in the Lateran into rejecting the myrrh that has already been unloaded in Ravenna, and is on its way to Rome under armed escort. According to my information, the contract is so drawn, that any supposed defect in the myrrh can provide grounds for repudiation.

'Now that these rumours have taken hold on the market, the share price has fallen by around a quarter. In a very short while, another rumour will be set in motion: that His Holiness has died in Naples.'

I looked quizzically at him. The pope dead? What from?

'Please be assured, young man,' the diplomat continued, 'that His Holiness is alive and well, and – according to information that I have and even the dispensator has not – is at this moment hurrying secretly back to Rome. You see, the volcanic mud cure has done wonders for him, and he wants to be back here to get on with preparing for the consecration. He will arrive tomorrow. However, while it is believed that His Holiness has most unfortunately passed away, shares in the company will drop further, perhaps to a third even of their presently deflated value.

'Of course, if the death were to be officially announced, the shares would utterly collapse. It took Caesar nine months to get round to confirming Boniface as pope. Bearing in mind what is currently happening in the East, Rome might easily be years without a confirmed universal bishop, were Boniface to die. No pope, you see, no consecration. The dispensator could stand in for a temporary absence – but not to fill a semi-permanent void.

'But I cannot arrange for such official confirmation.'

'So,' I said, 'you want me to help you buy some shares while they are low?' I'd picked up some elements of finance from our lavatorial conversations. This was supplemented by the frequently sharp practice I'd seen from the traders who'd accompanied the missionaries to Canterbury, and by my small but select study of mathematics.

Of course, I had other things now on my mind beside making money. On the other hand, the comparative little I'd already picked up had transformed my life – perhaps, I'll grant, not wholly for the better. And I'd need more if I were to go ahead with my ambitions for the English mission. I was willing at least to hear the man out.

'You want me to buy shares?' I repeated.

'No, Aelric, not shares.' The diplomat picked up a jewelled relic case and hugged it. 'I don't get out of bed to buy shares. We buy options.'

For those of you who have barely followed the above – and if you're a monk, that's probably you – I should explain what the diplomat was after. He didn't want me to go off with him and buy shares in the company. A share, by the way, is part ownership. Even down from one solidus to a quarter of that, you'd need to tie up a lot of gold to make a real killing. What he wanted to buy was the *right* to obtain shares on a future date at a certain price. We could have that right per go at a tenth of a quarter of a solidus.

Now, let me spell out the meaning of this. For one solidus, you can buy the right to acquire forty shares that, when all the depressing rumours have been discovered, will pass again at one solidus each. You can turn one pound of gold into forty. You can turn five pounds into two hundred. You have to deduct from this any costs beside the exercise price; and there may be special bribes to the Exchange authorities. But the only limit to this rigging of the market is how many options you can buy before you get rumbled. Oh yes, and you need to make sure that you don't entirely bankrupt the poor fool you get to sell you the things: do that and you may lose your payment up front. I suppose it helps also if you can square enforcement with the authorities.

The diplomat assured me this would be no problem. We weren't manipulating the price of myrrh – that would have got the Church involved at every possible level to stop our game. We were only manipulating shares in the company that was shipping the stuff in. The Church would be indifferent. The prefect could be trusted to do all that was needed to save himself the trouble of trying any action against us. That, or a straight bribe, would keep matters out of court.

The diplomat had thought of everything. Today was the Hebrew Sabbath. This meant the Jews would be at home praying and counting their gains from the previous six days of labour. They wouldn't be around to smell the rats we were planning to loose. The market would be hogged by the Africans and a few Syrians. It would be wide open to our assault.

'Where do I come into this?' I asked sharply. Was this some elaborate double fraud, with me as the ultimate victim? It was common knowledge in the house that I was in funds.

'You will buy the options,' came the reply. The diplomat went over to a locked chest. He fiddled with a key around his neck and withdrew five bags of coin. He emptied one onto the table. I looked at the pile of misshapen lumps I'd last seen in France. They were barbarian versions of the solidus. He'd made sure the gold was pure enough, he told me. But this stuff was so clipped and variable, it would pass purely by weight.

My job was to pose as the son of some rich pilgrim from the barbarian kingdoms. The diplomat would arrive first at the Exchange with a troubled look on his face. He'd ostentatiously buy options on shares at something like their normal value, talking loudly about his invite to the consecration. While he was doing this, his secretary would be got up in hood and gloves to hide his black skin – but not got up well enough – and would be selling actual shares at whatever price he could get. A little into this pantomime, the rumour would pass round that the pope was dead. The market would go into a selling frenzy.

Just into this frenzy, I'd turn up, gawping at the dealers and speaking a mangled, semi-comprehensible Latin. I'd show a written authority to buy options at four shares to the solidus, which by then should be an attractive price. This being said, I'd have several letters of authority – all with different prices, and I'd select which one to use in the precise circumstances. I'd do the business and leave and the dealers would congratulate each other on covering themselves against the official news of the death. No one would think to connect us until it was too late.

'You have some barbarian clothes?' the diplomat asked. I shook my head. Those horrid old things I'd worn all the way from Canterbury I'd ceremonially burned outside Rome. Maximin had nagged me that there were poor youths in Rome who'd give their teeth for such finery. Not surprisingly, I'd ignored him. A pity, I now thought.

'No matter. We can get something from one of that Frankish merchant's slaves.' He was referring to another of Marcella's guests. 'I've got some nice Frankish jewellery you can add to it. You'll pass as shabby rich in the barbarian mode.'

We turned now to the matter of what was in this for me.

'A twentieth part of the profit,' he answered suavely.

'Not enough,' said I. 'Do you suppose these men will simply smile as they hand over their last coppers? I've already just avoided a knife in the back. I want half. And I want this in writing. If you try to cheat me, I'll take your letter to the prefect or the dispensator or the pope himself.'

We started an interminable, circular argument. The diplomat cried that he'd done all the preparation work – months of thought and research, planting of rumours, getting a reputation for himself on the market as a shady and incompetent player. All I had to do was look stupid for a while before lunch. Surely he had a right to the main profit? If need be, he could use someone else.

But I was inflexible. You see, I had time on my side. This morning was the only opportunity, and I'd dawdled much of this already. He'd never get anyone half so reliable in the time that was left. The pope was getting closer to Rome by the hour. How long before this was noticed?

We settled on two-fifths of the profit. I could have held out for the full half, but the diplomat might come up with other schemes that required my involvement. Why be too greedy? While he wrote in his own hand, I dictated a short letter of confession. Show that to the authorities, and his black and distinctly heretical face wouldn't be welcome in Rome another day. As it was, his exact status in Rome as a Monophysite with no apparent diplomatic interest to represent was somewhat ambiguous. Since he'd taken to the place at least as much as I had, this would be a disaster for him.

30

The financial district of Rome used to be across the river from the main city. Nowadays, the Saracens have destroyed the trade on which the markets relied. Some years ago, a fire took the buildings. When I was first there, however, it was one of those districts of Rome that retained more than a shadow of its former glory. The streets were broad and clean. There was plenty of running water, and this kept the sewers in going order.

The Great God Mammon places heavy demands on the time of even his humblest devotees. But he also imposes an order on their minds that is often reflected in their surroundings. I could almost see the money behind the blank walls of the houses. At every corner, private armed guards were stationed. There was no need here of the prefect and his haphazard keeping of the peace. The riffraff was kept securely out. Any thief who did get through risked being beaten half to death and tossed in the river.

Otherwise, there were some magnificent churches. There was even a synagogue. This was the first I'd ever seen – built in the most extravagant oriental style, a Star of David topping each minaret. From within its walls I could hear the strange wails and chanting of the Jews.

The main Exchange was in a tall, circular building roofed with two domes. It was the most prominent building in a square lined with churches that couldn't all be for the True Faith of Holy Mother Church. There was another synagogue placed between two of these. So long as nothing was advertised, I think every known faith and variation on it was catered for in that square.

In this part of Rome, I could see, the only differences men recognised between each other were solvency and insolvency.

The inside of the Exchange was mostly a single room. It was smaller than the temple I'd visited with Lucius, and had no gorgeous marble on the walls. But it was in similar style. It gave plenty of space for the jostling, shouting crowd of dealers who spent much of their waking lives there.

In the middle of the room, I saw a circle of boards facing outwards. On these, slaves were hard at work chalking up the latest prices. Within the circle, on a high platform, sat an official dressed in blue silk. Behind him was a water clock in working order. Hung on these were icons of the emperor, the pope and various saints.

The diplomat's plan didn't go quite as expected. The rumour of the pope's death was quickly disbelieved. The shares fell by a little, and then began to recover. They were helped by a counter-rumour that Athens and all the Greek cities had declared for the exarch of Africa and closed their ports to Italy so long as it stood by Phocas.

The shouting of offers and counter-offers mounted to a steady roar. I looked round, confused. What little the diplomat had told me about the markets hadn't prepared me for the chaos around me. It was as if I'd stepped into a riot. For a moment, it looked even to me that the plan would have to be called off. If the shares rose back to their unmanipulated level, no one would sell options to buy for less.

Then everything changed without warning. Other rumours began to circulate. They passed in quick succession from one chattering dealer to another. I couldn't keep up with them. They came so quickly that no one believed them. The only question now debated was who was coining the rumours and for what purpose.

Now suspicious and confused, the dealers began to mark all the prices down. They fell steadily. The slaves rubbed the boards and scraped wildly with their chalk. I later realised that this was one of those rare opportunities when nerve and ready cash can bring in a rich harvest of gold. At the time, I didn't understand a tenth of what was going on. But I had fixed in my head the notion of the unmanipulated price of the shares in question; and I could see that the market price was heading firmly downwards.

As agreed, I went over to Silas, a monstrously fat Syrian with a suspiciously black beard and gold rings sunk into all his fingers. You see, the diplomat had heard he fancied my type, and might be too excited to ask many questions. I showed him one of my letters of authority and asked him to help me buy the options. I flashed him a broad, open smile that screamed stupidity.

'A nice boy like you needs to be careful in a place like this,' he said, breathing garlic into my face. 'But you've come to the right man. I'll see you right, just you trust me.'

And he did. I got options to buy at about three-fifths of the unmanipulated price. Silas weighed the coin while a clerk drew the contract. He took out some of the less regular pieces and tested them between his teeth. A few of them he tossed back to me. I replaced them with an equal weight of the imperial coins in my own purse.

He looked oddly at these. But I fluttered my eyelashes and asked admiringly about the icon of Saint Simeon Stylites set up on his counting table. That took his mind off the good coins I'd handed over.

He reached out and dabbled his podgy fingers over my bottom. I could feel the patting through the tight fabric of my trousers. I forced out a dazzling smile and tried not to shudder. His face sweaty with lust, he told me I'd done a brilliant deal – especially since he might not be inclined to be hard on me should I need to sell them back at some point. He was sure we could 'come to some agreement'. He crossed himself and kissed the icon.

I didn't need to take up his kind offer. A shouting crowd had surrounded the diplomat. His secretary's disguise had been un-covered in short order, and he was being pressed to explain his subterfuge. He looked wildly around. He caught my eye, and pulled hard on his crinkly beard. That was the message we'd earlier agreed. The planned actions were all off. I was to use my initiative. I heard him shouting loud above the surrounding roars of dis-approval. The pope was expected back tomorrow, he cried. There were no other shipments of incense, from Athens or anywhere else. He was ever so sorry for any trouble he'd caused.

'In the name of God and the double nature of Christ,' he looked at the Syrians, 'not forgetting His Single Directing Will, be merciful with me. I am but a poor black from the land of Kush. You have discovered me. Let that be my punishment.'

One of the dealers made a gesture of wiping his arse with one of the options he'd lately bought. He sneered a question at the diplomat: would he be able to execute without selling his horse?

More than ever, rumour clashed with rumour in that great trading room. The dealers ran about like disturbed ants, clasping hands when they met one another, and exchanging promises and slips of papyrus. The slaves scrubbed madly at the boards, chalking and rechalking the prices. The presiding official alone sat silent and serene.

In this commotion, the shares rose sharply. They went straight back to par and then rose to one solidus and a tenth. As they headed towards one and a fifth, I sold my own options on to an Armenian. He sold them straight on for more. I could feel the sudden rush of confidence in the room. Every price was rising.

I was tempted to spend some of my own money on what seemed an attractive forward contract on some Spanish slaves bound for a silver mine. But I knew enough about the markets to be aware of how little I yet understood them. I kept my purse resolutely closed.

Looking over at him, I saw that the diplomat had suddenly lost his crestfallen look. He hadn't made the absolute killing he'd described to me, but was somehow looking very perky. He was producing document after document before the other dealers. These had stopped shouting at him. Their laughter stilled; they were now pulling on their beards and looking nervously over at the Exchange officials. Some of them had gathered together under a clump of icons, and were talking very quickly in a language I didn't know.

I now realise the diplomat had been involved in an immense double or even treble bluff. My own part in the plan had been to help in a diversion from the main business of ripping off everyone in earnest. At the time, I suspected something of the sort, but lacked the understanding of the markets needed to say exactly what was going on.

But I had no cause for complaint. I had a draft safely in my tunic for over a hundred pounds of gold. I'd seen for myself what fertiliser a few lies could be with just five pounds of the stuff. I'd had the draft made out to me. Once it was cleared at the Papal Bank, the diplomat could have his share. But I'd harvested a straight, easy, forty-five pounds of gold for myself.

No more moonlit frauds for me, I thought. From now on, I'd do them all indoors. And every ounce of gold thereby gained would go on securing me from the common vicissitudes of life, and on preserving every ancient book I could lay hands on.

I can now see where the diplomat had ostensibly gone wrong. His own part of the fraud was too gross to be believed. What he should have done was to say that the pope had been advised to put off the consecration to the autumn. That would have been more credible, and would probably have still sent the shares down before the truth came out. He also should have planned for a sudden rebound.

But all this is irrelevant. I had been involved in a fraud that was meant to be uncovered. The real fraud was something much larger, involving many more securities besides the incense shipment. While the other dealers were laughing at him, the diplomat had made a killing on the markets. At the time, it really was all beyond me. Still, I hadn't done badly. I'd saved the day where the secondary fraud was concerned. Perhaps I could even still insist on half. Bear in mind, I had all the takings in my own name.

As I was balancing the certainty of keeping more of the gold, if I had a mind to, against the prospect of further riggings of the market with the diplomat, an old man sidled up to me. Short, thin, clean-shaven, he addressed me in a passable English of the Wessex dialect.

'I know who you are,' he said with a wheezing laugh. 'You're that boy whose friend was killed the other night.'

'Where did you learn English?' I asked nervously.

'In England. Where else?'

A reasonable answer. Where else would anyone want to learn such an unimportant language, and learn it well?

He explained he'd lived there for several years, handling the local business for a company based in Carthage. He'd picked up pretty child slaves for rich profligates out East, and a few of our black pearls. He'd paid with dyed silks and pepper.

'Good business in England,' he said. 'I hear Holy Mother Church is doing well there. Do you think King Ethelbert might want to borrow some money? You get me an introduction, and I'll pay good commission. Kent has its moments in the summer months, and I'd like to see the place again.'

I said I'd consider his offer, asking him to keep our little secret from Silas, whose face I could see at twenty yards was turning the colour of a roof tile. The diplomat and I had worried I might be recognised, but had decided to risk that – bear in mind, I'd only been out in Rome dressed as a noble, and had never before ventured across the river. Most dealers never left their own district.

I thought to add to the old man that I had some good contacts in Wessex who probably wouldn't hang him if he turned up with a bale of silk. At that moment, though, I saw through the open door that Martin stood in the square.

At first, I thought I must be mistaken. But as I pressed my way through the tight crowd of dealers towards the door, I knew it was him. He was dressed in nicely pressed white linen. He was holding hands with a very pretty young woman. Dark, braided hair, obviously pregnant, she was gazing up at him with a look of happy trust on her face. Martin looked back at her.

It was because of the expression on his own face that I thought I'd mistaken him. I was used to the reserved, often sullen look of a slave. Now he smiled, his face creased with the happiness of a day out in the sun. He pointed at the Exchange.

I dodged behind a pillar and continued to observe. They carried on walking until I could no longer see them through the open door. I came out into the square, but they were disappearing into a crowded side street. I would have followed, but the old man had caught up with me.

'Bad business with your friend,' he said. 'Still, he's soon to be a saint of the Church if I hear right. But a bad business, all the same.

You know,' he continued, 'you should be careful with the Column of Phocas. They're a bad lot. They did for your friend. If you get on their wrong side, they'll do for you.'

'What is this "Column of Phocas"?' I asked, spinning back to him, Martin forgotten. 'What do you know about the Column of Phocas?'

'All wise men know about the Column of Phocas. The wisest men don't speak about it.' He laughed at his epigram.

I pressed him, but he'd closed up. I offered him dinner with Ethelbert. I did think to threaten him with a beating outside. But he'd closed up.

'Beware the Column of Phocas,' he said, slipping back into the crowd, 'if you ever want to pray with me in the church at Canterbury.'

31

'Have you any notion of who this diplomat is?' Lucius asked over lunch. 'Did he tell you anything about himself?'

He'd taken me to a select place in one of the restaurants in the Market of Trajan. Being higher than the Forum, this was still in use. We sat in the open with a canvas overhead to keep the hot sun at bay. There was a fine view over the upper parts of the Forum. In the bright sunshine, it didn't look too derelict.

'I really have no idea who the man is,' I said. 'I know he spends a lot of time at the Lateran. Otherwise, he sits in his rooms, thinking of ways to defraud the Roman dealers.'

'We know that he spoke with Maximin on the day of the killing,' Lucius said. 'We have only his word for what was said.'

I asked Lucius if he really thought the diplomat might have been involved in the murder.

'I think nothing,' said Lucius. 'The man has been in Rome some while on a mission that no one is able to explain. If he's from his local king, he should be in Constantinople, addressing himself to the emperor.

'One rumour I picked up is that he's working for the exarch of Africa. If old Heraclius can get the Western Church on side, that's all the worse for Phocas. But I think nothing of rumours in themselves. All I know for certain is that he's been flashing money all over the place, buying horses and various luxury goods. You now tell me how he gets his money. . . . Oh, yes, and don't forget – he was the last person known to have had an extended conversation with Maximin. I say you should keep an eye on him.'

Lucius asked me to explain again what I'd been doing with him in the markets. It still didn't seem to go in. He knew enough about the law of property, and had been forced by circumstances to learn about the intricacies of the testacy laws. But financial speculation was beyond him. And I got the impression he thought it all somewhat demeaning. I let my words trail off.

We turned back to the assault on me the previous evening. While I was going once more over the story in outline, a slave returned from the place of the attack. No bodies, he said, but plenty of blood. He held out the slashed, bloody cloak I'd left there. No one to identify, I groaned to myself. The one I'd injured must have come back with help. Someone at least was showing an unusual interest in keeping the streets uncluttered.

'From now on, my dear Alaric,' Lucius said, 'I want you to promise me you won't go out again at night by yourself. I should have sent back that escort for you. It was wrong of me to go off and leave you like that. Worse,' he smiled, 'it was careless. Nevertheless, I think we can now be sure those letters are still about somewhere.'

I agreed.

'And I think we can say that those men weren't sent to kill you. I don't doubt for a moment you can be good with a knife. But one of you against four experienced street scum – they'd have had you before you could realise if murder had been on their agenda. They wanted you alive. Someone wanted you to take him to those letters. The question now is, who wanted you?'

'It was the Column of Phocas,' I answered. 'Our column isn't a thing of stone and gilded bronze. It's a group of men.'

As you ought to know, my Dear Reader, the Latin word 'columna' means 'column'. But it also can mean general support. 'Columna Phocasi' can therefore be translated into Greek as 'Movement for the Protection of Phocas'.

I was pleased I had uncovered more of the mystery – and had done it without help from Lucius. For the first time, I was taking information to him. I was less pleased that Lucius was so sure I hadn't been in serious danger from those men.

I suddenly felt less happy with myself. I hadn't told him about the stranger who helped me. And I'd decided to hold back on my sighting of Martin. The first made my side of the fight less impressive. Revealing the second might only get Martin into a trouble I didn't feel inclined to inflict on him.

We sat awhile in silence. I looked past Lucius, over the terrace, down past the shabby or ruined or still fine buildings, to the Forum, and to the gleaming statue atop its column. I looked back to a polished wine pitcher on a table just a few yards from us. Though distorted, I could see myself in the reflection. I'd got those crude barbarian things off me as soon as I'd got back to Marcella's. I was now dressed in my one good remaining suit of clothes. This was of heavy linen – white with no colour for the border. I looked decidedly beautiful. I felt better at once. I had to resist the urge to get up and go looking for a better reflection.

Now I was even richer, I'd have those tailors stitching through the night for an entire new wardrobe. Perhaps I'd go for the heaviest grade of silk.

'It looks,' said Lucius, breaking the silence, 'if what you say is correct, as if we're dealing with some secret imperial security service. I'm surprised, I must say. I never thought our lord and master in Constantinople was up to running anything like that. I thought straight executions with a bit of torture beforehand was his limit.

'Now, Alaric, this means we're up against something big – really big. Something very fishy was going on at that rendezvous outside Populonium. You and Maximin got in its way. He's dead because of it, and those letters are still missing. You tell me now those letters won't lead us straight to the killers.'

He stopped and pulled at some bread. 'On the other hand, it doesn't do to get involved in imperial politics. Few come out alive. Your friend didn't. My uncle didn't – assuming he was ever in them. You and I need to be decidedly careful from now on. I heard this morning that one of the sons of the exarch of Africa has just laid siege to Alexandria. The other son is ready to set sail for Asia.'

This was interesting news. I wondered how it might play on the markets. But I forced my attention back to Lucius.

'The only forces Phocas has to send against them,' he

continued, 'need to be taken from already losing wars with Persia and the barbarians. He can't move openly in Rome against anyone. But he does appear to have a reliable gang of cut-throats at his beck and call.

'Yes, let's go quiet on this for the moment. Don't suppose I've been scared off our enquiry for good. But I am now scared. And so should you be. I need to sit down and think how best to proceed. Do, please, come to me for dinner this evening. For the moment, though, let's carry on as if things have settled down.'

As we parted, Lucius came back to the matter of the diplomat. 'In view of what you've now told me,' he said very quietly, 'I'd be very careful of that diplomat. If he is working for Heraclius, he might be just as dangerous to us as the Column of Phocas. Do not, I beg you, suppose you can get close to the truth by playing these people off against each other.'

After lunch, I decided on another visit to the library of Anicius. After banking the draft, I collected Martin from the Lateran, where he told me he'd been all morning at work with the secretaries. I let his deception pass. I had no reason for complaint. Some of the books were already copied. I checked these against the originals, and was happy with them. They were mostly perfect copies. Where they deviated was usually for the better – a silent correction here, a marginal comment there. We were dealing, after all, with the semi-educated. They would welcome the occasional help with difficult words or obscure facts.

As we wandered over to the Quirinal, Martin was less taciturn than I'd previously known him. He'd changed back into the drab clothes of a slave secretary, but something of his earlier happiness lingered about him. He told me about himself.

'It was in Ireland, sir, that I was born,' he said. He paused, looking deep into his memories of childhood.

'You've seen the great seas that lie beyond the Mediterranean,' he continued with a sudden jerk back to the present. 'But you have to see the clean, cold waves of the Atlantic to know what an ocean truly is. I was born on the west coast, and my grandmother used to have servants place her chair high on the cliffs so we could look together to the edge of the world.

'No fisherman had ever seen it, but all agreed that the convex dish of the world ended just a hundred miles beyond those waves.'

'You'll find,' I said with a superior look, 'that the world is round. This being so, it has no edge.'

'As you please, sir,' Martin said with a bow that I thought slightly satirical. I was glad he didn't ask the obvious question about how people at the antipodes didn't fall off.

He went on to explain that he came on his father's side from a family that had left London when my people turned up. They'd run off to the Celtic enclave in Cornwall, and then, after constant raiding by us, they'd continued across the water to Ireland, far from the dangers we presented.

'I suppose, looked at from your point of view,' I said, 'my people must have been rather disruptive. But it was you who invited us. You brought us in to do the shitty fighting jobs you'd forgotten how to do for yourselves. It was only natural we should take over once there were enough of us.'

I stopped by an open shop and looked at a very nice cosmetic box. From the stiff look I could see coming over his face, I'd started this conversation badly as well. I envied Lucius and his way with slaves. It didn't matter if they were older than he was or better looking or brighter. They all deferred to him.

'You need to be aware,' I added with an attempt at starting over, 'that Fortune is on the side of the strong. It was your land. Then it was ours. Perhaps we shall ourselves one day be dispossessed – if we ever forget that a territory belongs to a people not by pre-scription, but simply by willingness to fight. But I really don't think anyone need fear or hope that for a while.'

What was I saying? I hadn't meant to say that. I hadn't even drunk much that day. I put the box down and thought of opening a negotiation for it. Though Lucius seemed to scorn it, many Church dignitaries from the higher classes wore make-up, and I rather fancied playing with different colours for my face.

'If you don't mind my saying, sir,' Martin whispered softly, 'that trimming isn't ivory, but just bleached ox horn.'

I stepped back hurriedly from the box and gave the shopkeeper a dirty look. You have to be careful with some of these people.

We continued on our journey. I made sure to thank Martin for his advice. This let me start over with him yet again. This time, I'd keep a curb on myself. 'Tell me,' I asked, offering him one of the dried olives I'd just bought from one of the cleaner hawkers, 'how you got to Constantinople?'

I ignored Martin's sullen comment about what a fine city London had been before we broke into it. There was no point in telling him about my own family's part in the killing and looting, creditable though it may have been. Instead, I began to prod him for his own story.

'Do have one,' I prompted him. 'I seem to have bought far too many for me.'

Martin had been educated in the local monastic school that his father had endowed, he now explained, with additional lessons from his father. He was intended for a priesthood in the Celtic Church. Then his father had committed some internal dereliction that he never would explain, and had decided to leave Ireland as his penance. Though a small boy, Martin had gone with him. Martin and his father had turned up at last in Constantinople, where they'd opened a school to teach the Latin language and Greek literature.

'He was the best teacher in the city,' Martin said proudly. 'He had all the learning of the ancients and all the wisdom of the True Faith. We had more students than we could teach. We turned away all but the best.'

But it was scholarship that had got his father and Martin himself into trouble. The Greeks didn't like having their business shown to them by a barbarian from places never conquered by Rome. If that weren't bad enough, he'd got into an argument about the correct pronunciation of Greek by the ancients.

Martin went into some detail about this – a mass of technical stuff about voiced fricatives and diphthongs and the like. It meant bugger all to me at the time, though I later realised his father had been absolutely right. The moderns are corrupt in their pronunciation. Worse than that, like the modern Latins, they speak an everyday language that is removed from the ancient language, but not far removed enough to let them learn it properly. Of course, the Greek scholars were at a disadvantage.

'What happened?' I asked.

'It was when my father began giving public readings of Homer in the recovered pronunciation that the Greeks turned really against us. They accused him of heresy. When the authorities had cleared us of that, they just told all the parents anyway that we were secretly spreading heresy, and we lost students.'

The bills had mounted. Credit was obtained and overstretched. Eventually, when Emperor Maurice put through his last round of tax increases, the credit lines had snapped. The school went bankrupt. Martin was rather vague about the legal process involved. Interested in these things, I pressed for details.

'It was all documents,' he said with quiet despair. 'I don't know what my father signed. I don't know what he got me to sign. I was young. We went to court again and again. The judge kept refusing our applications. The lawyers never made anything clear.'

He explained that enslavement for debt had been long since made illegal. Even so, whatever they'd signed had overridden that law. Martin and his father were sold into slavery. The father had died of a broken heart on the very auction block. Martin was sold into the household of an Egyptian merchant, who'd carried him back to handle his Latin correspondence from Antinoopolis.

From here, the narrative became broken. I had to press and press to get anything at all. Even then, I had to read between the lines. I gathered that his skin had peeled off in the hot Egyptian sun, and he'd sickened near to death from drinking the Nile water. Then, he'd been sold off cheap to a pimp, who'd prostituted him all the way to Cyrene, where the sun was still unbearable but the air was healthier. He'd almost been sold as a galley slave – though small, he was now growing, and a few months pulling an oar might have thickened his body to be of use until a few years of toil had worn it out. But his learning had saved him. He'd been bought by the Church and taken to Rome to be trained as a papal clerk. He'd been given all the less confidential Greek correspondence to handle. Now that Ambrose was dead, he might be promoted to handling it all.

'Do you never want to see Ireland again?' I asked. A look of wild despair crossed over his face. He turned away. I felt stupid for asking the question. We walked on in silence.

'I do dream of home,' he said at length. 'I dream of the faces I haven't seen in years. I dream of the clean, fresh waves. I dream of the little monastery bell, and the songs of old men around the fire at night.

'But it was all so long ago. I have . . . I have friends in Rome. Even if I were to find the money to buy my freedom, what would I be in Ireland? I'd always be a foreigner. I'd always long for the patterns of gold and shadow that play across the broken squares of this still great city.

'Can you go back to England, sir?' he asked me. 'Would you go back? Is there anything for you? Are the people there still your own?'

'No,' I said softly. 'We are both refugees from our own land. We can never go back.'

I wanted to add that we could only look forward. But that would have been crass. I had come into riches great enough to buy Ethelbert and all his kingdom and hardly notice the expense. He was a slave, living for the moments he could steal from the Church to be with his lover and a child who'd be born the bastard of a slave. If the woman were free – unlikely from the look of her – the child would enjoy a purely formal status he didn't possess. If the woman were indeed a slave, it also would be a slave – the absolute property of a stranger.

The Church did sell freedom to its slaves. But Martin was right: where would he find the sum of money needed to buy an educated clerk out of slavery?'

'Listen, Martin,' I said suddenly. 'I offered you your freedom the other night. That didn't come off, but I want to reopen the offer. Let's get these books out of the way. I'll then beg you from the dispensator. I'm not his favourite Englishman, as you probably know. But he'll owe me for those books. I'll have to pay for a new building in Canterbury to house them all by the time we've finished. And I will pay for it. The dispensator will owe me, and I'll collect on that. With all these wars, there must be educated slaves aplenty I can buy from the East to replace you.'

I don't know what I expected. I'd not have been surprised by polite thanks, or enthusiastic gratitude – or even a kiss. Instead, he broke down in tears. He leaned against a wall, his body shaking with uncontrollable sobs.

I patted him on the shoulder. 'Martin,' I said, 'I promise you'll be free – free to go and do as you like. If you can think of the approach, I'll see the dispensator tomorrow. He prays in the Church of Apostles, I think. I'll catch him after the service.'

Martin pulled himself together. 'No, sir,' he said, controlling his voice, 'it's best to wait until you can show the first cartload of books. I'll have them bound just as soon as they've been pressed fully into blocks.'

We walked on to the house of Anicius.

32

The library was much as I'd left it – was that just three days before? It seemed like three months. Martin had arranged for collection of the pile of books I'd left on the floor. I'd now start pulling down more of those precious things.

What I really had in mind was a regular institute of higher learning in England. The Church wanted an army of educated clerics. I'd give that to the Church. Those young men could spend all morning copying manuscripts. In the afternoon, they could discuss the meaning of what they'd read. I'd make England the intellectual heart of the entire West – far away from savage barbarians, and stupid, decayed nobles, and imperial officials too weak and lazy to protect the civilisation that had spawned them as meat in the sun generates maggots, but too active and strong to leave it in peace. Our own youth would learn all I could send them of literature and history and philosophy and mathematics and science, and they would bring it back to the world that had lost it.

Looking round, I noticed an open scroll on the reading table. I didn't recall leaving anything there. I looked closer. It was another old book. Only this one showed greater signs of use and much evidence of care for its condition. It had been mended in all the cracked places. Some of the fainter ink had recently been gone over in a wavering hand. There was no title on it. I carefully pulled it back to the first column and began reading:

> *e tenebris tantis tam clarum extollere lumen*
> *qui primus potuisti inlustrans commoda uitae*
> *te sequor o Graiae gentis decus inque tuis nunc*
> *ficta pedum pono pressis uestigia signis . . .*

It was a rapturous hymn of praise to Epicurus, I discovered with a shock. It went on to explain how he had freed us from the fear of death, and thereby enabled us to live more happily.

It was an odd sort of poetry – none of the smooth perfection I'd been used to in Vergil and the other old writers. I later discovered it was by someone called Lucretius, who'd lived around the same time as Cicero. And he hadn't lived to complete his poem.

But what this poetry lacked in smooth refinement, it more than compensated for in overwhelming force. It swept over me like an oncoming tide, in wave after wave of didactic passion. We had no reason to fear death, it proclaimed. After death there was nothing, as Anicius had said, and death itself was nothing.

'As we felt no woe in times long gone when from all the earth to battle the Carthaginians came, so when we are no more and the mind and body are sundered, we shall feel nothing of what may happen then – not even if the earth is confounded with the sea and the sea with the sky.'

No voice like this can ever have proclaimed the nothingness of the soul after death. Not even Epicurus himself can have thundered this Gospel of Death so loudly. Not even the Church Fathers could have encountered this blast of impassioned eloquence without bending before it. Death is annihilation. Why therefore fear it?

I read the piece through. I rolled back and read it again. It's at times like this that spacing between the words might be helpful. I read it again, committing it all to memory. Seventy-five years later, I can still remember it. Perhaps I will write it down before I die. It would be a shame if the young students at Jarrow miss out on something so astonishing.

I looked up. Anicius must have been standing over me a long time. He'd put on a robe that was almost clean and, except for his breath, didn't smell today.

'Please accept my regrets for your own troubled mind,' he said. 'Your friend is at peace, however. On the eccentric principles of yourself and your master, his atoms will be reused, for they at least are immortal. They will form the parts of other living bodies. He is now nothing. We all come to nothing. But different lives will make use of our atoms. And, like runners in a torch race, these atoms will hand on the lamps of life.

'*Post mortem nihil ipsaque mors nihil.*'

I thanked him for the immense comfort he had brought me. In truth, all the bounce I'd got from surviving that knife attack without a scratch and reaping that nice harvest on the Exchange had been knocked out of me by his words. But I wanted to be polite. I also wanted the rest of the poem. From the last sheet inside the book, I'd found that this was Book Three of a longer poem. Where was the rest?

'There is more, and –' he waved at the racks – 'it may be in that lot somewhere. I'll not dig it out for you. Far better, I think, if you can find it for yourself. You may find other books there that will bring you to a better appreciation of the truth. Yes, my young scholar,' he sat down and glanced with a curiously soft look at the racks, 'there is an educational value all its own in browsing. I used to do that when I was your age. It brought me friends who have lasted nearly the rest of my life.'

He looked back at me. 'Tell me, my dear boy, what for you is the value of all this knowledge that you seek?'

'Knowledge,' I said, trying to choose words that wouldn't give him an excuse for his logic chopping, 'allows us to live happily. Knowledge of the world gives us power over the world, and enables us to arrange the world for our own convenience.'

Anicius sat looking at me for a while. 'And you found that in your Epicurus?' he asked at length.

As said, I'd found very little yet in Epicurus. I'd had to guess most of it for myself. I didn't answer, but waited for him to go on.

'Your Epicurus,' he said, 'believed that the sole value of knowledge was to dispel superstitious fear. He encouraged his followers to learn astronomy simply to let us know that heavenly phenomena are natural and predictable effects, not acts of Divine Intervention. Equally his defective theory of the atoms.

'But all other pure knowledge he despised. He taught against geometry and virtually all mathematics. They do nothing to remove fear, and so have no value.

'Your positive theory of knowledge has no echo in any of the great philosophers of ancient times. There is a story of the great Euclid. While he was lecturing one day in the Alexandrian Library, a student interrupted him to ask what use the particular geometrical proposition might have.

' "Give the man some money," Euclid said to an assistant, "and throw him into the street".'

Anicius smiled at the recollection of the story. He went on to make some sniffy comments about where Archimedes had gone wrong in using his mathematical skills to build 'mere machines'. He made a brief defence of knowledge for the sake of moral improvement.

He saw my look of polite disagreement. He leaned forward and looked closely into my face. 'Where are you from?' he asked.

I steadied my features against the blast of his stinking breath and told him about England. I used its old name, Britain.

'A strange people, if there are more like you,' he said with an uncomfortable laugh. 'You will come again, though, will you not?' he asked, suddenly earnest. 'There are so many books here that you will find of value. I will personally dig out some translations of Plato that my uncle made into Latin.'

He paused and looked at me. 'If you can tell me each time when you'll be back, I'll personally find the books you want. I'll take you through them – that is, if you can bear an old man's company. . . . Do take whatever you want. I'll mark the ones I want back after copying. The rest you can keep. I'll gladly—'

He broke off with a gasp of pain. He lurched backwards, and I only just caught him in time before he hit the tiled floor. Teeth chattering, his face white, he clutched at his lower belly. I later discovered he had kidney stones. By the time he'd recovered from the spasm, he was lapsing out of rational mode.

'But it's all worthless,' he said, back in the whining tone of our first meeting. 'I envy you your barbarism. Devoid of philosophy, devoid of religion, you are all so pure of heart and mind.'

He prosed on about that learned ancestor of his. So educated, he'd been, yet still he'd met his end by having a cord put around his forehead and tightened till the eyes popped out. 'Let there be an end to learning, and then we can all be at peace,' he concluded, hobbling off for what I took at the time, from his quickened movements, to be a piss.

By the door, he turned back and added, now more rational again – almost, indeed, humorous: 'Never grow old, my little Briton. It really isn't worth the effort.'

Martin was sitting at a table in one of the other rooms. He had several books open before him.

'What are those?' I asked.

'I've found the Greek section, sir,' he said, pointing down at a scroll written in black with headings in faded gold.

I looked hungrily at the text. 'What is that one you're reading?' I asked.

'It's the fifth book of Thucydides – his description of the Sicilian Expedition.'

'May I see?' I looked closer over his shoulder.

He stood up and gave me his place. I sat, making sure not to get dust on my fine clothes, and looked at the glued sheets. I could read some of the words, though they were written in a slightly different alphabet from the one Maximin had taught me by scratching in the mud on those French roads. I could understand words here and there. But the whole was in a Greek far more complex than I had learnt. It might for the most important part have been in a foreign language.

I looked up in despair. 'I can't read it,' I said. 'Can you teach me?'

'When would you start?'

'Now?' I suggested.

Martin went to the racks and brought back another book. 'This is by Xenophon,' he explained. 'The Greek is pure, but simple enough to understand if you can read the Gospels.'

He pulled up another chair, and began the lesson.

So I put myself back into school. Martin was a good teacher. If his father had been even better, no wonder the Greeks had hated them. He read each sentence, giving me his father's reconstructed sound of the words. I followed him with my own reading. He told me it was important for appreciating the pure language to forget the modern pronunciation I'd got from Maximin. The two languages were often so far apart, it was best to regard them as separate. I could easily switch back into the modern pronunciation for speaking with educated moderns. Then he turned to explaining those difficulties of grammar and syntax that would puzzle a student who knew only the spoken language of the moderns.

It was like swimming in the sea at Richborough – the water was cold, so that wading in was difficult and movement was stiff and awkward at first, but then gradually your strokes became more and more confident. I won't pretend that I ended that lesson with anything like a perfect grasp of those endlessly complex variations of tense and mood. But I could understand the rising excitement of those brave and resourceful Greek mercenaries who, after so many months of passing through the landlocked realms of the barbarian, at last reached the sea and knew that they would see home again.

As Martin rolled up the book, I asked: 'How long before I can read your Thucydides?'

'It can take years of patient study by the modern Greeks to write like him,' he said. 'The only modern my father said had perfectly succeeded was a Syrian called Procopius – and he'd studied Greek as a foreign language. But just to read him – I think, at your speed of progress, we can move to him long before the books are all ready for shipping to Canterbury. But you will need to work every day.'

'Every day and all day, if I must,' I said firmly.

It was dark outside when we left. This time, we were accompanied back by two of Marcella's big slaves. And still we were followed. No one else seemed to notice, and I decided to ignore the footsteps behind us.

As we arrived, it began to rain, and I could feel a storm coming on. I hadn't gone off as agreed to dine with Lucius. Should I set out in the dark and rain? No. I sent him a note of apology, and promised to come to him for breakfast.

33

I'd decided on dinner in the common room that Marcella provided for her guests. I would get Martin out of dining with the other slaves. In return for a decent meal, he could continue explaining some of the difficulties that had come up during our inspection of Xenophon.

As I was locking the door to my rooms, though, I was caught by the diplomat. He'd been dawdling in the long corridor that led to all the upper quarters, and I knew he'd been waiting for me. But he smiled as if surprised at a sudden meeting, and invited me to dinner in his own rooms.

I thought to go back and change. I was, after all, only expecting to eat with persons of little consequence – and not even that if Martin had gone off to be with his woman. But the diplomat was dressed with less than his usual magnificence, and was rather pressing with his invite.

I agreed and followed him directly to his rooms.

The dishes were all of gold, made in a style I'd never before seen. The food almost knocked my head off – all pepper and other spices I'd not yet encountered. As we munched our way through the various courses of burning and brightly coloured meats, I found myself downing pint after pint of that fizzy water.

'You will surely forgive my lack of wine,' the diplomat had explained as I sat down with him. 'Except for the Holy Sacraments – in which we are far more assiduous than either Latins or Greeks – it is something not permitted in my country to persons of quality.'

I made a polite comment. My spirits sank. Even Martin, down in the slave quarters, would have beer with the warmed-up leftovers from the common room.

But I couldn't fault the conversation. The diplomat now gave me a regular lecture on the science of making money on the financial markets. Forget what I'd picked up earlier from him and on the Exchange, this was my real introduction to the ways of the market. After five years in Alexandria, he knew everything worth knowing.

Of course, what he told me now merely scratched the surface of a discipline that only a study of many years would fully reveal. And he was deliberately vague about the nature of what he had really been up to at the Exchange.

I asked him about the Great Library of Alexandria – was it still there?

'There are libraries there,' he said. 'But you will find them filled with the vain learning of those who did not accept the Truth revealed by Jesus Christ. In my view, that it was not long ago committed to the flames shows how little the Greeks have really accepted of the Truth.'

From this, he went on to an account of the True Orthodoxy of his own national Church. Outside the Empire, the Ethiopians had fallen into just about every heresy dreamt up in the East. Monophysitism was the least of their derelictions. I wondered again what on earth he could be doing at large in Rome. But without any visible seam in his discourse, he drifted from the single, not fused, nature of Christ to the charms of the women in my own part of the world.

'If bathed long enough,' he said with an appreciative smack of his lips, 'and if correctly perfumed, your women can be quite comely.'

As the meal ended, one of the slaves brought us glass goblets filled with a hot blue liquid. The diplomat's eyes lit up at the sight. He drained half of his goblet with a hungry gulp.

I sniffed doubtfully at mine. Get through the generous helping of spices with which it was dosed, and it smelt like dogshit.

'But do drink, my young Aelric,' the diplomat said with a now measured sip. 'It does all that your wine offers and much more beside. Drink up and enjoy.'

My palate was now so seared by the dinner that I barely noticed the taste. All I noticed was an extreme sweetness over something bitter that left my mouth dry. After the first preparatory sip, I drained the goblet and set it down on the table. Having managed a whole dinner in the Ethiopian style, I wasn't inclined to show myself up with any barbarian delicacy in matters of drink.

The diplomat gave me an alarmed stare and muttered something about the need to savour his – I think he called it – *kaphkium*.

'I'll drink the next one more slowly,' I said, leaning back in my chair. I could feel an oddly serene energy spreading through my body. Whatever was in this stuff beat what both Marcella and Lucius had given me the other day.

'Now,' I said, sitting forward again with a bump of the chair, 'there are other things that need to be discussed—'

'Such as the division of our spoils,' the diplomat broke in.

'All in good time,' I replied. 'First, we do need to discuss how you came to know my real name. Everyone here calls me Alaric. Do say how you learnt otherwise.'

The diplomat smiled. 'It is my business, Aelric, to know everything that may be relevant to my purposes,' he said.

'That still leaves us,' I continued, 'with the matter of what relevance I may have to your purposes. For all it concerns our fraud on the markets, my name might as well be Henghist or Cholodowicus. So why have you made it your business to learn that much about me? And how did you learn it? You could only have got it from the dispensator or the prefect. The first originated the mistake that got me my name in this city. The second was probably too lazy to inspect any of the documents Father Maximin showed him.'

A feeble opening, perhaps. But it was the best one I could devise at the time. I was hoping I might get some correction out of the diplomat that would give a little more information about what was known about me and how.

'Yes,' the diplomat said, wrenching the conversation away, 'the Blessed Martyr Maximin, who will soon be the Most Holy Saint Maximin. His murder was a truly shocking business. Such things would never happen in my own country. There, we know the respect due even to heretical priests of the True Faith. At the very least, we question them before proceeding further than arrest.

'I do feel a certain degree of guilt that I was the last person who had a civilised discussion with the Holy Martyr. I saw that he was troubled in mind, yet passed up the opportunity to lighten his burden. In particular, I do very much regret that I only discovered after his murder that he was possessed of certain objects that might be of concern to a person of great and increasing importance in the Empire.'

The diplomat looked steadily into my face. I tried to look back. But whatever had been in that drink had set my mind on a course of wandering that it took all my efforts to control.

'You told me the other day,' I said thickly, 'that you had information that was of relevance to the matter of Father Maximin's death. Can you tell me now what that might be?'

The diplomat smiled and beckoned his slave to pour me another cup of water. 'You will find,' he said, 'that all I might have been able to tell you came out in yesterday's meeting with your friend the lord Basilius. I have nothing further to say beyond a repeat of my most earnest condolences.

'I am, however, *very* interested in the matter of those letters. I believe there were four of them. I knew soon after you arrived at this most charming residence of your good fortune to the north of Rome. I was not aware until too late of the attendant circumstances.'

'There were three letters only,' I said, hoping the needless correction would give me time to think of something that would be an answer, but would give nothing important away.

The diplomat ignored my correction. 'Have you any idea what they might have contained?' he asked.

I shook my head. The diplomat changed his approach.

'Can you tell me what you discovered at the House of the Sisters of the Blessed Theodora?' he asked. 'Did anyone there see the letters?'

'Maximin never got there,' I said. 'He was killed shortly after he'd set out to go there.'

'So the letters have disappeared,' the diplomat said, his tone half statement half question.

'They are sought by the Church and by *other persons*,' he added with a noticeable emphasis. 'But no one so far has been able to set eyes on them.

'As well as the Church and these other persons, I also am now seeking the letters.'

'You and your master the exarch of Africa,' I said. I wanted to show the man I knew something. 'I wonder how much they might be worth if you could take them to him?'

The diplomat smiled broadly again. His teeth shone white in the lamplight, the gap between as dark as a prison cell.

'Why don't you help me find out?' he asked. 'You were pleased enough with the trifle of money we picked up this morning. Can you imagine how much more could be yours in return for the right information? Have you any notion of what money can buy? Think of your highest price and double it.'

He leaned forward to me, his eyes shining. 'I don't know what those letters contain. But I feel they are worth much – to the Church, perhaps to the Lombards, and perhaps to all those who have or who want this Empire of the Romans for themselves.'

He controlled himself and sat back.

'So you are working for the exarch of Africa?' I asked.

Above his continued smile, the diplomat's face turned impassive. 'I work for no one beside the king whose maternal grandmother is mine also,' he said. 'It is my business in the Empire to know many things, and to trade information with those who can offer me and mine benefits in return.'

'Do you know what happened to me last night?' I asked, with another laboured effort to take control of the conversation.

The diplomat shed his impassive look and gave me another of his open smiles. 'You fucked a barbarian slave,' he said. 'I sampled her delights for myself when I arrived, but found her strong bodily odour a bar to true felicity of flesh.'

'Some toughs tried to murder me in the street,' I said, thinking it might do to slap the little whore about the next time we were alone.

'So many the dangers of this great but fallen city,' the diplomat replied. 'However, you did tell me this morning of your adventures. Was there anything else about them that you might wish now to share with me?'

He fell silent. He sat looking at me for what seemed a long time. At last, my will snapped, and I asked: 'You may not know, but what do *you* think was in the letters?'

'If I thought anything clearly, my golden boy from the North,' he smiled back at me, 'would I be so eager to learn it from you?'

'This conversation,' he said at length, 'is private. If you care for your new friend Basilius, you will keep all this to yourself. As for the letter you had me sign, bear in mind it is a sword with two edges.'

He called one of his slaves over with more fizzy water. By the time I staggered out of his suite, I was bursting.

34

I fell sweating into my bed. My mind was racing, and I thought for a moment I'd not get to sleep. But I no sooner had the covers pulled up than I was out like an extinguished lamp.

I had the strangest dream. I was back outside that wine shop on the Caelian Hill. It was night, and there was no moon overhead. I was with Lucius and Martin beside the broken sewer. Martin was holding a torch that burned without any noticeable flame. All around was still and silent.

The sewer was different. Rather than terminating about six foot down in a thick layer of earth and rotting filth, it was too deep to see the bottom. A cold draught blew steadily up at us, carrying the faint smell of something very old and frightening. A flight of worn steps led down into the mobile blackness. They went down and down, seemingly far beyond the range of the light from our single torch.

'Go on, Martin,' I urged. 'Go down there and have a look. We'll be up here for you, and you can assuredly trust us to come down if you get lost.'

Martin looked at me with doubt showing plain on his face.

'Go on,' Lucius joined me in urging. 'There might be something valuable down there, and we'll let you share it with us.' He spoke in the cold, peremptory tone he always adopted with slaves.

At last, after a brief shove from Lucius, Martin went down into the shadows. Before setting foot on the steps, he handed me the torch, and I saw his pale, scared face as he walked down into the endless blackness of the sewer.

We could hear his footsteps crunching lightly on the various mortar crumbs and other débris that lay on the steps.

'It's very dark down here,' he cried up plaintively. 'Can I come back up and borrow the torch? I can't see anything.'

'You've started now,' Lucius replied firmly. 'You've got to see it out.'

Down and down he went, until we could hear nothing more of him. There followed an interminable wait in which Lucius and I speculated on what might have happened below.

'Are you all right, Martin?' I called softly down. 'Have you found anything down there?'

No answer.

The darkness within the shadow of the sewer grew more intense, and I noticed that the torch was beginning to fade without burning out.

Suddenly, at what sounded an incredible distance, we heard footsteps ascending. These were not the light, hesitant steps we had heard going down, but a slow, regular tread crunching heavily on the steps.

'Is that you, Martin?' I called down nervously.

No answer – only the same tread coming steadily closer up the steps.

'It is him,' Lucius said with trembling voice. 'He's just trying to frighten us.

'I'll have him flogged when he comes out.'

At this point, the torch went out, and we stood in utter darkness.

The footsteps were now just a few yards below, and I could hear something brushing on the steps as if dragged behind. Without seeing or hearing or smelling anything new, I had the impression of something unspeakably old and unspeakably evil.

Lucius and I bolted. We ran back down the street, looking for the security of Marcella's house. There was a wall across the street where there had been nothing before. In the centre of the wall was a small gate. Lucius dragged it open, and we ran through into the clear street beyond.

The street was now filled with a dense, white mist. We ran forward and lost each other. I called for Lucius, but heard nothing back. I could now hear nothing except my own breathing.

I ran towards what I believed was the turning for Marcella's. I came to the gateway in. Gasping for breath, I pushed on the gate and staggered into what should have been the common entrance. Instead, I found myself back beside the sewer. If I'd turned back on myself, the gateway had somehow expanded into something much larger than we'd found the other side.

Though all was dark again, I could somehow see around me. I recall seeing the torch where I'd dropped it. Though all was quiet, I knew I was not alone. There was something very big and very powerful behind me. I dared not turn round.

I cannot describe the terror that I felt. It had been growing from the moment Martin had vanished into the darkness, and now it had overwhelmed me, depriving me of the ability or the will to do other than stand looking forward at the dark gash of the broken sewer.

I heard a rough scraping behind me, as of something heaving itself over the paving stones. I felt a chilled breath on my neck. There was a smell as of something pulled from a very old grave. And there were words as well.

I didn't catch these. As soon as I heard them, the mists closed in around me, and I was lifted suddenly away. Before all went black around me, I could see the rooftops of the Caelian glowing white under the moonless sky.

Unlike with the similar dreams I'd had back in Richborough, I was too old to wake screaming from this one. But it took some while after I did wake to assure myself completely that none of it had really happened. I lay alone in the darkness, freezing and unfreezing from the terror that still lingered.

I tried to get back to sleep. But my mind was racing. I lay alone, my thoughts turning again and again to that awful dreamscape.

I got up and put on some clothes. I did think to go out for a walk. But I'd have to wake the old watchman. Then I'd have the streets of Rome to face all by myself. I didn't want that. I stirred up the charcoals in the brazier, then lit a lamp from them. Some of the books I'd got from Anicius were piled up next door in my office. But, for all they'd enchanted me in the daylight, there was nothing there now that seemed likely to soothe my ragged nerves.

I opened the door from my suite into the corridor. All was dark and silent. Walking carefully, so as not to make any noise on the floorboards, I moved down the corridor. With the key I'd got out of Marcella, I let myself into Maximin's rooms.

Once the door was closed behind me, I turned up the lamp and looked around. The dispensator's men had swept it almost clean enough for re-letting. Still uncleaned from when he'd first set them out for me to trip over, Maximin's boots stood by the bed. A bronze pen I'd seen him use in Canterbury was neatly set beside some waxed tablets. I looked at these. They were new and had never been used. Otherwise, there was nothing to show the room had been occupied by Maximin.

I sat on a chair and looked at the boots. 'Why didn't you tell me about those fucking letters?' I asked softly. 'Why did you have to keep them to yourself? At the very worst, we'd have been killed together. Even that would have been better than this. But you know we'd have come up with something. You know we always used to come up with something. We could have burnt the letters. We could have sold them to the highest bidder. We could have . . .'

I trailed off. I pulled my indoor clothes closer to me against the night chill and sat now in silence, looking at the streaks of uncleaned mud on the boots.

My thoughts wandered back to happier times. There was our first day of really good weather in Italy. We'd crept round the Alps, hugging the sea on our way in from southern France. At some point along the road, we'd come to a worn boundary stone, showing that we were now within the ancient provinces of Italy.

These had, Maximin explained, once been uniquely privileged in terms of citizenship and immunity from tribute. Rome had grown from a city state to the head of an Italian federation. And it might have remained the capital of a united Italy, but for a course of rapid conquest that had stretched its limits from the Tees to the Euphrates. Now, the conquests were long since reversed. Even before then, the unique status of Italy had been abolished in a world of universal citizenship and liability to taxes. But the stone remained.

'It makes no difference to me,' I'd said, looking at the invisible line Maximin had drawn across the road. 'The trees on each side are the same. The rain is still coming down like it does in Kent, and from skies the same colour.'

'Just wait,' Maximin had said.

I had waited. A few days later, I'd crawled from under the trees where we'd dossed for the night, and looked into a morning that reminded me of the lightest and most sparkling cider. It was like that morning I've already described on the road – but I was seeing it for the first time.

I don't know how long I'd stood wondering at the glory that Nature had strewn unexpectedly all about me. But Maximin at last had come up beside me. 'Didn't I tell you Italy was worth a look?' he'd asked with the pride of a native.

'Why did you ever set out for England?' I'd enquired, holding up a hand to shield me from the light of the rising sun.

'We all have our reasons for leaving home,' he'd answered with a faint smile. 'It's for each of us to say whether we go to better or to worse.

'Which will it be for you?'

I hadn't answered. But the sudden joy and hope of that morning in early spring was all the answer anyone could wish for.

We'd set out along the road with renewed energy. Maximin had even sung, and I'd croaked along beside him with the closing uncertainties of my late-breaking voice. It had seemed we were advancing into paradise.

Now, I sat alone, amid the ruins of this city of cities – and perhaps amid the ruins of all hope. 'I will avenge you,' I said to the boots.

The boots said nothing back.

'I will avenge you,' I said again, speaking up to try and fill the void of silence all about me.

The problem was that I was no longer clear that I could avenge him. With every step I'd made on the road to knowledge since I'd sworn to Maximin's body, my conviction that I could grasp the final truth had ebbed further away. Whatever facts Lucius and I could bring to the growing structure of knowledge, who had killed Maximin and why remained mysteries wrapped in the deepest shadows.

I knew he'd been killed for those bastard letters. But it was plain whoever had killed him hadn't managed to lay hands on them. It was plain the letters contained important matters of state. The emperor's agents were after them with frantic determination. The exarch of Africa's man was promising untold wealth probably for just a sight of them. I had no doubt the Church was after them – why else strip these rooms so bare? Just as plainly, no one had yet found them.

What had Maximin done with the things?

As for what they contained, I couldn't begin to think of an answer. Even Lucius couldn't tell me that. I knew he was fussing on about not making hypotheses without evidence. But it struck me he was making a virtue of necessity – refusing to speculate on matters that were as much beyond his understanding as mine.

What I needed, of course, was some solid fact. The letters would certainly help. If I could know what was in them, I'd be able to work out why they were so important and to whom. In the absence of those, I needed something else that would at least point me clearly in the right direction.

'What did you do with the fucking things?' I asked out loud of the boots.

No answer.

It was now that I heard a scratching at the door. It was very gentle, and I thought at first it was a mouse in the room. But it was on the door. I froze, my thoughts wandering stupidly back to that dream. Then I heard a movement of the latch, and the door was pushed cautiously open.

'Oh, it is you, sir,' Gretel said with relief in her voice. 'I heard noises from downstairs. I was frightened thieves might have broken in.'

Not much of lie, I thought indulgently. The slave quarters were far distant from the guest areas of the house. I'd have needed to make a great deal more noise than I had for anything to reach her.

And what would a lone woman be doing if thieves were a genuine fear?

'Shut the door,' I said, 'and get those clothes off your back.'

She gave me a startled look. 'But, sir, surely we should first go back to your own rooms.'

'No,' I said, 'I . . . I don't feel comfortable tonight in my own bed tonight. I . . . er . . . think there's a draught in the room. We'll use this room.'

'In the Saint's bed?' she asked, her shock at my suggestion for the moment overbearing the obsequious consent to whatever the free might command.

'The Saint is with Jesus,' I said firmly. 'Undress yourself, and then undress me.'

The diplomat's drug had now cleared my head and filled me with a pure, glowing energy. Such was the effect of the diplomat's *kaphkium*. Next morning, be assured, I discovered why the man spent so long on the toilet.

35

Next morning, as predicted by the diplomat, the pope made his surprise return to Rome. All the bells had finished for the Sunday service by the time Gretel could shake some life back into me. As I staggered out of bed, they began again. I heard the distant sound of trumpets down at the Lateran. I groaned and clutched at my head.

'Good business with the Jews,' said the diplomat as he came out of the stables and flopped down beside me for a shit. Evidently, he'd been up some while.

'They're buying futures on silk. But I think prices will drop when Alexandria falls to the exarch's forces.'

His voice flattened. 'When can I have my share of the money from yesterday?' he asked again.

'Tomorrow morning,' said I, 'when the bank opens.'

He grunted and said something about an evident lack of trust where I came from.

I changed the subject. 'What do you know about the Column of Phocas?' I asked. Despite the headache, I was, you'll observe, more with it this morning.

'I don't think the statue will be up there much longer,' the diplomat replied smoothly. 'I hear there is already a bid for the bronze. The dispensator is just waiting on events in Alexandria. If the city holds, the statue remains in place. If not, it comes down.'

'Not the thing,' I said, 'the movement.'

Either he knew nothing of this, or he was keeping quiet. Almost certainly the latter. He gave me a funny look. Our conversation of last night was over. I'd told him nothing then. He'd tell me nothing now.

We drifted on to the price of Athenian olive oil. Then, as I finished my own business and got up to leave, he caught me by the sleeve.

'Remember,' he said, 'whatever you do find will be shared with me to your considerable advantage. Whatever we did together yesterday was as nothing to what could easily be.'

Because it was a Sunday, I'd given everyone the day off. There would be no copying or binding at the Lateran. The secretaries could go to church. Martin, doubtless, had other plans.

I'd been in Rome only six days, I told myself. Was I even the same man who'd entered so exultantly with Maximin through the Pancratian Gate? How short a time before then had it been when Maximin and I camped down for the night on the Aurelian Way between Populonium and Telamon?

Have you, my Dear Reader, ever drifted in a little boat down a broad, slow river? Have you then ever hit sudden rapids? Have you ever noticed how what before was a short time has extended to equality with the whole previous voyage, as you've darted this way and that to keep yourself off the rocks? Such had been my first week in Rome. I felt I had been there longer than my journey took from Canterbury.

Lucius was sitting down to a late breakfast when I arrived at his house. He'd been exercising outside in the sun, and said I'd soon be able to inspect his tan.

No bath, however.

'Fucking slaves,' he snarled. 'They haven't gathered enough wood even to cook dinner for tonight.'

But he recovered his temper. I decided to say nothing about dinner with the diplomat. I wanted first to see if I could fit any of it for myself into a scheme of explanation. If it did fit, or if sharing it would help him, I'd certainly share the information with Lucius. For the moment, though, as with the stranger who'd saved me the night before last, I'd keep silent.

Lucius wiped his mouth on a napkin. I could see his hands

tremble slightly. 'I wish you every good luck on this, your nine-teenth birthday,' he said with forced brightness.

He clapped his hands together. A slave appeared in the room with a long, narrow box under a cloth. He bowed to me and held it out for me. I lifted the cloth and opened the plain wooden box beneath.

I took out the new sword within. I drew it noiselessly from the scabbard of polished black leather. The blade was of dark, shining steel – about two foot six long, and as sharp as a razor. The hilt was of curved bronze, the pommel ridged to give a reliable grip.

I weighed the sword in my hand. I took up a fighting position and lunged and sliced at the air. It was perfectly balanced.

'You didn't give me notice enough to commission anything special,' Lucius said hurriedly. 'As it is, I had to comb every smith in Rome yesterday to find this. I . . . I hope you like it.'

'Of course I do,' said I, embracing him. 'It's lovely.' I kissed him.

And it was lovely. You can forget those fancy things all covered over with silver and precious stones. They won't slice through flesh a jot cleaner. The most they'll do is get you knifed in the back for the value.

I had a sentimental attachment to the old sword I'd picked up in France. But this was the one I'd from now on carry with me all over Rome. It would never do for regular warfare, but it was just the thing for cutting someone up in the street.

Lucius helped me fix the thing to my belt, and stood back to admire the effect. 'Until you start shaving properly, you'll look too sweet to terrify on first sight. And that pure and quite virginal robe you've put on again only adds to the effect. Even so, I'd not like to find myself on your bad side.'

We laughed. I sat down and pulled at the bread. A slave filled a cup for me.

'Do you fancy going off to see Boniface this afternoon?' Lucius asked brightly. 'The prefect will receive him in state at the Basilica. It's a custom that goes back to when the bishop of Rome was less important than the representative of the emperor. Even though the positions are reversed, the custom remains. It will be quite a show.'

243

I drank more wine to wash down an olive stone I'd swallowed. 'You mean, we'll see the prefect do something?'

'Oh, these Greeks are always good for making up speeches. They go through the full rhetorical course in their schools – I often wish I had. He'll do well enough on his feet, even in Latin.'

A slave brought in a sealed letter. Lucius tore it open and read the contents. 'Fuck and damn these bloody lawyers!' he shouted, throwing the letter back at the slave. 'They don't piss, but they charge you for it.'

To the slave: 'Tell him to wait another month.'

'Lucius,' I said, 'I know this will embarrass you. But I'm very flush at the moment. If I can help with expenses, please do just say.'

He looked at me. 'No,' he said, smiling. 'I do have money coming – perhaps more than I expected until recently. The man can wait. And he will wait. I used to think debts were a mark of gentle slavery. But when you owe as much as I do, they become almost a source of power. All my creditors, I have no doubt, were hard at work in church this morning, praying for my continued good health.'

He changed the subject to exercise. 'Your occasional riding and sword practice have their benefits, I don't dispute. But there really is nothing like a good session out in an open gymnasium. I must insist on your company tomorrow morning. You won't believe until then how constricting clothes can be on the movements of a body.'

'Of course, tomorrow,' I said.

Another slave came in with a message. Lucius grimaced, muttering something about a day of rest for everyone but himself. Then he smiled and looked up. 'I'm in luck today,' he cried. 'My richest tenant has decided to pay his service charge in full.

'Listen, my golden Alaric, I must go off and thank the man in person. He's a greasy creature who makes his living from selling blood sausages. But cash is cash. I won't ask you to see me in humble mood with him. So, until I return, please make free with my house. Have the slaves show you the room I want to offer you. Regard all that is mine as yours.'

With that, he was off.

I went again through all the rooms that were still habitable. In daylight, the house was shabbier than it had appeared on that first lamplit inspection. The room Lucius had in mind for me was, however, splendid. It took the full morning sun. The marble on the walls was stained in a few places. But the paintings on the plaster were still vivid, and there were three very beautiful nude statues of the Old Gods. They'd recently been cleaned of the paint the ancients had used to make statues more lifelike. I preferred the honesty of the white marble. The ancients were often rather garish, even to the point of spoiling what they had made perfect.

I eventually settled myself in the library. As I've said, the books Lucius had were mostly worthless. What sensible man could risk the penalties attaching to treason for this mass of childishness? If even a hundredth part of those spells and incantations were effective, I wondered how Christianity could possibly have become the established faith of the Empire. But there were a few volumes of obscene verse there to brighten me. These rivalled the most stupid magical stuff for wear and tear. I sat sniggering to myself at their witty and abusive pornography.

Outside the door, some slaves were talking. I put the book down and strained to listen. There were two of them. I think one had been with Lucius when we'd met by the Tiber. But it was hard to tell, as slaves hardly ever spoke in his presence.

'Are you getting the stuff packed?' one asked.

'Haven't you heard?' came the reply. 'The master's put everything off. There'll be no trip to Ravenna until further notice.'

There was a pause and a muttering of obscenities. Then: 'Well, that'll be a mercy. We're short-handed at the best of times in this place. With all his extra demands of the past few days, I just don't know how we'd get the master ready to face the exarch.'

A pause, then the reply: 'Do you think he's having one of his funny turns again?'

The other laughed softly. 'Have you got shit in your eyes?' he sneered. 'Why else do you think he's been sniffing round every magician in Rome? Much more of this, and it'll be hellfire for the lot of us – that's if we're not all up for blasphemy first.'

They drifted further down the corridor. I thought to get up and go closer to the door. But I was concerned the boards would creak and I'd be heard. I went back to the book.

I supposed Lucius had devised yet other plan for charming back some of his family's confiscated property. Perhaps, with Phocas soon to be out of the way, he'd have more success. I decided when the time was right to ask if I could go too. Except its location was dreary, I'd heard nothing but good about Ravenna.

And it was where Maximin had been born and brought up.

36

Because of his rank, Lucius and I got seats at the front just to the right of the big statue of Constantine. This gave us a fine view of proceedings. I'd taken the unintended hint about the lack of colour in my robe, and had borrowed a bright red band for tying my hair. As we walked over to our places, several heads turned, and there was an appreciative buzz.

And it seemed all Rome had turned out for the occasion. The Basilica was crowded with the better sort of citizen. They sat or squeezed against the walls behind in their best and cleanest clothing. On the high marble platform just in front of the big statue, the prefect sat impassively in his white and purple robe. His secretaries stood behind him, holding icons of the emperor and the imperial family. Before him was placed the silver inkstand that was the symbol of his office.

For the first time, I could see what the Basilica had been intended to accommodate. Like bright insects, the crowd scurried about within that vast covered space. From the crowded floor, the animated chatter floated serenely up to the majesty of the vaulted ceilings far overhead. Except for the gold leaf gone from the statue, all looked much as it must have so long ago when Rome was still Capital of the World in the fullest sense.

A cheer from the still larger crowd outside indicated the pope's arrival. I later heard he'd travelled over from Naples in a closed carriage. His cure hadn't been that effective, and the Lombards were still on the prowl. But he'd pressed on with a minimal guard, only getting out of the carriage as he reached the Colosseum.

He entered the Basilica to a deafening blast of trumpets. The sound rose to the high ceiling, and was echoed back to us before the next blast. Before him came the papal guards in their silver and black armour. They marched in through the great doorway, fanning out to left and right as they entered, and forming a double line of drawn swords within which the rest of the procession would move.

Behind came a multitude of Church dignitaries in their white and scarlet robes. These were the Lateran officials, plus all the various bishops and deacons normally resident in Rome, or presently there for the consecration of the new church. Among these, I saw the dispensator. He moved behind the bishops – a reflection of his low place in the official hierarchy of the Church. I was pleased by the sour look on his face as he pretended to smile back at the rhythmical, shouted greetings of the spectators. He would no longer have Rome all to himself, I could see.

Behind these came a whole army of monks in their dark, hooded robes. They looked threatening in the mass, and I'd heard the stories, even if I didn't yet know at first hand, of how nasty they could turn given the right excuse. They were chanting one of the more triumphant psalms and they carried case after case of relics and other devotional material. I was too far away to see the individual items, but I imagined the nose of Saint Vexilla was among the mass of holiness. Soon enough, I didn't doubt, they'd be showing off bits of poor Maximin.

There was a trail of incense from the silver burners that some of them carried. It was a welcome cover to the smell of their unwashed robes and bodies. It was also cheering to see how much of the stuff was being used for even an impromptu occasion. I might yet buy shares in the importing company, and this time hold onto them.

The universal bishop himself walked alone in the middle of all this. A small man with a grey beard, he walked within a cleared space of about six feet around him. He walked slowly, resting on his ceremonial crook for support, his face lined, his eyes dull. I could see from his wrists and neck that he was swathed in bandages under his gorgeously coloured papal robe.

This was the man in whose name England was being won over to Christianity. This was the man the simple mention of whom had saved me all those months ago from Ethelbert in full rage. He dealt on terms of equality – and more than equality – with all the kings and bishops of the Earth. Even when not backed against a wall, the emperors in Constantinople played wary of him.

He was the universal bishop, the servant of the servants of God, the undisputed successor of Saint Peter. He was the holiest and most powerful man in my world.

And I was on my feet, within speaking distance of a little man who, under those robes, I had no doubt, was still sweating pus.

The procession came to a halt. The monks knelt on the hard floor. The pope and other dignitaries mounted the platform cleared for the occasion. He took his position in the highest chair, now vacated by the prefect, who'd taken another seat lower than the pope but higher than anyone else. The prefect stood before this chair with head bowed.

The monks ended their chant with a final menacing shout. There was a clashing of steel as the guards sheathed their swords. The great hall fell silent.

The prefect stood forward. When he was sure of the general attention, he lifted his head and began his speech of greeting. 'In the name of His Most Holy and Imperial Majesty, the benevolent and ever-triumphant Caesar Phocas Augustus, Lord and Emperor of the World, before whose awesome power the universe bows in hushed respect, and in the name of our Lord Smaragdus, Exarch in Ravenna, and in the name of the mighty People of Rome – the Eternal City within which Saint Peter and Saint Paul bore witness to the True Faith of our Lord and Saviour Jesus Christ, the only begotten Son of the Father – I bid welcome to Boniface, Patriarch, Universal Bishop . . .'

And so on and so forth. Lucius was right. These Greeks could put on a good speech, even in Latin, at a moment's notice. It was largely the stereotyped flattery Greek boys learn to rattle out in school. But it was said in a nicely modulated voice, and there was a kind word for all assembled, all the way down to nothings like me.

When he'd finished, the pope heaved himself up and gave a brief and pained oration of thanks. He mentioned the return of Saint Vexilla's nose, and how wondrously his cure had turned after he'd been given the news. He refrained from scratching. But every so often, a hand would go up to rub one of the sorest parts of his diseased body. Throughout, he took little sips of something poured by one of his doctors.

After this, the dispensator got up. I could almost hear the inward groans of the crowd as he opened his mouth.

'Normal men need to piss twice before he runs out of breath,' Lucius whispered to me. A Frankish diplomat standing behind us poked him in the back and hissed to show some respect. His long moustache quivered with outrage. We fell silent. I tried to listen to the dispensator. But even his long digression on the miracles said – with the most undeniable proofs – to have been worked by Maximin couldn't hold my complete attention.

I looked around the crowded Basilica. Even though the day was blistering outside, it was cool within. The great hall was lit by a golden, diffused glow from overhead. I looked at the design of the building, marvelling how everything was both beautiful and structurally essential. I ran my eyes over the crowd opposite. There was the diplomat, wearing his yellow robe. He saw me looking at him and smiled back, raising one of his icons in further greeting. Behind him, I saw someone I'd met at the Exchange. Here and there, I saw other faces I recognised. I was fitting in well in Rome.

I stopped my survey of the hall. I focused. I looked hard. I drew a sharp breath. Over on the other side of the hall, half behind a column, but looking straight at me, was One-Eye. He was dressed in black, and what I could see of him was half in shadow. But I could see him clearly. I'd never forget that patch over the left eye, nor the livid scar. He was nearly a hundred yards away, but I'd have picked him out at twice the distance.

I looked slowly away. 'Lucius,' I whispered, trying not to move my lips, 'if you look straight ahead, by the third rear column from the left, you'll see One-Eye. Try not to let him know you've seen him.'

Lucius didn't even move his head. 'I was wondering if that was the man. I'm going outside to gather my slaves. Don't move until I come back in and cough twice.'

With an easy movement, he was pushing his way through the crowd to the great doorway. He caused hardly a ripple of attention as he pushed through.

One-Eye saw him just as he approached the doorway. He darted back to the wall. I could see the forward motion and hear the whispered rebukes as he forced his own way through. He'd be out first.

I ignored Lucius and began to make my own way out. The stir I caused made the dispensator pause in mid-sentence. I could see his eyes fasten on me with a look of thorough distaste. He raised his voice and continued as if there were no commotion. 'For as our Lord and Saviour Jesus Christ himself said, "Compel them to come in" . . .' I heard his voice booming as I eventually got free of the crowd and forced my way out of the Basilica.

I met Lucius gathering his slaves. One-Eye had got out just a moment before him, he explained, and had gone off towards the river.

The slaves went before us, pushing the common people aside so we could pass easily through. Beyond the Basilica, the streets were empty and silent in the hot afternoon sun. But there was the dark figure, moving alone and with rapid strides.

'The only exit from that street is by the Aemilian Bridge,' said Lucius urgently. 'You and you,' he spoke to his slaves, 'get down the short route past the Shrine of Saint Glabrarius. I want you at the far end of this street before he gets to it. I want him alive,' he called after them.

We followed down the long street to the river. There were no side streets. There were no particularly ruined houses to let him off the street. Unless he could force a door open, we'd have him. It would be two against one at worst – four against one if we didn't catch him before the junction with the embankment.

We ran over the smooth, reasonably uncluttered paving stones. One-Eye never looked round. He ran ahead, his black cloak billowing around him like the wings of some great bird. For such a large man, he moved very fast. We could scarcely keep pace with him.

'Stop!' Lucius cried. 'We need to talk with you.'

A feeble instruction, you'll agree. It was still better than the mouthful of obscene threats I'd had ready.

We rounded a corner. Before us was the end of the street. Beyond was the embankment and the bridge. There were the slaves standing guard.

But One-Eye was now on horseback. How he'd left his horse unattended with any expectation of coming back to it was a mystery to me. But he had. With a clatter of hooves, he was off. The slaves put up their arms to stop him. He knocked them down as a storm flattens an old tree.

He was across the bridge in moments. We stood impotently, watching him canter off to our left along the Via Portuensis. He stopped once and looked back at us. He raised his riding whip in the now familiar gesture. Then he was off.

'Fuck you pair of incompetents!' Lucius swore at the slaves. 'Get me a fucking horse. I'm giving chase.'

But there was none to be had. The streets were empty of traffic. One-Eye was soon out of sight into some trees.

Back at his house, Lucius punished the slaves with his own hand. While they cowered screaming before him, he flogged them until their blood spattered his face and hands. His eyes blazed with anger. I'd never seen him like this.

'Please, master,' one of them cried. 'Don't hurt us. We did our best. Please don't use us like the others.'

But Lucius only beat all the harder, his face like black stone.

'Take them away,' he gasped at length to his steward, dropping the soaked, now broken cane. 'I want them in chains for the next month. Permanent latrine duty. Only bread and water. I want them brought to me for another flogging every time the weals scab over. They'll bless me at the end if I don't sell them into a lead mine.'

I looked on, appalled. You don't treat even churls like that – well, not unless they've done something really bad. And these had tried. Could you stop a mounted man twice your size?

Over an early dinner, Lucius recovered some of his composure. I suggested he might have been rather harsh with his slaves.

'Alaric,' he smiled, 'you really don't understand anything about the management of a household. I will make sure to educate you fully in this before you set up your own house here.

'Slaves may look like human beings,' he lectured me. 'But they aren't. They are in all respects an inferior breed. Everyone agrees on that. I know the priests witter on about the equality of all human souls. But even they don't actually believe that. If they did, the Church wouldn't have several hundred thousand slaves, or however many it is, getting with their sweat and blood all the gold that pays for their spreading empire of corruption over the Earth. Slaves are lower creatures. They are kept in line by force and the threat of force. Even today, do you know how many slaves there are in Rome? Can you guess at their ratio to citizens?

'They are there to do as they are told, and when they are told. It doesn't matter what instructions you give them. It doesn't matter whether they can or can't be carried into effect. If a slave disobeys, he must be punished. Flogging is normal for that. If he betrays you, or raises a hand against you or any of your own interests, you proceed to mutilation or burning. You rule by terror, or you don't rule.

'If you ignore this simple truth, you'll be lucky if you're simply laughed at. Do it too often, you'll wake one night with a knife to your throat.'

'But will you go all the way and sell them into the mines?' I asked.

'By the Twelve True Gods, of course not!' he laughed. 'I'd not get much of a price for city-bred trash like them. And I'd only replace them with worse.

'Since it seems to trouble your tender heart, I'll knock them around a bit more, then show clemency at a meeting of all the household. How does that suit you? Call it another birthday gift.'

A slave with an impassive face refilled my cup.

'All this and more, my dear Alaric, I'll do for you,' Lucius added, a pleading note now in his voice. 'Just say whatever you want, and it's yours.'

Well, friendship has its obligations as well as advantages. Lucius had done so much for me these past few days. All I'd done was to take. Indeed, I'd now withheld a fair bit of information.

'It isn't late,' I said, 'but it's been a long day. I can't take it permanently yet. But I'll gladly take up your offer of a bed for tonight.'

Lucius smiled and leaned back complacently into his chair.

37

That night, I committed with Lucius what Maximin had always called 'the abominable sin of the ancients'. The punishment, by the way, is castration, plus the usual confiscation of goods. I have known the law to be enforced in Constantinople – but only against those who've already got on the emperor's bad side and against whom no other charges are likely to stick.

We woke naked in each other's arms. A slave was standing over us with clean water to drink and some raisins. I couldn't get free from his embrace at first, and I thought for a moment Lucius would start the same enquiries about my feelings for him as Gretel had taken to making. But he grabbed at the dish and sent the slave on his way. I slid free and stood stretching in the early sunlight.

After this small refreshment, Lucius taught me the use of his gymnasium. He'd been right. It was so much better than the barbarian forms of exercise. I don't except any of these, even sea bathing. I resolved as we shared a cold tub afterwards – still no wood for the big furnace – that this was another civilised usage I'd adopt.

I was glad Lucius had said no more about the investigation. I was feeling increasingly guilty that I'd advanced more than a little by myself, and was revealing none of it. Then again, he had seemed alarmed by the discovery of a political angle to the murder. It was probably for the best if he didn't yet know the exarch of Africa was now sniffing about for the letters.

From Lucius, I hurried back to Marcella's to collect some papers. I was delayed there awhile by the delivery of yet more clothes. I hadn't time to try them on properly. But Gretel helped me into some of them, and swore I looked like a god. She danced around me so provocatively that I tore everything off and ravished her on the floor. It was an unexpected pleasure, and it really set me up for the day proper. Afterwards, she got water for me and suggested a touch of face powder to cover the sunburn I'd picked up going with the diplomat down to the financial district.

Then to the Lateran, where the copying was back in full swing. Martin showed me the first completed books. They still hadn't dried well enough to risk opening them. Even if they were wholly devotional, they looked very good.

I'd go over to the Exchange later. I'd sniff the financial air against the day when I went there as a dealer in my own right. I'd also look for that old man with experience of the English market. I could discuss the mechanics of shipping books to Canterbury. And I could press him again about the Column of Phocas. He'd known more than he was saying. I needed to know what that was.

I worked everyone until some while after the normal time for lunch. I let Martin go with a guilty pang, and took myself across the river to the financial district.

Before getting to the river, I dodged into an empty side street and put on the hooded robe of a monk. I was almost used now to being followed in Rome. It seemed to involve no danger during the daylight. I was even a little flattered by the constancy of the attention. Nevertheless, I wanted a bit of privacy for what I was to do. The robe covered me entirely. I left through the other end of the side street into a crowd of pilgrims and shoppers. There were at least a dozen other monks of one kind or another. For my first time in Rome, I might now count on being unobserved.

The Exchange when I got there was in uproar. I took advantage of the milling crowd and stripped off the robe, throwing it into one of the containers set up on every corner so that rubbish didn't have to be dumped in the street. Unless someone had guessed I was going there, and had sent spies ahead, I was unobserved.

Fat Silas, I was told, had been murdered in the night. Armed men had waylaid him as he staggered home from a brothel and cut his throat. That explained the uproar. This was the first serious crime the district had known in living memory, and the Jews and Syrians and others were in a blind panic. They'd forgotten all differences of religion and nationality, and agreed on setting up a committee of enquiry in the smaller synagogue – you see, this was close enough by the Exchange to let dealers run back and forth to keep an eye on the prices. There, they were issuing joint offers of rewards for any information that might lead to the killers. There seemed to be no question of involving the prefect.

This was a strange crime, I heard from the Armenian who'd bought my options. He was leaning alone against a pillar, making notes into a book of waxed tablets. He seemed quite pleased with himself. He gave me a queer look at first, but soon cheered up when he realised I didn't yet have the full story. Silas had been murdered, he explained, but his purse and jewellery hadn't been touched. This raised the matter from a property-related crime to something possibly much more alarming.

'Good thing I dumped those options,' he added thoughtfully. 'Perhaps I shouldn't have bought them in the first place. But at least I got out ahead. The poor sod I sold them to will have a hard job collecting from the estate.'

Well, this was unconnected with any of my business. Even so, it wasn't nice to wander into what I'd thought the safest part of Rome outside the Lateran, only to find myself in another murder investigation.

For all he didn't share in the general panic over Fat Silas, the Armenian was annoyed by the continued movement of prices. Following some vast, hidden intervention the previous day, they were still all over the place. The diplomat, on his earlier visit, had been observed in close conversation with some of the Jews. That had set things off again. The Jews weren't saying anything. Everyone else was still trying to guess what he was really about. Since I had nothing to say on this, the Armenian soon lost interest in me and went back to his waxed tablets.

Inside the Exchange, I found the old man. So far as I could tell, he was arguing over the terms of a mortgage he was negotiating to

257

buy. The seller had the golden hair and ruined complexion of an African Vandal. I waited for the transaction to finish, then made my presence known.

'Hello, Aelric,' said the old man in the buoyant voice of someone who's just got himself a bargain. 'Come down from the Caelian to make even more cash?' He also didn't seem that worried about the murder.

There was no point in asking how he knew my real name Instead, I asked for his advice on transporting books to England. We sat down privately together in the shade of a small portico just by the Exchange and bought some wine and hard biscuits from a passing vendor.

Ordinarily, he explained, the most secure transport would be by land. It would be slow, but there'd be no chance of saltwater contamination of the leather and parchment. This had to be taken into account when considering the lower costs of sea transport.

However, he was getting involved in a tin shipment from Cornwall, and there would be a big, heavy ship leaving from Marseilles in July. If I had enough books ready by then, they could travel in the ballast, at a very low rate, and in reasonable safety. I could get them to Marseilles on one of the grain ships from Sicily that was planning a triangular voyage.

The only drawback was that the ship wouldn't put in at Richborough, but at one of the Wessex ports, and the books would have to be carried overland. Then again, an armed escort wouldn't cost much for something like books, which hardly anyone would want to steal. Either that, or Ethelbert could be got at through his wife to stump up an armed party.

I asked about tin prices.

'Pretty firm at the moment,' he said. 'There's an expectation of all-out war in the East, and for a long time. Whatever happens between Phocas and the exarch of Africa, the Persians mean business. Getting them out of Asia will take hard fighting. I expect tin and all other goods related to the military to go up and stay up.'

I'd heard this already from the diplomat. 'How secure are

shipments out of Cornwall?' I asked. 'I've heard there hasn't been much doing there for a while.'

'You need to dig quite deep nowadays there,' he said, 'and that means some danger of flooding, which slows down extraction and raises costs. But prices will soon be high enough to cover that risk. So long as your people don't decide to raid the mine and steal everything or kill all the slaves, I see good profits there.'

After some very stiff bargaining, I put myself down for a twentieth share of the cargo. That got me free shipment of the books. It got me a chance of at least a tenfold profit. It also allowed me to probe for the information I really wanted. 'How long do you think the emperor can last?' I asked in English. There seemed to be free speech here on all political issues so far as they affected business. But what I wanted to lead into wasn't for anyone to overhear in Latin. I avoided using the name Phocas, instead using the English word 'cyning' for emperor.

'Most say he'll be out by Christmas,' the old man replied in English. 'I think it could be longer. He'll lose to the exarch eventually. But there are differences within the exarch's own side. His son and his nephew are in a race. One is invading the East through Egypt, the other by sea. Whoever gets first to Constantinople will be the one who deposes the emperor, and therefore takes his place. Because of this deal, each young man is quietly slowing the other down. I think the emperor will last a bit longer yet.'

I asked if Phocas had much support in Constantinople.

'Not much. The man is feared, which means there won't be open moves against him as there were against Emperor Maurice. But my information is that the whole administrative machinery has withdrawn its active support.'

'Does that mean the Church as well?' I asked.

'Have you ever been East?' he asked in reply. I shook my head.

'I didn't think you had. Until you've been in Constantinople, you won't believe how controlled the Church is there. It's almost a department of state. It's not much different in the other Eastern patriarchates – for all the trouble they have with heresy. The

Church won't lift a finger against the emperor so long as he keeps his palace guard on side.

'Here, it's very different. Pope Boniface sends long letters of support and not much else. Oh, he pays the costs of defence against the Lombards, but he'd have to do that in any event. No one else will or can pay those. But he makes sure little of the money he sends to Ravenna leaves Italy. In the meantime, he keeps in with the exarch of Africa, and is waiting on events.

'That statue of the emperor in the Forum will be up a while longer – but not that much longer.'

I ignored the opening for the moment. 'Does the emperor still have the support of the –' I paused and cast round for an English phrase for '*Agentes in Rebus*' – 'of the security services?'

The old man thought a little about the meaning of the words I'd used. Spies are for the civilised. Barbarians get by on gossip. 'Not the active support,' he said at length. 'It's the same all over the administration.'

Even though there was no chance we could be understood by anyone else in the square, he leaned forward and dropped his voice. 'I heard there was a letter intercepted last January in Syracuse. It's believed it came from King Chosroes of Persia to King Agilulf of the Lombards. I don't know what it said. What matters is that it got that far. It was only intercepted by accident. The security people in Constantinople have always been very careful to shut off contacts between Persia and the West. That letter got as far as it did because it was allowed to go through.'

This was my chance. 'That's why the emperor now has his column, isn't it?' I asked.

The old man sat sharply up. 'What do you know about that?' he asked. 'I shouldn't have told you about it. You'll get us both killed if you aren't careful. I saw Fat Silas boasting yesterday about those coins you gave him. Next I knew, he was dead in the gutter. You be careful.'

'But I already know about the column,' I lied. 'Because he can't trust the regular service, the emperor has set up his own personal security service. It's operating here in Rome.

'What do you know about a man with one eye?'

The old man got up. His face had closed on me like a town gate at dusk. 'We've spoken quite long enough now about matters that don't concern the likes of us, young Aelric,' he said. 'If you don't want to end like poor Silas – or your friend, the Saint – you'll stop asking these questions now.'

As he walked away, he turned and said, still in English: 'Within the next year, there will be a new order of things in the East. When that happens, this column will amount to nothing. Until then, regard it as an armed and dangerous conspiracy of the Greeks against the peace. Its spies are everywhere. It won't rest until the exarch of Africa and his boys are dead, or until they have defeated the emperor.

'I warn you, Aelric, stick to your books. Stick to the price of tin. Make money. Educate your people. Keep your nose out of politics. You may end by losing that and much more besides.' He walked off back to the Exchange.

What had I learnt from the conversation? Not much new, I supposed. But much had been confirmed. Phocas was up to something in Rome. The only question remaining was what it could be. Lucius was right: those letters really were the key to our locked door.

And that gold seemed to be cursed. I aside, everyone who'd owned to touching the stuff was dead – those two bandits on the road, the other ten, Maximin, and now Silas. And I was being watched and had been attacked.

A superstitious man might have considered giving the gold to the Church. I took a comforting grip on the pommel of that nice sword Lucius had given me.

38

I nearly bumped into Martin as I passed one of the Syrian churches in the square. We were in a crowd of dealers and professional men. He didn't see me at all. He was smiling absently when I saw him.

'Hello, Martin,' I said patting him on the shoulder. 'On a mission for the dispensator?'

Of course, he wasn't. He'd been with his woman and unborn child. Where could they be staying? This must have been an expensive area for renting.

He blushed a bright pink. 'Yes, sir,' he lied very badly. Then he remembered his place. He set his features into the required expression of cringing respect.

I smiled and clapped him harder on the shoulder. Martin was a rotten liar – most unlike the others of his race. But what was it to me if he had a woman? I hadn't believed Lucius in his wider claim. Yes, slaves might need a harsh discipline to keep them in line. But that was because, fundamentally, they were human beings, with the same desire for personal freedom and autonomy as the rest of us. Martin wasn't my slave. He was on loan from the Church. So long as he oversaw that copying, that was the limit of what I wanted from him. I had no complaint about the copying. So what if he ran off now and again to be with his woman?

I suddenly thought that Edwina would now be heavy with child. I felt a pang of remembrance for what I had lost. And I felt a degree of sympathy for Martin.

We walked on in the bright sunshine. Dealers and vendors and other men of business hurried around us. There was the occasional litter carrying one of their ladies. We passed through the financial district and across the bridge, back into the semi-ruined main areas of Rome, where the quality of those around us dropped correspondingly. Across the river, we turned right towards the Lateran.

We began a conversation about the sound of Greek and Latin in their better ages. You need a pretty uncritical nature not to realise that the sound of Latin has changed between ancient times and the present. Nowadays, there are more letters than sounds, and there has been a softening of sounds that once were hard. The question is, what was the ancient pronunciation? And, of course, is it really important to appreciating the writings of the ancients if the sounds have changed? Martin's father was convinced he had answered the technical part of the question for Greek, and was convinced that the correct pronunciation *was* necessary to appreciate the ancients.

I pushed and pushed with Martin to know more of what his father had told him. We spoke. We argued. We gave illustrations of our points as we walked on past the ruined Forum towards the Lateran, where our project of saving these arguments for another generation to settle was going smoothly ahead. But underneath, I was feeling increasingly troubled. I could sense a vague darkness in my mind.

'Martin,' I asked in as normal a tone as I could command, 'you said at our big meeting in Marcella's house that you had been with the dispensator on the day that Maximin vanished. Yet I spoke to the dispensator, and he said he hadn't seen you since attaching you to the copying mission.'

I didn't have my notes with me, and I'm willing to grant I was misunderstanding what both had said to me. Martin hadn't actually said he was with the dispensator, only that he had not heard from him about the summons that Maximin had received. As for the dispensator, all he had said was that he'd found himself in need of Martin after his attachment.

If Martin had turned and told me that he had met the dispensator, but was not at liberty to reveal the nature of their conversation, I'd have gone straight back to the question I was forming about the use of the dual cases in Greek. If he'd flushed red again and muttered something nonsensical, I'd have concluded he was with his woman again – though had he ever been gone long enough to get all the way to and back from the financial district? I wasn't sure at the time about the number and duration of his absences on that day. Instead, he stopped in the street, his face suddenly grey and sweating.

That vague darkness firmed in shape and colour.

'Martin,' I asked, now with a harder tone, 'whoever visited Father Maximin that last afternoon first stopped him from going to the dispensator, and then called him out as night was falling. Yet only four other people knew he had been summoned. There was the dispensator. There was Brother Ambrose. There was me. There was you. One of these leaked that information. Was that person you?'

This was embarrassing. I liked and respected Martin, and I was questioning him like this with the greatest reluctance. I wanted him to stop me. I wanted him to show impatience and even offence. My line of questioning could have been stopped dead by some kind of reply, however feeble it might have sounded in a regular investigation. How could I be sure no one else had known about the summons? I wanted not so much answers as reassurance.

Instead, Martin was babbling about his 'great regard for the reverend father', and almost having to support himself against a broken pedestal.

I pressed on, the dark shadow in my mind spreading. I asked where he got the money to buy fine clothes and support a woman and her unborn child in an expensive area. Instead of owning to the standard bribes that all clerical slaves take from petitioners, he nearly puked into the gutter.

Every response raised another question. Every question arranged more of the facts into an internally consistent pattern. I began myself to feel sick.

I took firm hold of his arm. 'What do you know about Maximin's death?' I demanded. 'What was your part in his murder? You knew he was dead when I offered you your freedom. I well recall how white your face went. You knew he was dead when you told me he wasn't in the convent. You finished cleaning the words off that parchment letter. It still carried recognisable text when the old woman handed it to you. It was you who scraped it and went over it with vinegar.

'I want to know what happened. Did you kill Maximin?'

'No . . . no, sir,' he gasped. 'Surely, I was with you when he was killed. I couldn't have killed him.'

A wretched answer. It only confirmed that I had been with him when the body was found. I had no idea where he was before I got late back to Marcella's. I looked at his feet. Were they the same size as those bloody prints? Lucius had taken the measurements. It would be easy to check.

'I want the truth out of you, Martin,' I said, tightening my grip on his arm until he winced.

'Please, sir . . . please,' he babbled. 'I don't know anything.'

'So tell me where you went on Maximin's last afternoon.' I fought to keep my voice from rising too loud.

'Please, sir – I can't. Please, you're hurting my arm.' Martin's voice was a ragged whisper.

'Hurting your arm, am I?' said I, grimly. I was angry. More than that, I was horrified. 'I'll hurt more than that if I have to. I know you've been fucking some girl. I know her belly is full of your trash. Do you think I give a shit about any of that? I want the truth about you and Maximin's death. Do you understand?'

Martin twisted ineffectually in my grip. I had him too tight. 'Please, please,' he cried, 'don't bring Sveta into this. She knows nothing. Please, sir!'

'You're coming with me,' I said, now squeezing on his arm until I felt the bones. But where to, I thought? To the prefect? What a joke! To the dispensator? What was his role in the murder? Where to? It was obvious.

'You're coming with me to Lucius. We'll have the truth out of you.'

Martin blenched again. 'No, sir – not to the lord Basilius. Please, not to him.'

Indeed not. I could imagine what Martin was thinking. Lucius would have the back off him without putting his wine cup down or raising his voice. If that didn't work, there were the spiked whips and red-hot pincers, or whatever else he kept in reserve for particularly naughty slaves.

I turned with him and began marching him away from the Lateran, now towards the house of Lucius. 'You'll tell us all you know about the Column of Phocas – who is in it, and how much you were paid. You'll also tell us about those letters. After all, that's why you volunteered yourself for the copying mission, isn't it? Your job was to help get those letters.'

Thump!

'Urgh! . . . Fuck you!'

I'd misjudged Martin. Just because he was weedy and didn't know how to use a sword didn't mean he was incapable of violence. He'd suddenly raised his knee and got me in the stomach. I doubled over, gasping for breath.

And he was off.

He was lighter than me, and his legs were longer. He was off like a rabbit before I could straighten up. But I gave chase. So long as I kept him in sight, I'd run him down. Then it would be off to Lucius and whatever it took to get the truth out of the man who'd killed or had some part in killing Maximin.

'Stop that slave!' I bellowed at some barbarian pilgrim further down the street. 'Stop him!'

The barbarian smiled and reached out a heavily muscled arm to scoop Martin as he tried to run past. I could see the gleam of the gold band on his bicep.

But Martin was deft as well as fast. He dodged the outstretched arm and continued running, his speed hardly broken. We both followed, shouting at others in the street to join the chase.

Martin ran and ran. We followed. As I'd expected, he had speed but little stamina. He was like my horse on the road from Populonium. He wasn't built for a long chase. He ran down long, almost empty streets, jumping here and there over the fallen ruins. But we followed close behind. Little by little we gained on him. I could hear his rasping breath as his energy began to fail him. He rounded a corner.

266

'It's a dead end,' the barbarian called exultantly. 'We've got the worthless cunt!'

He was right. It was a dead end. The street was blocked with a sheer, ten-foot-high pile of fallen rubble. No one could get over that without slowing to a crawl. We'd have him.

But there was another of those bastard sewers open. Martin stepped straight into a hole in the grating, and was gone. We were there within a few heartbeats. But he was gone.

'Fuck! Fuck! Fuck!' I shouted, looking down. 'Fuck!' This one wasn't blocked. I pushed my head through the hole into a cold, shitty draught. Of all the sewers in all the streets in Rome, Martin had chosen to escape into one that was still in working order.

Neither I nor the barbarian could follow. At its widest, the hole in the grating was only about fifteen inches wide. Even without the muscling piled on top, we both had those big Germanic shoulders. We pulled at the rest of the grating. But time had set it into the road as if it had been concreted in.

I looked around. There were others now with us. But they were all too big to fit through.

'Where does this lead?' I cried, looking round.

Someone told me it led down to the river, but that it might also connect to the great main drain that led underneath the city.

'Stay here!' I shouted to the barbarian. 'If he comes out, grab him. There's a price on his head.'

I raced back down to the river. I looked at the series of holes issuing from the embankment. Some were choked with weeds and filth, and were probably backed up solid. Others still ran clear into the Tiber, just as they had in the old days. Which one had Martin used for his exit? Had he come out?

I asked some fishermen who were washing their nets over the side of their little boat. They had seen no one come out. I offered them a price for catching whoever did come out.

I ran back to the broken grating. The barbarian had seen and heard nothing. Martin might be cowering just a few inches underneath our feet. He might be sinking slowly into a swamp of semi-liquid filth. He might have got clear away. Whatever, we'd lost him.

I pulled my right arm back from the hole. I'd been poking a long broken spar in all directions that I could reach. In all directions, I felt nothing.

'Fucking little shitbag,' I snarled as I thanked the barbarian and gave him some silver for his trouble. 'I'll get the fucker yet. I'll have all the gates watched. I'll post notice of reward. You can't hide long in this city. I'll have him in these two hands – and he'll beg for death before I'm finished with him.

'Fucking Celtic shit-eating motherfucker,' I added to no one in particular as I walked off, trying not to show how baffled I was by the man's sudden escape.

I came face to face with two men dressed in clerical garb.

'You must come with us,' one of them said in a tone that didn't permit argument or delay. 'The dispensator will want to see you.'

39

I sat in the dispensator's office. He was on his feet, pacing about in a white anger.

'You have been in Rome one week,' he hissed malevolently at me. 'In this time, you have been associated with three murders. You have been a principal in a serious fraud on several of the Church's most useful financial intermediaries. You have assaulted a valuable – indeed, currently irreplaceable – Church slave in the street, and caused him to run away. You have been brawling in the street and, according to my account, killed three men.

'You have also associated yourself with a man of the most shocking reputation – a man with whom I am ashamed to be connected by ties of common blood. You have committed one unspeakable crime with him in the Colosseum. And, from the reports I have of your movements last night, you have almost certainly committed another at his house.'

He might have added – and doubtless he did in his mind – that I'd come close to wrecking his most important public appearance that year. But he contented himself with my less arguable derelictions in Rome.

'I've told you,' I said back to him, 'I will do whatever I must to find Maximin's killers.'

The dispensator stopped and looked down at me, a sneer on his face. 'So, Father Maximin – soon perhaps to be Saint Maximin – would have found blasphemy, fraud and sodomy perfectly acceptable instruments of law enforcement? I think not. And what have you found for all this? Have you found the killers? Have you even found the letters that you and my nephew seem to think so important?'

'I haven't found the killers yet,' I answered, looking away from that nasty, cold face. 'But I know who they were.' I told him about the Column of Phocas. I told him that Martin was connected with it.

His face contorted into a thin smile. 'So you know about the Column of Phocas. And you think Martin was connected with it. But you can't lead me to it, or to Martin, or to those letters. For all your frantic hoeing and trenching, you have not reaped a great harvest of fact.

'All you have been able to establish is that those letters are lost to everyone who might want them. This may not be an ideal answer to the question of where they are. I think, however, it is an answer with which all should be satisfied. Yes, perhaps all should be satisfied.'

He sat down behind his desk and straightened his tunic. 'The matter now remains of what I am to do with you. Whatever he may think, young Basilius is not untouchable. But I shall need a better case for proceeding against him than I presently have. Your Ethiopian partner is also lucky in his circumstances. It is not for you to know why a heretic from beyond the frontiers of the Empire is welcome in Rome. It is enough for you to know that I must for the moment overlook his speculative manipulations and those of his other accomplices.

'You, however, are an altogether less important irritation.' He pressed the fingers of both hands together, now beginning to enjoy himself.

'I am informed that Father Maximin wanted to use the gold that you both took outside Populonium for the endowment of a monastery in Rome. In your barbarian lust for gain, you argued with him. You suborned a Church slave to assist you in his murder. You both murdered Brother Ambrose. For reasons as yet unknown, you both murdered the dealer Silas of Edessa. The slave then blackmailed you into handing over a larger than agreed share of your unlawful gains, and you tried to kill him in broad daylight.

'I think the facts are reasonably consistent with this explanation.

You are a vain, greedy, stupid barbarian. If I put all this in writing to the prefect—'

'But you can't do that,' I cried. I was outraged at the sheer effrontery of the lies he was proposing to tell. I struggled to fight back the tears of rage and self-pity.

The dispensator slanted his eyes and looked at me as if I were some leprous beggar in the square outside. 'Young man,' he said with quiet menace, 'you have no conception of what I can do in this city – or of what I will do to protect the interests of the Church. If I write to the prefect, believe me that he will take action. He will act with a speed and thoroughness that will be the talk of Rome until he has finished his term of office.'

He rustled some loose sheets on his desk. 'However, I am not inclined to harshness over the indiscretions of youth. I fail to see what benefit would follow from the painful execution of a man whose abilities may still be of use to the Church. I will offer you an escape from the justice of the civil authorities.

'You have three days from now to arrange your affairs. I then want you out of Rome.'

'But . . .' I wanted to ask where I'd go. But the dispensator already had his answer.

'Where you go is not my concern. If it is your concern, it is one that you should have borne in mind before interfering in matters that are beyond your knowledge or control.

'Let me see.' He pulled out a sheet of papyrus. 'I am told you have a business connection in Marseilles.' I looked at him. Did he have spies everywhere? He continued: 'You will know from your studies that Marseilles was in ancient days a refuge for those who had failed in Rome. Let it be so again. I am told it has a most healthy climate, and is not too greatly troubled by the Frankish authorities in its internal ordering. You may appoint an agent here in Rome to oversee the copying of the books. You may oversee his work from Marseilles. You can be a modern – ah – Gaius Verres.' He paused and gave himself an almost visible hug at the supposed aptness of his allusion.

'But I do not ultimately care to which other place you take

yourself,' he continued. 'I only warn you that if I find you are still in Rome once your three days have elapsed, I will see to it that the prefect sets light personally to the fire on which you are to be roasted to death in front of his Basilica. Do I make myself clear, young man?'

I nodded, swallowing with a dry throat.

'Then get out of my office!'

As I left, he repeated ominously: 'Three days,' and held up three fingers as if I didn't already understand.

Before I was completely out of his office, he was back to work on his files.

As I described the whole calamitous series of events to him, Lucius had his slaves ply me with strong wine and set an iced poultice to my forehead. I reclined on his bed while he stroked my hand soothingly.

'Now, now, my beautiful, golden boy, stop the crying,' he crooned. 'You should see how the swelling spoils those lovely eyes.'

I'd burst into tears long before getting through my account of the day. It was such a short while since I'd been walking confidently about Rome, almost like a native. I'd been counting my gains and looking forward to a resolution of our enquiry into Maximin's death. Now, I was about to become an exile for the second time in a year. And being kicked out of Rome was far worse than having to leave horrid old Kent. I had to fight hard against dissolving into another fit of the sobs.

'I never did like that Church slave,' Lucius said, turning to seal a letter and handing it to a slave who stood beside him. 'He was always too full of himself. He never showed proper respect to his betters.

'I can't take you to the Column of Phocas. But I can issue instructions for the arrest on sight of Martin. We'll have him brought back here. I have cellars so deep, no one will ever notice his cries as I have the truth extracted from his miserable body.

272

'Now . . .' He turned to another slave and issued his instruction.

I'd held back nothing of what the dispensator had said to me. I'd also finally got round to telling him about my dealings with the diplomat and the full truth of what had happened with those street thugs. I'd expected Lucius at least to give me a hard look. In the event, he'd contented himself with a few questions to clarify my broken, tear-stained account of things.

The stuff about the diplomat did have one effect. Lucius ordered his library to be packed up and hidden in 'the safe place' and replaced by a copy of the Gospels he had somewhere, together with some of the devotional literature he'd managed to inherit from his grandfather and had neglected to burn. He also ordered the main altar to be taken outside for use as a support for potted plants. 'Icons in every room,' he added. 'There's a stack of them by the slave toilets.'

The house would soon look properly devout, should anyone come looking. There was a limit, even Lucius acknowledged, to his noble immunity. 'There's an undeniable smell now of politics,' he said. 'You don't take any chances when that miasma rises.

'As for you, my golden, beautiful object of adoration,' he said, turning back to me, 'we must part a while – perhaps just for a few days – but we must part. The dispensator is right. There is no human power that can for the moment stand against him in Rome. But I have friends in Ravenna who will keep you safe.

'I'll send the letter of introduction by fast courier tonight. The exarch is of much sterner stuff than this broken-down fool of a prefect. Though also a Greek, he's very nearly a gentleman – and, in the religious sense, is quietly one of us.'

Lucius paused and chose his words before continuing. 'I'll warn you for when you meet him, he's a touch over the wrong side of madness. So don't try saying anything too clever. But he's undoubtedly one of us. You can rely on his protection. You can stay in Ravenna, while I press on here with what I can of the investigation. At the very least, I can have that slave caught, and I will gladly send you the various parts that I cut with my own hands from his twisted, still living body.'

Lucius went back to issuing the necessary instructions. I was to leave the day after next. He could have his lawyer recommend an overseer for the copying. I was to load as much as I could fit on two packhorses. Whatever else I had could be left with him. I was to be provided with all supplemental letters of introduction. I'd be in Ravenna for a while – though I might like it so much, he said, I'd never want to leave; then he would try to settle matters for my return to Rome to claim the justice that was rightly mine.

'There is one more matter to be discussed, my glorious Alaric,' he said as the last slave left the room. 'I said on the first day of our investigation that there are two sources of knowledge. We have tried a patient collection and judgement of facts. We have found much, but not enough. And time is now running out. We need therefore to take the more direct approach, of an appeal to the Gods. They have never failed me – not, that is, when I've asked with a pure heart. They will not fail me now.

'Go back to your lodgings, Alaric. Arrange your affairs with Marcella. Whatever now may happen, you must take advantage of my protection here in my house. I will send for you at nightfall. Tell no one where you are going. Do exactly as my slaves require of you. I promise we shall have some kind of answer before dawn.

'Just in case, though, do start packing for Ravenna.'

The diplomat had already had his interview in the Lateran by the time I sat down beside him in Marcella's latrines.

'Such harsh and undiplomatic language from this Chalcedonite heretic,' he said mournfully, referring doubtless to what the dispensator had told him. 'I really thought to remind the dog of the kings whose blood runs in my body.'

But he hadn't, and I couldn't blame him. He explained at length how hurt he was by the accusations made against his honour and his alleged abuse of diplomatic status.

'I hear you will be leaving us,' he said at length, untensing his abdominal muscles. I waited for the continuation. It came: 'Do you think we can settle any matters outstanding before then?'

I reached into my cloak and pulled out the draft I'd earlier arranged at the Lateran. He gave it a close inspection, looking up with a benign smile. 'The God Who Reigns in Supreme Majesty – always allowing for the status of His Son, which precise status is best not discussed with those who accept the formulations of Chalcedon – will surely bless your honesty.'

He looked over at the sun, now coming low through the toilet window. 'Do you know when the bank closes?' he asked.

'Late, I think,' I replied.

He rapped an order to his slave that sounded halfway between a gargle and a vomit. There followed a frenzy of wiping. The diplomat stood up. 'I do hope this is not to be the end of a wonderful and productive friendship,' he said. 'But you will forgive me if I neglect the formalities, bearing in mind how urgently I feel drawn to the Lateran.'

He stopped and looked back at me. 'Do not on any account try writing to me,' he said, coming back to speak in a low voice. 'However, if anything regarding those letters should come to your knowledge, I shall be happy to receive a messenger from you.'

We briefly shook hands. Then he stopped again and looked back. 'Remember, Aelric,' he said, 'the Evil One takes many forms. This has not always been the city of God. Take care to put yourself in God's hands.'

He went off towards the stables. Some advice he'd picked up from Maximin? Who could tell? I shook my head.

I sat alone, trousers around my ankles, and wondered what was to become of me.

40

Just as the last rays of the sun faded and the sky turned to purple, the slave escort arrived from Lucius. I received them in my rooms, where I'd been hard at work packing. In just a week, I'd managed to accumulate about ten times as much as I'd brought through the walls on that first morning. Nearly all of this I'd have to leave for the moment. I'd paid Marcella a month up front for the rooms, and she agreed to keep them free in case I should make a sudden return. Lucius could arrange at his leisure for the collection of whatever I left.

Gretel had folded and packed the best clothes. Then we'd had a long parting fuck. She'd come close to ruining this with a sobbing fit over my departure, as if she'd not be hopping into another bed the moment my back was turned. But it did somewhat recover me from the stresses of the day. Still, I felt decidedly low as I looked over the rooms that I'd entered in so different a mood and in so much happier circumstances.

The biggest slave bowed low before me. 'Sir,' he said, 'my orders are to dress in your own most distinctive clothes. I will then walk with three other slaves down towards the financial district, where I will spend the evening examining the illuminated frescoes in the church of St Diabathrarius. I will then make a very slow return here by way of a brothel run by a reliable associate of the master.'

He repressed a lecherous smile and handed me a bag. 'You, sir, must put on these miserable but clean rags of the master's household. Together with Antony, you will carry two of your bags back to the master's house. Antony will know if you are followed, and will advise you on the necessary evasion.'

Antony led me to the house of Lucius by a route I'd not yet taken, down very long, quite empty streets. The building was apparently still sound, but looked abandoned. But for the joyous squealing of the rats, we walked together in complete silence. Every so often, Antony stopped to listen for any sounds, however faint. Each time, he shook his head. Only once did he look worried. But there was no other sound.

For my first time in Rome, I could be sure I wasn't followed.

The house when we arrived looked empty. We entered though a small door at the back, and passed along a musty corridor to the main living quarters. I could see hardly anything, but I felt the wood flooring crumble beneath my feet.

Dressed in black, Lucius received me in his library. The books had already been replaced. On the far wall hung an icon of Saint Peter, a silver crucifix placed on a table beneath it. All was now as any priest might have wished.

He darted a look at Antony, who shook his head. 'We came alone, master,' he said. Lucius waved him out of the room so just he and I remained.

'Look, Alaric,' he began, omitting the usual epithets, 'you know that I'm counting on your total cooperation in this matter. You know the usual pattern of a sacrifice to the True Gods. But this one will be slightly varied from the norm. We shall be opening a direct communication with beings of unimaginable power. They can give you whatever you seek, or can blast you dead on the spot.

'You must promise me you will not step out of the sanctified zone of protection, and that you will say nothing unless called on to speak. Have I your assurance?'

'Yes,' I said, trying not to appear too sceptical about the outcome of this latest ceremony.

'Then let us begin.'

I dressed in the black suit of clothes Lucius had prepared for me. As I stood naked before him, he stepped forward to embrace me, but pulled back, muttering something about the need for purity of heart and body. He led me across to one of the smaller book racks against the wall. He pulled at it, and pulled again. With a gentle creak, it swung into the room on concealed hinges. There was a narrow doorway opening to a flight of steps that led down. Every few yards, a lamp shone dimly in its recess.

Lucius made a gesture of antique devotion and stepped through the doorway. I followed into the darkness.

We descended about fifty much-worn steps, our feet crunching as we walked on the unswept dust of many ages. The temperature fell and the air became damp and oppressive as we went. The lamps glimmered more and more dimly, and guttered as we passed.

At the bottom of the steps, a narrow corridor stretched forward into the darkness. Lucius took up one of the lamps and walked confidently forward with me close behind. The flame of the lamp was reflected back from the dripping, concreted walls.

At last, we came to the end. As before, Lucius knocked gently on the door, giving his name. The door opened. We stepped into a low but wide chamber of vaulted brick. At the far end was another doorway, locked and barred. In the middle stood a small brazier, burning low in the stale air. Before this, together with his assistants, stood the priest I'd first met in the Colosseum. He was dressed in black, arms folded and head bowed.

'It is all as you have commanded, O Great Lord Basilius, most noble servant of the Ancient Gods,' he said, looking up. His resonant voice filled the chamber. I shuddered.

'As ancient custom requires,' he went on in a voice still deeper, 'I ask if you are truly prepared for this most certain yet dangerous consultation?'

'I am prepared,' said Lucius, his voice dry and nervous.

'Then let it commence, according to the ways of our ancient fathers.'

The priest waved his hand over the brazier. It suddenly flared up, filling the room with white, acrid smoke. At the same time, the room turned still colder. No breeze accompanied this. It was as if someone had uncovered a block of hidden ice.

Lucius stepped back, a panicky look on his face. I resisted an urge to burst out laughing. I hadn't been able to see what the priest had concealed in his hand. But I'd seen this trick any number of times in Kent. Maximin had been quite adept in scaring audiences into conversion. The cold I couldn't explain. But every trickster has his own way of exciting wonder in the gullible. Where miracles are concerned, you need know only the part of how they're produced to dismiss the whole effect as a fraud.

I looked on with set features, now resisting the conditioned reflex to cross myself in a pretence of pious wonder. I tried not to think the worse of Lucius for his now clutching at my sleeve with an evidently rising terror.

The priest leading, the assistants took up a chant in the most archaic Latin I'd ever heard. It was in short sentences, the stress on many words moved unnaturally to the first syllable. Frequently, I could only guess the meaning from compounds in the pure language. Some words I couldn't understand at all. I wish I had been able shortly after to sit down with a clear head and record this chant. I doubt if it exists in written form, and I've now forgotten all of it, except for the reiterated claim: *Cume tonas Leucesie prae tet tremonti*, which I took to mean: 'When thou dost thunder, O Lord of Light, men do tremble before thee.'

But there was much more – all about the attributes and goodness and power and genealogy of the various Old Gods. At the end of each stanza, a silver bell would be rung, and the priest turned three times.

At the end of all this, the priest did his trick again with the hidden combustible. I could feel my teeth begin to chatter in the still growing chill of the place. He motioned the rest of us to take our places within circles traced on the ground with white meal. Then he walked firmly over to the locked door. One of his assistants unlocked and unbarred it, before darting back within his own circle.

The priest looked through the door. There was a small light within.

'Is the victim purified?' he asked.

From within, the answer came: 'It is.'

'Is the victim willing?'

'It is.'

'Has the victim been bled sufficiently?'

'It has.'

The priest stood back and turned to us. 'The communication is about to be opened,' he said in a low, sinister voice.

Two other assistants entered through the doorway. With them, they carried what I took at first for a statue – a statue, indeed, of Christ taken down from the cross. It had about it the same twisted, bloodied whiteness as something I'd recently seen in a church.

But this statue was still breathing. Carried into our presence, naked and bound to a wooden post, was one of the slaves who'd failed to stop One-Eye the day before last.

The assistants set the post down a few feet from the brazier, and got within their own circles. The naked flesh shone pale in the dim light. His head hung down on his chest. Blood dripped in a thin trickle from great gashes on the inside of each forearm. The gasp of his breathing came high and shallow.

'The victim stands between life and death,' the priest cried triumphantly. 'He sees us, and he sees the Gods. Through him, we speak to the Gods, and they speak to us. It is all as ancient custom requires.

'Ask what you will, O Lord Basilius, most noble and most pious.' He turned back to the brazier and muttered some nonsense that I didn't fully catch.

I stood rooted to the spot. I hadn't known what to expect as the culmination of this ceremony. But the last thing I'd expected was a human sacrifice. My own people used to go in for this sort of thing. But they had the excuse of being savages who didn't know better.

I once read that Julian the Apostate – the emperor, that is, who tried to restore the Old Religion fifty years after Constantine had established Christianity – sacrificed humans before setting out on his disastrous invasion of Persia. His palace in Constantinople, apparently, was found after his death stuffed with decaying bodies.

I don't believe this. Julian has a bad reputation, and the Christians have made up endless stories about him to drown out the rumours that they had him struck down from behind in his last battle. I know all Julian's writings, and I don't believe these stories. He may have been a superstitious pedant. But he wasn't a murderer.

Equally, though, human sacrifice was one of those things about the Old Religion that its devotees have always been rather coy about. And you can remember this if ever anyone comes at you with a word of that crap about the world of light and reason that the Church is said to have brought to an end. The Church may be a fraud. But it's never done this.

For a moment, I was torn. Lucius was my only friend in the world. He was doing this for me. But would Maximin have wanted this? Even had there been the slightest chance that this wretched human being was headed anywhere but into the blackness of death, could I have accepted the slightest scrap of information he might relay?

Non tali auxilio nec defensoribus isti, I thought to myself – 'Not by such means, nor with these defences.'

'Stop this at once!' I cried, stepping forward. 'I'll have no part in bloody murder.'

I took hold of the slave's arms and raised them to shut off the remaining flow of blood. He looked up to me, a weak, frightened look on his face. I saw his glassy eyes focus. He licked drily at his withered lips. 'I haven't been confessed, sir,' he whispered. 'Will God send me to Hell? I was a very bad slave – most inattentive to my duty. Will God punish me, sir?'

'No,' I said in a firm and priestly voice – the sort of voice that could banish all doubt by its very tone. 'In the name of the Father and of the Son, I absolve you of all your sins,' I continued, improvising. 'You stand on the verge of eternal bliss. Say with me this final prayer – say with me: Our Father, which art in Heaven . . .'

The slave croaked along with me, looking intently all the while into my eyes. As we finished those words, which for the first time sounded so marvellously sweet, I felt him begin his last rattling breath. He died with the 'Amen' upon his lips.

I dropped his arms and turned back to the shocked, silent gathering. The assistants were all on their bellies, knocking their heads against the floor in some scared, rhythmical prostration. Still on his feet, Lucius looked back at me with a white, terrified face.

'The Gods of the Underworld are loose among us,' the priest said with shaking voice. 'They will punish us according to Their Offended Will. This trespass into our holy rites of the Galilean Blasphemy they will never forget, and may never forgive.'

'There are no Gods – in the Underworld, or anywhere else,' I shouted at him. 'You're just a fucking murderer.' I glanced about the room. 'I'm looking for one decent reason not to drag the whole damned pack of you off before the dispensator. He'll see you punished, right enough.'

Of course, the man wouldn't look too kindly on me either. And I was in no position to drag half a dozen scared, reasonably strong men so much as an inch in any direction. That was reason enough.

I contented myself with kicking over the brazier. The charcoals flared up briefly and then dimmed again.

'The barbarian has profaned—' I cut off the priest's whine with a massive kick to his balls. He went down spluttering and gagging at the pain.

I walked out of the room, back along the corridor towards the light that came down from the library. As I walked back, every one of the recessed lamps went out exactly as I reached it. I was walking into light with darkness behind me. Draughts can be peculiar things.

4I

Lucius was onto his second jug of wine. I walked up and down in front of him, still trying to hold back the full weight of my anger.

'But Alaric, my love,' he wailed, 'desperate times call for desperate measures. We cannot go any further by the unaided light of reason.'

'Then let us go no further at all,' I snarled. 'I'm leaving Rome tomorrow. I'll take the first ship to Marseilles that I can find from Naples.'

'But the Gods—'

I put my face very close to his and said slowly: 'Lucius, there are no Gods. There is nothing but matter and space and time. There is no divine providence. There is no Judgement. Death is one eternal sleep.

'Certainly, your Gods don't exist. If they did, do you really suppose they would have given in so easily, that you people have to scurry round like rats in the sewers to worship them according to "ancient custom"? If there is any God at all,' I added flatly, 'it is the God of the Church.'

'That mass of corruption?' said Lucius, suddenly more effective in his argumentation.

'Yes, that mass of corruption. The Church may be rotten. But it is triumphant. Unless you look at the purely human causes, do you suppose anything so rotten could survive century after century – let alone flourish – without the continual, direct intervention of God?

'Those stupid books of yours give you as much ability to speak with the Gods as they show you how to make gold – and I haven't seen you do much of that in the time I've known you.'

I waved a contemptuous hand at the decayed grandeur of the library. As if in answer, I heard a gentle scurrying of mice in the still open doorway. No one else had come up. Either the others had left through another exit, or they were still down there, desperately trying to appease the imaginary demons I'd unleashed on the world.

I stood up. 'I'm going back to my lodgings. I'll send tomorrow for my bags. Let this be our parting. I'll get myself back alone.'

Lucius followed me to the main entrance. I stepped out into the fresh darkness of the night. Though full, the moon was clouded, but still gave sufficient light to get me through the streets. My sword would do the rest.

I walked a few yards. Then Lucius was beside me. His normal composure quite gone, he spoke from the heart. He was sorry – deeply sorry – for the horror I felt and for the shame he'd brought on himself. Yes, perhaps he was overly committed to the Old Gods. Perhaps not everything in their worship was seemly or desired by them. He'd been assured by the priest this was the truest way to unravelling the mystery. His own doubts had been broken down by that assurance. Now, he could see, there had been no divine presence in that underground chamber.

But he'd only had a slave killed – and his life was forfeit in any event. If I wanted, he'd have the other one set free from his chains and forgiven. He'd even free the man completely. Everything he'd done was for me. Didn't I realise how utterly devoted he was in all respects to me? Did I feel no atom of reciprocal affection?

As I describe his urgent pleading and protestations of love, they don't sound much excuse for the disgusting ritual I'd been too slow in breaking up. Here was a man who – whatever the exact legalities might have been regarding slaves – had just had a man murdered. I didn't for a moment believe it had all been on the priest's advice.

Behind that cool, ironic façade, Lucius was a man of brutish, ungoverned passions. Forget the sacrifice – I'd seen him tyrannising over his wretched slaves after One-Eye had got away. He was just like those wolfish ancestors of his who'd sat day after day, picnicking while men gored each other in the arena for their entertainment. For however short a time, he'd brought me to a better appreciation of the Church and its mission of genuine civilisation.

But you never met Lucius, or felt the bewitching effect of his charm. He was a superstitious bigot. He made that dreadful uncle of his in the Lateran another Epicurus by comparison. And I never could accept or understand his instinctive belief in the subhumanity of anyone who'd been unlucky enough to stand once on the auction block.

But he was Lucius, the smooth and wonderful Lucius, whose charm was like the rising sun. Phocas aside, who could ever resist him? He was all I had in the world. And I did love him after a fashion. Everything he'd done, I told myself, was done indeed for me. And – my pen hesitates in its course, but I will continue – he'd acted in good faith.

I stopped at a street corner, under the shade of one of those porticoes, now broken, that had once kept the sun and rain off the head in all the main streets. I embraced him.

'Oh, Alaric,' he wept, 'I thought for a moment I'd lost you. I promise you, I'll never do this again. I'll sacrifice again to the True Gods – but never again anything like this. And promise me that we shall never argue again.'

We stood hugging at each other and sobbing our reconciliation. Any street thieves who'd strolled by would have had an easy double target. But we were alone in the cool night air, the moon and a few stars overhead.

Marcella had been firm about no visitors after dark. But this wasn't a visitor, it was Lucius.

'Gretel! Gretel,' she cried, as we followed her billowing nightgown up to my rooms, 'wine for the young gentlemen – wine and refreshments against the cold air of the streets.

'And put your back into it,' she snarled, lifting her cane. 'When I'm visited by other persons of quality, we don't have them served like what is with the common trash.'

'That will be all,' I said to Gretel as she seemed inclined to linger in the main room. My tastes didn't yet run to threesomes, and I was beginning to suspect Lucius had no interest whatever in women. I changed back into my own clothes and took Lucius down the corridor to Maximin's old suite.

Lucius stretched his legs in the chair he'd taken and drank a little to clear his throat. He was back to business as usual. 'What he may have thought is a mystery into which we cannot enter,' he began. 'But we know all that Maximin did during his last day. He was called to the Lateran by the monk Ambrose. He was probably stopped by another message, sent by person or persons unknown. The slave Martin was involved in this deception, but I doubt as a principal. His function was to carry information back and take instructions. Maximin was then sent another message – almost certainly by the same – that probably called him again to the Lateran just as night was falling.

'We know his movements in some detail from this house down to where he was jumped and then taken off and murdered. We can also imagine why the body was placed beside the Column of Phocas – it was meant as some kind of offering to the emperor. We can be sure those letters that both the dispensator and the Column of Phocas want – assuming, of course, they are not one and the same – were not with Maximin at any time during his last day. He hadn't burnt them: there would have been evidence of that. But we can also at least suppose that he had read them the night before.

'The letters weren't with him on that last day, because he'd have had to hide them somewhere in the house. And we know that the house was searched by the professionals sent out by the dispensator who came for all his papers. Therefore,' Lucius sat up, a bright smile dawning on his face, 'therefore, he must have got rid of the letters some time between reading them and the beginning of our knowledge of his movements the following day.

'What a fool I am not to have seen this. It's so obvious. The Gods, it seems . . .'

In probable deference to me, he trailed off. I knew he wanted to claim that the Gods had spoken to him in their own way, after accepting his sacrifice.

He continued: 'Did Maximin go out the previous evening?'

'I don't know,' I said. 'I was with you. So, by the way, was Martin for much of the evening.'

But wait . . . I looked at the uncleaned boots over by the bed. It's strange how you can look at things and not see them for what they are. Maximin must have gone out! Hadn't I tripped over these boots, put out for cleaning, as I staggered in from the sacrifice? Maximin couldn't have been wearing those boots when he was murdered. No – he'd been wearing his nice boots, and they'd been taken off with his body to the Lateran. Hadn't it rained early the previous evening? Hadn't it rained the evening when I had taken as read that he'd been in all night?

I explained this to Lucius. He sat, looking for all the world like a clever schoolboy. 'I say, then,' he cried softly, 'those letters are with the Sisters of the Blessed Theodora. That's where he went the night before he died. Why else would he have said he was going there when he went out to be murdered? Anything else, and he'd surely have had the letters with him when attacked.

'No, Maximin was ordered in that last message to take the letters down to the Lateran. Before he could do that, he had to collect them. That meant going back to the Sisters of the Blessed Theodora. I don't like jumping to conclusions, as you know. But I'll break that rule tonight for my own reasons, and because the evidence is at least highly suggestive. He was going to the Sisters of the Blessed Theodora on his last evening because he'd already been there the evening before.'

He took another sip of his wine, repeating once more, and now with contemptuous relish, the name of the place. 'If only the Column of Phocas could have been a shade more patient, whatever was in those letters might by now be before the whole world.'

'But the abbess denied Maximin had been at the convent,' I said.

'Even if she had, why believe her unsupported word?' Lucius asked with a curl of his lip. 'Besides – though I don't have our notes with me – she didn't say that Maximin had *never* been to the convent. She only said he hadn't been there *on his last day*.'

'Then we must question her again,' I said. 'We can go as soon as the sun comes up.'

'We haven't much time,' Lucius agreed. 'But she might well tell us a direct lie if we ask a direct question. And then where does that leave us? Is there any objective evidence that Maximin was there?

'I think we should get Marcella back out of her bed this moment, and start reconstructing Maximin's probable movements from the time you and Martin left him.'

I thought suddenly of that slip of papyrus Maximin had used as a bookmark when I'd found him reading. What did this say? Was it blank? Was it some final message from him? Or was it the message that the child had brought?

I'd forgotten about it until now. It had passed me by in the confusion. But I thought more and more that it might have something to say that was valuable in one way or another.

'Is the library here unlocked?' Lucius asked after I'd told him about the thing.

It was unlocked. We crept in with a couple of lamps. If the old watchman were still awake and sober, he might come snooping. But this was only a guest looking up a reference. And the lord Basilius was with him.

I pulled down a book at random. It was an account of someone's journey to the shores of the Baltic. It looked interesting in its own right, but was hardly the sort of reading material to satisfy Maximin. I looked along the titles on the bookcase, taking down everything that was religious and about the size of the book I'd seen with Maximin.

We found the slip in – of all things – a life of Saint Vexilla. It marked a passage in which she made her long defence before Diocletian of the double nature of Christ – as if the old tyrant would have cared one way or the other about that: it simply dated what was said to be a contemporary record to after the beginning of the Monophysite dispute a hundred and fifty years after her alleged death.

I moved the lamp closer and strained over the faint writing: 'It was so good to see you again, and share memories of our dearest Jacob. You can trust absolutely in my discretion.'

There was no name at top or bottom of the message. I turned it over. In much fainter writing, I saw:

> *. . . tua nunc opera meae puellae*
> *flendo turgiduli rubent ocelli*

Lucius had been right about where Maximin had been. We had the woman! Serves the pious old philistine right if I now turned her convent upside down.

'What now?' I asked Lucius, back in my rooms.

He looked again at the message. 'My slaves will be back at dawn from their all-night deception,' he said. 'Until then, I suggest we sleep. It's been the most dreadfully long day, I'm sure you'll agree. I, at least, am quite fagged out. Who knows when we'll sleep tomorrow?'

Fully clothed, we lay down on my bed. I doubted I could sleep in all this excitement. But I was asleep almost before I was comfortable.

42

As agreed, the slaves returned just after dawn. They made a racket that got everyone up who wasn't already awake, and they stank of wine and cheap scent.

Lucius and I washed and took a private breakfast in my rooms. The sun was glinting at us over the tiles of the wing opposite.

'I don't think we should send ahead,' he suggested. 'The more warning she has, the more she may think of another deception.'

I agreed. But how could we get me again out of the house without being seen and followed?

'Confusing is deceiving,' said Lucius.

The slave who'd dressed in my clothes was to go out again alone, his head covered. Another was to go out with Lucius and the others, his head covered. Lucius would borrow another slave from Marcella to make up the number. Meanwhile, I was to slip out alone through the back door. If I thought I was followed, I was to make my way to the house of Lucius, who would think of another stratagem.

If I was successful at the convent, I was to hurry back to Lucius with reasonable but not paranoid caution. He would send slaves close by the convent to cover me as I came away. He'd make sure they were slaves I could recognise.

Though I couldn't be absolutely sure, I thought I got to the Convent alone. I knocked again on the door. The old man peered out through his little slot overhead.

'I have urgent business with the abbess,' I said. 'I come alone.' This time, my voice didn't allow of opposition.

Still dressed in black, the abbess was on her seat in the ruined library.

'Young man, this is most irregular . . .' she began.

I pushed the message under her nose.

'Father Maximin came to you the night before he was murdered,' I said harshly. 'He left property with you that is now mine. I want it back.'

She looked alarmed. She opened and closed her mouth. I thought she would call for assistance. Then her whole body seemed to relax. She looked back at me, the firm, Roman look on her face melting insensibly into despair.

I pulled up a chair from against the wall and sat down just opposite her.

'Your brother Jacob was a friend of Maximin's,' I said. 'I think we came upon his smashed monastery outside Populonium. All that happened to us after that followed from our encounter. You knew Maximin when he and your brother were students here in Rome.

'That is one reason why he came to you the night before he was murdered.'

I'd expected a denial, followed by a long argument. Instead, she was weeping. Her body didn't shake with sobs, but the tears ran in a continuous stream down her withered face.

'He was with you,' I said. 'You spoke carefully at our last meeting. But he was with you the night before.'

'We were young, so long ago,' she said when she could control her voice. 'You knew Maximin when he had grown into every inch the fat, jolly priest. I knew him when he was barely older than you. He was so intense and so devout – and yet so human . . .'

She spoke haltingly on – perhaps to me, perhaps to no one at all – about the brief yet passionate affair that had set their lives on different paths in search of the same redemption for their sins. She had retired to her grandfather's palace, hoping that endless piety and the destruction of ancient literature would atone for her weakness. He had become a missionary priest – for many years working among the village pagans who still spoke Greek in the south of Italy, and volunteering at last for the mission to England.

She spoke about their midnight assignations, about the thrill in her heart as he'd reached out for her, about the emptiness of all her life since then; about the joy that had rekindled on his last visit, and the chaste kiss they had exchanged as he stepped out of the convent to go off to his death.

'He spoke to me of you,' she said, looking up from her recollections. 'He was so proud of you, so very proud of your bright mind and essential goodness of heart. You know, you were the son we might, but for our callings to God, have brought ourselves into this world.

'When I saw you, a few days ago, I knew at once he was right.'

I forced back the lump that had come into my throat.

'Reverend Mother,' I said softly, 'We both loved Maximin. He was at all times everything the Church could want of a priest. If I could have taken his place on that final, dreadful evening, I would have done so with firm spirit. But the property he gave into your keeping will lead me to his murderers. I must ask for its return. I ask you to hand it into my own keeping.'

She rose and went to a locked cabinet. She opened it and drew out the leather bag I well remembered from that evening outside Populonium. It had been crudely stitched shut and sealed across with the sign of the English mission. She held it a moment, and then gave it to me.

'I know not its contents, but Maximin died to keep this safe,' she said. 'I know there has been a trail of death marking your return to it. I do beg you to be careful. Do you think Maximin would want you to throw away your own life in avenging his? There is a time for revenge, and a time for putting away revenge. I say this for Maximin, and I say it for myself.'

I took the bag into my hand.

'Do you think,' she asked as I left, 'that Maximin will be made a saint?'

'Yes,' I said. 'The miracles will undoubtedly be attested.'

I looked back at her from the doorway of the library. Still seated, she looked back at me. She had the sad eyes of the very lonely. She had lost and lost and lost.

*　　*　　*

With a flourish, I dumped the bag down in front of Lucius. He was seated in his library. With his own hands, he was cleaning off a phallus he'd once drawn on a page of the Gospels. A slave stood beside him with a battered relic box.

'We may expect a visit later today from the dispensator's men,' he explained, looking concerned. He turned to the slave. 'Remind me – who was that procurator of Judaea who put the Galilean carpenter to death?'

'It was Pontius Pilate, sir,' the slave replied, looking rather pleased with himself. As Lucius turned back to me, I saw the slave actually smile and kiss the relic box.

Lucius waved him out of the room. 'Well, this bag has a fine, letterly feel to it,' he said with sudden ebullience. 'Let's have a look inside.'

I broke the seal on my bag with my sword. I drew out the three letters to which I'd given so little attention, when the shortest glance could have saved four lives. Their seals had been broken and then resealed – again with the mark of the English mission. There could be no doubt now that Maximin had read the letters, and that he'd thought them just as important as we'd guessed.

One was a mass of elaborate squiggles that looked as impressive as it was meaningless. Another was in Greek. So far as I could understand the complex style, this was a translation of the first out of Persian. The third was in Latin. Lucius and I pressed close together over the table to read the tiny writing that covered the skin side of the parchment.

It was a letter from the pope to the Lombard king. It had all the right seals, and was drawn in exactly the same form as the copy letters I'd seen in Canterbury written to Ethelbert and his queen. I won't try to duplicate the windy recitation of titles with which these things begin, or the pompous language in which they are written. As it was, I had to read it twice to get the full meaning. I will instead summarise in a few words what was there expressed in a mass of words.

The pope was proposing a deal to the Lombards. Phocas was increasingly beleaguered in Constantinople. All the Eastern

Churches were on the edge of heresy or at least schism. Smaragdus, the exarch in Ravenna, was both mad and incapable of defending the True Church against its internal and external enemies. Bearing in mind the whole drift of the East, whoever replaced both emperor and exarch would be still less satisfactory as the civil power in Italy.

The pope therefore proposed that King Agilulf should lay close siege to Ravenna. This was impregnable from the land side, so long as it had unbroken access from the sea. But it could be cut off from all communication with northern and central Italy. This done, he should march on Rome. Outside the walls, he should convert before his whole army out of the Arian heresy into the True Faith of Rome. The pope would then allow him into the city, where he would be crowned emperor of the West.

The pope had this right of election, he claimed, on account of some grant of power by Constantine, which gave him supremacy throughout the West.

Standing together in the Lateran, the pope and new emperor should declare a twenty-year toleration of Arianism, during which time all peaceful means should be employed to convert the Lombards to the True Faith. In return for this election to the purple, the pope should get written confirmation that the Church was the supreme spiritual power in the West, and all military assistance possible to assert this status over any refractory Churches in France and Spain.

The cities of Italy, excluding Rome, should be ruled by joint councils of the Church and the Lombards, the surplus of any revenues to be shared equally. There was to be a common citizenship of the new Western Empire for all inhabitants of Italy, and a common obligation of service in both administration and army. All were to swear allegiance to pope and emperor jointly, and utterly to renounce allegiance to Constantinople, whether civil or military or religious. Rome was to be ruled jointly by pope and emperor, both of whom were to live there. It was to be the capital of the new Italy, with a revived Senate of Roman and Lombard nobles, who should be urged to intermarry and become a single order, and from which would be drawn all the highest officials of Church and State.

The pope had been in contact with Great King Chosroes of Persia, and with the Eastern barbarians. These were prepared, on acceptance of the terms proposed by Agilulf, to mount a coordinated attack on Constantinople. If successful, this would entirely destroy the Empire in the East. The imperial forces there, as directed by Phocas, would be outnumbered and outclassed. And there would now be no hope of reinforcements from Italy. In any event, the combined assault in the East would prevent reinforcements from being sent to Italy. There was also a strong possibility that the Ethiopians could be brought to invade Upper Egypt, thereby tying down still more of the imperial forces.

In token of his good faith, the pope signed his own name to the letter. In addition, he sent with it a sealed letter from the great king himself, together with one of the most holy relics of the Church and thirty pounds of gold. This would pay the first expenses of the march on Ravenna. A further three thousand pounds would be handed over once Agilulf had sealed his declaration of papal supremacy.

The letter was dated a few days before that encounter with the bandits on the road between Populonium and Telamon. The combined attack on the Empire was proposed for the early autumn.

The letter in Persian I couldn't read. But what I could follow of the Greek translation said enough. Great King Chosroes had written to Agilulf, confirming the proposed deal from the pope. He swore he would so far as possible tie up all imperial forces in the East, and would open full diplomatic relations with any emperor of the West on the same basis of equality as had long existed with Constantinople. Within a mass of Oriental flattery, he hailed Agilulf as his 'dearest brother' and 'Joint Eye of the World'.

43

We looked and looked at those letters.

I looked up first. It all made perfect sense to me. The emperor was clearly unable to protect Italy from the Lombards. But he was able to keep the Lombards from the peaceful enjoyment of what they had conquered. An alliance of pope and Lombard king would give Italy its first chance of peace in forty years. Indeed, with the Greeks sent off to fuck themselves, it would return Italy to the good old days of King Theodoric – only this time without the problem of heresy that had brought his experiment in coexistence to an early end. Who in Italy could object to this?

Lucius, I could see, objected. He was furious. I'd never seen him show the slightest concern for the common good. Now, he banged his fist on the table and was shaking with anger. 'Those shitty clerics!' he shouted. 'I should have guessed they were up to something like this. They'd make a pact with the Jews – no, they'd make a pact with their devil – if they thought it would advance the interests of their Church.

'You know something? When Alaric – the first Alaric, that is – was outside Rome, the pope of the day was told the city could be saved from sack by propitiating the Old Gods. Did he turn the advice down? Did he fuck! He said the ancient sacrifices could go ahead, but only if they were held in private to save his face. Because of that, Rome had its first foreign conqueror in a thousand years. Of course, there was a private deal before he was let in, and Alaric spared the churches.

'These people don't believe in anything but power! You know how they fuss on about heresy. Well, here they are, coolly offering to tolerate what they've always denounced as the most damnable heresy of all. So long as they get their hands on the full machinery of state, they're perfectly happy to share it with a bunch of Arians.' He paused and looked down again at the papal letter.

'But Lucius,' I protested, 'this would mean no more Phocas.'

He turned savagely to me. 'For all we know, sitting here, Phocas is already out of power. Whatever the case, he'll be out soon enough. If it isn't the exarch of Africa or his relatives, it'll be someone else. It'll be another of my noble relatives. He'll then set affairs right again.

'Yes, I'm no lover of Phocas. That doesn't mean I'll stand by and watch what's left of the Empire that my ancestors won with their blood and sweat handed over to a pack of fucking barbarians and clerics. It's bad enough to have barbarian kings in Italy. A barbarian emperor – a barbarian emperor tied by every possible interest to the Church? Never!'

He stood up and grabbed the letters, stuffing them back into the leather bag. 'I've been thinking for a while of a trip of Ravenna. Now, I'm going there with you.

'I had a message from the dispensator first thing this morning. He said he was sending men over to examine me for apostasy and blasphemy. The fucking nerve of it! Well, the next time I see him and that stinking old wreck Boniface, they'll be shitting themselves together in Ravenna as they face charges of treason.'

He turned to me and lowered his voice. 'And it might have all gone to plan if you hadn't stepped off that road outside Populonium. By now, those letters and all that went with them might now be with Agilulf.'

I broke in again: 'But surely, the exarch's men were on to this in any event? We ran straight into them.'

'And can you be sure they would have got there in time?' Lucius asked. 'Your One-Eye was well ahead of them. How do you know he's with the Column of Phocas? What do we really know about him, other than he's been hanging round you? Perhaps he killed Maximin. Perhaps he was up to something else that night.

'No, I can see now why the Church was so desperate to get those letters from Maximin once it was known he had them. As for the

Column of Phocas – as for that, you'll need to ask Phocas himself if you want an answer.'

'I don't think it's so uncertain as that,' I said, speaking slowly as I gathered my thoughts.

I'd known awhile that rendezvous outside Populonium was a big thing. I'd never imagined it involved the fate of the whole world. I knew nothing yet at first hand about high politics. One thing, however, was already plain. Little people who get involved in them see their lives changed fundamentally. Most often, their lives come to a sudden end. So it had been with Maximin. How much did I want to join him?

'Maximin wasn't killed by the Church,' I continued. 'All the dispensator wanted was those letters back. He could have had that from his summons to Maximin. It was the Column of Phocas that was so desperate to get the letters. Those are the people who stopped Maximin from going out. Those are the people who prevented the second summons. They called Maximin out eventually. They killed him.

'Why should I give the emperor's men what they killed Maximin to get? Why should I lift a finger against the Church that he died to protect?

'I say we burn the letters,' I insisted. 'We now know what happened. I say we burn the letters and forget their contents, except as may be required to get the bastards who killed Maximin.'

Lucius put the letters down in front of me. His hands shook still, but he now controlled his features. 'They are your letters,' he agreed. 'You must do with them as you think best. But let me put this to you. If Maximin was really trying to protect the Church, why didn't he burn these letters himself? At the least, why didn't he take them off unbidden to the dispensator? He'd have had the thanks of the Church, and in all likelihood preferment. A truly faithful Son of the Church would have had his reward in the simple handing back. Why did he seal them up again and put them somewhere safe? What was he intending to do with them?

'I'll tell you why, Alaric. Maximin was trained in Rome, and ordained into the Roman Church. But he was born in Ravenna, a citizen of the emperor. You say he was troubled on that last morning? Well, that's obviously because he felt a tug of loyalties – between pope and emperor. That's why he became so drunk and rambling as the day wore on. He couldn't decide where his real duty lay.

'Maximin is now dead. You are at least morally his heir. You owe it to his memory to make the choice he hadn't time to make for himself. I don't think destroying them is an option.'

Lucius reopened the bag and took the letters back out. He spread them in front of me. 'Let me now put this to you. If we take these letters to the dispensator, what will he do? He might say, "Thanks very much, my lad. Stay in Rome to your heart's content, and good luck with the investigation. Never mind the further trouble you cause me."

'Rather more likely, he'll have the pair of us done in before we can draw breath. He's already got a case against you. He wouldn't have trouble getting one against me – it's even now on his list of things to do for the day. Why should he let us get out alive? With or without those letters, we have information that could drag him straight down from that cushy eminence. I know how these clerics think. He'd watch the pair of us beheaded, and wouldn't miss a night's sleep over it.

'One thing I do promise, though,' Lucius said in a tone of finality. 'Even if the dispensator doesn't kill us, he's in no position to tell us who killed Maximin.'

He was right. What was it the dispensator had told me? 'You have no conception of what I can do in this city – or of what I will do to protect the interests of the Church.' He'd have us put out of the way, sure enough.

The exarch of Italy, on the other hand, might now benefit from the murder of Maximin. Almost certainly, the murderers were either his own men or men on his side. But put those letters into his hands, and there was more chance of getting to the bottom of the mystery than the dispensator could provide. The exarch had no reason to kill us, nor any to refuse me – if I were to help him now – whatever private revenge against his men I might care to demand.

Burning the letters was, indeed, not an option. It simply removed valuable evidence. I was faced with a choice: to whom should I give the letters? Pope or emperor? Exarch or dispensator? I cared little enough for any of them. If I were forced to choose, with no personal interest at stake, I'd have chosen the pope. At least his men hadn't laid hands on Maximin – not so far as I could tell. Moreover, I'd eaten his bread, and my life mission was now connected with the success of the Church mission in England.

But I wanted a truth that the dispensator couldn't give me, though the exarch might.

I replaced the letters in the bag and with a resigned sigh pushed it back to Lucius. 'We go to Ravenna,' I said.

Lucius turned and pulled some papers out of a cupboard. 'We leave today,' he said. 'We leave now. You've got enough luggage with you. I'll get you a horse.'

Lucius shouted for his slaves. In a moment, the house was in uproar, as they ran about filling bags with things for the journey.

The plan had been to send me off with a slave escort for protection on the road. Now, we were to travel light and alone. The dispensator would know almost at once what had happened. By then, however, we'd be out of Rome. By the time he could order armed guards to give chase, we'd be miles along the Flaminian Way. With our horses, and without armour to weigh us down, we'd easily outrun them, and keep ahead of any couriers sent on to intercept us. Fifty miles outside Rome, the temporal power of the Church began to fade. We could then trust in the letter of safe conduct he'd got from the exarch for his earlier journey.

Once in Ravenna, Lucius would show the letters. That would stop the whole plan. Whatever happened in the East, Italy would be saved from the unspeakable humiliation the Church had in mind for it. And I'd be at least closer to the truth about Maximin's death.

As I got myself into the riding clothes Lucius gave me, I heard the clatter of horses being led out of his stable.

44

Though, like all the other great roads of Italy, it starts from the Forum, the Flaminian Way ran fairly close by the house of Lucius. Because it is the main road to Ravenna, it was kept clear and in good order. We had to dismount a few times as we hurried down the side streets that led onto it. Once on the road, however, we were very soon at the Flaminian Gate. No message had reached the guards there, and we passed through unhindered. I didn't suppose even the dispensator could act that fast. Nevertheless, it was as if a weight had fallen from me as we passed through the heavy gate, the guards standing to attention for the lord Basilius.

Once out, we set a steady gallop. As we reached the great Milvian Bridge over the Tiber – the place where Constantine is said to have had the message from God that converted him – I looked back. I could see the high walls of the city, but as yet no pursuit. Within the walls, I could see the tops of the higher buildings.

I'd stopped noticing how bad the air was in Rome, or how built up the place was, even if much of it was ruined. Outside the walls, it was almost a shock to breathe clean air again, and to have an unbroken view all around me.

As before, the road was raised above the surrounding country-side, running straight and white into the distance. On our left was the Tiber, sliding further away from us as we travelled north; on our right the ruins of a civil order that had once reached far outside Rome.

Unlike on the Aurelian Way, we weren't alone. There was a thin but continuous stream of traffic: wagons laden with food and other goods for the Roman market, pilgrims coming in for the consecration or just to worship in the existing churches, the carriages and litters of the great. We passed a convoy of imperial couriers, bringing letters from the exarch. Covered in dust from the long journey, they now rode slowly, laughing and chatting. They called out a greeting as we passed them.

I looked back after a few miles. I shaded my eyes and squinted to see past the sun, which had risen high on my front left. My heart skipped a beat. There was a little cloud of dust in the south. The dispensator had at last got wind of our intentions, and had sent out a whole mounted brigade to ride us down. Another chase on a road. How would this one end?

Lucius looked back and laughed. 'They're too heavy and too far behind,' he cried, waving his cap joyfully. 'Unless they can grow wings on their horses, they'll never catch us.

'Come on! We'll be out of their reach by nightfall.'

This time, I was with a skilled horseman. Lucius rode beside me, explaining the proper use of the reins and spurs, and showing me the correct posture. We didn't seem to ride as fast as I had from those English mercenaries. The horse never once panted, let alone foamed. I didn't feel any jarring of my back or straining of muscles. But we kept a smooth, steady pace along the road. Every time I looked back, the cloud in the south was a little more distant.

'Even light armour is a drag on horses,' Lucius said. 'And they're keeping in formation.'

He pointed at a few tiny clouds of dust closer towards us. 'Those are the riders we need to watch,' he said. 'They aren't meant to stop us. Instead, they're to ride straight past and get an intercept at the next military station. If we try to stop them, the others will have a chance to get closer. We must keep well ahead of them.'

We rode on. There was a light breeze behind us to keep us cool in the hot sunshine. Lucius had a good look at everyone who rode past us in the opposite direction. He told me the advance couriers would co-opt every fast horseman they encountered. We'd soon have a small army on our backs. But we met no one who seemed to give him cause to quicken our speed.

After another few miles, we came to the first military station. This was based around a little fort built of reused materials. It stood on an earth mound, dominating the road and country. Some imperial foot soldiers lounged by a bar at about waist height that closed the road.

'Important business with the exarch,' Lucius called as we approached. 'Get that bar raised.'

The officer in charge darted a glance at the letter Lucius held under his nose. With a barked order, the bar was up and we were through.

'No horsemen back there or fresh mounts,' he said quickly. 'The Gods are with us today.'

We rode on through the afternoon. We stopped briefly a few times to water the horses and to stretch ourselves. As we got further away from Rome, and as the light of the late afternoon began to fade, the traffic grew thinner. There were fewer ruins along the road, and the countryside became wilder, with larger and larger clumps of bushes and small trees to give cover should it be needed.

As the light faded entirely, I looked back along the road from a high ridge. Could I see a small cloud in the distance? Or was it a trick of the dying light?

We came to a fortified post inn. In those days, Italy was still covered with these. They had been built in ancient times every so far apart along the main roads. There were fewer of them on the roads with every return journey I made there. I believe they are all ruined now. On my first visit, they were still in something like their old operation. This was the road that connected Rome with Ravenna.

All around – often very close – were the domains of the Lombards. The road had at all times to be kept open for communications. Every strategic point was fortified and controlled. The post inns were important links in that chain of control. They were also places where ordinary travellers could get a meal and a safe bed for the night. For those on official business, there was the added benefit of being able to change horses. Every inn had its stables and its many horses in continual readiness to speed those travellers with the relevant influence. The prohibitions of using the posts for private business had long since broken down. The whole operation now ran on a cash basis. But Lucius showed his letter from the exarch, and this got us the pick of the horses available.

Inside the gate, I could see that the inn had been built on a generous scale. On two storeys around the main courtyard, it offered individual rooms for travellers of quality, with descending levels of comfort for the humbler, and a good kitchen and eating area on the ground floor.

It was crowded when we arrived. The Lombards were still on the prowl after that cold winter, and everyone who could scrape together the minimal price of entry had squeezed himself in for the night. No stopping for us, however. A satchel of bread and wine and a change of horses, and we were off again. With the dispensator's men in hot pursuit, we'd take our chance with the Lombards. We were two powerful men. We had fast horses. We were armed. It would be a desperate raiding party that tried to interfere with us on the road.

'We'll ride as long as we can through the night,' Lucius told me. I suggested hamstringing the other horses in the stable. But there were too many, and we might be caught. We paid and rode off.

We rode until the moon was high overhead and until little puffs of steam came from the horses in the chilly night air. We stopped in a small grove high beside the road. This allowed a fine view back along the road. We didn't bother with a fire, but sat down on a fallen tree and ate what we'd bought.

Lucius questioned me again about my life in England. I told him of the broken-down house in Richborough, and Auxilius, who with his loving pedantry had given me a key to the world beyond. I told him of the humiliations that had attended our fall from nobility and the increasingly desperate shifts by which I'd supplemented Ethelbert's dwindling charity. I spoke of my dead mother.

'Not that much difference between us, then,' said Lucius when I'd finished. 'We both come from families pushed below their proper station in life. The Gods willing, though, we'll rise together all the way back to what we were born to, and – who knows? – we'll die higher yet.'

He told me nothing in continuous narrative about himself. From the disjointed anecdotes he gave me instead, I gathered his parents had died in one of the plagues when he was very young. He'd then been handed around various grandparents and uncles, getting scraps here and there of an education, while his family had wondered what to do with him.

At last, the plagues had done him a favour. 'It was like an invisible beast,' he said, 'the sort that comes again and again, but always takes others and never yourself.' While he grew up without a day's illness, all his relatives had sickened and died. His grandfather made sure to give the bulk of it away to the Church in his will, but Lucius had finally come into the full remaining wealth of the family. And he would have had more, but for those charges of treason laid in Constantinople against his one genuinely rich relative.

'The man is trash,' I agreed, hoping to deflect him from another of his denunciations of Phocas. 'But when you came back to Rome, was it to be forever?'

'Don't forget, Alaric,' the reply came, 'I am a Roman. The city is my world – this city and all that is natural to it.'

He'd come back to Rome, he then admitted, with no apparent alternative to settling into the life of a decayed noble. Except for his deep – if inconveniently placed – religious feelings, he was no different from any other member of the Roman nobility. He repeated himself: 'I am a Roman, and the city is my world.'

He'd thought at first to refuse the invite to that dinner party. It was too painful, he said, to look at what he was sure he was now fated to become. All that had got him along there in the end was the chance to see the learned yet deadly barbarian from far-distant Britain. And he had met me.

'And now,' he concluded, 'we are both fugitives from Rome on our way to what I hope will be a hero's reception in Ravenna. The Old Gods have a sense of humour – and, I think, of justice.'

When the moon had risen high above, we took turns at sleeping, the other keeping watch. A few night birds aside, and the rustling of nocturnal animals in the undergrowth, I heard nothing. As I lay down to sleep, it was for all the world as if Rome had been a bad dream, and I was still travelling there with Maximin. Except the weather was far more clement, it was like any other night we'd spent camping out in the open.

'They're still following,' said Lucius, prodding me awake. 'But they are a long way behind.'

I heaved myself up in the first light of morning. Whatever dreams I'd been having vanished beyond recall. I was stiff and cold. But the sun was rising in a clear sky. This would be another lovely day, though a little cloud cover would have been better for the horses.

I looked beyond the arm that Lucius extended back along the road. Far in the distance, I could see the faint glint of armour in the pale sunlight. For some while, we'd been riding uphill. We were passing into the range of hills and mountains that run down the centre of Italy. Far below us, shining like ants after a storm, our pursuers toiled forward in search of a quarry they themselves couldn't see. But still they came.

Lucius bent and stretched some life back into his stiff muscles. 'If we can keep ahead of them till nightfall,' he said, 'we'll be far outside the zone of papal influence. They can keep following, but their ability to command help will be at an end. By tomorrow, I'll be able to use the exarch's name to slow them down, or even have them turned back.'

We still had to look out for the lighter, faster pursuers. And we were making slower progress as we rode continually uphill. But there came a moment when, though we looked back, we saw no one in pursuit. No matter how I squinted back into the sunlight, I saw no pursuit.

'We haven't outrun them,' said Lucius during one of our little stops. 'They're still back there, and any delay on our side will bring them back into sight. Don't forget how desperate they are. But they'll need all the luck in the world to catch us now.'

Because these high lands had never been much settled even in ancient times, there were fewer signs of recent devastation. I saw a few abandoned villages and a few broken temples. But these were so weathered and overgrown, they might have been out of use for centuries, perhaps even before the making of the law to close them all down. I wondered if the inscriptions that covered the fallen columns were in Latin or in that older language I'd seen in Populonium. But Lucius made sure to keep me moving on the road.

We spoke about women. As I'd thought, Lucius had no taste for them whatever. He'd once considered marriage. But this had been purely for cash. And her father had broken off the engagement when a more substantial catch arrived suddenly from Carthage.

He'd found release in his better-looking slaves, and sometimes in the boys who were laid on for anyone in the nobility or higher offices of the Church who wanted their services. Then his friend the priest had persuaded him to a life of semi-continence – he'd been assured it made him a more fitting instrument for the will of their Gods.

Either the adherents of the Old Religion had cleaned up their act in competition with the Church, or those declamations I'd read against their lustful ways were just lies. Whatever the case, his own priests weren't unaware of how sex blunts the religious sensibilities. That may be why I've had so few of them – not even when I was posing as a bishop. Lucius had learnt to contain himself. Then he'd met me.

He asked me again about Edwina. Feeling the jealousy behind his playful tone, I spoke lightly of her. I said nothing of the love that had burnt – and still sometimes did burn – in my heart.

Though the sun shone bright overhead, the air was crisp. We passed streams and waterfalls. These were swollen with the snow from the mountains that rose about us. The tops of the mountains shone white in the sun. Even from a distance, I could see how densely the tops were fringed with the deep greens of the trees.

The rains and ruin of winter were over. All around us, later than on the plains, I could see the world coming back to life. Not for the first or the last time, I was forcibly impressed by the wondrous beauty of the nature in Italy.

Once, we passed a group of free peasants, taking their produce to some town along the road before us. We bought some food from them. For a few silver coins, they agreed to climb up to an outcrop above the road and force a rock fall that left a ten-foot-long band of jagged rocks. It took a while to supervise the work, but probably bought us much more time than we spent. It would take days to get that lot clear. Just getting horses over it would take long enough.

Onwards and upwards, the road extended. It cut through peaks and ran on bridges across the deeper ravines. Hardly once did it deviate from a straight line, and then only to skirt something that even the ancients didn't think it worth trying to overcome. It must have taken years and whole armies of slaves to build. Lucius had barely any of the historical knowledge of Italy outside Rome that had allowed Maximin to bring the vanished past to life. But I could imagine the settled, populous Italy of earnest officials and competent engineers who had strained every nerve to push these lines of domination to the farthest corners.

We rode all day. In the evening, we stopped at another post inn. This was smaller, but otherwise just like the one at which we'd stopped the previous evening. We ate a meal of meat and bread. After a change of horses, we were off again. As before, we took turns to sleep and keep watch in the open. As before, we were undisturbed.

45

We ran into trouble on our third day on the road, this being a Thursday. We were just coming out of a particularly wild and quiet stretch of road. We were deep into the afternoon. The sun shone. The birds sang. There was no other noise but the sound of our horses, as their hooves clattered slowly on the road, and our few words of desultory conversation.

We rode over a small hill and down into a shallow depression. As we reached the bottom, I heard a sound to my left. It was the bridling of a tethered horse.

Lucius reached over and clutched at my arm. Before us, the road was blocked, just before the peak of the rise out of the depression, by eight men. Big, with the usual plaited hair and long moustaches, they were lightly armed irregulars. Whether they were Lombards or imperial mercenaries was impossible to say. They might even have been bandits, in search of valuables from the few passers-by. It was impossible to tell. They all looked alike in those days.

They weren't bandits. That much was soon clear. We'd come on them by surprise. They were still wandering about after a slow lunch. But, if they hadn't expected us just at that moment, there was no doubt they had been expecting us. Though on foot, they blocked the road in a broad, muscled mass.

One of them stood forward. 'Lucius Decius Basilius and Aelric of England,' he said in a thick Germanic accent, 'we have orders to apprehend you for returning to Rome. You will dismount now and lay down your weapons.'

He spoke with an easy confidence. The men behind him drew their swords and grinned. They knew their business. They wanted none, but were prepared for trouble. Dead or alive, we were to be taken and sent back to the dispensator. What he'd do with us I could hardly guess.

I looked round. There were now two men behind us. On our right was a sheer cliff, on our left a gentle descent through trees so tightly packed together, I could hardly see beyond the tethered horses.

There was no point in denying who we were. We were trapped. If we were to escape at all, it would be by going back – and we knew what was back there. Even if we did make a dash for it, we'd be in the jaws of a closing trap.

'How the fuck . . .?' I heard Lucius mutter.

I thought the same. How could anyone have got ahead of us? Our pursuers must have been twenty miles back, if that close. There was no shorter route than the one we were taking. Lucius had joked about growing wings on horses. It seemed the Church had managed just that. Was this some genuine miracle of the Church?

'Dismount now and lay down your weapons,' the leader repeated, now louder.

Lucius pulled the reigns of his horse tight and drew his sword. I did the same. I'd left that heavy old Frankish sword behind in Rome. I had with me only the shorter sword Lucius had given me. But I tested its balance again, and looked at the bright gleam on its sharpened edges.

The men stood about ten yards before us, now spaced out on the road two deep. They knew exactly what they were doing. Breaking through might not be impossible, but would require great force and as much speed as we could manage uphill.

If anything in my narrative so far may have inclined you to despise the Roman nobility, let me assure you it doesn't apply to Lucius. Whatever else he had of his great ancestors, he had all their courage and cool nerve. Lucius had many faults. But he was no coward. If he was to go back to Rome, it would be as a corpse tied across the saddle of his horse. Alive, he'd go on to Ravenna.

Even before the leader of that group had stepped back to take his place in the picket, Lucius had spurred up his horse. He shot forward and upwards like an athlete starting a footrace. I followed close behind.

In a moment, we were on them. In a single, fluid motion, Lucius raised himself on his stirrups and leaned over to his right. With a bright, slashing arc of his sword, he had the head clean off the leader of the men. The head flew into the air. Spurting blood, the body continued standing. It must eventually have buckled and fallen over. But I didn't see this. What I did see was like watching corn cut with a scythe.

Lucius twisted his sword upright and struck hard with the pommel at another who tried to clutch at the reins of his horse. He got a massive, bone-shattering blow to the man's head, and was through, whooping and yelling as he picked up speed. Before anyone could turn, he was over the ridge and shooting down the other side.

I followed. I wasn't so skilful or lucky. I got one of the men. But it was one of those glancing blows to the collarbone that has a recoil. I had just the briefest moment of instability. But that was enough. Two pairs of hands grabbed at the bridle of my horse. I felt another hand from behind dragging at the saddle.

I wheeled the horse round and tried to scatter the men. But they stood just away from me in a tight group. Whichever way I looked, they stood in a close mass not six feet away. They saw no reason to push their luck as individuals by coming closer. But there was no chance of gathering the momentum to break through them.

I came to a halt in the middle of the group. I looked round at the sweaty, grinning faces.

'We've got you, my lad!' one of them gloated. 'You're coming back with us.'

'There's business waiting for you in Rome,' another said in English. I should have guessed from their appearance and efficiency that they were my people, and not just any old barbarians.

There was a laugh behind me. It had no words attached. But the meaning was plain. It needed no words. I might try and pretend I was some stuck-up Roman, with my good riding clothes and fancy Latin. But what was I really but another English barbarian on the make? I was no better than them. And they'd do their best to make sure I was soon much worse.

I was annoyed. I was frustrated. But I wasn't frightened. I'd wanted to go on to Ravenna with Lucius. But the important thing was that he'd got away. Taken back to Rome together, I didn't doubt the dispensator would have seen to it that our headless bodies were washed up in Ostia. But Lucius was going on to Ravenna. This put me into a different position. The dispensator might try at the worst to use me as a bargaining counter with Lucius and the exarch. He was far too intelligent to give in to any temptation of revenge.

I lifted my right foot from its stirrup as I prepared to swing myself off the horse.

There was a sudden clatter behind me of hooves on paving stones. The men just in front of me clutched at their swords.

'Eat shit and die, motherfucking scum!' I heard Lucius cry from just behind me. I heard a terrified scream that bubbled and stopped. Even before then, Lucius was in front of me, slashing to right and left.

I steadied myself in the saddle, striking out at one of the men who'd turned his back on me. I felt the heavy impact of steel on bone as I got him on the neck. I got the sword free and steadied myself again.

Lucius was twisting in his saddle, and was slashing out to left and right. As if they'd been a team all its life, the horse danced beneath him, sometimes trampling the fallen, sometimes avoiding the obstacles of their bodies. I saw the wild bloodlust in Lucius's eyes as he sliced at the men, shouting obscene abuse in Latin and in Lombardic.

I got myself alongside him, and cut down another of the men. It was a good blow that took his sword arm off at the shoulder. I followed this with a raking blow across the throat that started another fountain of blood.

'No survivors from this, I think,' said Lucius in a conversational tone, as he steadied my horse with his free hand. 'We get them all.'

I needed no encouragement. On horseback, ten against two would have been decisive in their favour. Even the four left still on their feet outnumbered us. But if they had expected us, perhaps the men hadn't expected us to be with them so soon. Or perhaps they hadn't expected serious resistance. Whatever the case, the real fact was they were on foot. They'd been dismounted when we came on them, and hadn't had time to mount. That was their undoing. They hadn't even the slim advantage that so many footmen would have had against cavalry. They were too used to fighting on horseback. They'd almost have been more effective without swords than without horses.

They ran about as individuals, making a poor effort with their swords as they jabbed and waved without the familiar height and mobility. Lucius darted among the men, shepherding them back to the centre of the road, where we could ride them down, cutting off every escape into the cover of the trees.

I can't say how long the fight raged, or what my own movements were. I only remember shouting and slicing and stabbing at everything I found beneath me on the road. My horse jerked me around continually, and half my own fight was to stay mounted. A few times, I noticed how the sword Lucius had given me was short by a few inches of the ideal for heavy fighting. But I know I hacked and sliced and stabbed wildly in that depression of the road.

One of those men ran at me with greater presence of mind than the others. He made a stab towards the underside of my horse. I got him a stab right in the mouth. There was a splitting of teeth and grating of bone. Then I was through with my sword. I pulled back the blade, and he went straight down, threshing out his lifeblood on the road.

At last, there were only two men left standing. They gave us a final, desperate look, and made a dash for the side of the road. I screamed something nasty in one of my various languages and spurred my horse forward. Lucius followed.

We each caught one before he could get to his horse. Lucius made short work of his. I cut mine about horribly before he fell down. Then I got down myself and pushed with all my weight through his ribs until he stopped moving.

While I sat gasping and waiting for the red mist to pass from just inside my eyes, Lucius made a tour of the carnage on the road. His face expressionless, I watched him cut the throats of the wounded, carefully stepping back each time to avoid the gush of blood. One tried to avoid the knife with a wail of terrified pleas. It might have been the cry of a stricken deer for all the effect it had on Lucius.

He passed from this to an examination of the tethered horses. I looked at him and then back at the road. In the golden sun of late afternoon, the paving stones of the road were a deep and slimy red, and were littered with bodies and body parts. I saw one body lying with its head split in two from crown to jaw. I'd done that, I vaguely remembered.

It was a fine sight, I suppose. I'd so far killed about twelve men – forgetting the churl I'd accidentally pushed over a cliff above Dover. That was a good total for a man of my age and quality who'd never yet fought in a regular battle. This kill had been a good one, almost worth commemorating in verse. But it didn't register. I was as if in a dream. All it meant to me at the time was that I wasn't going back to Rome until I was ready.

As cool as iced water, Lucius counted the horses and assessed their power and speed. He found nothing written in their bags. Again, he ignored my suggestion to hamstring them. Instead, he cut away the leather ties that attached saddles and bridles. They would be unharmed but useless to anyone who found them. Then, with a shout and a few jabs from his sword, he drove them off into the woods.

He turned to me. 'Mount up, my Alaric,' he said. 'Don't ask me how the dispensator got these men ahead of us. But if he can get some ahead, he might get others. Let's press on.'

We mounted and galloped forward along the road.

In ancient times, some of the Greeks used to fill their armies with lovers. It made the armies into invincible fighting machines – though not in the end against the Romans. I felt the power of that force as we tore along the road. That moment of calm as I'd sat in the road had passed. Now, we raced through the late afternoon. My body was on fire with an exultation I'd never before felt. To speed over those paving stones with Lucius beside me was better than the best sex I'd ever had. We rode on and on, until the horses began to falter.

Then we stopped.

We stopped beside another of those little streams and watered our horses. As we washed the blood and gore from our own bodies, I noticed for the first time that I'd been wounded. The left sleeve of my riding tunic was slashed down to the wrist. There was a deep vertical gash on my arm underneath. There was another shallow puncture in my left side. How I'd got these I couldn't imagine. I'd felt nothing at the time, nor afterwards. Now, I sat beside the stream feeling suddenly weak and cold as the blood poured down my arm in a crimson stream. I could see the parted skin hanging loose in flaps.

Lucius washed and dressed the wounds.

'I don't think this will turn bad,' he said grimly. 'But I guarantee it will hurt by nightfall like nothing you've ever felt.'

'Thank you for coming back, Lucius,' I said feebly.

Lucius stood over me, looking down. 'How could you possibly think I would ever have gone off without you?' he asked. 'You are my beautiful young Alaric. You are the sun that illuminates my soul. So long as I live, I will never leave you, my golden love, my everything. We go together through life, or not at all.

'Fuck the letters in my bag,' he added, more lightly. 'I couldn't go off without you.'

'We made a proper mess back there,' I said. Well, *Lucius* had made a proper mess. All I'd done was blunder about like a drunk in a tavern. I took another gulp of the wine he held out, and looked at the notches cut here and there in my now blunted sword.

'You fought well,' said Lucius firmly. 'You have strength and speed. You have the courage of your noble fathers. All you need more is the practice that brings them together. We'll see to that in Ravenna, when everything else is over.

'And you'll soon enough have a lovely scar to show off in the baths.' Lucius grinned as he helped me back onto my horse.

I could have managed a longer rest. But Lucius was right. How the dispensator had got an interception party ahead of us was beyond our imagining. But if he could get one, there might easily be others. We needed to get out of the papal zone as quickly as we could.

46

I felt a decided chill as the evening came on. At first, I thought it was the change of temperature. Then I began to sweat. A concern on his face that worried me, Lucius kept looking at me in the failing light. I felt nothing in my side. But, as he'd promised, the wound on my arm had begun to throb, sending spasms of pain up into my neck.

We came to another post inn. Lucius dithered a while over the keeper's offer of a bed for the night. In the end, he showed the exarch's letter to get us fresh horses, and bought some food and some drugs.

I don't know if it was the drugs or the rising fever, but I rode on through the night feeling increasingly detached from my body. I began to sing snatches of ballads in English, alternating these with long passages of the Lucretius I'd read in the library of Anicius. They made an incongruous match – the unreflecting joys of battle and the hunt, and that sombre meditation on the futility of life.

Lucius tried to quieten me several times. But I was hardly aware of his company. I raved on in a feeble croak until my throat was dry as dust and I called for wine. Lucius gave me sips of water. Several times, I thought he was Maximin, and questioned him about the finer points of the Monophysite controversy. I shouted impatiently at him as he failed to answer my queries about the perfect union of God and Man in a single substance.

I then thought Lucius was one of my fellows in that raiding party I'd briefly joined on the Wessex border. I jabbered on and on in English about nothing in particular.

Then everything seemed to clear, and I was sitting on horseback beside that broken sewer in Rome. It was night again, and I could see without any moon above. Lucius sat beside me on the left. Again, there was the heavy crunch of footsteps on the steps. It was coming closer, and I could hear the rough, laboured breathing of something unaccustomed to movement, but still immensely powerful.

This time, we didn't turn and run. We continued to sit, looking down from horseback at the awful blackness of the sewer.

'There's nothing to fear, do be assured,' Lucius said. His voice shook, giving the lie to his words.

'We must see what it is,' I agreed. My teeth began to chatter.

Suddenly, Maximin – or was it the diplomat? – stood beside me to my right. Sometimes it was one, sometimes the other, sometimes both at once. I looked at the shouting face and felt the gentle breeze fanned up by the frantic gestures. But I heard nothing.

I turned back to the sewer opening. Something was coming out. It was big. It was dark. It was—

And now I was back on the road with Lucius. The moon was bright overhead, and I could hear the sound of eight hooves on the road. My teeth were chattering in reality, I was very cold, and Lucius was leaning over to support me.

I know that, after a while, I couldn't sit up on the horse. I felt as tired and as weak as a kitten. Lucius stopped and laid me across the horse. We rode on through the night at a very slow pace. We compensated as best we could by not stopping.

By the morning, I felt some return to coherence. Still very weak, I wasn't up to any galloping. But I could at least now sit on the horse and ride slowly beside Lucius.

At a watering place for the horses, we came upon an armed carriage. Its main passenger was a Greek official on his way to Rimini to hand in some cadastral reports his subordinates had made up for him. Lucius showed his magic letter from the exarch, and I was soon wrapped up in the back seat of the carriage. A slave woman dabbed at my fevered brow, and poured some poppy juice down my throat.

This was one of those carriages that you still saw in those days – partly closed, partly open. The main bumping of the road was kept away with leather straps that secured the seating to the main body. I was soon deliciously comfortable.

The Greek travelled on my horse to reduce the load and allow us to keep up a decent speed.

Lucius rode beside the carriage. As I drifted off into a drug-induced sleep, I asked him where he'd got his knowledge of the Lombard language. I thought he knew only Latin. He explained that he'd been taught to ride and fight by a Lombard captive when he was about my age. He didn't know enough to hold a proper conversation. Besides, everyone in the Lombard nobility had now learnt Latin rather well. And even the humbler Lombards could speak it after a fashion. But he'd picked up most of the riper expressions from his teacher, and these came out as if naturally in moments of great danger.

'Did you never think of a military career?' I asked him.

'No,' he said shortly. 'The days when people like me got given armies to command were over long ago. The Christian emperors made sure to downgrade our place in the world to serving in the civil administration, or to whatever scholarly or other leisure we could organise for ourselves. We were too unreliable for the new order that Diocletian created and Constantine perfected.

'The armies are for Greek professionals or barbarian mercenaries. My father was prefect once, and had regular meetings with Narses, the first exarch. He was a fine general, but he started out as a eunuch in the Imperial Household. Until Phocas popped up, it made for stability – even if, the occasional Narses aside, it didn't bring inspired leadership.'

I felt the longing and regret that Lucius hid behind his increasingly smooth flow of explanation. I know he'd have made a brilliant general of the old style. He'd have kept the Lombard out of Italy. Even now, he could have cleared them out. Was this why he'd been so visibly upset by the settlement proposed by the Church?

I slept. I was distantly aware of when we were passing over the compacted gravel that gave us a smoother but slower ride, and then over the great paving slabs that had us swinging and jerking about on our leather suspension.

We rode on. The road stretched on, seemingly forever. We came to a tunnel cut through the rock. We stopped awhile in its shade, and Lucius supervised a change of dressings to my wounds. There was no visible suppuration, I was conscious enough to notice, and the wound in my side was beginning to heal. But, even through the weak opium I'd been given, I could feel my arm stiff and burning. Lucius washed it himself with cold water and rubbed some ointment he'd bought at another of the inns from a travelling apothecary. He accompanied this with some muttered incantations. Either the little Greek on my horse didn't notice, or he didn't care.

In the evening, the fever returned with similar force, and we had to go very slowly. The Greek was in a hurry, and didn't like the delay. But the only person to my knowledge with whom Lucius never managed to pull rank was the emperor himself. Everyone else just fitted around him.

In between short waking spells, I dreamt fitfully through the night. I dreamt that Maximin was looking down at me from heaven. He sat beside a severe, iconic Christ; on his face the same troubled look I'd seen him wearing the last time I'd seen him alive. He spoke to me, but I was again unable to hear what he said.

I dreamt, or think I did, that a wolf came close by the carriage. Lucius and the guards chased it away with their drawn swords.

Then I was back in Rome, though not this time by the broken sewer. I was now with the dispensator. He sat in his office, looking at me with his usual slight distaste. He spoke to me, but no sound came from his lips. He spoke to me again. Still I couldn't hear or understand. Now impatient, he took me to the door of his office. The entrance hall and labyrinth of tunnels at the front of the Lateran had been abolished. The door of his office opened straight onto the square outside.

Again, I saw that slow, silent triumphal procession. The emperor was shrouded in purple. His carriage stopped close by me. He pointed and pointed at me, until I realised he wanted me to join the procession in my allotted place at the back with the other barbarian prisoners. The flutists and drummers never once stopped their silent, convoluted playing.

I woke bathed in sweat, with the first light of dawn stealing over the rocky landscape from our right. My arm still hurt, but I felt that I was recovering from the fever.

By now, Lucius was increasingly sure we were safe. Closer to Ravenna than to Rome, we were deep into the exarch's zone of rule. We were passing rapidly down towards sea level, and the air was became appreciably warmer and more oppressive.

We thanked the Greek, and I got unsteadily but with returning strength into my saddle. My last sight of them was far back along the road, where they'd stopped for breakfast.

At Fano, on the Adriatic coast, we turned northwest, following the coastal road towards Rimini.

That evening, there was no return of the fever, and we were able to take turns again at sleeping and watching. But we did this, Lucius said, from simple caution. Even if the dispensator had worked some other miracle, he could have us murdered, or perhaps kidnapped. He was no longer able to have us arrested.

We spoke awhile about nothing in particular. But Lucius was concerned that I should sleep as much as possible.

We passed the sixth day of our journey on the long road between Pesaro and Rimini. On our left, approached by long spurs from the main road, stood walled towns. I could hear the church bells ringing for the Sunday service. Needless to say, we didn't stop to go in and pray anywhere.

On our right was the Adriatic. Looking out over the flat, gentle expanse of water, I could see the stream of warships and trading ships that connected this outpost of the Empire with the gorgeous East. I could hear the dull, rhythmical thump of the drums that kept the naval oarsman in time together. The trading ships were decked with sails of frequently gorgeous colour.

The East itself was preparing for some struggle of life or death from which it might not emerge. Here, on the edge of the directly ruled Empire, trade and the process of such government as was possible continued as normal. This, I reflected, was how our myrrh must have arrived.

The road was filled with merchants and wheeled traffic and the litters of the wealthy. The occasional band of soldiers passed by us. They gave me an interested look, but returned the greetings Lucius called to them.

That evening, we stopped at another of those inns. Lucius spent a long time after dinner questioning the keeper and the other guests about the news from Ravenna and the East. The wars were going uniformly ill for Phocas. There were rumours of a joint attack by the Persians and barbarians on Constantinople itself. The city couldn't be taken with those huge double walls that surrounded it and its unbroken command of the seas. But how long could the Empire last with just the capital intact? The provinces, I was told, were either occupied by various enemies or falling away of their own accord.

The main topic of discussion was how long it would be before our exarch in Ravenna declared for one of the African exarch's sons or some other candidate. There was no fresh news from Carthage or Constantinople. We had a drink with some merchants from Antioch. They told us the city was dissolving into endemic violence between the Greek and Jewish communities. Meanwhile, the Syriac majority was growing more open in its heresy and preparing to receive the Persian king, whenever he should make his expected full descent on Syria.

This was news, I thought with a sudden rush of greed, that would convert easily to gold on the Roman markets.

We had no fresh news from Rome – not that anyone now could possibly have overtaken us. No one had even yet heard that the pope was back from Naples. Circuitously but at length, Lucius questioned everyone about any groups of armed men who weren't obviously connected with the exarch. There had been no one.

For the first time since leaving Rome, we bathed and passed the night in a bed. I cuddled up close to Lucius in the warm night air, feeling a vague obligation to have sex with him. But he was asleep even before I drifted off. I'd slept badly on the road, he hardly at all with the work of looking after me. I dreamt in disjointed flashes of Rome and the many comforts of Marcella's house. There was nothing frightening in my dreams.

In the morning, we exercised away some of the stiffness of the long ride behind us, and bathed again after a leisurely breakfast. I managed a small quantity of bread soaked in olive oil. Lucius allowed me no wine.

We set out on fresh horses. I could feel the definite return of health and strength, and I delighted in the warm sea breeze and my clean clothing.

We skirted Rimini. I could see from a distant inspection that this was still a substantial town within its walls. But Lucius insisted we shouldn't spend any time there. Except for our inexplicable brush on the third afternoon of our journey, we'd passed unchallenged.

'Best not push our luck,' he said, after pointing out the main sights that could be seen above the distant walls. 'You can tour to your heart's content once our business with the exarch is out of the way.'

In the early afternoon, we entered a small town. This had shrivelled to a core within its walls. Most of the buildings outside this core had collapsed, and some of the materials had been used again for the construction of churches or heavier fortifications. But it had a bustling market and a wine shop where we could sit down and eat our first proper meal in days. Lucius fed me some thin gruel sweetened with honey to cover the bitterness of the drugs he'd added. I managed to swallow most of this. He kept the wine heavily watered.

'Can't have you drunk as well as half dead,' he joked.

We went for a walk round the centre of the town. I demanded this much, and I leaned heavily on him as we inspected the surviving buildings. There was a fine basilica there, now used as a monastery. An inscription above the portico recorded that the building had been provided by the munificence of a certain Gordianus in the reign of Claudius the Goth Killer. It was an interesting example from a time when architectural styles were on the turn from the elegant but ancient to the more functional modern.

There was a public library. But Lucius flatly refused to let me enter. He'd never seen me at work in Rome. But he probably guessed how time could stand still for me whenever I found myself in a room with books.

There was also a tiny church built by the mother of Constantine shortly after his conversion. This had been changed and extended over the years, and now had a bell tower that stood incongruously beside it.

'Are you up to climbing this?' Lucius asked. 'I can show you something that will raise your spirits.'

I nodded. He helped me up the narrow steps to the top. I clutched with my good arm at the wooden rail, wondering at how little strength I could put into the grip. Even so, I could feel the gradual return of strength. Young bodies have the most wondrous resilience. The fever had not been great, and now it was passing.

At the top, Lucius leant over the northern parapet. 'Do you see that blur in the distance?' he asked.

I looked. Before me lay an immense flat waste, an embanked road leading through it until lost in the heat haze. Far beyond, almost on the horizon, I saw what Lucius was pointing at. It was a blur at first. But I focused and concentrated. Through the low, shimmering air, I could see a high and wide expanse of domes and towers.

There were miles and miles yet to go. But I'd had my first sight of Ravenna – that great, untakeable fastness perched between a marsh and the sea. From here, the last Western emperors had ruled Italy as best they could, safe from the general havoc that lapped or overpoured the walls of every other city. From here, the exarch now ruled, in continual touch by sea with Constantinople and the world that stretched far beyond the narrow confines of the West.

Within those walls lay the last undamaged fragments of the old Roman life – the palaces and libraries and bathhouses and trading marts, and the large remains of an urban culture to which all Italy had once been home.

'We'll be there tomorrow,' Lucius said. 'Once I've got you bathed and rested, we'll take ourselves to the exarch. I would have sent a slave ahead to alert him to our coming. In the present circumstances, it may be best for us simply to arrive unannounced at his door.'

Back down in the square before the church, I felt decidedly better. We'd outrun the dispensator's men. Another day, and I'd be in the fabled Ravenna of the exarch. And I could hope for the answers to which I'd been laying impatient and not always advisable siege since that awful dawn by the Column of Phocas.

Whatever it meant for me, I swore, I'd have those answers.

After a brief and merciful rest, we set out again on the road. Before nightfall, we'd be travelling through that great marsh within which Ravenna was protected from all enemies. Some time the following day, we could expect to pass through the immense fortifications.

Yes, I'd have those answers.

47

We were deep into the marshes that protected Ravenna on its landward side. Still straight, the road passed across on a high causeway. Every mile or so, we were stopped and questioned at one of the military checkpoints that blocked the only approach to the city. Each time, Lucius showed his letter of safe conduct, and we passed through.

The marshes went on for miles. We'd made our gradual descent onto them in the morning. Now I was grown almost used to their hot, stinking air.

I asked how the city could possibly survive in a climate so pestilential.

'The city itself has the most wonderful air,' Lucius explained.

Just before Ravenna, he continued, the marshes gave way to more solid ground. Part of the city was built on this, part on moles sunk deep into the coastal mud. The continual breeze from the Adriatic gave it an unexpectedly fine climate. The gentle movement of the tide washed sea water in and out twice a day through the canals that intersected much of the city. This carried away all the filth and other refuse that would otherwise have remained to fester into an epidemic. Such infections as did take hold in the city were carried in along the shipping lanes from the world outside. Even these were less terrible than when they reached Rome or any of the inland cities.

It was less fortunate for those armies anyone was mad enough to send against the city. Every one of these had sickened and shrivelled away. The only need for an armed garrison was to keep order inside the walls and to guard the causeway that led across the marshes.

'If it's churches you like, you'll love Ravenna,' said Lucius. 'The place has been filling up with them for centuries. Even I can appreciate some of the craftsmanship that went into their creation. One of these days, they will all be turned over to the worship of the Old Gods. Even then, however, I hope we can keep some of the mosaics in them. Some might have to be painted over. The rest, though, can be put to a more fitting use than they were designed for.'

Lucius explained his plan for rolling back Christianity. It required another Julian. But this one wouldn't throw his life away on trying to imitate Alexander the Great's conquest of Persia. This emperor would take up the failed project of complete religious toleration. All forms of worship would be protected. But the Old Religion would be again the established faith. Only its adherents would be allowed to serve in the army and administration. Only they would be allowed to teach in any institute of higher learning.

'And this is only fair,' said Lucius. 'How can someone who believes the Old Gods are demons possibly teach an ancient literature that was created to glorify them? How can he celebrate and encourage emulation of the lives of heroes who his Church insists are burning in Hell?

'It's really as if I were given the job of preaching the Gospels. With my best effort, I'd make a mess of it. So I'm hardly insisting on the unreasonable. Let them preach the word of their Jewish carpenter. I'd never dream of stopping them. In return, let them stick to that. Everything else must be for my people. Each to his own. What could be fairer than that?'

I thought of Saint Jerome in his desert, accused by those invisible demons of giving more time to Cicero than to the Gospels. I thought of Pope Gregory and his prayers for the souls of the pagan writers and heroes. There was a contradiction between the two cultures.

Lucius had a point, to some extent. The Church was at war with the past. At the same time, though, the Church had taken over the whole of ancient learning to a degree that he couldn't realise. The more educated clerics were able, in ways that I myself had trouble comprehending, to hold in their minds two contradictory views of the world without letting one contaminate the other. They could read Cicero in the morning, and preach from the Gospels in the afternoon. In the evening, if they felt inclined, they could write about the Gospels in a style sometimes admirably close to Cicero. I thought to explain the plan behind the English mission. But Lucius was continuing with his own explanation.

Christianity would be tolerated, he said. But every man of ability and ambition would avoid the Church once membership was no longer the path to worldly advancement. From the moment Constantine had established it, the Church had been filled with hypocrites. They mouthed one nonsensical doctrine after another, never believing a word of any of them. They didn't believe, but they supplied an essential weight of numbers without which the Church couldn't have triumphed. Take away that establishment, and the hypocrites would give their same essential weight to the restored Old Religion.

One generation of rigid discrimination would force Christianity back into becoming the lower-class religion from which it had started. The temples would reopen. The greater churches would have their uses changed. Once again, the smoke of sacrifice would rise from ten thousand altars, and the nightmare of the past three centuries would pass away.

But the new paganism wouldn't be the decentralised bundle of worships that Christianity had displaced. The Old Religion was true, but its organisation had failed it. The Church was based on the fraudulent raising up of a minor Jewish deity far beyond his proper station. But the organisation of the Church from Saint Paul onwards had been a work of genius. Long before Constantine, it had mirrored in its own structures the administrative machinery of the Empire. Before ever they had been given equal status with the civil authorities, its bishops had been trained in a school of government.

A revived paganism would learn from that. No longer a bundle of self-contained worships, it would be unified at every level. Each cult would be formally assimilated with the others corresponding

328

to it. The worship of Syrian Astarte would be combined with that of the Ephesian Artemis. And above the worship of the people, a class of philosophical priests would teach that the honour paid to every lesser deity was also honour paid to the single unmoved Mover of the Universe.

There would be a formal hierarchy, with regular councils to settle points of disputed doctrine. But, unlike with the Western Church, the civil power would predominate. The emperor would be *pontifex maximus*. There would be no room for patriarchs, let alone a universal bishop able to arrogate the imperial power.

Lucius spoke on, ostensibly to me, but mainly for himself, building his castles in the air as we trotted along that interminably long causeway. For a while, I thought he had caught some of my old fever. At last, though, he turned to the more immediate matter of our accommodation in Ravenna.

We'd turn up unannounced at the house of a friend close by the naval base. We'd rest. From here, we'd move on to the palace of the exarch. Even if he were up to his eyes in work, Smaragdus would receive us directly. Once those letters had been produced and read, there would be an immediate dispatch of enough soldiers to arrest every senior official in the Lateran and secure its archives. These would all be brought to Ravenna for the formal investigation of treason.

'And what then?' I asked.

'That depends on events that I can neither predict nor control,' said Lucius. 'But one thing I can promise is that we shall both have something at least of what we most want. And we can plan our future together.'

Our future together?

I hadn't thought of that. I owed an immense amount to Lucius. He had taken me up that day on the Tiber embankment and helped me on a journey to the truth I could never have mapped out for myself. He had saved my life. He was good in bed. But the rest of my life with him? How much had we really in common?

I wanted to read every book in the world that hadn't yet fallen to pieces. I wanted to see much of the world. I wanted to endow the mission to my own land with riches of knowledge and its supporting gold that would multiply across the centuries. In this last respect – and perhaps in the others too – I was part of a Church that he only wanted to see destroyed.

And what did Lucius want? He wanted, I had no doubt, enough money to get his palace back into its ancient glory, and to give him the undoubted first place in noble society in Rome. That was the only reason I could see why he had made that long journey to wonderful Constantinople. I knew he'd been in the Imperial Palace. I knew he'd watched some execution in the Circus that had sickened even his firmness of mind. Had he once stepped into those vast libraries? I knew he had barely a word of Greek, and had no desire to learn more.

Women are one thing. They look after the household and have children. They can even have a sort of equality in your life once you accept their lower nature. But where would be the glue in a long relationship with Lucius?

And what about the Church? In Rome, it had all appeared obvious once Lucius explained it. Maximin hadn't destroyed those letters because he wanted to use them to bring the pope and dispensator to justice before the exarch.

But had he? Did Maximin really want the Western Church to be despoiled and then made into a department of the imperial state, as it was in the East? Where would that leave the English mission? Was Ethelbert to become a vassal of the emperor? Was the race of educated Englishmen I was to help raise up to become pieces in a game played from Constantinople?

It had seemed obvious enough in Rome. I hadn't given any thought at all to the wider implications of what I was doing in the first and most exciting part of our journey to Ravenna. But I had, in my conscious moments while jolting along the road in that carriage, been able to give long thought to these matters.

I fell into a guilty silence.

'Are you feeling well, my love?' Lucius asked, giving me a look of tender concern. 'Does the air trouble you? We'll be in Ravenna before evening. But we can stop at an inn built over the marshes. We can rest there awhile.'

'I do feel rather tired,' I lied. 'If we can stop before very long, I'd appreciate the chance of a rest and a cup of wine.'

We stopped at the inn. This was a lighter structure than the other inns I'd seen. It rested on wooden supports sunk deep into the mud. Lucius and I bathed again and took a late, slow lunch.

'We can slow down as much as we like,' said Lucius. 'I suggest we don't put any further strain on your health in this climate. Whether we arrive in Ravenna this evening or tomorrow morning doesn't now matter. Smaragdus will thank us for those letters, but would never appreciate being got out of bed to look at them. He's getting old, you know. And he is just a little mad, I think I've already told you.

'Let's spend the night here,' said Lucius, now decided.

We ordered a room. We got into bed. I slept. Stronger than for several days past, I now had no dreams.

I didn't mean to sleep so long. I'd expected Lucius to wake me. But I eventually woke by myself as the first light of morning was stealing across the marshes outside. I could hear the big, wooden gate creaking open for the day, and the cheerful sound of men on horseback. From down in the slave quarters, I could smell the heated wine and hear the clatter of pots as breakfast was made ready.

Lucius was already up. For the first time, I saw him reading a book. He read aloud, but was keeping his voice down so as not to disturb me. I heard the slow, halting mutter of something in one of the more complex lyric metres.

'I never guessed you liked poetry,' I said, looking over to the window where Lucius had his book.

'Nor did I,' came the reply. 'I had a wretched education, and I'm beginning to feel I should do some catching up if I'm to be a fit companion for you. I borrowed the book from some deacon I was

331

drinking with last night. It's all rather difficult stuff, though, don't you think? I've been up half the night, and I'm only on the fifth page of this thick, heavy book.'

I got stiffly out of bed and stretched. Lucius gave me an appreciative look.

'I think I could do with a brief walk to get some movement back into me,' I said. My arm was still aching. But I'd removed the bandage, as the wound was nicely scabbed over. I reached for some clothes.

'If you're going down, could you sort out another change of horses?' Lucius asked. 'Get something fine. I've had our good clothes aired and pressed. We shan't be exactly splendid. But there's much to be said for making the best entry possible into Ravenna.'

I reached for my purse. So far as I could tell, Lucius had paid the whole cost of our journey so far. With all my riches – and if the dispensator had frozen these, they'd soon enough be unfrozen – I had a plain duty to pay some share of all this travelling.

'No, no, my golden Alaric,' Lucius protested. 'Take my purse with you. I absolutely insist.'

He got up and forced his purse into my hands.

Down in the stable, I chose a couple of black horses. They were a matched pair, and of good quality. But I thought they were rather expensive.

'This is Ravenna, mate,' the groom explained when I tried to haggle on the price. 'You aren't in some shithole pile of ruins now. This is an imperial city. You pay standard prices here.'

I wished I had brought my own purse. I was being forced to hand over almost as much as the previous six days had cost us. I sighed and opened the smaller compartment of the purse Lucius had grabbed up as we left his house.

I pulled out a couple of solidi. I looked at them. My heart froze. The coins all bore the head of the Emperor Maurice. On the reverse, the letters 'CONOB' were clearly stamped. The letter B was raised just a little above the other four letters.

I emptied the whole compartment into my hand, and spread out the smooth, regular coins.

'It's not that much, mate,' the groom laughed. 'Here, I can see you aren't up with real coin. Let me sort out the price—'

'That won't be necessary,' I snapped. 'Keep those horses to one side. I'll be back for them.'

48

Back in our room, I undressed and lay on the bed. I stretched out my arms to Lucius. He came to me. We fornicated for a long time.

Afterwards, I began in a slow, dreamy voice I'd been practising in my head.

'Lucius,' I asked, 'We'll be meeting the exarch later today, shan't we?'

'Yes. Probably in the late afternoon.'

'You say he's a bit mad. Does that make him dangerous?'

Lucius thought. 'Not really dangerous,' he said. 'The man is getting old, and the tendency to shortness of temper that he's always had is growing worse with age. I promise you'll get on with him – no problem.'

'But I'll need to be careful what I say to him – after all, he's the most powerful man in Italy.'

'Of course,' said Lucius. 'But you don't have to worry about that. Your speech and general manners are not in question.'

'Yes,' I continued, 'but I'll need to know the appropriate responses to what he says. In particular, I'll need to know the truth about those letters. The truth for the whole world is one thing. The real truth is another. And I must have the real truth.'

Lucius sat up. I continued lying, my eyes half closed, my good arm across my brow.

'Lucius,' I said, 'I know that you had those letters written. You got Martin and someone else to write them. You got them to those English mercenaries outside Populonium, and you set them up with the prefect's men.

'The idea was that they'd sit in their camp beside the shrine of Saint Antony, waiting for orders that would never come. Instead,

334

they'd be taken by the prefect's men, and the letters would be given to him. The pope would then be arrested before he could set out back from Naples.

'That's the truth, isn't it, Lucius? You are the Column of Phocas.'

Lucius was silent awhile. Through my half-closed eyes, I saw a range of expressions flit across his face.

'In a manner, yes,' he said at length, speaking cautiously. 'How long have you known this?'

'For a long time,' I lied. Or did I lie? As with Martin, the elements of the puzzle were assembling themselves into a chain of reasoning so firm that I could barely conceive of not having seen it from the beginning.

Lucius lay back and relaxed. He let one hand fall on my chest.

'Very well,' he said, 'I'll tell you.' He closed his eyes and began.

'There are details you haven't caught. In the first place, the letters weren't to be carried before the prefect. He'd only have sat on them or gone to the dispensator. The orders were that the mercenaries were to be killed and all that they had with them taken straight off to Ravenna, where the exarch would deal with the matter.

'I told you I was with Phocas earlier in the year. I gave you the truth about our public meeting. He sent me away with nothing worth having. But he called me back to the Imperial Palace late in the evening. That's where we first hatched the plan.

'As you know, the man is short of money. Armies and officials need to be paid. Indemnities and bribes to the Persians require hard cash. The Eastern Church is rich, but is too close at hand to be despoiled. Take money from the Churches there, and you'll have the priests leading insurrections in every city.

'But the Western Church is fabulously rich – and no one in the East gives a shit about the sufferings of Latin priests who've been getting on every set of Eastern nerves for centuries with their presumptions of supremacy.

'All we needed was a credible excuse to smash up the Roman Church. Any excuse would work in Constantinople – probably a

335

simple decree would satisfy people there. But we needed something that would absolutely paralyse opinion in the West.

'An offer to hand out the Purple to some illiterate savage, his hair stinking of rancid butter, would detach most civilians. An offer to tolerate the Arian heresy would detach the Churches in at least France, Spain and Africa. It might also cause uproar in Italy.

'I timed the release of the letters for when Boniface was in Naples, up to his neck in mud. The dispensator may be the real power in Rome. But he still needs the pope to mouth the words he prompts. He can't speak by himself for the Church.

'But for you and your friend, those letters would by now be old news in Ravenna. The fresh news would be the arrival for trial of the pope and dispensator. Even if they could talk their way out of those charges, a trawl of the papal archives would surely turn up something else for which we could nail the Church. One way or another, we were to get an excuse to lay hands on whatever property of the Church was saleable and within reach—'

I broke in. 'And in return, you were to get back your family estates in Sicily and Cyprus,' I said. 'But why make a deal with Phocas? No one believes he'll be around much longer. Even if he is, how can you trust a man like that?'

Lucius smiled. He took the hand from my brow and kissed it. 'Phocas and I hatched the plan together in Constantinople. That's how I got the gold and the letters in Persian and Greek. But the plan grew and altered as I made the sea journey between Constantinople and Ravenna. By the time I'd had dinner with Smaragdus, certain important details were – ah – changed.

'The letters were still to be intercepted and carried to Smaragdus. There were still to be arrests in Rome. But once we'd got our hands on the money of the Church, Smaragdus was to get himself declared emperor of the West. He has all the right qualifications, you know: birth, education, sufficient ability. He would denounce Phocas as a tyrant and an incompetent. He'd have stolen a march on the exarch of Africa, whose son and nephew still haven't worked out which is to be the rival emperor. An emperor in being is worth a dozen possible claimants. At worst, we could do a deal. Africa is expendable, now the corn supplies from Sicily are adequate.

'Most people in Italy would accept a Western emperor – someone at hand with the means and ability to throw out the Lombards. Though Smaragdus is a Greek, he'd govern through Latin ministers. Neither Phocas nor anyone else who might take over from him would be able to lift a finger to dislodge him.'

'And the Church?' I asked. 'Where does the Church come into this? Orders from Constantinople are one thing. No one in Italy can get at the emperor there. But how long could Smaragdus last in Ravenna as the man who plundered the Roman Church?'

Lucius shifted his position and looked wistfully up at the ceiling. 'My dearest Alaric,' he said, 'Smaragdus is an old man. As emperor, he might have at best a few years of power. From the start, he'd need a colleague. This colleague would be in all reasonable likelihood his successor. That colleague will be me.

'And that answers your question about the Church. Plundered by Smaragdus, disestablished by me, it would be in no position to make serious trouble.

'So, Phocas offered me some estates. Smaragdus has given me a future claim to all Italy.

'And I don't think I have to persuade you that I don't want this for myself. I am the right man to throw out the barbarians, keep out the Greeks, restore the Old Religion, and generally give Italy back to itself. Just imagine that: all Italy united, and without all the imperial entanglements that got my ancestors distracted from the real prize. We could start again. A united Italy, Rome its capital.'

'How did you get Martin to help in this?' I asked.

'The man is a slave of the Church,' Lucius answered with a sneer. 'He hates the Greeks who ruined his father and had him enslaved. He hates the Roman Church for something to do with doctrine or your people or whatever. He's got some woman with child. He wanted freedom and money. The Gods led me to him, and I offered him what he wanted.

'He did a good job on that papal letter. I watched your face closely as you read it. I don't know when you stopped believing.

337

But you certainly believed then. He also stole the relic. He was on the dispensator's staff, and had easy access to the Church of the Apostles—'

'It was your slaves,' I interrupted, 'who attacked me that night in Rome. You got yourself called away on some fake appointment with your lawyer – and I wondered how that slave found you so easily. You relied on me to refuse the escort you offered. Those were your slaves in the street. And that's why you couldn't get the wood for the bathhouse boiler. After I'd killed three of them, you were short of slaves.'

Lucius spoke sharply: 'Alaric, I want you to know that those slaves had strict orders only to frighten you and then run away. I had to get your mind focused on those letters. You must understand how I needed them back, and how only you could lead me to them.

'When I heard your story, I had the survivor beaten to death – him and one other who stood in the main street. I would never, under any circumstances, have had you harmed.'

So that was what the beaten slave had meant when he called out about 'the others'. Was this fifth slave the one who saved me? I didn't ask. Instead, I asked about Silas of Edessa.

That, Lucius explained, had been a mistake. He'd grown alarmed at what I'd heard in the Exchange about the Column of Phocas, so ordered the death of the old man. Unfortunately, the slaves had come across Silas boasting about the money I'd given him, and had killed him instead.

At last – and I'd dreaded this – I turned to Maximin. Why kill him?

Lucius looked away from me and spoke softly.

'I was waiting all night and much of the next day on the Aurelian Way. The plan was that I'd intercept the prefect's men as they rode back with the captured articles and have them taken straight off to Ravenna. I'd bought one of the officers.

'Instead, the men rode by with just you and Maximin. There had been no interception, he said, nor battle, nor frustrated exchange. There had just been the rescue of a priest and his barbarian assistant from an attempted robbery. The priest had the relic. There was no mention of anything else.

'I nearly panicked. I thought of riding right off there and then to Ravenna. Instead, I went back to Rome, to see what would happen, and what opportunities might still be available. I sacrificed to the Gods outside the city walls. They gave me a favourable answer.

'In Rome, I had Martin check your movements. You didn't tell the prefect about the letters. You didn't give them to the dispensator. Either you were holding on to them for some reason of your own, or you hadn't bothered to read them. Martin soon guessed it was the latter.

'Martin got himself assigned to you so he could watch you, and perhaps steal the letters back. When he learnt that the dispensator had called Maximin to an unexpected meeting, we knew he'd got wind of something, and would soon have the letters in his hand. That would have ruined everything. He already knew I was up to something. This would give him all the proof he needed. He'd dig and dig. Eventually, he'd come up with enough of the truth to get me and Smaragdus had up ourselves for treason. We had to get those letters back.

'I arranged for the messenger who cancelled the meeting. I killed the monk Ambrose. Martin then wrote the letter that got Maximin out just as dark was falling.'

'Did you kill Maximin?' I asked.

'No!' Lucius spoke firmly. 'Look Alaric, I'm telling you the whole truth. You must believe me that I didn't kill your friend.

'The plan was to jump him and grab the letters. I'd be home in time to arrange dinner for you. He'd get up the next day with a sore head. There was no need to kill him. You came into the plot without realising. You'd have been out before you realised.

'But it all went wrong. First, Maximin put up the most tremendous fight. It took two big men and one smaller to get him off the street into the shade of that portico. Even then, he fought like a maniac.

'Then, we ourselves were attacked from behind. It must have been the dispensator's men. It can only have been them. If so, your One-Eye is one of them. But we were attacked, and there was a general fight. From those bloody footprints, you might think it was a premeditated killing. But it was much more confused than that. I just don't know who struck the killing blow. It might not even have been one of us.

'Maximin was down. We had no time to search him. We ran off. The next morning, I heard about the killing. I heard how the body had been carefully placed beside the Column of Phocas – a warning to us, I took this, from the dispensator. I heard from Martin about the search of your lodgings. I grew more and more convinced that the dispensator's men hadn't got the letters either.'

'So you came looking for me,' I said. 'When you found me sleeping in the sun, you sat beside me and waited for me to wake up.'

Yes, Lucius had used me like a clever hunting dog. He'd helped me gather up and connect the fragments of evidence available into a credible and largely true narrative. In return, I'd taken him steadily closer to the moment when he could set hands on those letters again. The dispensator would have no evidence. The plot could begin over again – only this time, with me to vouch for them and a trail of bodies, the provenance of the letters would be all the stronger for the brief delay. Losing the gold was well worth the additional prize.

Lucius had acted his part in the drama with a smooth conviction that I'd never once doubted in my waking moments. Even as he handed out knowledge he already had, he'd made it look freshly uncovered.

Did this mean . . . did this mean everything had been a lie?

Lucius must have understood the look on my face.

'Alaric,' he said, 'I was attracted to you in the physical sense when we first met at the dinner party. Then the Gods told me at the sacrifice that you would help me achieve the great purpose of my life. Even then, though, I was still prepared to use you and move on.

'It was the next day, when I found you sleeping by the river, that everything changed. You can't know how long it seemed when I sat watching you sleep. You can't imagine the longing and tenderness and desire for moral cleanliness that welled up in my heart. I can't feel your touch, I can't look at you, but my whole body and soul catch fire.

'I didn't tell you the complete truth, Alaric. I couldn't tell you that truth. But I love you, Alaric. And so long as I am alive, I will never be apart from you.'

I moved my body close against his. We were both already sweating lightly from the heat of the day outside. Lucius moaned gently and ran his hands over the muscles of my upper back.

'Alaric, in just a short while, we shall be in Ravenna. There are libraries there so great, you will not comprehend their size until you have seen for yourself. As a co-emperor's consort, you will have open access to every library in the city, public and private. With Phocas out of the way, I can arrange Alexandria and Constantinople itself. Every piece of knowledge you've ever wanted will be yours for the having.

'By all means, send books to England. But also have them copied for the new Italy. We shall build a great future – but on the foundations of our great past. We need to recover that past, now most of us have lost it. That includes all our learning. But we shall need new libraries, and teachers to explain the meaning of the ancient writings placed there. Who could be better as my minister for learning than you?'

Lucius used the phrase '*magister scholium*' – 'master of the schools'. I wasn't just to be his bed companion – his Antinous. I was also to be an integral part in his plan of renaissance. There were to be statues of me in every city, and my name on the pediment of every new school and library. I'd be . . . I racked my brain for a parallel. Except I'd be the younger, I'd be to him what Plato had tried to be to Dion of Syracuse.

'A place in the imperial government,' I said. 'Every library in the world open to my direct or indirect inspection. An army of secretaries and architects and builders. The revival of learning in Italy, and me to supervise! You tempt me, Lucius.'

'I don't tempt, my love. I promise. Together, we will create a new order.' Lucius sat up. 'But we must be on the road again. We must get to the exarch before I can deliver on anything.'

'Come to me, Lucius,' I said smiling. I held out my arms. 'Lucius, I love you.'

I took his head in my hands as he sat beside me and kissed him long on the mouth. Still holding his head, I twisted my hands suddenly, one jerking forward, one back. I heard the snap of his neck like a dry twig.

Lucius died at once, with a slight convulsion, his body flopped forward onto mine. The last thing he could have known was the unbounded happiness flowing from the surety that I loved him.

49

I don't know how long I sat cradling his naked body against mine. I wanted to think this was another of the opium dreams – that I'd wake up beside him in another moment, and he'd send me down with a purse full of debased silver to negotiate a last change of horses; better yet that I'd wake and find myself still bumping along the road in that Greek official's carriage, while Lucius fussed about with ointments and charms.

But no – I was awake just outside Ravenna, and Lucius lay dead in my arms. The wonderful, glorious Lucius was dead. Lucius, whose charm, it turned out, had not failed him even with the emperor. In my arms had died the last of the Romans – and perhaps the first light of a new Italy. And I had killed him. And I now sat alone.

Since then, Italy has gone from bad to worse. In those days, the embers of the old world still faintly glowed. They are now extinguished forever. I can't say how many cities that were then just about surviving are now mere heaps of overgrown ruins. An age of chaos and destruction stands between that world and whatever will finally emerge in its place.

Did I contribute to that? Did I, to revenge the death of one man, help bring on the death of many more?

I don't think so. Lucius was a great man. He had almost every ability needed to do great things. One thing only he lacked, and that was common sense. At the level of high politics, I have no doubt he could have defrauded Phocas – and perhaps also the exarch – out of Italy. He could have done over the pope and dispensator as individuals. But did he seriously think he could replace something as solid as the Roman Church with a revived paganism led by a few eccentrics and vagrant magicians? I think not.

All his noble plans would have been brought to grief in very short order by his proposal to base his new order on the rubble of the Church. He might have got as far as deposing Smaragdus in one palace coup. With every Italian of substance – no, every Italian – against him, I doubt he'd have lasted six months. At best, he'd have been another Julian. And he'd not even have left that legacy of interesting writings and speculations on what might have been. More likely, he'd only have accelerated a collapse that was already under way.

But it wasn't politics that went through my head as I sat alone with the body of Lucius. I tried to adjust the long lock of hair that fell down from his forehead, and close the dulling eyes. All I managed to do was push the loose head from one unnatural angle to another. The eyes and mouth hung open in expressions of blank horror.

Lucius was dead, and I had killed him. For all I loved him, for all I clung to him, for all he had done with and for me, I had to kill him. Because I loved him, I had made his death as sweet as any man might want. He died in the arms of his love, just moments away from a triumph after which all else would surely be disappointment. I sent him into the darkness with all hopes undimmed. But I had killed him, and he lay dead in my lap.

I think the sun was heading towards the west when I heard a rattling. 'In the name of the Church, open this door!'

It was a harsh, urgent voice. Still looking down at my poor, dead Lucius, I gave it no attention. 'Open, or I break it open.'

The voice was louder and more menacing. Still I ignored it.

There was a great crash and splintering of timber. Fragments of shattered door hung loose on the hinges. The men who'd smashed it in stood smartly back. In their place, filling the doorway, stood One-Eye. Sword in hand, he was, as ever, dressed in black.

He looked at us awhile with his good eye, taking in the situation. 'Get dressed,' he said at last in a quiet, neutral voice. He gave orders in an Eastern language I didn't understand. His assistants went downstairs, where I soon heard cries and protests of diminishing volume.

He threw my clothes over at me. 'Get these on you,' he said, now with a hint of anger in his voice. He leaned forward, speaking quietly again, though there was no one to overhear. 'Your life is in the hands of the dispensator. He alone will decide your fate. But my orders are that, if at any time between now and our arrival in the Lateran, you speak a single word to anybody, I am to kill you on the spot. Do you understand? One word of any kind, and I kill you.'

I nodded.

'Then get dressed, and be fast about it.'

As I finished dressing, One-Eye had his assistants pack everything up. The room was to be left empty, all trace of our presence there erased as if it had been a sheet of misused parchment. He made sure to take the obvious items into his own possession.

At last, he scooped Lucius up and wrapped him in some of the bedding. He threw the body over his shoulder as if it had been a carpet.

On the ground floor, everyone else at the inn had been forced at sword-point into the kitchen, where great and humble stood alike, all protesting at the violation of their rights. The door to the kitchen was guarded by the three assistants One-Eye had with him, also dressed in black.

There were other armed men in that place, and these might have resisted. But the dispensator's warrant, it seemed, was valid even to the gates of Ravenna.

'God save us, master!' a voice cried in rough Latin. One-Eye stood out in the courtyard, with me close beside. He was awaiting the final gathering and loading of our horses. He stiffened at the cry. From outside the main gate came the sound of many hooves. A whole party of men was tearing up or down the road towards the inn.

One-Eye put a hand on his sword. He called out more orders in that unknown language. Then he turned to me. 'Remember what I said,' he repeated. 'One word and you die. One step beyond where I set you, and you die.'

He turned back to face the riding party as it pelted at full speed into the courtyard. It was obvious at once they'd been coming up from Rome, not down from Ravenna. One-Eye relaxed the grip on his sword, but kept it covered.

It was a party of five men. Covered in dust from the long ride, the cloaks that covered their heads had turned from dark to streaky white.

The leader of the party continued forward a few yards after the others had stopped. After a momentary pause to take in what he saw, he jumped briskly down and walked confidently over to us. He staggered just a little as he pulled back the hood of his cloak, but recovered his balance at once, and continued over to us as if just back from a brisk morning canter.

The diplomat looked at One-Eye and smiled. He let his eyes linger a moment on the rolled-up bundle. 'It seems, my friend, I am just a moment too late.'

Except for his black face and the high, accented Latin, he might have been any other shabby horseman we'd encountered on the road. He looked back at his four assistants. He looked at me and smiled. 'You would be the luckiest man alive, had I only got to you first,' he said. 'As it is—'

'As it is,' One-Eye took up in a voice of flinty grimness, 'you are too late. Ride on towards Ravenna if you must. The exarch might not hang you. Or go back to Rome. In either case, you can get message back to your master in Carthage that you failed again.'

The diplomat looked again at me. Silent, he bowed. He turned back to his assistants. They'd ridden like the wind up from Rome. They'd checked every inn along the road. But it had been too late.

He called something at the others in their own language. Then he laughed. The others following, he led his horse into the stables.

Unseen by anyone else, Lucius and I were taken back out onto the road. I was given a horse – something big and unfamiliar that it alarmed me ever so slightly to ride. One of the three assistants rode close beside me. Without speaking, he gave me to understand that the orders they'd received would be carried out to the letter if need be.

They buried Lucius in the marsh. The city walls were just visible in the distance. Otherwise, I looked over a flat, dreary waste. There was no tree nor rise of the land to break up the monotony. Not even a bird sang. They gouged a shallow hole by the road and threw the body in. It landed unwrapped with the head by chance at a normal angle. The eyes looked at me from a face that carried some ghost of its living expression. I ignored the command to get back on my horse, and looked steadily down until the black, stinking mud had closed over him forever.

Lucius had come so far. Now he lay in an unmarked grave by the long causeway that led from Ravenna.

I wept. I wept so that I could hardly stand. I was made to remount, but I wept on, oblivious of the horse that moved beneath me, taking me further and further from the one I had loved.

The journey back from Ravenna was less dramatic than my journey there. We didn't bother with the Flaminian Way. Instead, we cut straight across country, riding on little, often unmade roads. In the winter and early spring, I don't doubt, they were impassable. By now, the hot sun had done its work, and they were as hard and smooth as if they'd been paved.

We crossed at some point into Lombard territory. We were met at the frontier by an armed guard bearing the insignia of the Lombard king. They gave a formal salute as we crossed over, and rode with us in close formation. They deterred any armed attack on us, and waved us through any official delay.

We passed through regions of devastation more utter than I'd ever seen before. We passed also through regions of surprising prosperity. Some of the towns were just as large as, and no more apparently ruined than, those in imperial territory. But we didn't stop at any inhabited point. Each evening, we camped in the open. I slept beside the fire, always under close watch. I said not a word. Beyond the minimal instructions that One-Eye rasped at me, no one spoke to me.

I think we made still-better time across country than I had with Lucius.

We crossed the whole northern width of Italy, coming at last to an isolated inlet somewhere on the western coast. A fast ship awaited us there. Propelled by strong slaves who kept time to the rapid beat of the drum, we made an uneventful passage to the south. I looked over the left side several times, thinking I made out some of the landmarks I'd seen coming along the Aurelian Way with Maximin. Once, I was convinced I saw the shrine of Saint Antony rising above the surrounding cover.

On the tenth day after setting out from the marshes of Ravenna, we docked in the port of Ostia. Bathed in sea water and clothed in the white linen Lucius had urged on me for my reception by the exarch, I looked over the crumbling docks and semi-deserted town that had once served as the sea port for the greatest city in the world.

One-Eye spoke earnestly with the captain, every now and again casting a look with his good eye in my direction.

We transferred to a boat with a bottom flat enough to get us through the now silted estuary of the Tiber. We arrived in Rome early the next morning, disembarking by the island on the Tiber. I was taken in a covered litter straight to the house of Marcella. This was occupied by more of those dark guards. Neither Marcella nor the slaves spoke to me. Gretel darted me a concerned look as she hurried by. I smiled weakly back.

Except they had been thoroughly searched, my rooms were more or less as I'd left them. It would have been painful, had I not still been so numbed, to look on those familiar things I'd left behind. There were my books and papers spread out on the table. There was the green stone Edwina had given me.

Once more, I wished and wished I could have blotted out all the previous days. Only, I couldn't know how far back I wanted to go. Was it to the day before Maximin was murdered? Was it to the morning when I'd sat beside Lucius to question the household? Or was it to the day when Lucius had given me the chance to burn those letters? He'd known I wouldn't burn them. If only I had, things might have turned out so very different. What had been going through Maximum's mind to keep him from burning the things? I'd never know.

But time moves on like the pen of a rapid scribe. And not prayers nor act of human will can bring it back – nor any tears wash out a word of it. What had happened had happened. Only what might happen next was still in issue.

I sat and tore at the loaf that had been set for me, and drank the whole jug of wine that came with it. For the first time in days and days, I began to put my thoughts in order, and to plan for that mystery of what would happen next.

50

The lamps were being lit as I was ushered into the dispensator's office. He sat at his desk with One-Eye, who was interpreting and comparing the Greek and Persian letters. Over in the corner, sitting so still I barely noticed him, was a new monkish secretary.

'Sit down, Aelric,' the dispensator said. His voice and face were carefully neutral.

As I sat in the chair he indicated, he returned to the forged papal letter. He read awhile. At length, he looked up. 'I want you, Aelric, to tell me all that you know about these letters. Do not assume either knowledge or ignorance on my part. I want the whole truth as you know it.'

For the first time since I left the inn outside Ravenna, I opened my mouth and began to speak. I did as I was asked, telling the truth exactly as I've given it to you. I held nothing back, no matter how embarrassing to me or criminal it might have been.

I spoke for a long time. The dispensator interrupted me only twice, and that was to silence me when a slave came in a couple of times to adjust the lamps. The secretary in the corner took a full shorthand note of the narrative.

I finished. The dispensator looked at me. One-Eye brushed his sleeve gently, drawing his attention to some words in what I took to be his own written report. The dispensator read and nodded some agreement. He looked over at me and spoke.

'We had known for some time that Basilius was up to something. Our problem was that we didn't know what. We had a spy among his household slaves. That allowed us to know that he was in communication with the exarch. And we knew that he had been involved in the murders of Father Maximin and of Brother

Ambrose. But our spy was not privy to the secrets that Basilius shared with an inner ring of slaves. We were not even aware until very late that he had recruited Martin to the conspiracy.

'We knew that he had arranged something outside Populonium. We knew that you and Father Maximin had accidentally wrecked that part of his plan. But we had no idea of what had been arranged.

'Simon –' he indicated to One-Eye, whose name I mention but think it rather late to start using – 'did speak briefly with two renegades from those English mercenaries stationed outside Populonium, but was unable to gather from them as much information as you seem to have managed. By the time he was able to piece together from other sources that there was to be some kind of exchange by the shrine of Saint Antony, you and Father Maximin had been there first.

'Simon followed you to Rome. He arranged for both of you to be closely followed.'

So it was indeed One-Eye who'd been following us! I asked about the botched attack on me that Lucius had arranged. It was One-Eye again who'd intervened to save me just when I really needed help. I nodded an acknowledgement of his help without thanking him for it.

The dispensator continued: 'It was, as you rightly gathered, towards the end of our first meeting in this office that I was given a further report from Simon. Because of some delay for which I may blame Martin, this was handed to me a day late. In it, Simon informed me that there might have been letters with the mercenaries, that these had apparently disappeared, and that you and Father Maximin were the most likely present possessors. Because of my own delay in opening that report – I blame my own excitement over the return of the relic of Saint Vexilla – I was not able to call for Father Maximin until the following morning.

'A further lapse on our part, though I cannot blame Simon for this, is that we lost sight of Father Maximin the evening before he died. You may recall that the pair of you were invited to a gathering of some of the more decayed Roman nobility. We were aware of this invitation. When Simon saw you go out with another dressed in Father Maximin's cloak, he did not realise until too late that you had gone out with Martin. This meant that we had no more notion than you had of what Father Maximin could have done with those letters. It never occurred to us he did not still have them on his last day.

'You know the rest of the story. I can only add that you and Basilius were watched closely throughout your investigation. The disguise you adopted to visit the financial district was penetrated at once, though Simon was not able to keep track of your movements on your last night in Rome, when you were directed by Basilius.

'It was my decision to leave you and Basilius to the investigation that he must so richly have enjoyed. I knew that, sooner or later, you would lead him to the letters, and that Simon and I would not be far behind.

'It is testimony to his resourcefulness – and to yours – that we were not able to keep up with you at the critical moments, and that the interception we asked our Lombard friends to arrange on the Flaminian Way was less successful than we hoped.'

'Your Lombard friends?' I asked, looking closely at his face. I saw no change in its bland, official expression.

'Yes, our Lombard friends.' He picked up the forged papal letter and looked briefly at it again. 'This is a most ingenious production,' he said, dropping it lightly in my direction. 'Martin has a fine grasp of the diplomatic style. We really should have used him for more important work than we did.

'Of course, what would have given the letter away as a forgery is the touch about toleration of the Arian heresy. I doubt if anyone would have believed that. It would have exposed the whole letter as a forgery.

'Even so, it would not have done for this letter to get into the wrong hands. It might have been used to our brief but considerable disadvantage. A search of our archives would reveal much that we do not yet wish to be revealed to the world. Be assured, the Church has thought much about the future of Italy and the corresponding safety of Rome and the Lateran. Not all that we have discussed has been carried into effect. Much of it cannot be carried into effect. We have never considered the toleration of heresy. But there is little else we have not considered.

'And yes, we do hope for some eventual full accommodation with the Lombards. For the moment, we try to keep relations with their kings as open as we can. Our accommodation may involve a wider political settlement – perhaps with the Lombards, perhaps with some other force. But this is not presently an option. For the moment, we remain good and loyal subjects of His Imperial Majesty in Constantinople, whoever this may be.'

He looked again at all three letters. 'Most ingenious. No, too ingenious. If I knew not better, I should assume that Martin had got himself access to our most secret archives.'

He picked up the letters and stood. He dropped them into a metal box on the floor of his office. He poured in hot lamp oil and dropped in a lighted taper. The room filled with smoke and the acrid smell of burning parchment. Soon, the letters were reduced to crackling ash. Before they went out, as if as an afterthought, the dispensator added the papyrus note of our meeting and One-Eye's report.

'These letters never existed,' he said firmly. 'This meeting discussed no matters pertinent to any alleged existence of these letters. The lord Basilius has unaccountably disappeared. Bearing in mind the desperate state of his finances, this will surprise no one.

'You, Aelric, have been out of Rome on confidential business connected with the English mission. Tomorrow, you will return to the scriptorium here, to continue supervising the work of copying that has proceeded regardless of your lengthy absence.'

'So, I'm not to be killed.' I didn't ask. Rather, I made a statement of possibly doubtful fact.

The dispensator threw up his arms. For the first time that evening, he smiled. 'Goodness, no, Aelric! What could possibly have given you that idea? Ours is a Church of perfect love and forgiveness. We can have no blood on our hands, nor ever will have. For some offences, of course, we will hand over malefactors to the secular authorities for punishment according to secular law. But ours is a Church of peace and love.

'I do not see what offence you can have committed to justify your handing over to the prefect. In any event, considering all the circumstances, I do not think it would be appropriate to send you before the prefect. And – again considering all circumstances – I do not think you would ever be foolish enough to take yourself before the prefect or any other official of the emperor.

'Nor,' he raised a finger in emphasis, 'would you think to share any information with another person, presently absent from Rome, who acts for an entirely separate interest.'

The dispensator examined the front of his tunic. 'I did, at our last meeting, suggest that you might find the air outside Rome somewhat more to your liking. But this was purely to encourage you to give more attention to the work of finding those letters. And now you have tried the air outside.'

I stood up as if to leave. I thought everything had been said. The dispensator stopped me. I could think of nothing more to say. As ever, he could.

'There is one matter outstanding,' he said. He nodded to One-Eye, who went to the door. There was a whispered instruction. A bound prisoner was pushed into the room. I could smell the filth clinging to the body and dirty rags of a man who'd been on the run in the sewers of Rome, and then in some disgusting prison cell.

I looked at Martin. He looked back at me, a desperate resignation stamped on his dirty, unshaven face. The red hair he'd always been so particular about dressing was a mass of clotted filth. His arms were cut and bruised from the leather straps that held him fast.

'Martin was arrested some days ago as he tried to leave Rome,' the dispensator explained. 'He was careless enough to arrange a last meeting with a young person whose movements we had been following. We arrested him just before he reached the meeting place. Even as a slave of the Church, his life is forfeit. As said, we can do nothing ourselves to visit on his body the punishment allowed by law. But he can be handed over to the justice of some other person or persons.

'We could resign him to the care of the prefect – the laws of the Empire and of the Church do permit this. Or we can give him up to some other person.

'I have decided to make a present of him to you. Call it a reward for what you have done to advance the work of the English mission.'

One-Eye grinned as he pushed Martin towards me. Again, we looked at each other. I could do anything I liked with him. I recalled the grisly punishments Lucius had insisted were owed to slaves who had trespassed far less. But I recalled also the words of the abbess: 'There is a time for revenge, and a time for putting away revenge.'

I hadn't asked Lucius what part Martin had taken in the killing of Maximin. Were his the light footprints? Had he struck the killing blow? But how many deaths had those letters caused over the past month? Lucius had been the originator of the plot. He and I jointly – he deliberately, I negligently – had set in motion the chain of causes that led to the death of Maximin. Now Lucius was dead.

Let that be an end of the matter. Revenge is an infinite cycle only among savages or the demented.

I struck Martin a light blow in the manner that I supposed was still prescribed by law. 'Martin, I free you,' I said in a firm voice.

He looked back at me, a look of disorientation on his face that at any other time I'd have found funny. I don't know what he had expected. Certainly, he hadn't expected this.

I turned to One-Eye. 'Unbind him, if you please.'

One-Eye took a knife to the tight straps. Martin stood before me, rubbing life back into his arms.

'Go back to Marcella's. Get a bath and a meal. Or go elsewhere if that is your wish. In the morning, get a lawyer to draft the necessary documents. Bring them to me in the scriptorium.'

I handed him my purse. 'This will pay any drafting fees. Keep the rest as a wedding present.'

Martin opened his mouth to speak, but could think of nothing to say. He hurried past me out of the office.

I turned again to leave. But there was still one more matter. The dispensator cleared his throat. I turned back to face him.

'Aelric,' he said, 'you came here to do penance. Penance you have now done.'

He stopped me again as I reached the door. 'I know you have your doubts. Let me assure you, however, there is a God. And He often works in mysterious ways.'

And that was it. I walked out of the Lateran into the warm night air. There was no moon overhead. But there were lights on the stalls selling cooked food and souvenirs to the pilgrims who now crowded the square. I could smell the blossom on the trees and the cooked food and the smoking charcoal of the fires.

And that is it. I did see the dispensator again the following afternoon. But that opened a new chapter in my life. This one is closed.

As you know, they did make a saint of Maximin. I was at the consecration of the Church of the Virgin and All the Martyrs. He was canonised at the most dramatic moment of the proceedings, the pope officiating before the exarch and a mob of assorted dignitaries. I can tell you, it was all of the highest magnificence. The Church did itself and Maximin proud that day.

The robe he wore when killed is on display in Canterbury. I've never been able to bring myself to look at this. But I'm told it still works the occasional miracle.

I went into the chapel last night, here in Jarrow. I lit a candle and thought to pray to the Holy Saint Maximin. Perhaps I did pray. In the darkness lit only by that single flickering light, I felt for just a moment so close to him that I could almost reach out and touch him and hear his loud and cheerful voice.

But the moment passed. And I was just an old man, alone in the gloom, waiting for the final darkness.

Richard Blake

The Terror of Constantinople

THE EASTERN PERIL AND THE BATTLE FOR ROME

The Emperor Phocas, a bloodthirsty tyrant, is preparing for the greatest battle of his life. Enemy armies are racing closer to attack his fortress the golden city of Constantinople and traitors within plot his downfall. He clings to power by masterminding a campaign of terror, executing 'traitors' and confiscating property, but he is running out of funds, allies and time. He has only one card left to play.

Aelric, a naïve and ambitious young clerk, is sent to Constantinople ostensibly on a mission to copy old texts for the Church of Rome. On his arrival though he realises that danger lurks behind the shining streets and glittering facades. A pawn in a secret conspiracy that will change the course of history, he must use all his wits, charm and strength to stay alive.

AVAILABLE FROM HODDER & STOUGHTON IN FEBRUARY 2009

HODDER &
STOUGHTON